THE
BINDING

THE BINDING

A Novel

NICHOLAS WOLFF

G
GALLERY BOOKS
New York   London   Toronto   Sydney   New Delhi

G

Gallery Books
An Imprint of Simon & Schuster, Inc.
1230 Avenue of the Americas
New York, NY 10020

First Gallery Books trade paperback edition June 2016

GALLERY BOOKS and colophon are registered trademarks of Simon & Schuster, Inc.

For information about special discounts for bulk purchases, please contact Simon & Schuster Special Sales at 1-866-506-1949 or business@simonandschuster.com.

The Simon & Schuster Speakers Bureau can bring authors to your live event. For more information or to book an event, contact the Simon & Schuster Speakers Bureau at 1-866-248-3049 or visit our website at www.simonspeakers.com.

Interior design by Davina Mock-Maniscalco

Manufactured in the United States of America

10 9 8 7 6 5 4 3 2 1

Library of Congress Cataloging-in-Publication Data

Names: Wolff, Nicholas, author.
Title: The binding : a novel / Nicholas Wolff.
Description: First Gallery Books trade paperback edition. | New York : Gallery Books, 2016.
Subjects: LCSH: Plague—Fiction. | Horror fiction. | BISAC: FICTION / Horror. | FICTION / Occult & Supernatural.
Classification: LCC PS3623.O559 B56 2016 (print) | LCC PS3623.O559 (ebook) | DDC 813/.6—dc23
LC record available at http://lccn.loc.gov/2015046668

ISBN 978-1-5011-0271-4
ISBN 978-1-5011-0272-1 (ebook)

To Tim Hartigan

Man is wolf to man.

—*Latin proverb*

PART ONE

THE GIRL IN THE SHAN

CHAPTER ONE

If there's a time to visit my little corner of Massachusetts, Dr. Nat Thayer thought as he walked quickly along the darkened path, *January isn't it.* When friends were thinking of journeying to his small city of Northam, he always told them: Come in May, when you can hear the knock of baseballs on aluminum bats from three blocks away. Or early fall, for the foliage and the hand-pressed apple cider. Half of New York City does. Northam was famous for that crap. Get your cider at Johnson's stand, not from that fraud Matheson, who laces his stuff with brand-name stuff from Stop & Shop, and head back home with an image of the golden Berkshires to last you awhile.

But get out by the end of November, by all means. That's when the smart ones shutter their vacation homes and take their L.L.Bean duck boots and their mountain bikes back to Boston and points south, and the population settles back to around four thousand souls. The smart ones *know.* You don't come here in winter, especially if you're prone to black thoughts. Here the hills block whatever sun we get and soak it into the loam along with the dying leaves, the locals turn inward, and the alleyways between the quaintly named bars get splashed with blood. The thin church steeples rake the sky like a handful of knives held blade upward.

No dementia caused by inbreeding up here, Nat thought as he walked briskly toward city hall. *We're not Southern Baptists or anything, just good old God-fearing Yankees.* But plenty of doom-ridden landscape and seasonal depression. And just . . . darkness. Of every kind.

The little valley Nat was coming up from was stripped of all colors except black and stone gray, the hills plunged off to his right into darkness and mist, the color in the trees now sunk back into the ground, replaced by its opposite, the bottomless night of rain-soaked birch trees against a darkening slate blue sky. He could see a half-moon low in the eastern sky as he walked, caught and sliced to bits by a dozen black fingers of branches.

This was another city now from the one you saw in summer. *This* was the place Margaret Post had left, violently and unwillingly, only two nights earlier.

———

Three hours later, Nat was sitting in the satellite office of the Northam Mental Health Clinic in the basement of city hall, rubbing his hands together like two dry sticks and cursing the town fathers. Jesus Christ, it was cold. It was like sitting in a puddle at the bottom of a stone quarry. The three-hundred-year-old granite walls conducted cold and wet like steel did for electricity.

10:14 p.m. "What the hell am I doing here?" he whispered as he blew a breath into his hands.

Getting money for Buenos Aires. He always got out of Northam every winter, at least for a few weeks. God knew how dark his mood would get without that dose of sunlight and rum cocktails. And no one else in his life was going to spring for a South American vacation. Nat had no family to speak of left in Northam, except for some distant cousins, and they didn't speak at all. His friends were broke or married, which usually amounted to the same thing. He was the end of the line, old man. And he liked it that way.

A sudden chattering noise nearly snapped him out of his chair. It was his cell phone on the desk, rattling like a skittering pebble, giving the low growl that meant an incoming text. Nat picked the phone off the imitation mahogany.

Suicide: . . . the message said.

Nat frowned. It was from John Bailey, his oldest friend, now a detective with the Northam Police Department. John was working a double shift on account of Margaret Post's murder, the same reason Nat was here at the clinic. All part of an effort to calm the citizens of Northam into believing that her killer was far away, heading to Boston after his stopover in their sleepy little burg. Psychiatric outreach, they called Nat's night job here. Personally, he believed the town fathers were hoping whoever did it would wander in to his little office and confess.

The phone buzzed in his hand with the rest of the message.

Boned Maggie Voorhees.

Nat's frown changed into a sly grin. He and John had invented this game in high school. It was called Northam Suicide Note, or Suicide for short. They'd been bored back then. Hell, maybe morbid, too, typical outsiders in jock-ruled Northam High.

The aim of Northam Suicide Note was to re-create the last words of someone driven to kill himself for any particularly local reason. They'd write the note on a piece of paper—*Suicide: Ran over Ma with snow blower, oh God, the blood* or *Suicide: Maggie Voorhees just smiled at me all sexy-like*—and pass it to each other. Poor old Maggie got mentioned a lot, being the ugliest girl in school.

But it had been years since he and John had played the game. What had made his friend think about it now, on a Friday night in the dead of winter?

Nat typed out U dated her freshman year. Repent. and hit *Send.*

Outside he could hear the wind start up with a low shriek, that shrill inhaling sound announcing one day it would rise and rise and you'd never hear the top of it because the stones would have fallen in on your head.

Something began to ring in another part of the building.

Nat checked the little TV screen by the side of his desk. It showed the locked outside door that led into the clinic. Nothing but freezing rain on its small black-and-white screen, plus a small cone of bright white light and beyond it the darkness of the back side of the hill, descending downward to the Raitliff Woods. Who the hell was going to come out on a night like this?

Nat almost wished someone *would* show up, ring the bell under the bulb at the end of the wooden walkway that would sound in his office. Company would help pass the time. Still, only forty-five more minutes to go before he was done for the night.

Buzz. He picked up the phone and read the screen. Exactly why I should KM. *Kill myself,* part of their old code they'd used in high school to avoid teachers freaking out over their notes. Now John had to watch what he said on department time.

Strange. The messages didn't sound like good, yeoman-solid John Bailey. He must be out of his mind, parked in an unmarked car in this horrible weather. John had mentioned he'd be staking out the college entrance where Margaret Post's body had been found, in hopes the killer might return to the scene of the crime. Nat had walked by there himself yesterday on his way to the hospital and felt a chill zigzag up his back. The stakeout must have John reverting back to the old days. Next he'd be making a joke about seeing Margaret Post's sliced throat . . .

He caught himself. *Too soon, old man.* Nat wouldn't be able to stop himself joking about it eventually, of course; it was his nature to make light of even the most horrendous events in life. But the girl's murder was still too fresh. How goddamn awful it must have been. Walking home, alone, the comforting stone wall of the college to her right. Margaret had been twenty yards from the big Wartham College gate, with the words *Terras Irradient* inscribed in stone on an archway twenty feet above the ground. Just inside the gate sat a little security booth with a guard inside 24/7. But she'd never made it.

Judging by the grip marks on Margaret's left arm, the killer came up from behind, grabbed her, and dragged her into the bushes just short of the gate, then hung her on an ash tree next to the wall. But not before doing something to her so terrible that the newspapers could only hint at "disfiguring wounds."

Over in the psych wards at Mass Memorial, his day job, Nat wasn't exactly known for his empathy. Sometimes he wondered if he'd gotten into the wrong profession. *Your curiosity and your need to stay interested,* his mentor, Dr. Francesci, had once written on an evaluation, *overwhelms your recognition that this is a human being in need in front of you.* Touché.

But he could still feel for Margaret Post. All joking aside, they needed to catch the freak who had killed her.

The phone rattled on the desk. John again. All OK? the message read. Any takers over there?

Nat scooped up the phone and walked to get some blood flowing to his toes, which were quickly losing feeling. The disembodied messages out of the ether were starting to spook him. He felt like calling John. But Nat typed instead as he walked out into the dark hallway.

Nope. Yankees hate psychs. Rather drink.

Nat paced, walking up one flight into the tall arched hallway of the building. It boomed with a low, full-bodied echo; the place was old, built in 1729. In the gloom of the exit light, Nat passed the black-and-white archival photographs of famous Northamians: mostly sea captains or whalers (they were only forty miles from the ocean) or old codgers in top hats standing over some cornerstone or inaugurating the water mill. There were even a couple of public hangings in the town square depicted somewhere near the front entrance. Ghoulish fun for schoolboys.

It was, if that was physically possible, even colder in the hallway.

The phone buzzed in his hand.

Ur not psych. Ur bait. Be careful.

Nat caught his breath in surprise, then laughed. It could be true. The town was locked up, windswept, seemingly deserted. He'd been the only one out tonight in the ten minutes it took to walk from his condo to city hall.

Well, send him in, Nat thought. *As long as he has an extra blanket and a bottle of Jack.*

He thumbed the phone's keys.

Suicide: Found out best friend John secretly married to Maggie Voorhees. Shame too much.

It took thirty seconds by Nat's count for the little balloon to appear with his response.

I'm serious, Nat. Watch urself. Had reports . . .

Nat waited.

But nothing appeared under his little text window. Nat frowned. *Reports of what, John?*

He stared at the phone, then watched his breath disappear into the gloom. Damn it, what was John saying? He gave the phone a little shake, as if the extra letters were stuck somewhere in the circuitry and would tumble out with a little coaxing.

Nothing but the boom of the wind outside.

What was John up to? He felt a little fissure of concern. Maybe he should give the guy a—

DDDDDRRROOOOMMMM.

A huge metal tone boomed through the hall, then sank lower. Nat ducked and wildly looked up. He had forgotten how deep and melancholy the clinic bell was. Scared the hell out of him.

Nat hurried back, taking the steps two at a time. He walked into the clinic office, leaned over the desk, and shot a look at the security monitor. There was a man standing there, waiting outside the door in a dark green slicker and narrow-brimmed hat.

Nat's heart froze. The man . . . he had no face. Beneath the dark cone of light was a completely featureless expanse of blank skin. A wave of repulsion swept over Nat as he stared, horrified, at the eyeless and mouthless oval.

Then he looked again and let out a long breath. *Jesus Christ, get a hold of yourself.* The visitor was turned away from the camera and the sharp relief of darkness under the brim wasn't his face but the back of his bald head.

But somehow Nat kept thinking of it as a face—a *no-face.* He stared at the back of the man's head, but the guy didn't move. Rain splashed off the top of his hat and the shoulders of his slicker, danced briefly in the light, and then disappeared. Odd.

Nat walked out of the office and turned left toward the outside door. As uncanny as it was, that image of the faceless man faded as he headed down the darkened hallway. It had been replaced by a thought that disturbed him even more:

Why the hell is he watching the woods?

CHAPTER TWO

Nat hurried upstairs and turned left again at the corner. The heavy gray metal door was twenty yards in front of him, down a hallway with cupped lights set high in the wall. The man was still out there, the plunging gloom of the forest behind him. He didn't seem to have moved.

Maybe it really is about his face, Nat thought. *Maybe he doesn't want me to see it? Like he's missing a nose or has a terrible deformity?*

Between Nat and his visitor was a fire door with metal-threaded, double-paned security glass, nearly soundproof. No-face wasn't going to get in unless Nat allowed it. Regulations. He walked quickly to the door and pressed the intercom button.

"How can I help you?"

The man didn't move. Up close, he was about six foot two, a couple of inches taller than Nat, and his body seemed tense, as if he were on alert.

Nat thumbed the button again. "Sir?" He could hear his voice boom out into the rainy night.

No-face remained staring at the woods. Nat felt a wave of revulsion crawl over his skin. The man was spellbound.

Slowly, Nat approached the safety glass. He felt he was approaching a captive lion at a zoo; he knew the lion couldn't get to him, but he didn't quite *believe* it.

The raindrops danced off the man's shoulders, sparking in the overhead light.

Come on, Nat thought, and a surge of anger went through him. He knocked firmly on the glass.

The man's head now rose, and he turned crisply to face the window. Nat felt a shock, as if a wave of heat had passed through the metal-threaded glass and swept over him in the cold hallway.

The visitor was in his sixties and had a long, angular face, dark skin with deep creases running from the edges of his cheekbones to the corners of his mouth, and thin red lips that seemed fixed in a sneer.

Nat met his eyes. They were . . . He searched his brain for a description. *Diseased*, he finally thought. They pushed out slightly as if some internal pressure were forcing them slowly from the sockets. The whites were the color of an old tobacco stain—yellowed, dingy. They were shot through with red veins, and the irises were a flinty blue and intense. He looked like some army colonel who'd gotten a gutful of viruses in the tropics and had come home to die right on this goddamn doorstep. But not from a wasting disease, not malaria or a dose of yellow jack.

No, something that drove you crazy with fits. Lunatic energy.

Nat's eyes instinctively twitched down to the visitor's right hand. No weapon there, he was relieved to see. Just a big bare hand dripping with rain.

What had John said again? Reports of what?

Nat went to the intercom. "Can I help you?" rang out on the other side of the door.

The man just stared at him, studying the lines of his face. Then he met Nat's gaze and mouthed something, two fast words, but through the glass Nat only heard a smear of an urgent bass voice.

"What?" Nat asked.

No-face said it again, baring his teeth on the second word. He looked enraged, or frantic that Nat wouldn't let him in.

Nat pointed to the left side of the door. "Use the intercom," he said.

The man's pencil-thin lips—the only real color in the whole scene framed in the window—opened, and he stepped closer to the window, the dark eyebrows beetling over the sick eyes. Nat took a step back, then jerked his finger down toward the intercom. Finally the guy understood. He reached his right arm over to the bell.

"SHE'S SLEEPING" boomed into the hallway and echoed past Nat into the area upstairs.

Nat waited for more, but the man only drilled him with his gaze.

"Okay . . . ," Nat said, pressing the button. "What's your name, sir, and how can I help you?"

The guy looked angry now.

"You can open the door for me," he said through the intercom.

Nat frowned. *This is my rodeo, Sally.* Protocol said the patient had to tell the psych what the problem was before entering. Especially when people were being murdered in the general vicinity.

"State your name and business, Mr.—?"

The raindrops danced off the man's shoulders.

"Prescott, Walter Prescott. And I need to talk to you about my daughter."

Satisfied, Nat reached over and hit the buzzer. Prescott reached out and grabbed the handle. The little rubber gasket around the metal door popped, and a gust of cold air rushed over Nat. As Prescott came forward, Nat stepped back to give him room. The man's frame blocked out the light for a second in a blot of shadow, and then suddenly he was standing in the hallway, dripping.

Walter Prescott smelled like old medication. Stale but sharp somehow, like a piece of old gauze with a spot of fresh ruby blood at the center.

"Mr. Prescott, is your daughter in need of immediate medical attention?" Nat said. That one was state law.

"Med—?" Prescott said, worry lines bunching on his forehead. "No, no, nothing like that."

"Okay then. My office is one floor down. After you."

Nat held his arm out, headwaiter-style, toward the stairs at the end of the hall. It was something you learned your first year of residency. Let the crazies go first. Self-preservation.

Prescott frowned, then started toward the stairs.

"I assure you, Doctor—?"

"Thayer."

"*Thayer?*" Prescott stopped. "An old Northam name."

The voice was more formal, more cultured, than Nat had expected. *He sounds like a historian giving a talk at the local women's club. The voice doesn't match the eyes.*

Prescott smiled, a hideous thing of yellow teeth.

"I assure you, Dr. Thayer, it's not me you have to fear."

"Well, that's a relief. Straight ahead, please."

The two men walked single file down the stairs to the basement. Nat pointed right to the little glow outside his office. Prescott walked to it slowly, as if Nat were nosing him into a trap, then entered the office and set his dripping hat on the desk. Nat followed, walking around the desk and looking with distaste at the wool hat. A small puddle was forming around it.

Nat pulled open a drawer and fished out some heavy paper napkins.

"Let me get that," he said. He wiped the desk clear of water, went back to soak up the last drops, then tossed the napkins in the wastebasket. Then he sat down.

Prescott folded himself into the bare metal chair that sat in front of Nat's desk but said nothing.

Nat studied him for a moment. "You came out on a hell of a night, Mr. Prescott."

The old man pursed his lips. "Your family," he said finally. "You're one of James Thayer's sons?"

Nat took a breath, then gave Prescott a look and let it hang there for a second. Were they really going to play Old Yankee Social Call?

"No. Nathaniel's."

"Ah." Prescott's eyes sought the desktop. "A tragic story."

In the South, Nat had heard, they will offer condolences four decades after a "tragedy." In New England, you get one year maximum, and then it becomes town history, and any stranger can discuss it in front of your face as casually as if he were talking about the fat dude on *American Idol.*

Nat sat back in the cheap business chair that the town fathers had provided and gave the situation another couple of beats. He was an employee of the state of Massachusetts. He was contractually obligated to give Walter Prescott a hearing. He didn't, however, have to exchange family histories.

Prescott merely stared. Now that he was inside and had Nat's attention, he seemed in no rush for psychiatric outreach. Finally Nat broke the silence.

"But . . . not one we're here to discuss, is it, Mr. Prescott? Let's talk about what's bothering you."

The look, sickness—and what else?—returned to his eyes.

"It's my daughter."

Nat nodded.

"She's sleeping now. I felt it was safe to come away."

Prescott talked like someone out of the books Nat had read in high school. *The Scarlet Letter,* maybe? It was interesting enough. He'd gotten his wish of company for the night.

Prescott then stood and went to the window, just staring and saying nothing. The clock on the wall ticked away. Nat steepled his fingers in front of his face and waited.

He was familiar with the problem. Something drives a man like Walter Prescott to Nat's office. The man goes there full of hope, as if Nat has a cure sitting in the corner. Big old jar of Thayer's Fear

Killer. Lozenges specially formulated to melt away your childhood terrors. Jumbo shots of Thayer's Anti-Bad-Mother Medicine. But when the patient arrives, he finds a six-foot dark-haired stranger waiting for him. A man not warm by nature who lets the patient do most of the talking. Then he has to admit the demon is inside him, and he is afraid to speak its name.

Nat's phone buzzed, startling them both. Nat reached over, gave the screen a quick look—another message from John—and flicked the side switch to silent mode before sticking it in his pocket.

"Your daughter, you were saying?"

"Becca. Yes."

Nat continued waiting. The ticking of the clock. The sound of rain. Prescott's view out the office window was of the west corner of the Raitliff Woods where it met Main Street, and a street lamp whose yellow was, Nat saw, vibrating in a gust of wind.

The radiator knocked.

"Becca is the last of my children."

Nat *mm-hmm*-ed, glancing at the old man's profile. Prescott's right eye had a faraway look.

"Perhaps you've heard part of the story," he said, turning to look at Nat with a hint of disdain.

Nat spread his hands wide. "No, Mr. Prescott, honestly I haven't."

The man swiveled back to the window, too fast for Nat to see if he was disappointed or relieved.

"My eldest boy was named William. He was in his junior year at Amherst when he came home for the summer six years ago. I could see that he was . . ."

Something seemed to have gotten caught in Prescott's throat.

"Changed," he said finally.

Jesus Christ, were they going to do the whole family?

"I thought you came here about Bec—"

"Her story is *their* story," Prescott said, and there was a note of steeled anguish in his voice.

Nat frowned. *Buenos Aires*, he thought, *Buenos Aires, Buenos Aires, Buenos . . .*

"Changed how?" he said.

"His spirit was gone. He was a rower, rowed lightweight at Amherst. Debate club, treasurer at Chi Psi, he was a joiner." Prescott dropped his head, as if he were reading off his son's résumé. "Glee club even," he said, his voice almost embarrassed.

Is that his way of saying William was gay? Nat wondered.

"But when he came back that summer, he seemed like he didn't have an ounce of energy left in him. He walked around the house in a daze. He didn't have to get a job, but I would have preferred it. Both summers previous he'd worked in a Boston law firm . . ."

Something in his throat again.

"He was losing weight. Wasn't eating right, or eating at all, and he couldn't sleep. I'd hear him roaming around the house late at night, just walking from room to room. I even heard him banging his head on the doorpost upstairs one night. Scared me to hell."

Prescott looked at Nat; then his gaze fell to the floor.

"And then, one day in August, when he should have been getting his things together to go back to school, he came to me in the kitchen . . . and he told me . . ."

Silence. Five more ticks of the clock.

All you can do is wait them out.

Prescott gave Nat a ghastly smile.

"He told me that I wasn't his father. And that his siblings were not what they appeared to be. We were all imposters."

A name flitted in the back of Nat's mind, a French name from his postgrad course in psychoses. But he couldn't quite remember it.

Prescott paused. *Oh, don't stop now,* Nat thought, suddenly interested. Every psychiatrist is a prospector. And what Prescott was describing was gold. Rare, extremely rare.

Prescott continued. "He insisted we weren't his real family, and what's more is that he didn't appear to be shamming. He truly believed that we were strangers to him. I'd catch him studying my face from the side, as if he was *trying* to recognize me, actually wanting me to be his father. You see, William was a dutiful boy, never gave me trouble."

"Did he get treatment?"

"I made an appointment with a psychiatrist in Boston. A friend of the family. We were scheduled to drive up on Friday. On Thursday, William jumped off the Drammell Bridge."

Nat had expected something dramatic, but in that little office, it was like a blow to the chest.

He stared for a moment. And then his mind rebelled. *Really?* The rain-swept night, the frightening text messages, the man facing the dark woods, and now the perfect little gothic ending. Was John Bailey outside the door, laughing? Was Walter Prescott just some cop buddy he'd sent in with this macabre story? He looked like an ex-cop. If that bastard John—

But one look at the old man stopped Nat's thoughts dead. Prescott wasn't faking anything. In fact, at that moment he looked like he would gladly slip his neck into an executioner's noose. His neck muscles were strained, and his thin lips were twisted into a false smile that expressed the opposite of mischievous pleasure.

"I'm so sorry," Nat said.

"And then the same thing happened with Ch—" Prescott said mechanically, his voice falling away.

Nat felt a small chill run through his blood.

"Were you going to say Chase?"

The old man met Nat's gaze, and suddenly Nat understood.

Nat could feel fear seep into his bloodstream and shoot straight to his heart. *Jesus, he is the father of Chase Prescott.*

But he had to make sure.

"This is the Chase Prescott who . . ."

Prescott looked down. "Go ahead and say it out loud."

Nat's face grew cold.

"Who shot those men in Williamstown."

"And?"

Prescott seemed to enjoy dragging the details out of Nat. His eyes were lit up. *What pleasure could a man get from hearing about the people his son murdered?* Nat wondered.

"And then killed himself."

"That's right. That was my Chase. I knew you'd have heard *some*thing."

Nat shrugged. His lack of empathy—his weakness at the comforting side of psychiatry, the bedside manner and all that—was showing. He knew it, and it didn't bother him.

"Hard to avoid. It was very sad. I'm sorry."

Eight more ticks of the clock.

"Can we—" Nat said, but the old man suddenly raised his head, interrupting.

"Do you know when the Prescotts first came to this area, Dr. Thayer?"

Nat waited.

"A few years before your family, I'd guess," Prescott said.

This was the second-oldest Massachusetts game, after Old Yankee Social Call: When Did Your People Get Here? It bored Nat to death.

"I'm sure you're right."

"If you look at that cornerstone in the northwest corner of the hall"—his voice boomed as he pointed, his finger shaking—"you'll see the first one. Jacob Prescott. 1708."

Nat didn't bother following Prescott's finger. "What happened to Chase?" he said instead.

The name stopped the old man's rant. His hand dropped to the armchair as he swiveled back around, his body seeming to deflate.

"The same as my eldest son."

"The insomnia, the night walking, banging his head?"

"Yes."

"And the conviction you were not his father?"

"Yes. That always came last. Which is why I'm here."

"And now Becca," Nat said, the name strange on his lips. "She said the same thing to you?"

Prescott seemed visibly paler.

"This morning. It's the final sign, Dr. Thayer."

"We can get to that later. Why don't you tell me about Chase in the meantime?"

Prescott came around to the front of the chair and sat. He closed his eyes. Four more ticks of the clock. He opened his eyes and began.

"One night back in 2010, about this time of year, I was asleep in my bedroom. It's on the top floor of our house, three stories up. And I clearly remember that I was dreaming about Korea. I'd been there after the war, '61 and '62, a place called Pusan. Cold like you've never experienced, Dr. Thayer, colder than the worst winter night you ever lived through around these parts. Once, this Korean peasant came running out of his little hovel carrying some metal thing. I thought it was a bomb. I trained my gun on him and was about to blow his head off—there were saboteurs everywhere, even on the southern side—when I saw that he was carrying a pot. It was hot soup. I nearly killed the son of a bitch." His eyes were fogged and distant. "Anyway, that night, in my dream, I could even hear the choppers that ferried in those MREs to us out in the field, or carried the officers back to base camp."

His left hand made a little cutting motion into his right palm. "*Chop. Chop. Chop.*"

The hand continued cutting, but Prescott was silent, still far away. Finally, he snapped back from wherever he'd been.

"Anyway, when I woke up, I saw that the window in my room was open, the one facing back to the woods. The cold air was streaming in. The helicopter sounds were the snapping of the curtains. *How the hell did that get open?* I wondered, and I wrapped a blanket around me and got up to close it. I wasn't three feet away when I saw the eyes."

He stopped.

"Chase," Nat said.

"Yes. Chase. Standing behind the curtains."

"So, he'd opened the window."

Prescott dropped his gaze.

Nat could put the rest together easily enough. *So that he could push you out, dear old Dad, when you got close enough.*

"Yes."

"Did he say anything?"

"He said, 'Who are you in my father's body?' Chilling, I can tell you. Not just because of what he said, but because it was an echo of William's words. The two boys had never sounded that much alike, but just then—"

Prescott gave a visible shudder.

"Chase was . . . stronger than William. A hellion to be honest. Drove a motorcycle that sounded like the coming of the Antichrist when he drove up the street. He raised Rottweilers in a little shed out back from our house. Now, we are not the kind of people who raise Rottweilers, Dr. Thayer. Setters, maybe, or Irish wolfhounds from a good northeastern breeder. But Chase was different. We butted heads, I can tell you. But that boy had grit! He was battling whatever was happening to him, and hard, too."

They were far beyond any diagnoses now, Nat thought, deep

into Prescott's grief-dimmed conception of psychiatry and madness. You don't "battle" chemical imbalances or genetic tendencies.

"Do you understand, Dr. Thayer? William let it take him over, but Chase *fought*."

"And then he went to Williamstown?"

Prescott winced. "Yes. He said he was going to visit a friend. I didn't know of any friends he had there. I don't know what drove him at the end. I didn't recognize my son. The"—Prescott's eyes locked on Nat's—"*illness* had taken him." The ghastly smile returned.

"You don't think it was an illness, do you, Mr. Prescott?"

The eyes bore into Nat's. "No, I do not. I think it was something much more insidious, Dr. Thayer. Much, um, older."

"Like what?"

Prescott looked away. "I couldn't say."

Nat stood up and felt his back muscles ache. He hadn't realized they'd tensed up until now. The wind seemed to attack the windowpane, and it rattled in its mortar.

"And now you believe your daughter is suffering from the same condition?"

"Yes. But with one difference." Prescott leaned forward. "It . . . can't . . . have . . . Becca."

Prescott sat there, leaning over in his chair. He seemed to be transfixed again. His sick old eyes focused on the eggshell-blue paint of the office, and his lips moved slightly, though he said nothing.

"Mr. Prescott?" Nat said. "Mr. *Prescott*."

The old man started, his hand rising as if he were grasping at the lip of a cliff's edge to pull himself up.

"You need to bring Becca to Mass Memorial," Nat said, enunciating clearly to cut through the man's mental fog. "I have visiting hours there. I'll speak with her, and we can get her the treatment she needs."

"*No!*" Prescott yelled, startling Nat. His voice boomed down the hallway, and Nat heard the echo from the big stone room outside. *No, no, noooooooooo.*

Prescott breathed heavily, and his throat worked. "If I let her out of my sight, the same thing will happen to her. Don't you understand that? I won't let her leave the house."

Nat felt the time for gentleness had gone.

"Your sons committed suicide because they went untreated. If you want her to get better—"

"I've taken precautions, Dr. Thayer. Very careful precautions."

Nat stared at the man. He had a vision of a young girl strapped to some kind of medieval halter, up in the attic, being fed slop from her father's unsteady hand. In his present condition, Prescott seemed capable of almost anything.

"I hope you're not telling me that you're restraining her in any way. If you are—"

"I do what I please in my—"

"If you *are*," Nat said, bearing down on the last word, "this becomes a police matter. Do you understand me?"

The old man stared at Nat like a stubborn child. Nat stared back. Finally, Prescott nodded.

"What do you want me to do for you and your daughter?" said Nat.

"Come and see her. Speak to her. Find out what has taken hold of her mind. Before it's too late."

Prescott was more cunning than he let on, Nat thought. Now that he'd hinted that Becca was locked up, Nat had to make sure the girl was okay.

"Today's, what, Thursday?" Nat said with a sigh. "Will you be home tomorrow?"

Prescott stood up. "If I'm alive tomorrow, Dr. Thayer, I will be waiting for you at 96 Endicott Street."

CHAPTER THREE

Nat watched Prescott leave on the little TV screen. The old man stepped outside, pulled on his hat, and stared at the woods for a full twenty seconds before starting away left and out of frame. He was heading to Endicott Street on the other side of the Raitliff Woods, the area known as the Shan. Short for Shantytown, a leftover from the waves of Irish immigration in the 1800s. Ancient history—there were some beautiful houses there now.

Nat glanced at the clock: 10:50 p.m. Just ten minutes to go.

Prescott's story had unnerved him, he admitted to himself. Slightly. As a psychiatrist, he'd lost count of the competing symptoms Prescott's children—and their father—were presenting. But his son Chase was clearly psychotic at the end. There was no doubt about that.

Nat remembered the murders two years before, the black-and-white photo of the bloodstained sidewalk on the front page of the *Northam News*. He even vaguely recalled the school photo of Chase that had accompanied the article. He had his face tilted back, like Marlon Brando in some '50s motorcycle movie, with a thick, muscular neck the width of his head, a drift of dirty-blond hair over his face, a wash of stubble over a heavy jaw. Physically, he looked like any of the linemen Nat had shared the halls with at Northam High.

The difference, though, was the eyes. That and the viciousness of the crime was what had kept the picture alive deep in the recesses of Nat's brain, and he briefly tried to summon the eyes again. At first, he couldn't bring Chase back. Couldn't even re-member what color the eyes had been. Then, with a rush of dread, the face came welling up from his memory like some sea creature surfacing from the depths. Chase Prescott had blue eyes like his father's, but in his newspaper photo, they were filled with a kind of rapturous horror that had struck Nat as beyond strange even then, before he knew the full story. Chase looked like some nineteenth-century opium addict caught by a slumming photographer deep in some sordid den, staring at a vision of complete, engulfing terror, a demon rising six stories high, invisible to everyone but him—and Chase looked as though he welcomed it. Embraced it.

Can you be terrified and utterly joyful at the same time?

Monster of Northam, read the headline, as Nat recalled.

Madness is not contagious, he said to himself. Just because her brother was a psychotic didn't mean that Becca had the same patterns. Maybe her father was a kind of Munchausen's case, inducing madness in each of his children by turn. Maybe there was a good reason the children had stopped recognizing Prescott: because he had stopped acting like a father to them. But if Becca had one-quarter of what was in her brother Chase's eyes, she might be doomed to life in one of the few remaining state institutions in Massachusetts.

As eleven p.m. finally rolled around, Nat picked up his brief-case and locked the office. The freezing rain had turned to thick flakes of snow. The moon had now risen, and the clouds that scudded across it looked pale blue with a core of dark, smudged gray. Nat walked fast, eager to get home to his warm condo and his bed. He remembered John's text and dug in his pocket for his phone. He looked at the message on the screen.

Suicide: Too dark. Cold, cold, cold.

Not funny, old man. Not funny at all.

CHAPTER FOUR

On Friday morning, John Bailey drove along the twelve-foot red wall of Wartham College, its bricks glowing mellow in the midmorning light. John flicked the pages of his notebook while stealing glances at the road. Finding the right page, he noted something written there, then tossed the notebook onto the passenger seat. The name of the girl he was going to see was Ramona Best. She'd been BFFs with the dead girl, Margaret Post.

He wondered if Ramona knew how Margaret had died. God, he hoped not. Even though, as a proud townie, he was supposed to disdain Wartham, resent its airs and the privileged assholes who sent their daughters to it, he still felt protective of the young women who came from all over the world to study there. To know about how Margaret went out . . . Well, that wasn't something any twenty-one-year-old should be burdened with.

The red wall sweeping by slowly on his right ran around the entire length of the campus, rising and falling with the hills like some Great Wall of Massachusetts. It had been built in the late 1800s, when industrialization hit the town and turned it from a stagecoach stop on the way to Boston or points west into a small, dirty, ambitious city. The Blackstone Canal that linked Worcester and Providence had provided the power, and the locals had remade themselves into entrepreneurs: making wire and manufacturing rifles. That's what had transformed Northam from a little bumpkin town full of farmers and lawyers into a place of smokestacks and grime: wire and guns.

Back before the wall, Irish immigrants had flocked to Northam to work its mills and its factories, crowding into old mansions in the Shan that had been divided up into tiny apartments. Wartham College had reacted with horror to the dumb unwashed micks who had propositioned its upper-class girls as they walked to town on a Saturday for an ice cream or sarsaparilla or whatever the hell you went into town for back then. But you couldn't arrest the micks for talking to a girl. They just didn't understand the social code; they thought they'd left all that behind in County Clare. Unbeknownst to them, in Northam, the rules were a little more mysterious but just as hard.

So the college trustees decided to build a fence. Not an iron barrier like they had at Mills College, another all-girls university twenty miles away. That wasn't good enough for the caretakers of Wartham because the Irish could see through it and leer at the bodies of the girls, put their dirty-ape mick faces between the bars and have themselves a good look. The men's gazes polluted the atmosphere at Wartham. So the trustees had built a high brick wall.

Maybe that was the start of the Mills girls' rep for being wild. *Mills to bed, Wartham to wed* was the saying around town. Wartham girls were the ones you took home to California or New Jersey to meet your family at Thanksgiving, while you went to Mills to do drugs and have threesomes with budding lesbians. Who knew if that was true anymore, or if it had ever been true to begin with? It was something John had overheard in bars from loud frat boys visiting from colleges across the state.

The saying about Mills and Wartham girls only applied if you were some rich kid down from Amherst or Williams for homecoming weekend. They were the ones who swarmed into the little red beehive of Wartham, plundered the freshmen, then wandered out drunk as dogs, engaged to some dentist's daughter. If you'd grown up in Northam, like John Bailey had, you were local scenery, like the trees and the bell tower. A Wartham woman would rather marry a retarded midget than a local.

All John knew for sure was that Mills College had built an iron fence around its campus, allowing for the girls to be seen, and Wartham had gone with brick twelve feet high.

Little good it had done Margaret Post. John got the sense she wasn't the kind of girl who showed herself much—a loner, wearing a long coat the night she was killed. No flesh visible. But something had attracted a vicious killer.

John pulled up to the tree where he'd found Margaret Post hanging two nights earlier. He parked the car and looked at the tall spindly ash. The police tape was gone; the ground had been left as it was, muddy under where her feet had been dangling.

He'd been the third man on the crime scene. Those moments, beginning at 1:14 a.m. Tuesday night when he got the call, seemed to have been traced in his memory with acid. Wartham College was the biggest taxpayer and second biggest employer in Northam, so when you got a call about one of its students, you blew red lights all the way to get there. That was understood. He'd arrived on scene at 1:22 a.m. and found Dunlop, a patrolman, standing by the tree, along with the college security guard, an old guy wearing a pea green cardigan and orthopedic shoes.

"You call it in?" John said as he got out.

"Yeah," Dunlop had said. John was pulling on a pair of latex gloves. He could hear a branch creaking, as if it was under stress. There was a light crust of snow on the ground, but no ice on the branches. He reached back into the car and got his flashlight, clicked it on.

"Anyone see anything on the street?"

Dunlop seemed frozen.

"Dunlop?"

"Yeah?" the patrolman said faintly.

The wind stirred the tree branches, and there was the creaking sound again.

"Did anyone see anything?"

Another headshake.

"You sure?"

"Yeah, I'm sure." Dunlop's voice had been so low John had to strain to hear it.

Margaret Post had been hanging on the bottom branches of one of the ash trees that lined the border of the brick wall, her feet six inches from the ground. The college had planted the trees years ago to make the wall seem less forbidding, to make the fact that they'd built a barricade between themselves and the town seem less harsh. And Margaret was hung on one of the original ashes, her limp hands making a V above the branch.

John had walked up, still rubbing the sleep out of his eyes, not knowing what the security guard was pointing to so dully. He shone his flashlight up into the branches. And he'd seen the two hands above the tree limb, tied at the wrists with rough rope, the body hanging straight down, the head perched between the upraised shoulders. It didn't look right. The head was too low. It made it look like the thing had been severed and then hurriedly stuck back on between the shoulders, as if it corrected things. Margaret's mouth was open, her tongue black and sticking out of her mouth, and in the light of John's flashlight her skin was one shade paler than the snow on the ground.

John stopped, then moved toward her. Margaret, her name was Margaret Post. School ID in her pocket, the dispatcher had said. Clearly, the security guard had reached into her pocket and fished around for it. John hated when people messed up his crime scenes.

He'd touched her face, and suddenly an electric shock had gone through him. Like you get when you walk across a carpet and touch something metal. He dropped his hand immediately, and the old duffer of a security guard looked at him strangely.

"Something stick you?" he said.

No. It was as if a sliver of Margaret's fear had shot into his body. As if there were something still alive in her. Electrical charge. Leftover terror that hadn't been fully spent when she died.

But bodies don't have leftover electricity, John knew. No way, no how. No training in such things. No entry in the detective's manual, *Beware of stray shocks from corpses*.

He'd given the latex gloves another tug and lifted up her chin. When he did, the neck wound opened and the two flaps let out a wet sound. Her eyes goggled at him and her mouth hung open.

"Did you hear that?" he said to Dunlop.

"Hear what?"

John lowered his voice. "Did you check her pulse?"

Dunlop gave him a look. "Check the pulse?"

He was right to say it, John thought. Check the pulse when the woman's head was cut half off? What goddamn sense would that make?

Little bulbs of pink flesh were visible where the knife had gone through, washed in dark blood. And blood had fallen from the neck wound and soaked her kelly green blouse with the small white flowers, all the way down to the waist of her jeans. The smell of blood was in the air, like an aerosol that had been sprayed only minutes before.

The face was so chalky white it looked like she'd applied talcum powder for a Halloween party.

John sat in the car now, remembering that night. Trying not to look at the tree. Or think about what he'd seen on the tape from the Wartham security camera.

CHAPTER FIVE

After a late breakfast, Chuck Godwin walked out his back door, across his snow-covered yard, out the screechy gate in the fence, and into the Raitliff Woods. He liked to get out in the morning before heading in to work at his office on State Street. Divorce law wasn't the kind of thing that got you out of bed, charged up with purpose and inner fire. He needed to hear the forest streams and the crunch of moldering oak branches beneath his feet before he plunged into the raw human misery of his work.

The morning mist hadn't yet been completely burned away by the pale sun. He was glad he'd stayed in the Shan, in his part of it, at least—"his" because Chuck's family had been walking these trails since 1789, back when the Wampanoag tribes still came to the door asking for bread for their tawny little babies. It was wild, undeveloped land. Usually he loved wandering through the old paths that he imagined the Wampanoag had walked down two or three centuries ago. Sometimes in summer, he even took off his shoes and let his big pale feet toughen up on the trails. It connected him with the old place. He cherished that.

But Chuck's mind wasn't on Indians today; he walked purposefully, slightly out of breath, rarely looking up at the jaybirds swooping through the old-growth trees. He was taking a secret back trail that would lead him on to the back of Mary Reddington's house. The girl he should have married forty years ago instead of Stephanie. The girl he would have married, except he hadn't expected to live so long.

The land slanted away from him. Up ahead, Chuck saw a stand of birch trees—rare in this area—through the parting mist. Their thin white trunks caught in the mesh of fog always seemed to him like the bones of the Wampanoag dead, having been sucked from their burial grounds by the mist and now hanging in midair like an accusation. Haunts. Spectral, whiter than the gray gauze of the dew. They sent a chill up his spine, but he made as much noise as he could to dispel the spirits, snapping branches with his Timberland chukka boots, the branches' severed spines sending shots crackling through the woods. Only when he approached the Reddington house would he grow quiet. Mary couldn't know he was there. It would ruin things.

Chuck Godwin had never crossed the lawn that separated the tree line from Mary's house. He'd only stood at the forest's edge and caught glimpses of Mary as she got ready for her day. She was a widow now, all alone in the big house, her shadow visible on the pale upstairs curtains, then her face in the downstairs ones as she made breakfast for herself. But he felt the need growing in him to stride across the lawn. He'd once even emerged, drawn to Mary's profile in one of the upstairs windows covered with a strawberry-dotted curtain. It wasn't fear that made him turn and disappear back into the forest; it was that the thought of what he was about to do had been so exquisite that he'd grown weak with anticipation. Next time, he would be bolder. He'd march on over and tell Mary how he felt, that they had to be together again.

Chuck could hear the sound of running water, the stream at the bottom of the hill. His boot steps echoed like muffled gunshots as he clumped down the path. The burbling sound of water fast with runoff from melting snow grew louder. He turned right at an enormous oak, and the stream was in front of him with a small homemade bridge that had been here for generations, set deep in the banks.

Chuck was walking across the bridge, his bird-watching binoculars smacking firmly against his sternum, when something caused him to turn and look upstream. Suddenly he felt someone was out there, on the bank, watching.

The sun was hidden behind a thick stand of trees, and the riverbank was covered in a gray gloom. The pale trunks were encased in darkness. He could see nothing out of the ordinary in the feeble light of early morning.

Someone is following me, he thought. A tremor seized Chuck's heart, and in that moment, he wanted to run away.

Buck up, Chuck, he told himself. It was something his father used to say, not unkindly. *Buck up, son, buck up, Chuck, buck up.* He remembered it so vividly because when his father had gone off and hanged himself, Chuck had wondered to himself why the old man couldn't take his own counsel. But he knew the answer: it was because his father hadn't believed it himself. His dad's watery blue eyes looked like they wanted to cry even as he gave Chuck that ridiculous advice. He thought his father was laughing at him, toward the end of his life, with those stupid words. *Buck up.* As if there were any such thing.

Chuck stepped quickly across the bridge, and his boot sank to the leather in the soft loam of the bank, and the soil gave a tiny moan and then sucked at the rubber sole as he pulled it out. He would stay away from the deep woods and follow the path of the stream all the way to Mary's house, keeping out in the open.

He began to walk along the bank. The mud slurped. The water rippled. And as Chuck bent forward and tried to increase his speed, he thought he heard a third sound disguised in the noises around him.

Whispering. He was certain of it, as if there were lips a few inches from his ear.

He caught his breath and stood panting on the waterline. Nothing but stillness and bird cries.

"Who's out there?" he shouted. These were *his* family's woods. A trespasser was an unwelcome thing.

He scanned the tree line, the birch trunks and the heavy pine branches. Suddenly, the top of the pines to his right began to move, shivering as if someone were gently shaking the tree limbs. Chuck watched, his heart skipping beats, as the green branches jerked and bucked. There was no wind blowing across his face.

Run, he said to himself. *Quickly.*

He took his foot out of the hole it had just made in the mud and took a step backward. The tree shivered, and Chuck's mouth fell open in an O of horror.

An enormous bird came bolting out of the tree and flapped its wings. A sleek night-black crow. It gave Chuck a piercing look and headed upstream.

Chuck was shaking. He realized he'd been holding his breath.

He began to walk again. *Buck up, goddamn it. Just an old bird, for Christ's sake.*

He spotted the open space to the right that meant he was near the backyard of Mary's house, which itself was set back a hundred yards from the road. He crossed the stream, the water rippling over his boots and reaching almost to the top of the leather. The flat rocks underneath his feet were slippery—he felt as if they were covered with some gooey substance, as if he were walking on jellyfish—but when he looked down, the stones seemed clean. He made it safely to the other side, but a sudden repulsion puckered his skin.

Between him and the house was a thick patch of young birches, surrounded by a line of dry scrub. The path that he usually took was visible even in the bad light, but Chuck headed to the left of the trail, stepping onto fresh snow that crunched loudly in the still air. For some reason, he had the uncanny sense that, if he took the usual way, he would meet someone on the path. Someone that he didn't want to bump into.

Chuck leaned forward, pushing through the virgin snow. He stamped his way through a line of bushes that came up to his thighs, then found himself inside a circle of rustling birches. A cool breeze swept up from the floor of the little grove, and Chuck shivered, walking on. Now that the little stream was behind him, the sound of whispering grew in his ears once more.

It isn't real, he kept saying to himself. *I'm just nervous. Stop it, Chuck.*

He saw a curtain of brightness ahead. The sun had come out from behind its cloud and was now shining down on the field that backed onto Mary's house. The yellow light was so intense, in the way it often was after a rain shower, that it seemed to have set the field on fire. The burst of light was framed between two enormous birches that Chuck was now headed toward. A song came to him—"Rocky Mountain High"—and he hummed it tunelessly, his lips itchy with the vibration, to drown out the murmuring if it came back.

He came to the thick birch on the left, and he rested his forehead against it. The house looked so perfect, a deep bisque color with white trim nestled on its half-acre plot. *This is where I should have been*, thought Chuck. This was where he should have spent the last forty years, being happy and making love to the pert, gamine-eyed Mary Reddington, instead of locked in with Stephanie, who was so boring in bed and so uncharitable outside of it.

A shadow seemed to cross the sun, and a wave of dread seemed to wash the light out of the air. It was as if some huge invisible beast had come striding through the forest, sucking away the cheeriness and the warmth.

Chuck felt eyes on him. He *felt* them, from the west. But he would not turn to look.

Buck up, you fool. Nothing bad can happen if you keep your eyes

*on the house. Watch for Mary. She'll be coming out of her shower soon
and walking downstairs to start the coffee machine. Watch for her
profile in the kitchen window. Watch.*

A pain began to build in his head. It felt as if he were in a kind
of pressure chamber and the dial was being turned up, up. Almost
pleasant at first, but quickly becoming painful. Higher. *Goddamn
it, make it stop.* Another notch. Chuck blew a breath into the air,
leaning hard now on the birch.

Do not turn away from the house. Eyes on Mary. She will save you.

But the pressure inched up and his teeth gritted as if he were
having a seizure. "Oh God," he panted. He took a rasping breath
and his eyes slid away from the house and he saw the thing immediately. Staring at him.

The man stood straight in the shadow of thick elm. He was
wearing a uniform, a pressed khaki one that Chuck hadn't seen
since he was a boy. The man's head was bare and the side of his
face as pale as alabaster.

But the eyes . . .

They were snowman eyes, black as anthracite coal, with a tiny
spot of orange at the center. Against the paleness of the skin, they
seemed to spark with a cold light. The thing was looking at him
with a hatred so intense, he felt it as a wave of hot, foul air.

"God, no," Chuck cried out, but his feet were rooted to the
ground and he couldn't move.

An animal screamed from the woods to his left, and he heard
the tread of it tearing through the underbrush. Chuck tried to
scream, but his voice was lost in a smear of terror. His gaze was
being pulled into the blackness of the man's insect eyes, around
and around the edges toward the tiny orange flame at the center.

The man's lips, which had been set in a grimace, began to
move silently. Chuck watched them, feeling as if he were in a
trance. As the lips formed words, an echoing voice sounded
clearly in his head.

The rope . . .

A tremor of fear loosened his knees, and he pulled his feet free and stumbled back before turning to run. He was moving in slow motion. He raced back toward the sound of water, pushing the tree limbs away from him, the needles stabbing his cheeks. Finally he reached the stream and headed toward the bridge.

The rope . . .

His right knee suddenly gave way. He fell heavily into the stream, and the sound of the running water blotted out the other noises around him. But he knew that the man was walking toward him. He could feel a cold spot in his back expanding outward with each passing second.

. . . is in the basement.

He couldn't turn. If he turned and looked, the man would snatch his soul away.

Beneath the stairs.

In the burbling of the brook, he could hear other noises, heavy footsteps approaching and a strange moaning.

"Leave me be!" he cried out over his shoulder. He got up to run, freezing water streaming down his legs.

The voice spoke, and he flinched as if the lips had touched his ear.

The rope is in the basement.

His throat tightened.

Beneath the stairs.

The cry of an owl. Chuck looked up, and the sun was breaking through the clouds in the little circle of treetops. He knelt there, frozen, waiting for the man's cold hand on his neck.

Buck up, Chuck thought. *Not too late.* He staggered up and began to run again, reaching the path after a few steps, his boots striking the ground with the sound of a blow on thick leather.

If I don't look, I'll be safe, if I don't look, I'll be safe.

He saw the dun-colored fence of his own backyard rise up

out of the landscape twenty yards ahead, and his breath caught in his throat as he used his last bit of strength to race toward it.

If I don't look...

He grasped the top of the wooden gate and swept it wide, forcing his freezing legs through the gap. The wind was whipping in little vortices, tossing leaves into the air in his broad yard and whirling them around in dissolving circles. Chuck stood up straight, the icy spot throbbing at the base of his spine, and turned slowly around.

There was nothing out there except trees and silence. If it had been following him back home, the apparition was gone.

CHAPTER SIX

John Bailey swung the old Crown Vic into the entranceway at Wartham and waved to the guard there, the same old man who'd reported Margaret hanging in a tree. The man was wearing the same pea green cardigan he had two nights before. He looked at John but didn't wave back. Just licked his lips as John cruised past.

John felt a little out of his depth coming to Wartham, to be honest. He'd been out of college for thirteen years, and he knew how rich and secluded this place was. The old social awkwardness he'd felt since high school—which had made his friendship with Nat Thayer even more of a miracle—stirred inside him.

The press had been kept off the campus, for the most part, but they were baying like bloodhounds outside of it. The *Boston Globe* had sent one of their better crime reporters, now ensconced at the local Red Roof Inn, and he'd taken to calling the department at least twice a day, demanding information. There were TV reporters doing regular stand-ups from the entrance to the college or just in front of the ash tree; John had passed one on his way in. Margaret Post's parents would surely be filing a lawsuit once their daughter was buried and a suitably relentless attorney was hired. The longer the case remained unsolved, the more prospective students Wartham would lose to Smith and Holyoke, the more social media would produce wilder theories and fresher suspects, the more the department would look like a bunch of small-town yokels, and the worse John's life would become.

He slowed down to 20 mph as he cruised through the twisting little streets on campus. Girls strolled by in their long winter coats, collars pulled up against the morning chill, some chattering in groups, others alone cutting fast across the quad. John parked in front of Smith Hall, where the Post girl had lived. Ramona Best lived in 2C. A single, John guessed, just like Margaret. He got out of the car, walked across the stiff frost-hardened grass that gave way reluctantly beneath his size-13 boots.

He thought of his first questions, but they only brought back the memory of Margaret's face, the ash tree . . .

Blood everywhere. Blood soaking into the ground, running down the wormholes in a rush. Blood in your mouth and lungs, breathing it in.

He pushed open the door and walked into the first floor. Someone was playing "Positive Vibration" down the hall, and he could smell the faintest tinge of sinsemilla in the air. *Jesus Christ, nothing ever changes.* They must give every incoming freshman a Bob Marley greatest hits playlist and a nickel bag.

Some of the doors were propped open. A girl emerged from the last one in a ratty green bathrobe, her hair tied up, her legs naked below the knee. Bailey averted his eyes, but he'd seen the flush of red covering her neck. At least he had his badge hanging by a chain around his neck, which made it clear he was on official business.

Still, he felt like a damned rapist in here. Any man would.

John found the stairwell and climbed up to the second floor. The second door on the left had a plain black plate on it at eye level that read 2C. John knocked. The Marley music from downstairs had switched to "Stir It Up." John caught himself nodding along to the opening chords.

He knocked again.

The door opened suddenly and Ramona Best was staring at him. Black, bright-eyed, short, dressed in a green-and-white sweatshirt and jeans.

"Yes?"

"Ms. Best?"

"Ye-es. Can I help you?"

"I'm Detective Bailey with the Northam PD." His ID was in his right hand, and the leather flap fell away to show his unsmiling picture. "I had a few questions about Margaret Post."

Her eyes flicked down to the ID. "I spoke to the officer the night . . . the night of."

"I know. And it was very helpful. But I have to ask a few more questions."

She frowned, deciding whether it was within her rights to close the door. "Come in, I guess," she said finally.

Bailey stepped inside what was a typical dorm room—a cluttered desk by the window, a tie-dyed sheet hanging on the wall with the name of some band he'd never heard of written on it, and a couple of plants dangling over a bookcase filled with paperbacks and course books.

There was a wooden desk chair with yet another plant on it. Ramona put it on the floor, then looked over her shoulder at him.

"Thanks," he said.

The girl pulled out a second chair from under the desk and sat on it, facing him. Her face looked heavy, as if she'd been sleeping.

"I'm sure the other officer told you this," John began, "but anything you can tell us—no matter how minor it seems—could really help. I just want to catch this guy."

Ramona nodded.

"Can you tell me about Margaret's friends?"

"You're looking at her."

"She didn't hang out with anyone besides you?"

Ramona made a face. "This girl in the glee club, Tessa. You know, Margaret was a music geek—she'd always imagined coming to Wartham and singing glee and traveling to Yale and having wild sex with sensitive poets there. That was before she realized that Wartham was just as bad as anyplace else."

"Just as bad, how?"

"Cliquey. There are about twenty girls who can either make your life wonderful or make you want to kill yourself."

"Was Tessa one of those girls?"

"No, not even close. Tessa is an outcast, just like us. But even she broke Margaret's heart. She was supposed to take Margaret to her house for Christmas, but the invitation was mysteriously rescinded."

"Was there anyone else? Men?"

Ramona shook her head.

"Not even . . ." *Can you even say* one-night stands *anymore?* "Casual acquaintances? Guys from town?"

The girl's face wrinkled up, as if she'd smelled a skunk. "Guys from *town*?"

John felt his face flush. Ramona realized her mistake and looked horrified. "Oh, I'm sorry," she said, her voice softer. "But, I mean, no."

"She didn't mention anyone?"

Ramona shook her head. "And believe me, she would have told me. She told me when the UPS guy looked at her more than three seconds. Margaret wasn't getting noticed. She won't be—" Ramona caught herself. "She wouldn't . . . have . . . been until we graduated and got away from here."

"What about her behavior? Did you notice a change lately?"

Bang. Ramona looked like a gaffed fish.

"No."

He said nothing for a few seconds, then: "Ramona."

She got up and began to straighten up some books there. John could hear the first synthesizer chords of "No Woman, No Cry" floating up from the first floor. Ramona took a book from the bottom and placed it on the top.

She was working something out. Clearly Ramona was loyal to the dead girl. John liked that, respected it.

"You talked to Margaret's parents, right?" the girl said finally.

"Yeah. I told them the news. They're in Brazil, doing missionary work there out in the boonies. They're trying to arrange a flight."

"I don't want any of this getting back to them."

"We can do that."

Ramona took a deep breath. "Margaret felt she was being . . . watched."

John didn't like the sound of that. What he wanted was a clean and simple stranger murder, a crime of passion. Not a stalker who might turn his attention to another Wartham girl. "Watched how?"

"She wouldn't say. But she was scared. She said that she could feel someone . . . following her."

"Did she ever give a description? This someone was male?"

Ramona nodded yes.

"Young, old?"

"That's just it. She never actually saw him. But she was convinced he was out there. She couldn't sleep. And then . . ."

"Yes?"

Ramona frowned and came around the chair and sat down. Her eyes had changed somehow. Were the irises smaller? Or was John imagining things?

She's afraid, John thought.

"I went over to see her last week. I hadn't heard from her in three days or so, and that was unusual. She hadn't even come over on a snack run at night, and Margaret was a stone-cold carbs junkie, especially after eight o'clock. Had to have something. I kept cookies for her over there."

John looked and saw a box of animal crackers on a shelf next to a Spanish dictionary with a torn white cover.

"She was killed on Tuesday. What day would this have been, Ms. Best?"

"Last Friday."

John made a note.

"So I knocked on her door."

He watched her. So easy to see when someone was telling the truth. They forget about you. They go back to the moment.

"And I heard something inside. I thought I heard Margaret talking to herself. Before I knocked. Over and over again."

"Saying what?"

Ramona looked out the window down at the quad.

"I don't want you to tell her parents that she was a crazy person."

"I won't."

Ramona sighed. "She was saying . . ." Her eyes came up to his. "'*I will not . . . submit.*'"

John swallowed.

"To you?" he said finally.

Ramona shook her head.

"To someone in the room?"

Ramona shook her head again.

"How do you know?"

"Because I saw."

Ramona's eyes were slanted down to the floor, as if she didn't want to witness again those things head-on, as if she wanted to keep them *there*, off to the side, safely away from her. She hugged her arms to her chest and shivered.

"I knocked and said, 'It's me, Ramona, you dumb cow, let me in.' And then I heard her voice again, but I couldn't make out the words. She was starting to freak me out. I tried the handle again, and when I looked down, I saw something in the doorway."

John waited. Ramona Best wasn't in this dorm room anymore; she had, for all intents and purposes, left her body and was now seven days before, staring at something in Margaret Post's doorway.

She said something. John leaned in.

"Excuse me?"

"*Salt.*"

"Salt?"

"She had poured a line of salt across the doorway."

"Why?"

Ramona's eyes went big. "Do I look like I know? What, all black people know 'bout potions and powders?"

John sat back, flustered. "No, no, no, it's not that. I mean . . ." He collected his thoughts. "Did you ask her then about the salt?"

"I couldn't. She opened the door. She was pale and she looked . . . out of it. And the door was open enough for me to see past her. There was no one else there. Whatever *it* was, it was in the room with her."

John made a note. "So what happened next?"

"Nothing. She didn't come out of that room for the next three days. Wouldn't answer her phone or e-mails. Something had her scared to death."

"But then, on January second, she went into town."

"Exactly."

"Do you know why?"

Head back and forth. No.

"Did she go into town often?"

"Once in a while. We would catch a movie at the Northam Twin. They have double features on Wednesday nights, old classics and oddball movies that the owner likes. A lot of students here go."

John closed his notebook. "I get that you don't know why she went to town. But what do you think? If you had to take a guess."

Ramona hugged herself tighter, looking at the floor. "I'm sure

I don't know. And furthermore, based on what happened, I don't *want* to know."

John took a deep breath and leaned back in the chair, tried on a friendly smile. "You graduate this year?" he said.

She looked at him warily. "Why?"

"I'm just making conversation."

"Yeah, well, cops don't just 'make conversation.'"

"I do."

"Yes, I graduate this year."

John nodded. "And you don't want anything to mess that up?"

Ramona looked up, and he saw a kind of feral ambition in her eyes. And fear, too. "Nope," she said.

He looked at her, his eyes steady. "I understand that."

The young woman didn't respond, but her eyes said enough: *Do you, Detective? Do you really?*

CHAPTER SEVEN

Nat slept until eleven that Friday morning. Today was his day off in the flex schedule and his condo was nice and heated, so he lingered, staring at the ceiling, listening to the traffic noises from the street outside. Finally, still dressed in a pair of shorts and a ratty T-shirt, he got up and rooted around in the cupboards until he found the pancake mix, added water, whipped up three extra-light flapjacks—he hated anything burned—and was relaxing with a large mug of tea, looking at the clouds raking over the top of Grant's Hill, when the doorbell rang.

It was John Bailey, dressed in street clothes. His reddish-blond hair was tucked under a Red Sox cap, his growing belly slipped over a brown leather belt, and he was wearing a thin leather jacket for such a frigid day. The man was always warm.

"What's up, stranger?" John said.

"Hey. Come on in. Pancakes?"

"Nah, I just had an Egg McMuffin. I'll take some coffee, though."

"You have to wait a few minutes then, as I need to make it."

John walked in, nodding at the exposed brick hallway, the clean hardwood floors, and the minimalist leather furniture of the apartment. His broad farm-boy face still took it all in every time with mock wonder, though he'd been here a hundred times.

"Amazing," he said. "Simply goddamn amazing."

"Stop it, old man," Nat said, affecting the accent of some English actor. "It's just a little *pied-à-terre*."

"I'll never get my head around how you do it."

"Do what?"

"This! You're single. It's eleven thirty a.m. and you're just getting up. You bang broads and then never see them again. How do you do this?"

Nat laughed and lifted the bag of Starbucks Pike Place Roast to see how much was inside. Enough for a few cups. He poured out a heaping portion into the coffeemaker and went to sit on the leather couch facing the big picture window.

"How, old man? Absence of money," he said.

"Yeah, right. That didn't stop Leah."

"You're the one who proposed to her, dummy."

John threw up his hands. "But she accepted. Why'd she do that? Bitch."

"Well, she made up for it in the divorce settlement."

John gave a big sigh.

"So what got into you last night?" Nat said, taking a long pull on his tea.

"Meaning?" John said, turning his beaming cop face toward Nat.

"The texts."

"Huh?" John stared with complete incomprehension.

"Warning me to watch myself? General doom and gloom? Hello? The Northam Suicide Notes . . ."

"Ohhh, oh, *that*. Man, listen. I was just messing around. It had been a long day. And that Margaret Post case . . ." He blew out a breath. "Well . . . the whole department is spooked. Let me just say that."

"Were there reports of someone prowling around?"

John gave Nat a quick sidelong glance, then looked away. It was the *I wish I could but I can't* look that cops gave their friends. *You're not part of the club, pal. Sorry.*

"Come on, John, who're you kidding?! What was it?"

"Nothing, really. False alarm."

The smell of coffee was wafting out of the kitchen. John sniffed and a look of doglike anticipation came over his big face. "Ahhhhh. It's ready, bro."

Nat got up.

"Well, right after you texted," Nat called from the kitchen, "I had a visitor."

"No shit. Who?"

Nat didn't answer. John twisted around and looked at him. Nat gave him the *I wish I could tell you* face right back.

"Awwww, don't be a baby. Tell me."

"Doctor-client confidentiality."

"Horseshit."

Nat came over and handed John the coffee, black, in a chipped mug.

"Actually, maybe we should talk about it. What do you know about Chase Prescott?"

The innocent look of anticipation on John's face vanished and was replaced by horrified disgust. "Oh God. Dude, don't even talk about that guy."

"Why?"

"There are things . . . The whole family's bad news."

Nat sat down and stretched his legs out to the coffee table. "Drugs?"

"No, not drugs."

"Domestics?"

John took a sip and leaned back into the leather with a sigh. "'Domestics'? You sound like some old fart who listens to the police scanner for kicks."

Nat raised his eyebrows.

John shook his head, once. "Not 'domestics.'"

"Listen, John," Nat said. "I need to know this. For reasons that are none of your concern. And don't get ethical on me. It's not like you."

Actually, it was, but Nat liked to goad him anyway.

"Why do you want to know? Chase Prescott's dead, and good fucking riddance. The only ones left are the father and the daughter."

"How'd you know about that?"

John looked at Nat. "How'd *you* know about that?"

Nat shrugged. A game of chicken.

A school bus came lumbering up Grant Street, grinding gears as it climbed the hill's steep gradient. It passed under the condo window and made a left onto Porter. John watched it go.

"All right. What if I told you that there's been at least one violent death in that family every generation for the last hundred years?"

Either it was Nat's imagination or the light in the room changed. He looked out at the mountain, and a thick patch of cloud was coming over, obscuring the sun.

"You're kidding," he said quietly.

John said nothing.

"Why haven't I heard about it?" Nat said.

"My guess? Some of them were covered up. Your accidental drownings, or bad reactions to medicine. Nothing was accidental, believe me. But the family has money and friends in town. Or had. Once upon a time."

It was worse than Nat thought. A hundred years of mental illness, no skipped generations? That was impressive. And scary.

"Were any of them treated?"

"What am I, the town historian?" John said.

"Whoa. Why are you getting all bent out of shape?"

"Sorry. Long night. Listen, all I know is department scuttlebutt. Cops talk. Certain houses in this town get bad reputations. And the word on the Prescotts is that the family is cursed and has been since, like, forever."

"Any theories as to why?"

"Please don't tell me you're getting mixed up with them. Are you, Nat? I'm telling you, do not do that."

"Uh-huh. I love it when you get all superstitious and then order me around, one right after the other. Asshole."

John shook his head, turning his back toward the window. His shoulders slumped, and he looked worriedly at the hardwood floor. Nat watched him. It was so unusual for the guy to be depressed that it made Nat edgy just to see it. Finally, Nat leaned over and slapped John heartily on the back, leaving his arm draped around his best friend's broad shoulders.

"What's with you? Weird texts in the middle of the night, worrying about my health. Shoot me straight. Are you in love with me?"

"Shut up," John said.

"You can tell me. It'll be just between us girls. You should know that I have feelings for you, too."

"Why didn't you ever say anything?" John said, and they both laughed, the odd tension dispelling for a moment. Nat was glad. If good yeoman John Bailey was tense, something wasn't right with the world. John was Nat's reservoir of positive feelings about humanity; if John ran empty on optimism, Nat felt everything around him might shrivel up and die.

His hand lingered on John's shoulder, and he gripped his neck, giving him a crooked smile.

John laughed again. Nat dropped his hand.

"But I did get a call there once, at the Prescott residence," John said, and now his voice was quiet.

"Yeah?"

John took a sip of coffee. "Yeah. Report of a prowler."

"When?"

"After the oldest kid—what was his name?"

"William."

John was about to go on, but turned to stare at Nat, sharp-

eyed. Nat only smiled. John continued: "Yeah, William. But this
was before Chase went on his little killing spree. I was working
nights, and it came in at the beginning of my shift. Eight o'clock."

Nat watched him, expecting the punch line. *And when I
looked through the window, I saw Maggie Voorhees sucking you off,
Thayer.*

But he looked at John's face and somehow that wasn't going
to happen, that the story wouldn't end in a joke or some anticli-
max. Nat had the strange feeling—like last night, when he expected Prescott's tale to turn out to be an elaborate hoax, but he'd
recited one gruesome detail after another—that there was a pattern to the whole thing, one that insisted the grimmest possible
option would always come true. The normal variation of life was
missing. Everything would lead downward into darkness, re-
morselessly.

John had pulled up to the Prescott house in his patrol car, stopped
in front, and climbed the wooden steps toward the house, which
was perched up on a little embankment. The curtains in the windows downstairs and upstairs were pulled shut. He rang the doorbell. No answer. He'd knocked several times, then climbed down
the porch stairs . . . when something made him turn quickly and
look at the house again. He spotted a slight movement of the curtain in an upstairs window. Someone clearly had been looking
out. John went and rang the bell again and pounded on the door,
but without a reported emergency, he wasn't authorized to break
it down.

So he'd gone around back. The weeds along the sides of the
house were grown over, and pricker bushes, as they called them
in Northam, had grown over the flagstones leading to the backyard. He had to turn sideways and smash his way through with his
flashlight. The backyard had been nice once, with a large veranda,

but the big oaks were dead, their bark gray, the towering branches leafless.

He'd found Chase Prescott back there, shirtless, dressed only in jeans. Chase was staring off into the elms—the property went back a good hundred yards. John called out to him, saying "Police!" but Chase never moved.

"I came up behind him," John now said. "His chest was rising and falling and he was breathing hard. He seemed to be in a kind of trance, that's how I'd describe it. I asked him if he'd called 911.

"He never turned. He was *listening* to something. When I got round in front of him, I saw that his chest and belly were covered with scratch marks."

Nat frowned. Again the feeling came over him: *Nothing will turn out good again, nothing.*

"Well, the only sound was the wind blowing through the tops of those dead oaks. But then I began to hear something else. Sounded like someone moaning, but far away. I couldn't place it, and Chase Prescott was so out of it I thought he was tripping on—what's that stuff? The Indians use it."

"Peyote."

"Yeah, Chase looked like what I imagined someone who'd just done a big dose of that was. No smell of liquor, no meth teeth."

"The moaning," Nat said. "Did you figure that out?"

A look of disgust passed over his face.

"Yeah. The dog."

"A . . . Rottweiler."

John looked over at Nat, his eyes a bit hooded, unsurprised now that Nat knew intimate details of the Prescott family's life.

"Yeah. Chase raised Rottweilers. Loved 'em, as I found out later. He wasn't so good with human beings, but he bought prime steak for the Rotts at Stop & Shop every Friday."

"The dog had scratched up Chase."

John nodded.

"Where was the dog?"

John looked out at Grant's Hill.

"Buried."

Nat's eyes went wide.

"I followed the sound to a little mound with fresh dirt in it, near one of the oaks. Chase didn't dig the hole deep enough. I stood over that mound, and I could hear the dog screaming for its life, the oxygen going. He'd buried it alive."

John loved dogs. If his son, Charlie, hadn't been allergic, Nat knew, he'd have two at least. Charlie had bigger problems than dog-hair allergies; he had Heller's syndrome, which meant he couldn't talk. His brain just didn't work normally—there were hallucinations, loss of motor skills (very mild in Charlie's case), and social impairment, which meant that Charlie had zero friends. Nat had studied the rare syndrome when Charlie was diagnosed, and found its mysteries, and its lack of any hope for a cure, intensely frustrating. Thank God the kid had avoided the worst symptoms of the disorder—the loss of bowel control and the low-functioning intelligence. But, with Heller's, you don't want to add allergies to the mix.

John went on: "I ran around the yard until I found a shovel leaning up against the back door. I was yelling at Chase the whole time to help me, but he just stood there, staring into the trees. I'd grabbed the shovel and ran back and dug the fucking thing out. Meanwhile, the little mound had gone quiet. I got down to what was an old apple crate he must have pulled up from the basement, and I knew the thing was dead. Had to be. No movement or nothing. Then I had to fill in the hole I just dug. And the whole time it was all I could do not to go over to Chase and brain him with the shovel."

"He never moved?"

"Never. I didn't bother calling the EMTs. I wanted to let him suffer a little longer, to be honest. Found his jacket, put it on him, and put him in the back of my patrol car, took him to Mass Memorial for a psych evaluation. You weren't there yet."

He would have been at grad school in Boston. "What was the diagnosis?"

"When we got to the door, he had his head in his hands. Crying. Son of a bitch. He never gave a reason, but he checked out as normal and walked away three days later. Pled guilty to animal cruelty and served, I don't know, I think he got two months."

Nat picked up John's near-empty cup and walked back to the kitchen. Animal cruelty, as any armchair psychiatrist knew these days, was a marker for early disturbances. But that's in childhood, not when someone was in his late twenties, like Chase Prescott. Strange.

When he came back, John looked up expectantly.

"Quid pro quo?" Nat said as he sat down.

"Yeah, whatever that means."

"It means I owe you some info, old man. So, yeah, Walter Prescott came to see me last night. Said his daughter, Becca, was showing some of the same signs Chase and her brother showed before they . . . went off the rails."

John stared at Nat, his face puffy. "So you're going over there."

"Yeah."

John looked out at the clouds. "Can I talk you out of it?"

Nat laughed. "Have you ever been able to talk me out of anything?"

CHAPTER EIGHT

At five thirty p.m., after saying good-bye to John earlier and getting some work done on his laptop, Nat got into his Saab 900 and headed toward the Shan. It had begun to snow, that kind of light windless squall where the flakes are falling so slowly and soundlessly that it really does seem like an enormous goose-down pillow is being shaken loose a mile up in the air.

Nat didn't know the Shan well and had to use the Google Maps app to get to the address. The map showed the house fronting Endicott Street, with a large lot behind it, backed by a stream that ran diagonally across the back of the property. The houses nearby were widely spaced.

When the Irish had come to Northam in the mid- and late 1800s to work in the factories, they'd made the Shan their own. Many of the landed gentry who lived in the area had divided up their properties, sold out to the grimy-fingered men who would throw up the narrow houses for the immigrants, and left for Nat's side of town, where they built even bigger houses. Only a few of the old-stock landowners had stayed put, and were more tied to the land than any Southern plantation owner, some with their own family graveyards on the property.

Nat went over Bogg's Hill and the rusting railroad tracks that separated the Shan from Northam proper and immediately got lost. The blue Google Maps dot that tracked his car wandered through fields and across streams as if it had a mind of its own, and he had to pull over twice to figure out where the hell he was.

Finally, he asked a bunch of kids playing street hockey on the wet asphalt where he could find Endicott Street, and after giving him hard Irish stares, they pointed him in the right direction. He arrived in front of the house just shy of six p.m., as the early dusk was falling over the trees and the white snow-covered lawns.

As Nat pulled up, he saw the house rising against the black-furrowed storm clouds that were streaming west. It was an old, spiky Victorian, painted black and green, with a single turret coated in dark panels, like a malevolent Fabergé egg. *But houses can't be malevolent*, Nat thought. It's the relationship of the physical structure and its occupants that can press itself into the passerby's mind. When one senses an air of decay, two-foot-high grass and broken windows, that tells you that maybe the children raised inside were treated with the same kind of neglect and violence. Or a house where the lawn edge is straight as a razor and there isn't even a stray pebble out of place could indicate an overabundance of discipline.

Still, 96 Endicott did give off a whiff of something unclean, Nat realized as he walked up the path to the porch. Who paints a house black with green trim? Even the color that the Prescotts had chosen, that deep hue—Nat recognized it as what they called Dartmouth green—was the darkest on the market. It was picked by an owner who secretly wished to paint his house all black but knew that his neighbors will frown and whisper, *Do we have a devil worshipper in our midst?*, so he went with one degree above that with the darkest green in the hardware shop. Its light-sucking pigment made the looming mass of the house seem heavier and more massive against the sky as Nat climbed the steps. As he got to the top, he realized the porch and first floor were half hidden behind some spiky uncategorized trees that had started to grow wild.

The only other house visible on the street was a hundred

yards away. *Who called 911 to begin with?* Nat wondered, remembering John's story about Chase Prescott. *Who could hear the dog screaming?*

He rang the bell, and it seemed instantly that the double-wide door opened and a figure stood in the half darkness. Nat recognized the general shape of Walter Prescott, though the light was so bad his head was wrapped in a kind of gray murk.

"Mr. Prescott?"

"Yes?"

Prescott's features slowly swam into view. He stood there, staring at Nat, as if he had no idea who the psychiatrist was but was too afraid to ask him to leave. The old man's eyes darted uncertainly.

"It's Dr. Thayer."

Nothing.

"You asked me to come by?"

With this, Prescott's eyes found Nat's and stared at him in terror.

"To come by? Whatever for?"

Nat lowered his head, as if to say, *Are you serious, man?* "To talk to Becca. Your daughter?"

Prescott's lips moved soundlessly, as if he was repeating to himself what Nat had just said, or translating it from some other language. Then he looked up.

"Oh, Dr. *Thayer*. Of course. Come in."

Prescott pulled the door wide, and it swung back soundlessly. Nat walked into the echoing foyer, whose ceiling was lost above him in the gloom. There were no lights on in the first floor as far as he could see. The gleaming dark hardwoods of the foyer had patches of dusky light playing over them, illumination that came from a small stained glass window to the right of the door in the shape of a diamond. In front of Nat, there was a long hallway, with only a few feet of floorboards visible before they merged into blackness. To his left, a stairway with an elaborately carved railing zigzagged up to the second floor.

"Are you feeling all right?" Nat said, turning to Prescott.

Prescott shuffled around Nat in halting steps and reached out to the front door. When he closed it, the resulting sound boomed through the foyer and into the house's interior, a kind of sonic echo that revealed passageways Nat couldn't even see in the dimmed light. He'd never heard a house sound so dead, as if there were no furniture, no stuffed leather to reflect the sound waves as they traveled through the darkness.

Nat heard locks slam shut and the screeching of metal. Prescott was sliding a large metal rod along its sleeve. He forced the head of it through a circular iron latch that was bolted to the black door frame. When Prescott was done, he turned to Nat, his yellow teeth visible.

"I . . . I just woke up. I was up all night last night."

"Everything okay?"

Prescott was staring at Nat, who had the odd impression that the old man was afraid he was going to attack him, his entire body ready to flinch if Nat made any sudden gesture.

"We haven't had visitors here since Chase . . ."

Nat waited. "Yes. Since Chase . . ."

"Since Chase . . ."

Prescott's lips worked, and the eyes seemed to protrude even farther out of their sockets. He dropped his head quickly and whispered something to himself. It didn't sound like *died*, but a word or two full of soft sibilants. Whatever it was, it seemed to end the thought adequately for him, because he immediately headed left toward the stairs.

"Can we get some light?" Nat said. "Don't want to fall and break my neck. My insurance sucks."

Nat heard, rather than actually witnessed, the old man stop.

Then Prescott came back out of the darkness and whispered to Nat, leaning over to make himself heard. "I don't, usually." His eyes were pleading.

"Can I ask why not?"

"It . . . attracts attention."

"From *whom*?"

The old man smiled, as if Nat knew the answer. "Whoever might wish this place harm."

With that, Prescott went for the stairs, passing beyond one ray of sunlight and disappearing into the darkness except for a pale smudge and the sound of his feet whisking up the few first steps. Nat stumbled after the ghostly figure.

His foot kicked on the bottom of the stairs, and the darkness rose up in front of his face as he pitched forward. He caught the railing with his right hand before the polished wood knocked out his front teeth, then straightened up, took a deep breath, and slowly brought his next foot up. He reached a wide landing after three slow steps, then turned right with the railing and started up again.

The darkness slowly thickened as Nat climbed the stairs. He could hear the sound of Prescott's feet above him and then silence as the old man reached the top and moved off down the second-floor hallway into the interior of the house.

This is bananas, Nat thought. It was as if the house were weighing on Prescott, as if he were afraid of the wood and glass that made it up.

Nat hurried after him, suddenly afraid to be left alone in that echoing, malevolent house. When he got to the top of the stairs, he saw a light glowing dimly at the end of the hall. He started down it unsteadily, distance and depth seeming to have been altered in the murkiness. When he took a step, he wasn't sure if he would land on a plank of wood or drop downward into the basement. As he shuffled on, the light ahead seeming to grow no brighter, Nat felt ahead with his left hand. He could make out . . . *things* on the walls next to him, but he felt an urgency to get down the hall and only glanced once to his left. Through the dimness he perceived something, a paleness, welling up at him. He stopped and stared, and then the features came clear and it was a face, a chalky face with long, flaccid white cheeks and eyes that seemed blacker than the gloom. The eyes regarded him accusingly, and the face seemed to hang in the air, disembodied, no throat below it and only the hint of a hat perched above the severe brow.

A painting, of course, a family portrait of some kind, with a beady eye at the center that was not beautiful but recriminating, with some kind of white bonnet above it. Nat moved away uneasily from it and kept on toward the light and the profile of Prescott, head down, lost in his own thoughts.

Finally, after what seemed like a few minutes but could only realistically have been ten seconds, Nat was standing next to Prescott. The light fixture next to the old man's face was screwed to the wall at about six feet, the glass yellowed and rimed with dirt.

"This is Becca's room."

"Well, let's go in."

Prescott shook his head. "I can't."

Nat looked at Prescott. "What do you mean, you can't?"

"I can't bear the way she looks at me. She claims she doesn't know me, Dr. Thayer. If you ever have children, I hope you'll never experience that look of . . . distaste. I find it unendurable."

Prescott reached up and turned a key, then snapped a sliding lock across with a sound that exploded like a rifle shot in the passageway. Then another.

"Mr. Prescott, you can't lock your daughter up."

"Nobody is locked in here."

"Then . . ."

"These are to keep things *out*. Protection from outside is what is needed here. Becca is free to go wherever and whenever she wants. She only has to knock."

Prescott now seemed to have come fully awake. Genuine emotion worked in the old man's face. Nat remembered that he was here to treat his daughter for a nasty little mental quirk and decided to cut the guy a break.

"Okay, then. But I have to ask her about all this."

Prescott stood back.

"You do remember coming by last night, don't you? I wasn't dreaming?"

Prescott laughed thinly, but his eyes were uncertain. "What are you talking about?"

Nat stared at him. "When you came to the door, you didn't seem to recognize me."

Prescott's eyes went dead. "Of course I did," he said. "*My* mental faculties aren't in question here."

Nat studied him, then said: "I'll talk to you after I've had a chance to meet Becca. You'll be here, right?"

Prescott stared, then leaned in and lowered his voice. "Where else would I go, Doctor? Where else would I go?"

Prescott suddenly walked away and was swallowed up by the gloom, with only the sound of his shuffling feet coming back to Nat as he traversed the hallway.

Nat reached for the door. It was unlocked. He pushed it open and entered Becca's room.

CHAPTER NINE

Nat found himself in the typical room of a certain kind of teenage girl. More precisely, the kind who loves books. Rows of them were lined up in a white five-shelf bookcase to Nat's right, and more were packed onto shelving that lined walls covered in light green wallpaper. There were no posters of movies or bands or anything like that, but there on the pale cream-colored wall opposite him was a painting that might have done by a nineteen-year-old girl: a landscape with dark jagged mountain ranges and what appeared to be a man walking along a fringe of forest and entering the tree line at the bottom of the hills. There were two sconces on the wall, throwing light out into the small room, and two amber-colored candles on the windowsill, unlit. There was an old quilt on the wrought-iron bed and many pillows. Two stuffed animals—a zebra and a bear—looked down at the pillows from the window shelf. If Becca opened the window regularly, the bear and the zebra would have been moved somewhere else. So, like the curtains, the window remained closed.

The room smelled sweet, as though she'd sprayed rose water into the air sometime before he'd opened the door.

Becca was sitting at a small antique desk, the right side of her face in half profile. She didn't move, only stared ahead at the book she was reading.

"Becca?" Nat said.

She turned slightly in the chair to look at him. Her eyes were widely spaced, brown, and fixed on Nat with a kind of repressed urgency. Her nose was slightly flat and dented in the middle—like a young Ellen Barkin, Nat thought—her skin pale and her face oval-shaped. Becca was attractive, even if she was almost severe-looking, especially with her brown hair pulled back. She was wearing a white turtleneck and a pearl gray skirt that reached to the knees. She appeared . . . oddly composed, Nat thought. Not what he'd expected.

"Yes?" she said.

Nat breathed a sigh of relief. She didn't display the usual psychotic or schizophrenic affect, or appear to be entranced or possessed or zombified either. She was a nineteen-year-old girl whose brothers had committed suicide and whose father had lost himself in grief.

Nat Thayer's insta-diagnosis? A girl raised under sad circumstances.

"I'm Dr. Thayer. Can I talk to you for a minute?"

Her eyes seemed to blaze up for a few seconds, then calmly searched his face. She got up and moved to the bed, leaving the desk chair for Nat.

"Thank you," he said, sitting down. "I'm not sure if your father—"

She shook her head.

"He didn't mention I was coming?"

"No," Becca said. "I mean, he's not my father."

She said this with an unforced conviction, as if she were stating something so obvious that it almost didn't warrant mentioning.

"Okay, we can talk about that later," said Nat. "I came by to see how you were doing. I talk with a lot of people, and I'm able to help some of them."

She didn't ask, *Help with what?*—she just watched him. Her hands were pressed together and placed on her lap.

"So," Nat said, smiling. "How *are* things with you?"

Her gaze was steady and deep. "What do you mean?"

"How are things going? Do you feel happy with . . ." Nat spread his hands and looked around. "Your situation."

"How can I be happy?"

Nat frowned. "Well, we're happy when we feel that we're enjoying life, I guess."

"But that's just it," she said, and her pained smile said, *You've blundered right into it.*

"Just what?"

"That's the problem."

"Let's talk about that."

Her eyebrows arched, as if she was going to mention something a bit sad, though she didn't mean for it to be that way.

"I can't enjoy life," she said quietly, "because I'm dead. I died three weeks ago."

Nat felt a chill go through him at the matter-of-factness in her voice. Behind it, he heard the hum in his ears, the echoing low buzz of dark electricity in the house. But what frightened him was the look in Becca's eyes. A look of serenity.

"Why do you say that?"

"That I died?"

"Ye-es."

She brought her right hand up and smothered a laugh. Nat saw that the nails were bitten to the quick, and the pinkie finger was painted with a black cross.

Why are you horrified by this? her expression seemed to say.

Nat had come expecting a clinically depressed teenager. But there was something about Becca's confidence that unnerved him more than he could describe. For a second he believed her, and felt a little lunatic laugh run up his own throat. *She thinks she's met death and it's nothing to be afraid of,* he thought, before getting control of himself.

"That's a very serious thing, Becca. Death. Not something people usually find amusing."

"*Isn't* it, Dr. Thayer?"

Nat frowned and looked away. "I suppose it can be. I suppose it's even good to laugh at death. But in this—"

"Ah!" Becca said. "I see. Because my brothers died, I should be more respectful when talking about it."

"I'm not telling you how to feel, Becca."

Her eyes were mischievous. "Thank you, Doctor. But, you know, they weren't my brothers."

Now her eyes grew serious.

"If only they *were* my brothers. I would've loved them. I've dreamt about having brothers, to throw me in piles of leaves out on the lawn"—she pointed at the closed curtains—"and to go Christmas caroling with. To defend me."

There were tears in her eyes now, and her voice had a slight warble of hysteria in it. Nat watched her, unable to get a word out.

"But I never had one."

Something about Becca's maturity made Nat trust he didn't have to play games with her. And the fact that he was seeing her furtively—outside of his office, after the doom-laden visit from her father—tempted him to be unorthodox. It had always been a weakness of his. *I'm not saying you're not concerned about the patients*, his mentor, Dr. Francesci, at BU had once told him. *It's just that you like to make it interesting.*

All true. So let's make it interesting, then, he thought.

"So tell me, when did you die?" Nat said.

Becca seemed delighted by this. Her eyes were liquid in the gloom, and her head tilted slightly to the right, as if she was trying to recall, and then stopped. "December twenty-first, 2011."

"And what did you die *of*?"

Her eyes searched his face. She leaned toward him. "I was murdered," she whispered.

Nat felt the chill again. How had he come to be having this conversation with a nineteen-year-old girl? The still depths of her voice, the calmness of those eyes. It was eerie.

"By whom?"

"I don't know. Perhaps you can be my detective and find out."

"Perhaps I can. What happened on December twenty-first?"

For the first time, she hesitated. Her lips formed into an unhappy shape, and tears rimmed her eyelids. "I was in my bed. I dreamt I was choking, and when I woke up a man had his hands around my throat. So I believe it would be called manual strangulation."

Nat glanced at the turtleneck, and suddenly a memory came floating back to him from his childhood. When he was a young boy, six or seven, his father used to play a record for him, an old 78 in a cream-colored paper sleeve from a children's collection called *Scary Tales for Littl'uns*. It had been handed down from his grandfather, along with the upright record player with the musty webbed speakers that pulled out from the feet of the contraption on thin brown wires. Nat would sit in their basement, his ear close to the dusty speakers, and listen.

This particular record featured a story told by a male narrator in a rich baritone, about a beautiful woman who wore a black velvet band around her throat. The woman never took the band off, not even when she bathed or slept. She grew up with it around her neck, had her portrait painted with it on—the family had money. When she turned eighteen, she met a man who became her lover, and at first he was intrigued by the velvet necklace, but eventually he grew annoyed by it and asked her to take the band off once so he could see the lovely lines of her ivory throat. She said no. This made the lover angry. As time went on, he became consumed with fury, more and more obsessed by the velvet band.

He *demanded* she remove it. *No*, the woman told him lovingly. *If you love me, ask me anything except this one thing.* He insisted; she begged him to forget the velvet band. Finally, driven to a kind of madness, he screamed at her to take it off or he would do it himself. She said something debonair and eerie, something like *Very well, my love,* and with a smile, she reached up to her neck and pulled the band away.

And . . . off . . . came . . . her . . . head! shouted the narrator through the hisses and skips of the record needle.

Nat seemed to hear a faraway echo of the narrator's voice now, distinctly, in his head.

He shifted in the chair.

"But," he said, composing himself and raising an eyebrow at her, "I can see that you're breathing. If I feel your pulse, I bet I'll feel your heart beating."

The enigmatic smile again. "Yes. I'm aware that I *appear* to be living, but I'm telling you that it's an illusion. I can't explain how I'm still here when I should be in my grave."

I should ask her what was happening in her life before the "murder" occurred, Nat absently thought. About the relationship with her father. Did she feel isolated, perhaps, removed from life? But there was a shining intelligence in her eyes. *Let's play the game her way for a moment.*

"Who was the man who killed you?"

She looked at her hands. "I'd never seen him before."

"Describe him to me." Nat suddenly felt the urge to rough her up a bit verbally with a full-blown interrogation. She'd unnerved him—this whole house had unnerved him—and he wanted to get control of the situation.

"Dark hair, long hair, mustache. Sunburnt. And his eyes were . . ." It all came out in a rush, as if she'd memorized it.

"Were what?"

"All black."

"Interesting."

She shook her head jerkily and took a sharp inward breath, as if she'd just seen the man standing behind Nat.

"Becca . . ." he said quietly.

"Yes?"

"Is there anyone else living in this house besides you and your father?"

Her eyes went cold. "I told you—"

"He's not your father. Yes, I remember. Anyone else besides the old man, then?"

"I don't thi-iink so."

"Then why do you double-lock the door?"

"Because the black-eyed man came once, so he might—"

"But I thought you're already dead." *Checkmate, little girl.* Nat smirked to himself.

Her forehead was cut with two worry wrinkles. "But I feel things, Dr. Thayer. The sensation of his grip . . ."

Her right hand detached itself from the left and began to reach slowly upward. Nat watched it, an ivory, blue-veined hand with a bracelet of green stone falling down the arm as it rose. The hand came up, the fingers slightly bent. Her hair slid soundlessly off her shoulder until it fell in a glossy bunch and hung straight down.

Nat watched the hand rise as if it were floating of its own will. It finally touched the hollow where the neck met the breastbone, touched lightly the cords of Becca's throat that stood out through the fabric of the turtleneck, and then began to close on the neck itself. Becca's eyes rolled back in her head as her eyelids started to close. As Nat watched, her chin rose and she gave a little choking sound.

"Okay, I think I get it," Nat said. So she was a dramatic girl. She wanted to win their little game.

Nat could see the right finger press into the pale line of the carotid artery and the thumb press on the windpipe. He had never seen a patient reenact her own choking before and found himself paralyzed with fascination. He went to speak but no words came and he felt suddenly weak. The flesh of her thumb went white as she pressed down on the windpipe, and he heard her breath drawn inward in a gasp.

"Okay, Becca, you made your point."

As if through a fog, Nat reached out for her arm. He half stood and took a step toward the bed. His fingers closed on her thin arm, and he found the muscles were tensed, remarkably strong. He tried to pull them down from his crouched position but was startled to find that the arm stayed locked where it was, the hand pressing her neck harder and harder. Nat caught his breath and reached his fingers around for a better grip, the tips digging against the soft wool of her turtleneck and pushing into her right breast. Her whole body seemed to be filled with tremendous excitement.

"Enough!" Nat cried, his voice sounding drugged in his ears.

What the hell was going on here?

He stood up fully now, his body tingling as if he were standing in an electric field, to give himself a better angle. Becca's skin was going even paler, and it looked as though the flesh surrounding her eye sockets was turning blue. Angry now, Nat twisted his hand into her breast.

"*Becca!*"

She shook her head violently, and her lips parted but no words came out. With a grunt of effort, Nat wrenched her arm away. Becca's eyelids suddenly fluttered open. The arm went limp in his hand. No, not just limp but dead, the muscles going so slack that he could feel the bone.

He let her go. Becca's hands dropped to her lap. Her face was even paler now, not a transparency where the blue lines of her veins were visible but a kind of chalky pallor that seemed to glow with an unhealthy luminescence.

Nat sat back down, a little out of breath.

Her head was bowed in front of him, the back of her neck a patch of whiteness between the parted waves of her brunet hair. She looked as if she were waiting for an axe to clip into her spinal column. Docile.

Was she paralyzed with fear? What was she reenacting?

"Becca?"

She sat unmoving.

"Was this a nightmare that you had?"

Nothing.

"Becca, did you dream this?"

Her head swung back and forth, the hair following a half second later in a long swing, the light playing over its surface.

"It really happened?"

She nodded her head *yes*.

He had to consider there had been some attempt to strangle her. And the only person in the house was her father.

"The man who did this. Are you sure it wasn't someone you know?"

Nat felt like he was looking down a deep well at a girl who sat stock-still, surrounded by a circle of the blackest darkness. She wasn't moving, barely breathing, as he watched from above. What forms did she watch in that circle, their claws an inch from the band of light, circling her, waiting to tear her throat out if she so much as uttered a sound?

The shake of the head again, the face covered by gleaming shafts of hair.

"Did he have anything else in his hands?"

This seemed to catch her unawares. "*Wh-aat?*" she whispered.

The murder of Margaret Post had come into his thoughts, unbidden. He leaned in and lowered his voice. Their heads were now bowed together as if in prayer. "You showed that this man was choking you only with his right hand. Why? What was in his left? Was he holding something there?"

Nat felt a cold breath escape her lips and bloom against his face. It had no odor. It smelled of the house.

"NNNnnn...," she said, the sound trailing off.

"What was that?"

She looked up and her eyes were pleading. "*NNNnnnnn...*"

"Tell me—"

"*Knife.*"

Nat felt danger close now. A flash of dread. He reached out and put his hand over hers.

"Okay. Okay, a knife. But he didn't cut you?"

She shook her head. "He pressed. Here." She tilted her neck away, baring the flesh of her throat exposed above the turtleneck. She pushed a point on her neck just above her collarbone, her eyes closing as if the spot was still tender. Then she regarded Nat again.

A voice seemed to speak clearly in his mind. *Leave now.*

Nat blinked rapidly. He stood up and looked around the room. The voice had sounded as if it came from someone standing a few feet away. But there was no one in there with them. No one at all.

"I'll need to see you again," he said finally.

When she looked up, he detected something new in her eyes. Gratitude. Or maybe sympathy for him, for what he'd just committed himself to.

The two emotions could look very similar, Nat had found, when written on a face.

CHAPTER TEN

The door closed softly behind Nat, and he heard the snick of the metal arm entering its socket, followed by a hard click in the silence. He hadn't realized Becca had a lock on her side as well. He imagined her on the other side of the door, her hand pressed to the painted wood, waiting to hear if Nat would call to her. Then, when that hadn't happened, the grating of a bolt being pulled across and locked into place. And then silence.

The yellow light out here was still burning, and it cast a circular cone of solid amber that ended about three feet away from Nat, as if there were a black velvet curtain there. A choking sensation filled his throat, and suddenly he was sure that a hand was about to reach down and place its cold flesh on his neck. He felt the urge to run blindly toward the stairs. But instead he shivered and began to walk purposefully, his right hand feeling blindly against the wall. He touched the slick surface of an oil painting—could even feel the ridges of the painter's strokes under his finger. When he touched a patch of fur—Jesus, it must have been a mounted deer head—he dropped his hand, a cold sweat breaking out across his back.

A fucking horror house. The prison of the Prescott clan.

Nat reached the stairs, and his right foot went pitching over the first step before he caught himself.

"Mr. Prescott!" he called angrily. *Damn it. Why did he leave me out here to break my neck?*

Silence.

"Prescott!" he yelled.

He heard footsteps from directly below. Mr. Prescott walked into the center of the foyer, then looked upward, his face blank.

Nat glared at him and came down the stairs to the landing, then three more steps to the dark hardwoods of the foyer. He marched up to the old man.

Prescott waited, his eyelids half closed, for Nat to speak.

"Becca needs treatment. I'd like to see her tomorrow morning at my office."

His eyes flicked to Nat's. "She doesn't leave this house."

"Just bring her in, please. This atmosphere . . ."

Prescott raised his eyebrows. Nat suddenly felt that the old man was mocking him, somehow. He couldn't account for the change in the man's behavior from yesterday to today. Prescott was the one who had begged him to come, and then he seemed terrified that Nat had actually shown up. Now he was acting . . . vilely amused by Nat's concern.

"It's not conducive to any kind of recovery, Prescott. The things that have happened here . . . She's emotionally damaged, and vulnerable. You've created a kind of dungeon full of bad memories. I need to see her in a neutral environment."

"*I* didn't create anything. I have no such abilities."

"You're her father. Sign the goddamn order. I'll get her on a daily schedule and some medication, if necessary. We can keep here there for observation."

"I can't possibly do that."

"You wanted me to help her, right? Well, this is what helping looks like."

Prescott shook his head. "You have no idea what you're dealing with, Dr. Thayer."

"What am I dealing with, Mr. Prescott? It might help me to know if you told me."

"This," Prescott said, looking around, his look encompassing the whole house. "It's not my doing. It came about of its own accord. I suffer here, too."

Nat wanted to grab the old man's thin turkey neck and shake this gothic horror batshit nonsense out of him and take his daughter away to a clean, antiseptic facility that wasn't dripping with the accumulated paranoia of the last five fucked-up generations of the Prescott clan.

Prescott turned and walked away.

"I will be back," Nat called after him. Prescott made no gesture, just shuffled until the murk of the hallway seemed to swallow him up.

"Asshole," Nat muttered. He moved toward the front door, knocked the metal bar left out of its sleeve, turned the handle, and jerked the door open, slamming it shut as he left.

He felt drained and slightly dizzy as he climbed down the porch steps. Becca was clearly delusional; her father was so terrified of her joining the two brothers that he'd convinced her she was next.

You have to get her out of here, he said to himself.

He ripped the Saab door open, got in, and turned the key in the floor ignition. But he just sat there then, with the engine running, his foot pressed slightly on the gas. Finally, he looked back up at the house. The light was still on in Becca's room, and the curtains were pulled tight. He thought he could detect the presence of a human form behind the ivory cloth. It had to be Becca, but the material was too thick for Nat to be sure.

The figure moved away from the window.

Nat drove out of the Shan with the radio pumping loud. He nearly rear-ended an old Mercedes turbo on Narragansett Avenue, and glared back at the driver—a gaping old woman with a doughy face framed by gray curls—when she stared back at him. He felt aggressive, like some strong narcotic was washing out of his bloodstream, leaving him tetchy and spoiling for a fight.

CHAPTER ELEVEN

It was Saturday, but Daddy had to work, so Mrs. Finlay was in her chair in the living room, watching reruns. Charlie was allowed to stay in bed as long as he wanted, so long as his room was clean by the time Daddy came home. He lingered in the bed, watching the trees dance in the backyard as the wind tossed the branches this way and that. He loved his bedroom; he felt safe and warm here, no matter what was happening outside.

Finally, his stomach began to rumble, *hungryhungryhippofeed-mefeedmefeedme*, and Charlie jumped off his bed. He quickly pulled the Patriots sheet, with its footballs and helmets and goalposts, all the way up to the wooden bars, then did the same with the Patriots blanket. Charlie didn't really like football all that much—he was going to play lacrosse at Bishop Carroll, whose playing fields were just past their back fence—but his dad liked it a lot, and Charlie sat on his lap during games and wriggled when the Pats scored and Daddy squeezed him as they yelled and Charlie liked that even more. The sheet and the blankets were really for his father.

Charlie folded the blanket back, smacked the pillow, and made the bed as best he could. He didn't like Mrs. Finlay—she smelled like lotion and old cheese—but he had to go and say hi anyway. He grabbed his notebook and pen from under the Batman lamp on his dresser and wrote as he walked slowly into the hallway.

GOOD MORNING, he wrote, then walked up to the chair and tapped on Mrs. Finlay's arm.

"Good Lord, Charlie," Mrs. Finlay said, jumping. She stared at him and then at the notebook he was holding up to her, and she breathed out once shakily and tried to smile, but didn't get all the way there. Mrs. Finlay was wearing a blue sweater with a lace-looking design around the neck and watching some cooking show.

"Good morning to you, too."

BREAKFAST, he wrote.

"Do you need my help?"

NO, he scribbled quickly. He knew where the Trix was and the milk, and he didn't want her pancakes because she always burned them.

"Okay, then. Scoot along."

He headed down the long hallway that connected the two parts of the house. The light was dim in here, the walls painted red like you were inside a blood vessel in his book *This Is Your Body*. Charlie's bare feet made little *pat-pat* noises on the hardwood floor. He was only a few steps in when something made him stop.

The pictures. They were lined up on the left side of the wall, two feet above his head. The right wall was blank because all his mommy's pictures were gone now. She'd taken the photos when she'd left and gone to Portland, Oregon, to live with her sister who had a baby but no husband. Charlie was going to see his mom this summer in Oregon. He hoped she had the pictures up, because he missed seeing the faces of his other grandpa and his aunt Natascha, who lived in Australia, and all the others. It was like she'd taken one whole side of the family with her when she left. The right side of the hallway where her pictures had been was empty now, but you could still see the outlines of the missing pictures and the little holes where the nails had gone.

But he still had his daddy's side. Charlie approached the first picture. The man was wearing a funny hat that Daddy said hunters wore, and he was standing there with a big shotgun, leaning on it and looking into the camera with a big, tired smile.

Grandpa, Charlie thought. Charlie had never met him; he'd died in an accident when hunting deer up in the woods. *That's why people wear those orange vests*, Daddy had said. *So more grandpas won't die from pure stupidity.* Charlie guessed that meant that some other man had thought Grandpa was a deer and shot him by mistake. Charlie didn't want to go hunting in the woods, ever, and he shivered when he heard the echoes of gun blasts from the Raitliff Woods that came every fall when Daddy said the deer were running and the hunters were catching them.

He moved on, his stomach not rumbling anymore. Every time he came in front of a picture, he would whisper the name in his mind. *Great-grandma and Pops* were next. They were wearing dark, uncomfortable-looking clothes, and he didn't like to look at Great-grandma's eyes because she looked mad, but Daddy said she was just ornery. *Ornery* was an old-fashioned word for *mean*. Charlie studied Pops's weird glasses—the frames looked heavy and odd, as if they'd been made in a fire or something. Pops was fat and bald and had a bushy mustache and bushy gray eyebrows and he was smiling, and Charlie wished he knew Pops more than anyone else on the wall. He bet Pops ate apple pie—Charlie loved apple pie—and burped afterward like his daddy and liked to play marbles or some old-fashioned game, but Charlie would have been glad to learn any game to play with good old Pops.

Uncle Matt was next. Uncle Matt was ten years old in the picture, holding a football in his arm like he was going to make a run. He was smiling, too. Matt was Daddy's older brother. Charlie still didn't understand how a ten-year-old boy could be his uncle, but he liked the picture a lot because of the football and the fact that he was the only boy he knew in school who had a ten-year-old uncle.

Next came *Aunt Stephanie*. Charlie didn't know much about

her. She lived in Georgia, where they grew peaches and it was hot and they spoke with funny accents. He'd never met Aunt Stephanie and he didn't want to much, either—because his father got sad when he talked about her and Charlie guessed that Stephanie had done something mean to him when he was a kid—unless she brought a whole crate of peaches and told stories about his daddy as a boy. Daddy didn't like to talk about the time when he was a boy, and Charlie sometimes thought that he'd never been one, that his father had been a grown-up always, ever since he was born, and a daddy, too, who was waiting for his boy to show up, which was Charlie.

He moved down the line, skipping one or two who he'd forgotten or who he couldn't see real well, the ones taken from far away and the people in them were just stick figures whose eyes were tiny like little raisins. He would forget about the pictures for months, and then one day he'd feel that one or two of them wanted him to look up at them and say hello. Today, he felt that more than ever. Aunt Stephanie's and Pops's eyes were bright in the yellowy light, and they'd looked eager to see him. Maybe they missed the pictures across from them and were getting lonely in the hallway with photographs on only one side.

The last picture was his great-aunt *Middy*. Middy was dressed in black, and she had a doughy face with big round cheeks and a big chin that looked like a cue ball but with little dents in it. Her eyes were dark, and to Charlie it looked like someone was pinching her when the photo was taken, because she looked like she was trying not to yell out. Daddy wouldn't talk about her, and he'd heard Mommy yelling at him about it. It had been a month before Mommy left and they'd started arguing about a Merican Express bill, but as usual they'd ended up fighting about other things. Charlie had snuck up to their bedroom door, which they'd left cracked a bit by mistake, because they usually argued with all the doors closed. He'd only stayed for a second, because it sounded like Daddy was coming toward the door, but he'd heard his mommy say this: *Take it down, John. I don't want that thing looking at me every day.*

He didn't hear what his father said back, only the words *awful thing to say . . .*

Charlie stood in front of the photo now. Middy's face gave him fluttery feelings up and down the inside of his stomach. He felt sorry for her, but he was also scared of her skin that sagged and bunched in places and made her face all crooked and that eye, the right one, that was crooked—*East-West eyes,* they called people like that in school. The right eye stared out like it was made of glass, but at the same time it seemed like it was looking through you at something bad on the other side, waiting for you to turn. Or something inside you maybe.

A noise buzzed in his ear. It was like a voice was talking on a staticky station on the radio.

In his brain, Charlie asked Middy why she looked so sad, but she didn't say anything back. Middy's face looked like the dough before you poured the chocolate chips in and made cookies: soft, mushy, like she didn't feel well. The right eye gleamed under the ceiling light, and Charlie took a step backward. From here, the tiny black of her eyeball looked furious, like it wanted to scold Charlie, and he took back his question about why she was sad because he didn't want to know anymore.

You don't scare me, Middy, he thought. *You chased my mommy out of here and I don't like you one bit.*

Charlie felt the wall behind him, and inched over a little with his right foot. All of a sudden, he tore his eyes away from Middy's picture and dashed for the kitchen. When he got there, he closed the door behind him fast, pushing his bare feet on the brown tiles to keep the door tight against the door frame. He kept his back pressed against the wood until he'd counted to ten, and then he felt better and strolled over to one of the padded kitchen chairs, then dragged it over the shiny brown tiles that were gleaming in the sunlight coming in the window, dragged it over to the cereal cupboard. He put the chair up to the counter, then stepped on top and opened the cupboard and got down the Trix, his favorite. He reached all the way over and opened the dishes cupboard and got his Avengers cereal bowl out and then climbed down and found a big-boy spoon in the drawer.

His heart didn't stop racing until the first bowl of Trix was beginning to leak its colors into the milk he'd poured into the cereal. Charlie watched the cereal balls send long curling rivers of red and yellow and blue into the white ocean around them, and he tried to think about when they'd start playing baseball in the yard beyond their yard, because sometimes a stray foul would come looping into their yard and the left fielders from Bishop Carroll would come running up and he'd go to throw the ball back to them and one of the boys this year might ask Charlie to be the boy who collected the balls at the end of practice. He didn't think again about how Middy was a bad old woman or what her mean right eye might be staring at in the hallway out there, not until the Trix was almost done and it was time to go back to his room and get dressed.

CHAPTER TWELVE

Intake was busy. There was the droning voice saying "Ohhhhh-hhh" from behind a closed door. *Psychotic*, Nat thought absently. It was something that most psychs did almost unconsciously, starting during their residency—trying to diagnose patients on the fewest clues available: what they said (before the intake exam), what they looked like, even how they smelled. It was like that old TV show *Name That Tune*, which he used to watch when he'd stayed home from school as a young boy. *I can name that manic-depressive in three notes*. Totally unscientific, of course. But during his second year of residency, Nat had earned an unofficial success rate of about 65 percent, the highest in his class.

And that droning, wavering chant coming from down the hall? Schizo, for sure.

Nat stuck his head in the nursing office. An unhappy-looking black woman looked up from her computer.

"Greene?" he said.

"Who's asking?"

He smiled. "Nat Thayer. Hi."

"Oh, I wouldn't have known, seeing you didn't say hello or good morning or anything mannerly like that." The woman reached into an amber-colored glass bowl, pulled out a piece of hard candy, unwrapped it, and popped it in her mouth. She gave Nat a reproachful look.

"Forgive me. Good morning, Ms. Beth Annelisa Duncan, charge nurse of the intake unit. Now where's Greene, please?"

Beth gave the candy a few more circuits of her mouth, staring blank-faced at Nat as if she were looking right through him. Then she pursed her lips and glanced down at a list by her left elbow. "Says here, Iso."

Nat gave the door frame two sharp knocks. "Thanks."

He went to Isolation, dodging fast-walking nurses and patients in wheelchairs, the tips of their bathrobes dragging along the floor. The section was around two corners and through one security door. As he swiped his security card and pushed through, a host of sounds came rushing at him: an exhausted doctor talking on his cell phone; someone struggling on a metal stretcher, which rattled under his or her weight; calls and shouts from the locked rooms where the dangerous patients—dangerous to themselves or staff—were kept until they were stabilized.

And floating above it all a high-pitched, maniacal, and completely hopeless laugh. Actually, it was a despairing shriek disguised as a laugh. Nat winced.

Saturday was a busy day in Iso, especially in the depths of January. Postholidays were always a bad time for unstable people. And Fridays were drinking nights in Northam, which meant the inconsolable often washed up in the psych wards at Mass Memorial the morning after.

Nat scanned the room and spotted a nurse manager, a burly Scandinavian type named Ivor. Iso was the riskiest unit in the hospital, which meant it got the linebacker types.

He tapped Ivor on the shoulder. "The hell's that?" Nat asked.

Ivor made a blank face, as if to say, *What do you mean?* Then he heard the laughter.

"Para-phren," Ivor said, which was short for paranoid schizophrenic. "Fresh off the am-bu-lance. They found him walking in the middle of Cherry Avenue with one sock on and nothing else."

Nat made a face. "They going to be doing like that all day?"

Ivor bent over a chart and made a notation. "Why do you care? You don't work down here."

"But *you* do. And I care about you, Ivor."

"Fuck you, too, Thayer. What do you need?"

"Greene."

Ivor pointed toward the room from which the eerie laughter was emanating. "She got lucky."

Nat frowned. "Damn. How long has she been in there?"

Ivor glanced up at the clock, calculating. "Twenty."

"When she's done, tell her I'm looking for her, will ya?"

"Got it."

———

Half an hour later, someone knocked on Nat's office door.

He swiveled in a chair. Dr. Jennifer Greene stood leaning in, her hand still poised over the door.

"You rang?"

"Yeah, Jennifer, come on in."

Greene was wearing a lab coat, a neat blue button-down, and khakis. Her light brown hair with blond highlights was tied back in a bun. She leaned against the back of one of Nat's chairs.

"This isn't about the yogurt in the fridge, is it? I told everyone I was going to return it."

He smiled. "No, believe it or not, actual cases pass through this office. Please disguise your shock."

"Actual cases? I thought you were here just to give the women in the office a reason to show up for work. I mean, besides me."

"No, that I do as a public service."

She laughed.

"Can I ask you a question, Dr. Greene?"

"Absolutely. What d'ya got?"

He tapped on a yellow legal pad he'd been doodling on. "I remember you did some of your postgrad work on Capgras delusion."

Her broad face went thoughtful. "Yes. Fascinating stuff."

"Did you do anything on Cotard as well?"

Greene's brow creased. "Cotard delusion?"

"Yes."

A look of eagerness spread across her face. "Don't tell me you have a walker."

"I'm not . . . Wait, a what?"

"A walker. That's what we called them."

"Why?"

"Cotard patients walk in a daze, obviously. And they walk out on their lives. Listen, if you truly have one, you *have* to let me assist. I've never—"

"Why don't you just give me the basics for now? What was the gender breakdown on the cases you looked at?"

"Mostly female. Is that your patient?"

"Confidential. Please continue."

She made a face. "Most were in their twenties or thirties. Many had deep issues of abandonment relating to their families. One had been in an automobile accident and he believed he was dead. In fact, he swore that not only was he deceased, but that he was *putrefying*, that he could smell himself rotting at night. Kept a bottle of Febreze by his bedside, went through six or seven of them a month. Some thought organs had been taken from their bodies while they slept. I'd say about half had that delusion."

"What did the CAT scans show?"

"Abnormalities in the prefrontal, usually. But not always."

"How did they relate to family?"

"Generally speaking, very badly. One believed his mother was transporting his corpse to hell, when she had really just taken him to the Virgin Islands to try to cheer him up. In a couple of cases, the background showed there was parental neglect on a scale that's pretty hard to believe. One day they woke up—literally, these ideas came to them almost always in the morning—and they no longer recognized their loved ones. But it was part of a constellation of problems. Is your patient bipolar?" Greene said.

"All I can tell you is there are no signs as of yet. Not schizophrenic either, I don't think."

"Some pharmaceutical approaches have worked."

"I've read the literature. I may recommend one or two, depending. The individual isn't a patient here yet."

"Why not bring her in? I'd be happy to sit in."

"That works."

Jennifer's eyes studied Nat. "The home situation. For that kind of trauma . . . there have to be some deep pathologies in the parent. Parents?"

Nat turned in his swivel chair to look out over the town in the direction of the Shan. "There's a lot wrong there. Can't say much more than that."

Out of the corner of his eye, Nat saw that Jennifer had advanced to the corner of his desk and was now leaning on it.

"You did a home visit?"

Nat laughed.

"I appreciate your curiosity, Dr. Greene. Now get out of my office. And thank you."

She got up, walked back to the office, swinging her shoulders, lost in thought. She turned at the doorway, as he'd known she would. She put her hands across the doorway and held them there. "Have you gone back further?"

"Past the father? I hope to. I have to get the situation stabilized before I start going back in time."

She nodded. "Very deep pathologies, Dr. Thayer. *Very.*"

CHAPTER THIRTEEN

That night Nat Thayer brought home the printout he'd made at the hospital library. It was an article from the May 2002 issue of *Neurology*. He popped open a Stella and collapsed onto his leather couch, letting the foam surge up the bottleneck before taking his first sip.

He turned his attention to the article. Jules Cotard had been a neurologist—they wouldn't call them psychiatrists for a number of years—working in Paris toward the end of the nineteenth century. He'd been born in 1840 and interned at the Hospice de la Salpêtrière. *Funny name*, thought Nat. *The Saltpeter Hospital.* He reached over for his iPad and Googled it and found the place was an old gunpowder factory that had been turned into one of Paris's biggest hospitals, and one of its grimmest. A warehouse for prostitutes, the insane, the criminal-minded. It had been attacked during the September massacres of 1792, and some of its patients—the mad ones—had been pulled from their beds and slaughtered on the streets.

God, he loved this stuff. Psychiatry had been so much more interesting when they'd known only half as much about it.

Cotard had focused on stroke victims, diabetics, and—this was a departure—the delusional. That must have been what brought Mademoiselle X into his office in 1880, a woman who swore that she was dead. Cotard became fascinated by her case and called her affliction *délire des négations*. He was the first to describe the condition, so the medical authorities would give it the formal name Cotard delusion.

Mademoiselle X was clearly disturbed. Violently so. She not only denied the existence of God, which was a rather extreme position in Paris—even in 1880—but also told Cotard that she herself had died long ago. Interestingly, Cotard had done just what Nat had done with Becca; that is, pointed out the obvious. You're alive, you're standing, you're breathing. Mademoiselle X had replied that she'd been cursed, and so had to wander the earth. Her bodily organs had been stolen—she didn't say by whom—one by one. Her brain, nerves, chest muscles, intestines had all been taken from her body, leaving only the outer shell of skin and bones. Therefore, she felt no need to eat, as she was slowly decomposing and needed no nutrition.

I need a more detailed description of the interviews, Nat thought. Family background, a fuller listing of the symptoms, any earlier signs of psychoses.

He read on. The article had broadened out to a discussion of the delusion throughout history. Cotard was most common in elderly women suffering from schizophrenia, though cases had been found in the young, often accompanied by clinical depression and/or organic brain damage.

No mention of a hysterical form able to be passed on from one family member to another. Walter Prescott hadn't detailed any accidents or head injuries in Becca's past. He'd have to ask him about that. But somehow Nat didn't think so . . .

This paper was mediocre at best, a bare-bones survey. He was surprised that the *Neurology* editors hadn't demanded more detail. But the syndrome was so rare that it might have been pitched as the equivalent of a human-interest story, light reading for the clinical trade.

Nat tossed the paper on the hardwood floor, feeling a sore

throat beginning to come on. He took a shot of NyQuil and crawled into bed in the top floor of the loft as gray light darkened the room. The rounded shape of Grant's Hill outside his windows began to merge with the dusk.

He felt the sheets, cool on his skin. The room began to grow warmer. As his mind drifted away, he wondered if he'd set the thermostat too high again.

An image floated into his head, a black-and-white image in a black frame. Something from a book? A family portrait? He couldn't recall one like it in his house growing up, and the outlines of the figures seemed smudged, refusing to come into focus. Something from a museum maybe? He hadn't been to a museum since he'd been in New York two years ago. He let the image float away.

Then the beginnings of a dream. The face that swam into view as he sank into a pleasant stupor was his aunt, Aunt Sophie, his father's sister. Aunt Sophie. Funny, he'd always called her that, even when she'd become a surrogate parent to him. After the accident that killed both his parents.

Aunt Sophie had been a highly unwilling substitute for his father and mother. She didn't mince words, old Soph. She had her own money from a family inheritance that had kicked in at thirty-five and, ten years later, wasn't looking to take on a moody, sarcastic thirteen-year-old. As far as he could tell, Sophie had the perfect life down pat, the envy of her married friends. A closet full of designer dresses, beaus in Boston and New York, trips to Europe whenever she felt like it. She was brutally direct, beautiful in a dark aquiline way and not at all motherly.

He'd have to drop Aunt Sophie an e-mail over to France, where she'd moved "to get away from the Northam pond scum." Alone. Always alone.

It was the thing that Sophie had said to him, that first night in her sleek apartment off State Street, which had stuck with him. It was two nights after his parents' funeral, which he'd gotten through without shedding a single tear, much to the amazement and worry of his friends. But Sophie had tucked him into the bed in the strange room, which smelled of the perfumed clothes she'd stored there before he'd arrived, and studied his face on the first night of his new life.

"Do you know why your father died?" she'd said.

"No."

Sophie had leaned over, and he'd smelled the alcohol on her breath, something he would never detect again on her. Rich, dark, slightly intoxicating fumes.

"Because he got close to someone," she whispered.

Nat was speechless. He could only stare at her in the darkness, thinking that was a strange thing to say to a newly orphaned boy.

Sophie had leaned back, and the sadness in her face was soon overtaken by something else. Cunning. Ferocity.

"Never let people get close to you," she said, getting up and walking to the door. She held the handle, then looked back at him. "They're dangerous."

She'd closed the door and never mentioned the subject again. But he had to admit, the advice had stayed with him.

CHAPTER FOURTEEN

That Sunday morning, Chuck Godwin knelt in the dank corner beneath the stairs of his basement. He was squeezed uncomfortably between a three-legged chest of drawers and cardboard boxes of old magazines and newspapers. The smell was musty, moisture combining with the decaying remains of paper. If he dug down to the bottom of the stacks, he was sure he'd find mold growing on the waxy cardboard.

Chuck knew he was distracting himself from the true object of his search. He'd done a lot of that lately. Telling himself stories, little pep talks, saying to himself *Buck up, Chuck*, all to drown out the voices that were always there now. Even when he couldn't make out the words, he felt the hum like a small but powerful generator. Now the sound was growing louder, which is why he'd come down to the basement, to do something.

The rope . . .

He snapped his mind away from the thought. Or was it a voice? The two things had merged lately, his own thoughts and the whispery voice of the man from the woods.

A box tilted thanks to his rummaging, and suddenly its contents spilled onto the floor. Ancient *Better Homes & Gardens* magazines, dozens of them. If he didn't watch it, Stephanie would become a hoarder. Already she was "collecting" things like twine and papers and photo albums and other stuff that no one in their right mind really collects. The photo albums sat empty; they had no grandchildren to fill them up with pictures of outings at the beach, birthdays, graduation...

It was gritty down here. It smelled primeval, like iron and water. The arch of his shoulder began to throb, the bursitis kicking in.

...is in the basement.

Was it possible to make peace with the voices? To live with them? His father had gone through affairs, alcoholism, even taken up pottery making in what Chuck figured was a likely attempt to escape from the urgings from outside. Drown them out. He'd lasted a good few years before he'd stood in the little room in the basement of this very house with the sump pump in it, and hanged himself from an exposed rafter. The smallest room in the house. Dark, claustrophobic, reeking of earth minerals. A horrible place. Chuck never went in there.

The rope...

The pressure in his brain was increasing. He was afraid of seeing the man, the one from the woods in the khaki uniform. If Chuck had to face him, he thought he would run screaming from the house. Anything but that.

Chuck kept looking. It was here somewhere. He hefted one of the boxes—an old banana container now filled to the brim with stuff—and lowered it to the floor. JFK assassinated in Dallas, *Life* magazine. Everyone had one of those. Goddamn Stephanie saved the most obvious things.

He could feel the thing sitting at the bottom of the stack.

How does an inanimate object throw out waves of loathing and fearfulness?

But it did. He felt the waves of fear move through his chest.

...is in the BASEment.

The voice was louder now.

There it was, the thing he'd come to see. It lay in the half darkness, stained with oil. The rope, twenty shiny yellow feet of it. It had been his father's, along with this house. There were probably dead skin cells ingrained in the twine from when his father hanged himself.

Pick it up.

God knew Chuck had enough reasons to kill himself. The anniversary of his father's death was only three weeks away. But that he'd learned to live with. It was Billy, his only son, who'd crashed his car out on 95 South three Christmases ago, that truly haunted him. Billy being gone was the bad thing that outweighed every other bad thing in Chuck's life put together. The only fact that gave it any competition was that he'd been a terrible dad, by turns angry and withdrawn.

"It should have been me," Chuck said to the dank gray wall. His voice floated out into the basement, giving him the creeps.

Now.

He moved another box away, not caring when the top half of its contents went all over the floor. An old china gravy boat crashed to bits on the cement.

What Chuck really feared was that he would see the man's face again.

But this time it would have changed to Billy's.

CHAPTER FIFTEEN

Dusk was spilling over the craggy ridge of Grant's Hill. Nat glided down the condo stairs, looking up and down the street for his Saab. He had weekend duty all month, and he'd drawn the evening shift tonight, but unless he remembered where he'd parked the damn car, he was going to be late. As he scanned the street, shivering slightly in a bracing wind, he saw an unmarked black Crown Vic parked in front of a fire hydrant directly in front of his building. He ducked down and caught John Bailey's profile in the front seat. Nat went up to the passenger window and knocked.

John glanced up. A look—sadness, fear?—passed across his face, and then he gave a half smile.

"I was just coming up to see you," John said, rolling down the window.

Nat narrowed his eyes. "For what?"

"I want you to take a ride with me."

Nat paused, hands on his thighs, crouched down. "You'll take me to work after? I'm on second shift tonight."

John gave a smile, tinged with worry, and nodded. Nat swung his shoulder bag into the backseat, then opened the passenger door and got in.

"You look like shit, my friend," John said, eyeing Nat as he drove toward the center of town. "What's going on?"

Nat rubbed his eyes. "Freaky dreams."

John's perked up.

"Not that kind of freaky," Nat said. "Never mind. I think I need to get drunk. Frat-boy drunk. *Mark Prendergrast* drunk."

A smile tugged at the corner of John's mouth. In high school, Mark Prendergrast had gotten loaded on peach schnapps, undressed fully, and entered an unlocked house near the party they were all attending. It had been the home of the school's principal, the unloved Mr. Cameron. *Mrs.* Cameron had found him, asleep on their French love seat, the next morning. Prendergrast's first comment—*This doesn't make me a bad person, does it?*—had gone down in Northam history as about the funniest line possible in such circumstances.

Nat watched John make a sharp turn onto State Street and gun the engine. State led straight across Bogg's Hill to the Shan. He looked over at John.

"So where are we going?"

John met his eyes. "The Prescott house."

Nat tensed. "What happened? Is it Becca?"

"No, she's fine."

Nat breathed out, then looked up and down the street.

"It's the father," John said.

"The old man?"

"Yeah." John shot him a glance.

"What happened?"

"He hung himself."

Nat felt a wave—like the last pulse of a concussion from a faraway blast—pass through him.

"Jesus," Nat said quietly, thinking of Becca. "The whole goddamn family gone. He thought . . ."

"Yeah?"

Nat slammed his hand on the Vic's dashboard.

"Hey!" John said. "Easy, brother!"

"He thought Becca would be next. I didn't see it coming, but I should have. He was obsessed with the curse on his family, some bullshit to screen off his own depression. *Damn* it."

"How the hell could you see it coming?"

Nat stared grimly at the gray macadam falling away as they topped Bogg's Hill and headed down toward the Shan.

"Did he do it in the house?"

John shook his head. "No. Out back. In the woods."

"Same place you found Chase . . ."

"Yeah," John said softly. "Acting all crazy."

The road ran under the Vic. The Shan didn't see as much city money as the rest of Northam, and Nat could feel the gritty surface of the pavement vibrating through the car into his leg muscles. The two men were silent awhile.

"Well, FYI, that's not all," John said with a sigh.

"What do you mean?"

John stared straight ahead. "The old man's hands were tied behind his back."

Suicides were something that they both knew about—that and murder were the places where their two jobs overlapped. They both meditated on the implications of that detail.

They made the right onto Endicott, and Nat watched the houses begin to space out, the circular driveways, even a few colonnades of elms heading back to houses you couldn't even see from the street.

"Did she see it?" Nat asked.

"Who, Becca?"

"Yeah."

"No idea."

Nat was getting that feeling in the pit of his stomach—roiling, electric, and black—that he remembered from the last time he'd been to 96 Endicott.

John pulled into the driveway. They could see the neon-like reflections of the police lights shining off the trunks of the dark woods in the backyard. Red and blue flashes. Nat looked up at the house as they passed in front. The bare branches of nearby trees dipped and whirled to invisible currents, and the sound of torqueing, breaking wood filled the air. The gusts of wind whipped the dead leaves across the porch and a few had stuck to the panes of the first-floor windows, but everything about the house itself was completely still. It neither emitted light nor revealed the slightest motion. The curtains on the windows were closed, and the light by the front door was dark.

As they pulled past the front of the house and down the driveway, Nat felt a wave of repulsion come over him, and he reached up and wiped his lips with the sleeve of his jacket.

It was as if the house knew what had happened, but had sealed itself up to the public, damping its secrets, its malevolence, in darkness. The thought that Becca was up there, sealed within, made him want to go at it with an axe.

John pulled up to the bumper of the single patrol car and killed the engine. Nat got out and felt the wildness of the air. It was tossing back and forth, fitful and strong. He smoothed his hair down and looked down the length of driveway at the backyard. There was a flashlight shining deep in the trees.

He led the way back. The ground was slick with dead leaves, and he had to catch himself twice after tripping on exposed roots. Nat weaved through the dark trunks and heard the gales tossing the tops of the oaks high above. When he got to the patrolman, the officer—tall and lanky—was facing away, the flashlight held down by his left side, the light illuminating a pair of gray wool slacks with a black stripe and a pair of black shoes.

"Officer."

The man swung around, his right hand reaching to his side. His face was startled, the cheek muscles tight. "Oh, it's you guys," he said, straightening up.

"Were you expecting someone else?" Nat said, looking at the gun gleaming evilly by the cop's right hip.

"Uh, no, it's just a little spooky out here."

John's flashlight fixed the young cop in a cone of light. Nat saw that he was pale as a sheet of paper, the line of his stubble visible beneath shocked blue eyes. His Adam's apple bobbed up and down.

"Nat, this is Officer Pendleton. Pendleton, this is Nat Thayer."

They nodded at each other.

"Nice way to get shot," John muttered as he went by.

Nat heard something in the wind back here that was different, something added to the grand sweep of the trees dancing above. He knew it was the sound of a rope with something heavy on it.

"Who called it in?" John said.

"The neighbor," the young cop said.

They were three blue-black silhouettes lit up nightmarishly now and then by the flashlights. John shone his toward where the sound was coming from.

Walter Prescott's face suddenly loomed out of the darkness.

"Jesus," John said.

"Yeah," Pendleton said. "That's what I said."

Prescott's eyes were bulging wetly from the sockets. The mouth was open as if in midscream. The purplish tongue was visible behind the yellowing teeth. He was hatless, and the flashlight shone off his bald pate.

The body was facing away from the house, out into the deeper woods.

Nat had seen five suicides in his life: one cutter, one pill overdose drowned in a bathtub for good measure, a self-inflicted gunshot, and two hangers. He'd been struck by the expression on their faces, all except for the shooter, who'd apparently flinched at the last moment and turned the gun so that he'd lost the front part of his skull above the eyes. The others had looked exhausted. Not peaceful, but just *finished* with whatever had goaded them to get out the razor blade or the rope. Fucking done.

But Walter Prescott, swaying here slightly a foot above Nat's head, didn't look like that at all. Prescott had the appearance of being caught. If Protestants had put gargoyles on their churches, they would look like this.

Nat was staring so hard that he missed what John said next.

"I'm sorry, what?"

"I said, 'What'd he step off of?'" said John.

Pendleton shone his light on something near the foot of the tree. It was a cooler, bright blue with a white top, and for a moment Nat flashed on Walter and young Chase Prescott going down to cast their fishing lines from the shore, and Walter sitting on the chest, which contained sandwiches, with beer for him and root beer for the boy.

Maybe it had happened. A long time ago.

"Coroner coming?" John said.

"Yeah. Said ten minutes," Pendleton noted.

"Let's look at his hands," Nat said.

John glanced over with an expression that might have meant, *I don't recall deputizing you, asshole.* But from John, it was just surprise. Nat supposed he'd brought him to the scene to help in interviewing the girl; he didn't want to overstep his boundaries, but he wanted to know how Prescott had died.

John shone the light down on the old man's wrists.

Nat, relieved that Prescott's face was no longer a beacon of death in the dark forest, came closer to the body and around the back, his shoes shuffling through the mustard-colored leaves that glowed dimly on the ground from John's flashlight. The flesh on the wrists was swollen and puffy just above the rope, which was light tan and dirty. It was tied in a simple double knot, pulled tight.

"That's an old rope," said Pendleton.

"Mm-hmm," John said.

Nat took a half step toward the body and peered at the knot.

"Now how do you do that yourself?" he said.

"Doesn't need to be too tight," John replied. "Once you start struggling, you're your own worst enemy. With the right knot, it takes care of itself."

"I realize that," Nat said. "But could *you* tie that knot on yourself?"

John played the light over the tie, tilting his head. "Probably not."

Pendleton looked uncertainly from Nat to John.

"You think someone else . . ."

Nat frowned and replied: "I'm not saying anything, but it's a detail."

"Jesus Christ," John said softly.

Nat followed his eyes and swiveled. Through the tree trunks, he could see a window lit up on the second floor of the house. Through the muslin curtains, Nat thought he saw the outline of a body.

"Did you tell the girl?" Nat barked at Pendleton.

"What girl?" Pendleton said. "I knocked on the door but no one—"

John looked at Nat. "Would she talk to me?" he said.

"I'm not sure. I think I'd have better luck, at least to start."

"Go ahead."

Nat hurried off through the elms.

He ran through the dark trunks, dodging the trees. The cold seeped through his clothes and he began to shiver. Above him he could see the brightly lit window flashing into view for a second here and there.

Nat made it to the side door. He pulled open the screen door and grabbed the brass knob. It screeched as he turned it. He found himself in a small entranceway, with a coatrack to his left and a narrow stairway to his right, lit by a single fixture high up on the wall.

"Becca?" he called.

Something stirred above him.

He began climbing the stairs, the wood of the railing chilled under his hand. He ascended slowly, listening. There was a small landing, then stairs to his left, even darker than the lower section. He continued upward. As he got closer to Becca's floor, he could no longer see the stairs in front of him, only a matte blackness. He felt ahead instead.

He sensed something breathing on the stairs, someone pressed back into the darkness.

"Who's there?" he said.

It could be a breeze moving past. Is there a window open up here?

A board creaked.

"Damn it, who's there?"

He advanced toward the sound, feeling along the wall. His hand flinched, but it was just a stuffed animal head. The house was probably lousy with them. He couldn't make out the features, so he reached up to feel its thick tufts of hair. He had to know what the damn thing was, to visualize it. He slid his hand down, and his fingertips felt something hard under the fur. The jawbone, he thought. He saw the animal's face as his hand explored: a long snout; thick, bristly fur as coarse as any he'd touched; a small glass marble where the eye had been; and, finally, two large, curved tusks extending on either side of the snout that the taxidermist had left as sharp as small knives. At any moment he expected to feel the pulse of blood under his fingertip, to hear the jaw snap shut over his hand.

It was . . . a boar? Some kind of boar, maybe. He walked on. He felt a slick oil painting, and then the cool touch of glass.

Finally he came to a door, but it couldn't be Becca's, as this one felt rough under his hand. Something pricked his finger and he drew back.

"Becca . . . ?" He felt to the side. His hand finally fumbled on what felt like a light switch, and he took a breath and flicked it up.

The cone of yellow light flooded down and Becca's door

came blooming into view. Nat started, stepping back. Deep holes had been gouged in the wood, fresh hack marks glowing in long strips and cuts.

Someone had gone at the door with a kitchen knife or a small hatchet.

He looked at the locks. Splinters hung around them. Nat touched one of the needle-sharp pieces of wood; it came loose and fell away into the darkness at his feet.

Five more minutes and whoever had done this would have gotten through.

"Becca!" he said, and pounded on the door. It rattled in its frame.

Silence.

"I saw you in the window. Please let me in."

He heard a voice.

"What?!" he cried.

"How do I know it's not him?"

"Listen to me. You know my voice. This is Nat Thayer, and you and I are friends. Okay? Just please open the door. You're safe. No one's going to hurt you."

He heard a bolt slide back slowly. A lock popped, and the door opened a crack. Nat could see a line of yellow light, and then Becca's brown eye staring at him.

"Hey, it's okay," he breathed out. The rush of relief shook his knees.

The door opened and suddenly Becca rushed into his arms.

He didn't want her to see the door or how close the attacker had been to getting the lock dug out. He murmured comforting words and pushed her slowly back into the room, leaving the door ajar. She would have to get used to having it open.

"Are you all right?"

She nodded, her hair rubbing against his cheek. Her body was incredibly light in his arms.

"Okay, why don't you sit down. Everything's going to be okay."

She found the bed and quickly sat on it. Nat sat on the desk chair and glanced around the room.

"What the hell happened?"

She shook her head.

"You were locked in here?"

She looked flustered. "I'm *usually* locked in here."

Nat frowned, but his other questions were more pressing. "Did your father try to get in?"

"He is *not* my father." Her eyes flashed angrily and her voice rose.

"Okay. Just tell me what happened."

Her face, the slightly flattened nose, the rich brown eyes—he'd been seeing them in his head ever since he'd left this room, and he felt a lightness in his chest now that he was seeing them again.

She looked at him, her eyes wide.

"I was sleeping. That happens a lot these days. I thought I was dreaming, and it kept getting worse and worse. I don't remember what it was now, but through it all, there was a voice talking, describing something, describing horrible things that were being done to somebody . . . and the same things would happen to *me*."

"Go on."

"I felt heat. I was sweating and I . . . I . . ."

"It's okay, Becca."

"I felt I was trapped, like the walls were closing in. And through it all was the voice. But not that man's voice, the one who kept calling himself my father. Another one."

Nat frowned.

"And I heard banging. The branches of the tree outside my window, they knock on the glass when there's a storm. Maybe that's what I heard. But whatever it was, it woke me up."

Becca's eyes searched around the room. They went from object to object—bookcases, the oil painting of a jungle, the bottles of perfume on her table, and then Nat, seeming to look right through him.

"That light was on. But not the corner lamp. I woke up . . . I was so happy to be here. Safe. The room was nice and cool. I could hear the wind outside."

Nat came and sat on the bed next to her. "Did you hear anyone pounding on the door?" he said.

"I . . . I don't know. Earlier, I heard pounding, but I was still half asleep, and thought it was part of my dream."

Nat watched her. "Okay. In the dream, what was the voice saying?"

Becca's eyes went wide, but then she shook her head a little. "He wasn't speaking English."

"Really? What then?"

"It sounded like French . . . but it was so bad I couldn't understand it. Why?"

"No reason. Keep going."

"I could catch only bits and pieces. But it was a horrible, low voice. Like a chant."

Nat reached over and put his hand on her shoulder. Becca's body was tense. "Did you see anything through the window?"

"I looked out to see if the storm was over. I saw . . . the man who lives here. He was walking down there in the trees. That's all I saw."

"The man. Was he alone?"

She looked at him, then shook her head once. "I don't know."

"Okay. And then?"

"And then I heard a scream. After that, silence."

Nat sighed. "Becca . . . I have to tell you something. The man who lives here—"

"Yes?"

"He's dead."

"Good," she said, breathing out in a rush.

"Becca," he said, grimacing. "The man who lives here was your father. He hanged himself."

She glared at him, and a vein pulsed in her throat. Her lips slowly lost their blood. She was refusing even to say the words again. *He was not my father.*

"So why do you keep saying he was a stranger to you?"

Her mouth opened, and she gave him a wounded look that turned to disbelief. "What, you think I'm crazy? Do you think I don't dream of my father coming and taking me away from here? Don't you think I'd recognize my *own father* if I saw him? I would jump into his arms and never let him leave me again. But he deserted me . . . and he left me here to be murdered."

Nat stood up and walked to the window, feeling his craft escape him. She wasn't responding in a normative way—even for a psychiatric patient.

"Becca, growing up . . . did the man who lived here . . . did he ever touch you?"

"What do you mean?"

"You know, touch you. In a way you didn't want him to."

Becca was staring at him with an icy look that bordered on hatred. "What . . . do . . . you . . . mean?"

He didn't respond.

"No," she said finally.

"What about the man who . . . who attacked you on December twenty-first. Did he do anything else to you?"

Her eyes went cloudy, and she frowned, looking down at the bed. "He took things away," she said.

Nat's eyes closed for a moment. "What things?"

She only stared.

"Organs?" he said. "Is that what you're saying?"

She stood up, a look of horror spread across her face.

"How . . . how did you *know* that? Are you with the people who killed me? I thought you were—"

Nat took her hands in his. "Becca, I want to tell you something. I want to show you that your fears, as real as they appear to be, are *not* real. Will you let me do that?"

Becca watched him, distrust in her widely spaced eyes. *She's so young,* Nat thought. *I have to remember she's only nineteen.*

"Will you give me a chance?" he said.

The slightest nod.

"I know these things because other people have believed them, too. There is a psychiatric condition that is very rare and I believe you have it. It's called Cotard delusion. It was discovered in the late 1800s by a French doctor named Jules Cotard. A patient came to him and said that she had died. I wouldn't normally tell you . . ."

"So it's happened before," Becca said.

"Listen, she wasn't *dead*," Nat said. "She only *believed* she was. She woke up one day and couldn't recognize her family, and so she was under the mistaken impression that she was actually dead."

Becca's face was unreadable. But she was composed, her dark hair falling over her eyes. She had the stillness of a painting.

"Others have gone through this, Becca. They believe people have come and stolen their organs and that they've passed away. But it never really happened. It was all in their minds. And they've been cured."

"What was the name of Dr. Cotard's patient?"

"I don't really know. He called her Mademoiselle X."

"Nobody knows?"

"No, and it's not important."

"What happened to her?"

"I don't know. It was a long time ago."

Becca turned away, sudden bitterness in her face. "She died, though."

"Yes."

"While under the doctor's care?"

"Yes. But he didn't know what to do with her. *I* can help you."

"What did she die of?"

Nat cursed himself for ever bring up Cotard. "She hated herself, so . . . she stopped eating. She starved to death."

"Nobody cut her open?"

"No."

"They didn't take her liver? And her kidneys?"

Nat winced. "No, Becca. Like I said, it was a delusion."

Her eyes looked hopeful for a moment, but then they moved to his right and Nat knew she was looking at the door.

"Who was trying to get in the door?"

"Perhaps your father."

Becca's eyes looked at his, and he felt her intelligence alive in them. "Or no one," she said, her voice low. "Perhaps I heard the voices myself."

"I don't know that. In a way, it doesn't matter."

"Dr. Thayer, if I show you something, will you believe that I am not delusional?"

Nat studied her face. "You can try. But I've seen the door. Yes, someone attacked it with a knife."

"You're thinking I did that, too."

"No." He took a deep breath and released it. "Honestly . . . I don't know."

Becca smiled. He felt his body growing lighter, as if helium were filling his chest. He felt their closeness.

"You can't help me, Dr. Thayer. If I'm not really dead, that means I'm crazy—and not in any way you can fix."

She wore a smile that almost mocked him. But in her eyes there was something that contradicted the smile. Hope. A silent appeal.

"You're very much alive," he said. "And I can help you. We're going to get you better. I promise."

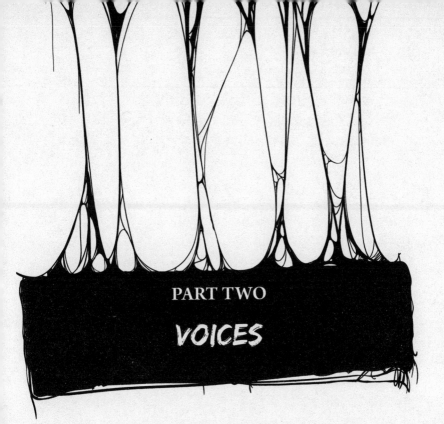

PART TWO

VOICES

CHAPTER SIXTEEN

The classroom at St. Adolphus was quiet Monday morning as Ms. Elizabeth Sena made her way through the desks. Her first graders were so bad this year, *so* unruly and *so* loud, that she considered moments like these—when all the little heads were bent over their papers, coloring—a kind of triumph. She didn't want to break the spell by even speaking.

It had been a long day, and it was shaping up to be a long year. There were going to be a lot of assignments like this one in the months ahead.

Today's assignment was to draw one friend as you saw them. It could be a parent or a grandma or a crossing guard, so long as the person was your friend. She'd made sure to include those categories because if she didn't, God only knew what the loners like Matthew Fudderman and Charlie Bailey would draw. Matthew had no friends because he was a fat, odorous bully. And Charlie . . . well, Charlie was just different.

She turned a corner by Rita Molino's desk, saw she was making something outrageously colorful, as usual. Smart girl, though the mother was trash from the Shan. Across from her, Marcus was gazing off into the distance, having completed just a big round head with triangle ears—was the boy drawing Dracula, for God's sake? Ms. Sena stopped above Marcus's straw-colored mop of hair and glanced down. Crisis averted. The boy wasn't drawing Dracula; he was just unable to form human ears. Marcus should have been left behind a year instead of being shoved into her class. His overbearing parents, both lawyers, would be the ruin of him.

She moved on. At least Marcus was drawing *something*. And the dome of silence was still intact. That was the important thing. She needed to rest her sorely tried nerves.

Strolling again, the only sound the whisk of her feet on the polished floor and the occasional "ummmm" from a student. She eyed Matthew Fudderman, coming up on the right. *Let's see who he thinks is his friend today*, she thought, *the deluded little fool*. Ms. Sena came up behind Matthew and turned to look down. The Incredible Hulk. The boy was actually drawing the Hulk. He was incorrigible. She'd stressed that the friend had to be a *real* person and *not* a superhero out of a comic book, but Matthew had a hard head. Ms. Sena paused over him, watching the green crayon rub furiously against the paper, the tip of the boy's wet little tongue visible in the right corner of his sloppy mouth, coloring the big green torso.

But no. She wasn't about to speak to Matthew, because his arms would fly up in frustration and his screeching would begin and the little dome of quiet inside the room would be destroyed. Ms. Sena felt she deserved a few minutes of calm. She began to think about the bottle of cabernet she'd left out on her kitchen counter before she'd turned on the radio for Jacks, her Pekingese, who'd be alone all day. It was 1:16 p.m. now, so that meant in about three hours, the first delicious pour of the wine would be rolling down her throat.

Ms. Sena walked down the last row. Charlie Bailey was at the head. Poor silent Charlie with Heller's syndrome. At the beginning of the year, she'd had to take a class on special disabilities just because of him. His father had fought to get Charlie into a normal classroom environment—the deadly stigma of the short bus was still strong, she'd learned—and so here he was. Charlie was sweet, but it wasn't easy accommodating him—the speechlessness, the notes scrawled in their capital letters. He tried, though. The boy did try.

He now looked up at her uncertainly as she approached. Ms. Sena raised her eyebrows, as if to say, *What do you have for me today, Charlie?* He was leaning over the paper, his right shoulder blocking her view.

She bent down.

"How's it looking, Charlie?"

The boy's eyes. As deep as an ocean.

Something quailed inside of her. She felt fear coming off of the boy in tiny wavelets. Like low-level radiation.

"It's okay," she said quietly. "Let me have a look."

Charlie shook his head.

"Uh, Ms. Sena?" It was Matthew.

"I'll be with you in a minute," she said evenly.

"Yeah, but is the Hulk—"

"I said one minute."

Matthew muttered something and his head went down again.

Ms. Sena laid her hand on Charlie's shoulder. It was trembling. The poor thing, he should really be in special ed, where they had the personnel to deal with things like this.

She applied the lightest pressure, pulling him toward her as if to whisper in his ear. As he came back, she peeked over his shoulder. Probably another Marvel hero.

"Good Lord, Charlie," she hissed, her hand tightening on his shoulder. A shiver of horror ran through her.

The face on the paper was black as coal. It had high cheekbones, a gaping mouth, and its eyes circled in, each like a whirlpool toward a center of bright orange. It looked . . . diabolical.

"Who in God's name is that?"

Charlie looked at her and said nothing, just stared at her with those big brown eyes.

"Charlie. You were supposed to draw your friend. Did you

not understand the assignment?" She had the sudden urge to send the drawing immediately out of her classroom. There was something . . . unearthly about it. A seven-year-old drawing a satanic figure and calling it his friend.

She reached down for the paper. She would throw it away. Or burn it.

Charlie swiveled his shoulders and pulled his drawing away from her outstretched fingers. She touched the corner of it, but he jerked it away, then angrily looked up at her.

Ms. Sena stood up straight, one hand on her hip, feeling a rush of heat coming up her neck.

"Charlie!"

He was looking down, afraid to meet her eyes.

"Who is this . . . person?"

Heads popped up. She glared at them, and all but Matthew sank back down. Charlie pulled the paper out farther onto the desk. He took a red crayon and began to scribble something under the thing's black neck. Interested despite herself, Ms. Sena watched.

The boy crouched over the drawing, blocking her view. She tapped her foot on the linoleum floor.

Finally, Charlie pulled back to show her what he'd done.

THE MAGICIAN, it read.

"Well, I don't like the looks of the magician," Ms. Sena said a little too abrasively. "Draw somebody else."

Charlie looked at her. The sadness in his face . . . Okay, fine, she would try. She bent down to him, putting a hand again on his little shoulder. "Don't you have another friend?"

He shook his head.

"What about your daddy?"

Charlie's head went still and the brown eyes regarded her.

"Just draw somebody else," she said, attempting not to hiss at the boy. "I don't care if it's Superman, for Christ's sake . . ."

She heard her own voice screeching. The little heads shot bolt upward all around the room, and two hands shot up. Ms. Sena cursed under her breath. She was letting her anger take control. The dome of silence was shattered.

Charlie's confusion mingling with fear in his eyes.

"Not like that," she snapped. "Turn the paper over."

Charlie did as he was told. And now just stared at the blank side.

She was going to speak to Mrs. Abruzzi as soon as possible. She'd had enough of little Charlie Bailey. It was time for him to go.

CHAPTER SEVENTEEN

John Bailey was driving down State Street when his phone buzzed in his pocket. The little screen read *Wartham Coll*. He stared at in puzzlement—*Is someone calling me from administration?*—before realizing that all calls from Wartham were labeled with the college and not individual rooms or dorms. He quickly pressed *Talk*.

A drifting wave of static sounded in his ear, rising and falling.

"Detective Bailey," he said.

The static dipped, and from the back of it emerged a voice. "Hello?"

"Yes, this is Detective Bailey. Who am I talking to?"

Sssshhhhhhh in his ear. *ShhhhhWWWWWOOHHHHHHH-HHHH.*

He thought he heard a voice. It was like one of those hearing tests when you're tensed to pick up anything and you think you detect a ping after it's sounded.

"This is . . ." The static rose to a moan. It was like talking to someone in space.

"Who is this?"

"*Rrrrr . . .*"

John pulled over in front of McGinnis's Hardware and jammed the car into park. Without the sound of the engine, he could hear deeper into the static.

"Yeah?"

"*Rrrrrrramo . . .*"

John frowned. It had to be the black girl. "Ramona?"

"... *essssss*."

"Ramona, where are you? The reception is terrible."

It was the reception, but it was something in her voice, too, in the middle of that storm of electricity. She sounded a little off. Almost panicked.

"I saw ..." SSSSSSSSSNNNNIIIIIISSSHHHHHHHH.

He banged the phone on the steering wheel. When he brought it back to his ear, the static was trailing off like a departing comet.

"Ramona? What did you see?"

"I saw ..."

The comet coming back, the hiss beginning to rise, popping in his ear. But there was an echo of a word carved into the noise.

John felt a little chill sweep over his arms.

"Did you say 'Margaret'?" he said.

"*Yessssssss.*"

The flesh on his back puckered and went icy. Ramona's voice sounded close now, as if she were sitting next to him in the seat. He could hear her breath ruffle in the holes on the phone's speaker.

"You mean you dreamt about her," he said, as if he were consoling his boy after he'd had a nightmare about the oogly-man, which is what Charlie called the boogeyman. The oogly-man had been coming by a lot lately.

Static beginning to build far off, like a sandstorm building on the horizon. It rose in volume, sweeping forward, and he imagined the sandstorm growing and turning his way, turning the sky black.

"No," came the voice, and then the static blotted out the rest.

He waited for the noise to end. *What the fuck is happening at Wartham? Some kind of hysterical mass illness?*

"Ramona?"

The static crackled, and he now slammed the phone onto his lap before pulling it back up to his ear.

"Ramona!" he yelled.

The static cut away, and he took a breath before he heard her say: "Margaret's not dead anymore."

CHAPTER EIGHTEEN

Chuck Godwin glanced into his living room. His wife, Stephanie, was sitting in the sun-yellow armchair by the fireplace, wearing a black-and-white knit cardigan and tan slacks, her feet bare. Logs crackled in the fire he'd started an hour ago. She was reading a hardcover book, open to about the middle. He couldn't see the title. He didn't want to know it anyway.

"Got to go to Stop & Shop," he said.

"What for?" she said without looking up.

"Milk."

Her eyebrows lifted into round arches, but gently. It was one of the first gestures of hers that he remembered. He'd found it so . . . intriguing forty years ago. It did nothing for him now.

"I thought we had some."

Chuck brought his right hand around the doorway. In it was an empty plastic milk jug, the half-gallon size.

"No."

That's because, two minutes before, he'd poured the milk that had been left in the jug into the kitchen sink, careful to bring the spout close to the drain mouth so as not to make any noise. Now it was his evidence, and he shook it.

"Oh, okay. Get some cheese, too," she said, her eyes drifting back to her book. "Muenster."

He backed away from the doorway, nodding and jiggling the keys in his pocket.

"No, Swiss lace!" she called after him.

He didn't nod this time.

Chuck shut the garage door behind him and got in his Volvo station wagon. He turned the car on and sat in the front seat, looking ahead robotically, *feeling* robotic. The voice was back there, behind the sound of the running motor. The rope was on the front seat where he'd placed it before emptying the milk. The morning sunlight shone through the windshield and caught the top loop. That piece of twine seemed to throb in his temples. It was as if the goddamn thing were *hissing* . . .

He put the car in reverse and backed out the opened garage door. The tarmac of the street gleamed wetly between the plots of snow that covered his and his neighbors' front yards. It was ten on a Monday morning, and the good people of his comfortable and peace-loving section of Northam still seemed to be slumbering deep in their beds.

He pushed the car into drive and rolled down his street, turning left on Willow, revving the engine as he did so. He checked his watch. It was 10:02 now.

The hissing was growing louder. Chuck kept his eye on the yellow line that split Willow Street in half and did not look over.

He was driving toward the Raitliff Woods, the voice growing louder no matter how much he raced the engine. Willow would take him right over to State Street and then the woods. But as he approached Minotaur Avenue, he shot his left foot out and hit the brakes and wrenched the wheel right. He began to breathe heavily.

Use . . .

He hit the gas and roared down Minotaur Avenue going 65 mph. Up ahead he saw the sign for 95 South, a shield-shaped glow of green. The road was nearly deserted, swept by spinning drifts of snow blowing in from the east. He hit the gas harder and jetted up the ramp, the Volvo lifting into the air as the road deposited him onto the highway. He landed with a rattle, and the car almost got away from him.

He looked over at the yellow twine. It was curled luxuriantly, one loop resting on the back of another. He reached over to grab it and to throw the rope in the back, but at the last moment his fingers twitched away and he jerked his hand back into his lap.

. . . the rope.

It was a trick of the light. But it had looked like the rope moved as he reached for it. Coiled away.

"Buck up, Chuck," he said in the silence of the cab, the only sound the humming of the wheels on the road.

The hissing rose in his ears. It was crackling now, like static, with words blurred behind it.

Unexpectedly, he began to pray. "Lord, look down on your wayward son. Lord, look down on *me.*"

He was approaching the exit for the next town, coming up fast on his right. He'd lost track of where he was and leaned forward over the steering wheel to make out the letters. But the sign blurred by so quickly he couldn't even read it—just a camera flash of green and white. Chuck leaned back and looked at the speedometer. Still 65 and climbing.

Chuck saw signs, more signs. Was he near Mansfield? Or was he past there, all the way to Attleboro? His phone vibrated in his pocket; surely a text from Stephanie asking him where he was. He pulled his foot off the gas and then suddenly a big Dodge pickup ahead of him veered left and Chuck shot up behind it and nearly rammed the son of a bitch. He went by the Dodge like it wasn't moving and saw a black hole of a mouth yelling at him in the driver's window.

"Buck up. Buck up. Buck up. Lord, look down on me."

The words of faith felt so strange on his tongue. He'd never been one for church, but who was powerful enough to fend off the thing worming its way into his brain if not God? He passed a tractor-trailer, its mud flaps shooting white spray over his windshield. The speed was increasing again, seemingly of its own volition.

The Volvo swerved, and then the wheels caught on the wet tarmac and shot off down the straight black line. The needle steady at 70. He couldn't hear the rope over the sound of the straining engine. He pressed the window button and the glass slid down and a gust of snow blew into the car.

Chuck stuck out his tongue.

The wild cacophony of the engine and the snow roaring in his ears drowned out everything else, but then he heard it inside his brain.

You're getting close.

Chuck clawed the inside of the windshield that was frosting over with the snow, rubbing a hole on the fogged-over glass.

"God, God!" he cried.

He rubbed a small hole in the fogged glass and saw more signs flying by. Chuck's eyes were wide, unseeing.

Very close.

Something ahead. Something he recognized.

Here!

His left foot shot out and stabbed the brakes. The Volvo bucked hard, the rubber screaming *SHEEERRRWWWAAAA-AAAAAAAHHH* on the wet pavement, and the car fishtailed right. He saw steel railings swimming into view through the passenger window, and past them, a huge valley of deepest blue. Chuck swung the wheel left and the tires squealed through the open window like they were getting ready to blow. He was drifting, drifting, the car like a figure skater flying over the ice. If only . . .

BBRRRRAAAAANNGGGG! Chuck's head racked off the door column. The car shuddered violently and then rocketed back across the road. It spun twice in full circles, whipping Chuck into the driver's door and then down onto the parking brake. He heard a snap, and a stab of pain cut into his side. Finally, the Volvo, groaning and screeching, backed into a curb and seemed to leap a foot into the air before crashing down on the highway, facing back the way he'd come.

The tractor-trailer went flying by on his right, the driver hitting his horn. The air bags, miraculously, hadn't deployed, perhaps because the right side of the car had taken the brunt of the impact.

But if anyone came now, they'd slam into him head-on. The air bag wouldn't save him.

The road behind him was empty. Chuck's left eye was battered shut and beginning to swell. His head felt three feet across, and he could feel bumps on it beginning to blow up like small balloons. His rib cage throbbed on the right side, and something seemed to jab into his lung when he took a deep breath.

Chuck reached across and grabbed the rope. He pushed the driver's door, but it was stuck. He bellowed like a trapped bull and slammed his shoulder into it. It sprang open.

You're so close. Go.

The radio was playing the Drifters, "Save the Last Dance for Me." He hadn't even realized the thing was on. Chuck pushed the door out farther, cutting his left palm on the broken glass that had sprayed onto the armrest. He got out.

A Cadillac shot by not three feet from his nose. He had the image of a woman, red lipstick and white skin smudged together into a carnival face. The car slewed by, then braked hard, and he saw it shudder to a stop at the end of the bridge about thirty yards away.

So *that's* where he was. On the Mackinaw Bridge. He grabbed the rope, pushed himself into a standing position, and began to walk across the tarmac. His bare hand reached out for the rounded steel of the top railing.

The woman stepped out of the Cadillac and stood in the road, watching him.

The rope was hissing again. And the voice was humming, the words no longer intelligible, just a hymn or a chant. His head was full of music.

He reached the railing, three thick round beams with a dark

abyss behind them where the river valley was swathed in mist. He looked down at the rope in his hand.

You know what...

Chuck took the end of the rope, the one marked with an old piece of black electrical tape, and held it tightly in his left hand. He felt its grain scratching the palm of his hand as he gripped it tight. He looked out at the void beyond the top railing.

...to do.

"Yes, I do," Chuck said out loud. He took the coils of rope and tossed them over the railing, letting the rope fall into the abyss that was sucking snowflakes down into its core. He still held the end with the bit of electrical tape snugly in his right hand.

The rope fell and then snapped, like a fishing rod with a trout on the end. Chuck felt the length of it swinging in the abyss, like he was falling all down the length of the rope.

Tie it tie it tie it.

Chuck's heartbeat was racing in his ears. His eyes were glazed. The blue air was sucking in the snow, sucking everything down to its icy heart.

You are...

Chuck opened his mouth wide. He was trying to pop his ears, like you would when descending in a plane on final approach.

...near.

Chuck roared and shook his head back and forth. If he could just pop his ears and clear his head. He held the rope between his two hands and wrapped the black-taped end around the cold railing. But he hadn't tied a knot into the loop. It was just hanging there on the steel. The rope wriggled in his hand, alive.

His ears finally popped.

Chuck went to tie the rope. The wind was pulling it toward the railing and the void, but he somehow had a nice loop around the top bar.

"Buck up!" he cried. And suddenly his mind was quiet.

Chuck bent down convulsively and swept the rope up into his arms, pulling it with short furious jerks. One, two, three, four, the thing came up quickly, only twenty feet long. The end of it slapped him on the cheek and he stepped back.

His eyes were wide and his mouth shaped into an O of fear. Then Chuck pushed the coils over the bridge, nearly tumbling into the misty depths in his eagerness, letting go of all of it.

The yellow thing fell, twisting and rippling. Chuck watched it. He swore it was wriggling like a snake.

"Fuck you," he said. Then he yelled it, baying like a hound. "*FUUUUUUUUCK YOUUUUUUUUUUUU!*"

He was laughing maniacally. He dropped his hands to his thighs and hunched over, taking big delicious drafts of the cold air into his lungs. He laughed again and turned back toward the road.

The voice was gone from his head. *I believe I have freed myself from this goddamn curse*, he thought. *Free at last, free at last.*

He whooped again. He looked up the road and saw the woman, who was still standing by the Cadillac, hurriedly get back in her car and start it up. He waved at her, his arm making a wide arc through the air. *Have a good day!*

Chuck was literally shaking with giddiness. *Thank God Almighty . . .* A white sports car went flying by him, and he danced back, still laughing. *I'm free at last.* He relived the moment again, that sudden spasm of madness. No, of courage!

Nothing echoed in his head. His mind was clear; he stood still a moment and dared the voices to come back.

Who knew it could be so simple? All it took was a little bravery. He had bucked up, just like his father had always told him to.

As he looked at the railing one last time, he heard the wind beyond the bridge railing. It was moaning, fluting between the little horizontal bars, causing them to thrum and sing. He listened for a minute, then returned to the battered Volvo.

CHAPTER NINETEEN

Ramona Best stared at the phone, then closed her eyes. She had done her duty; she'd warned them. So what if she had told a white lie? No, two. She wasn't at Wartham College, hadn't been for the last two hours. She was at a rest stop on 95, a quaint little gas station and snack shop in the middle of Connecticut that she'd reached after doing ten mph over the speed limit for the last fifty miles. She'd called the college operator and asked her to put her through to Detective Bailey, since she didn't have his number, and they had.

The other white lie was harder to talk about. It was about Margaret. About the way Margaret *looked*. Ramona Best was already afraid she was losing her mind, and she wasn't going to tell Bailey about hearing a dead girl talk to her, and the thing she'd learned from listening. Wasn't seeing Margaret enough?

She'd made the call from here at the rest stop. The little stone-clad building had shielded her from the traffic flowing south down 95 on this frigid morning, and now she leaned her head up against the side. It felt rough and cool, and it relieved for just a second her burning brain.

The phone began to buzz, and she knew it was the big, sad-eyed detective calling her back. He'd taken her cell phone number when he came to interrogate her that first time. But she'd already spent far too long in this little rest stop. Ramona slid the phone into her sweats and pulled the hood of her ankle-length black down coat until it drooped over her forehead. She jerked the strings, and the hood went *schwirp* and closed to a small circle in front of her nose.

Her car was a ratty old Altima that she'd inherited from her brother before he'd signed up for the air force, the idiot. Raford—both their names began with *R*, she and Raford, the two children of Edouarine Best—was just as smart as his sister. He could have gotten into any of the colleges she did; when he was a junior in high school and she was a sophomore, Ramona would even leave the brochures on his bed when she sensed a good fit for him. Ramona had collected those brochures like other kids collected comic books or baseball cards. She'd kept them in a big Adidas box under her bed and had read them for pleasure months before choosing Wartham.

But Raford was stupid—he wanted to join the air force and fly planes, even when Ramona told him, *Ray-ray, they're not going to let you fly planes, they keep those slots open for white boys who look good on recruiting posters and they'll tell you, Yeah, sure you can fly the F-24 Mega-Raptor or whatever you call the damn things, and then when they have you all legal and proper they'll say, Oh, sorry, you didn't meet our height requirement or our aptitude thingamajig or our pigment goals, and they'll have you loading the bombs under the wings and waiting on the deck of the aircraft carrier as the white boy who got your slot goofs the landing and brings the plane crashing down on the hot tarmac and the whole kit and caboodle goes up in a fireball and you die in the middle of the ocean, like someone with no sense.*

But Raford had gone to the recruiter on his eighteenth birthday anyway, his dumb face set into a man's scowl, and now she was alone. Ramona had always been close to Raford, and she cursed him now because he was strong and decisive, even when he was wrong, and more than anything, he believed her, and she wanted to sit on his bed back home in Roosevelt, Long Island, and tell him what had gone down at Wartham and have him believe her about that, too. What she'd seen back there on the common at eight o'clock in the evening on a perfectly nice Sunday evening.

But Raford was gone. Only her aunt Zuela would be home. And Zuela ...

Ramona looked through the little porthole of her hood. The Altima was angled into a parking space not four feet away, the gray sunlight gleaming dully on its blue hood. The next car was two spaces over, a Jeep Cherokee with blackened windows that she didn't remember from when she pulled in. Ramona stepped six inches out of the shadow of the building, and her eyes went to the people milling in front of the convenience store. She pretended to be searching in her pocket for change, but all that was there was a nickel and a quarter and her phone, still buzzing—*Damn that detective, couldn't he just go and do what needed to be done?*—but really she was going over each person in the little forecourt with her eyes. There was a Latino man in a black sport coat pumping gas into his Lexus, all spiffed up and shiny—*No one in the backseat, I don't think, but the left corner is all shadowy and who knows.* A white woman in skinny jeans and a brocaded jacket was walking out of the convenience store, her heels making sharp distinct clacking noises on the concrete as she shook a Snapple iced tea bottle in her left hand. Ramona got no vibes from her other than thinking the brocaded jacket was kind of cute on her. Then there was a white man on a motorcycle, just idling and staring at her through a pair of BluBlockers or whatever you called those corny sunglasses. He could be waiting for someone inside, she thought, and even though his BluBlockers were following the woman shaking her Snapple—the cords standing out in his neck as he turned his head—Ramona suddenly felt the eyes behind the glasses were watching *her.*

The fear rose up her throat like bile, and she stepped back around the corner.

Come on, you chicken. You've got to leave now. How far are you gonna get if every man with sunglasses gets you flustered?

Ramona took half a breath and put her head down and walked quickly to the side of the Altima. She reached for the door handle and she pulled it up and it clicked, but the door didn't open. Ramona realized with a freezing horror that of course she'd locked the car. A sheet of ice seemed to slide down her back as she rooted in her bag for the keys. She couldn't help but turn and look over her shoulder at the man on the motorcycle as her hand frantically touched gum, coin, lip balm . . .

He was watching her now, full on. The two black circles of the sunglasses were pointed directly at her.

Ramona's hand closed over the keys, and she had them in the door and pulled it open and nearly threw herself into the front seat. She pulled the door in after her, and when it shut with a solid metal sound and she locked it up, Ramona felt as if it had completed a seal of the vacuum inside the car. It was quiet except for the sound of her heart racing along in her ears.

She started the car and put it into reverse. Soon she was on the highway, the hum of the road under her feet—there was a rust hole about the size of a quarter that let sounds into the car and which she didn't have the money to fix, not unless she didn't want to eat for a while.

Ramona's eyes slid uneasily to the rearview mirror. She watched the cars behind her and then caught herself.

Ramona, please. Please get a hold of yourself now. That Detective Bailey had probably already put out an APB or whatever they call them on her. *Emotionally disturbed person, a filer of false and outlandish reports. Please detain if spotted.*

Well, I didn't want to see Margaret, she thought.

She leaned over and began tapping the radio tune button. The radio would make that garbled sound you used to get when you fast-forwarded a cassette tape. She remembered home again, taping those Prince concerts on the Maxell 90-minutes and swapping them with her friends Natasha and Girl—they'd just called her Girl at Roosevelt High because she started every sentence with the word. As in, *Girl, those shoes are . . .* So ghetto. But she missed Girl now, missed them all.

She was tapping the down button on the radio tuner when the image of Margaret Post swept into her mind. Ramona's hand hovered over the button and Jesus music flooded into the car. Ramona Best hated Jesus music, but her whole body seemed to be frozen in place, one hand on the wheel.

Oh, Margaret, why didn't you stay in the morgue? Why didn't you just stay in your room *and make it to graduation?*

She tried to erase Margaret's face from her mind by picturing her old bedroom back home, wondering if Zuela had done anything to it, and how exactly she would get revenge if her aunt had touched one single jar of Ramona's lotion. But Margaret's face didn't fade, and Ramona got a strange metallic taste in her mouth—like copper, like a copper penny—and soon she felt herself traveling to the night before. The scenes from the common were flooding back to her, unwanted, spilling into her vision as if they would blot out the road and the yellow line . . .

Ramona wrenched the wheel left, and the Altima veered toward the shoulder, a BMW blaring as it swerved past her on the right. Ramona hit the brakes, and the Altima slid on the gravel, the back of the car veering toward the highway before the wheels gripped and the car rocked to a stop.

Ramona sat there, breathing, her eyes wide with terror. *Goddamn you, Margaret Post. You're gonna drag me down with you.*

The pictures in her head would not stop coming.

CHAPTER TWENTY

Ramona Best sat in her Altima, cars rocking the vehicle on its wheels as they whipped by on the right. Her eyes were glassy, her mouth open. Her breaths were quick and shallow.

She'd been at the snack bar in the Keegan Memorial Building when it happened. This was her sanctum, her last-resort study nook. After getting her first B-minus in biology, she'd found a little corner table that was shielded from the register and most of the other tables by a frond-leafed plant that stood six or seven feet tall. When Ramona had to get her real work done, she came to this dark corner, where she could hear the frozen-yogurt machine churn at its twelve-minute intervals—she'd timed it. Next to the table was a tall window that faced out on the main common. That window was her TV. Excellent for people watching.

That night, she'd gone to the Keegan with one textbook: *Psychology* by David G. Myers, her latest bugaboo. Dr. David G. Myers was not a very clear writer; sometimes Ramona thought he intentionally muddled things up so as to make her life miserable. She'd worked on the chapter "Neuroscience and Behavior," hiding behind the big leaves of the plant. Just her and the round little table, her English breakfast tea in a stylishly colorful paper cup (medium), two sugars, no milk, and the window out onto the quad, which was brightly lit by modern poles fashioned to look like ancient brass fixtures.

There'd been a full moon that came slanting over the spires of the chapel and shone onto the tangled boxwoods lining the pathways cut between the two-foot snowbanks. When Ramona was tired of Dr. David G. Myers, she would look up at the girls crossing back and forth and absorb a little gossip about who'd become new besties and what freshman, *scandal*, was holding hands with which senior. Lesbianism was au courant at Wartham. Ramona had resisted, but she kept tally of who was smushing who like a baseball box score.

The machine had kicked in four times since she arrived. Forty-eight minutes. Which meant it was about 6:48 p.m. when she looked up and saw the girl under the boxwood in the northwest corner of the quad. She was wearing a shiny black anorak and jeans and black shoes, and she had the hood pulled up over her head and the drawstring pulled so that only her nose and maybe her eyes would have been visible if you'd been standing three feet from her.

But it was Margaret. On her mother's grave, she'd swear it was Margaret Post.

Ramona had felt her vision waver, and terror seemed to expand her heart so that she found it difficult to breathe.

"I know," she said to herself. "I know this cannot—"

And then the voice, soft in her ear.

Ramona.

Just like Margaret asking for help on her trig exam. Just like poor friendless Margaret with no aptitude for buckling down.

The taste of copper in her mouth. Ramona reached for the paper cup and took a gulp of the steaming tea and felt it slide down her throat. Then she looked back.

Margaret had moved closer. She was standing only thirty feet away now, just to the left of the statue of one of the school's founders. Ramona could feel her eyes burn into her own.

Help . . .

Ramona wanted to run, but the figure held her gaze, the moonlight creasing the black folds in the jacket.

And then something rushed through Ramona like a gust of wind. *Margaret doesn't know what's happened to her,* she thought.

...me.

Ramona's skin puckered with chill bumps. She wanted to scream.

How could Margaret be alive? Her throat had been sliced nearly to the spinal cord. She'd identified the body at the morgue at three in the morning on that awful night.

And then, as she stared out the window with fear spreading through her veins, Ramona saw Margaret's right hand begin to rise slowly, the cuff of the black jacket falling back, and the hand emerging and turning slowly, as if it were being pulled up. Even from the window, she could see the moonlight shine on the deathly white pallor of the skin. The hand was so drained of blood, it almost seemed to glow.

Ramona began to keen softly.

The hand came up and reached into the space under the hood, and Ramona saw the wrist turn and she realized that the thing, this body of her friend, was feeling at its face. Feeling along its face to see what it looked like, like a blind person.

Maybe Margaret doesn't know she's dead.

Ramona tried to answer the voice in her head with her own, but as soon as she formed the thought, a painful buzzing static— always for her the first sign of a migraine—throbbed in her head.

Clouds of dead sound sucking her thoughts away.

Now Margaret's voice coming through the static.

Please help me, Ramona.

Ramona's teeth began to chatter. She brought her hand to her mouth to stop it.

You're not Margaret, she thought. *You're some sorority asshole playing a stupid trick...*

Where...

Where what, Margaret?

Where am I?

The buzzing cloud descended, and Ramona twisted down in her chair. Then popping sounds and a moan that droned in the background.

Ramona closed her eyes. The coppery taste seemed to coat her teeth and tongue.

Panting like a dog, Ramona then sat with her head just above her knees. She didn't want to look. She'd just stared at the tiles of the floor and tried to listen for the frozen-yogurt machine. She willed it to kick in, to restart time.

Finally, the machine rattled to life with a jolt that Ramona felt in her chest, and she slowly inched her head up above the level of the window ledge.

Margaret was gone.

Remembering now, Ramona felt her body go cold. She closed her eyes, trying to banish the image of the hooded figure from her mind. After a moment, she opened her eyes, cupped her hands, and blew a warm breath onto her fingers, twice. Then she reached for the ignition and turned the key.

CHAPTER TWENTY-ONE

Ever since he'd thrown that cursed rope over the bridge, Chuck's life had seemed to brighten. The Volvo had started right up when he'd turned the ignition. A small miracle. He'd called Stephanie on his cell and told her he'd had a minor accident and would be home after he dropped the Volvo at the mechanic's. Her voice had edged up an octave, and she'd wanted to know the full details right there on the phone—was he hurt, were the police there, how badly was the car damaged?—but he told her he'd explain everything when he got home. Chuck had driven the Volvo to his mechanic's and taken a taxi home, where he found Stephanie waiting at the door, tense with worry. He'd explained the whole incident as the result of slippery roads, and said that the damage was sure to be below their $1,000 deductible, so he hadn't called Allstate. Nobody had been hurt, so he hadn't notified the police, either. After twenty minutes of questions, the tension in her voice had finally dissipated and he'd gone to bed, pleading a headache.

Best of all, the voices hadn't returned. His own voice had taken their place. "It's okay, Chuck," he'd told himself. *You're a good person. Why shouldn't there be one Chuck Godwin in this lousy goddamned world?*

The mechanic had called early this morning and told him his car would take only an hour or two to fix, but it would be a day or two before he could do the repairs. Chuck had rented a car, a red Toyota, driven to Mary Reddington's house, and parked just down the street. Then he'd marched up to her door—her *front* door—and knocked and gone inside and sat on her couch, done up in a bright floral pattern, and told her he'd never stopped wanting her. And, miracle of miracles, she hadn't thrown him out into the cold January afternoon. No, she'd placed her hand on his cheek and then kissed him full on the lips.

They'd restarted their affair—or, to be more precise, re-*ignited* it—because he'd never known sexual desire like this. Twenty years ago, he'd had a couple rolls in the hay with the redheaded Mary, their midlife crises seeming to hit emergency levels on the very same crisp fall weekend. Back then, they'd snuck off from the committee at St. Adolphus that they'd been cochairing and gone to the Lucky Clover Motel for hours of debauchery. What was the committee? The lawn council or some ridiculous thing. Deciding which kind of shrubbery to plant beneath the pastor's window. He'd sat there during the endless discussions about rosemary bushes versus rhododendrons and stared at Mary's flame-red hair, her gem-like green eyes. They'd slept together four times, but then she'd stopped answering his calls. He'd confronted her at the church, and she'd confessed that his bouts of depression were the cause. Her mother had suffered from melancholia and it had nearly torn her family apart. She was very much afraid of his black moods.

But now all that was behind them. Chuck laughed to himself. His father had farmed three acres of good soil when he was alive, fancying himself some kind of homesteader, and he would have said that his son had lain fallow for forty years. Four decades of depression and bad sex with Stephanie. Well, no longer. He was roaring back to life.

Chuck felt charged up, almost superhuman. The pads of his fingers, the tiny ridges of his fingerprints, seemed to be alive with electricity at the memory of touching Mary's skin. She was still so beautiful and, thank God, just as horny as he was. It felt good, yes, sir. He sat in the Volvo, looking at the long line of Willow Street

cut between the banks of hard white snow, the light on the whiteness soft and benevolent, the shaggy pines in the front yards and
the tops of the mailboxes gleaming, and it was as if he were seeing
these things for the first time.

Chuck didn't feel guilty about Stephanie. What his wife
wanted was his mind, his conversation, his comforting presence.
She'd been chronically undersexed her whole life. She sure didn't
know what she was missing. So his liaison with Mary was a guilt-
less affair, the best kind.

He was headed back to her house now in his little rented Toyota. They'd agreed that they couldn't wait another day to see each
other again. Who had time for patience when you were in your
midsixties?

Yes, it had done him a world of good, tossing that rope over
the bridge. He'd get up tomorrow morning, call in sick to his assistant, and spend the entire day cleaning out the basement of all
the accumulated trash that Stephanie had stuffed down there. He
was going to put a nice Rockler table saw in the corner, get back
to woodworking. The high whine of a quality table saw was something he'd always loved. Just thinking about it seemed to boost his
testosterone levels.

Chuck Godwin began to sing as he sat in the car. The only
song he could think of was "O Come, All Ye Faithful." The double
entendre didn't register with him. It was just a beautiful, beautiful
song.

"Joyful and triumphant," he sang in a passable voice. Chuck
felt alive, alive and grateful.

At 6:40 on Tuesday evening, Elizabeth Dyer was sitting at her
desk at the Northam morgue, slowly drinking a Diet Dr Pepper
and reading *Us* magazine. The morgue was in the basement of the
county administration building, and the place suited her. It was

cold, and she liked that. The corpses, too, were cold and silent, and after ten years of working here, she felt as much kinship with them as with anyone walking above.

Elizabeth had allotted a full hour to read the magazine cover to cover. She began at the back, as she always did. There a trio of snarky critics picked photos of the worst-dressed celebrities of the week and ripped into their fashion choices. She studied them for a while (Nicole Kidman didn't look *that* bad, she thought—*I mean they obviously just wanted to include her*), then paged ahead to the ads for awful products that she would never buy. Still, she liked to imagine being the kind of person who was confident and carefree enough to order spandex corsets without worrying about people finding out.

Then the really meaty stories: the cheating boyfriends, pregnancy scandals, and drug addictions that were slowly being revealed in the lives of American starlets. These Elizabeth read thoroughly, no matter if she liked the person or not. The idea that many of these beautiful people were sliding toward disaster despite their money and their fame appealed to her.

"Gosh, *her*?" she said, studying a full-page photo of an aging actress who'd apparently gotten hooked on meth. Elizabeth's laugh was cut short when she heard a noise from the outside room. The cavernous storage room here had originally been a cellar for the county offices before it was turned into the sleek modern facility for the processing of bodies. It was big and its ceiling was arched like a medieval wine cellar. Between the stone walls and the stainless steel equipment, sound traveled well.

Elizabeth stood up with uncertainty. It had been a low metallic sound, almost a screech. Her brow furrowed, and she came around the desk and walked to her door. She held the handle, her chin down, listening. Then she slowly pulled the door open.

The room was empty, just as she'd left it when she walked in this afternoon. She was the only one on duty today, besides

Jimmy Stearns and Claude, and they were out on a call. As Elizabeth stood in her open doorway, a metal echo vibrated in the air.

She listened. Nothing else. The echo slowly seemed to shrink away behind the tables—blue and glinting in the overhead lights. She frowned and dropped her eyes back to the page she'd been reading.

That sound again. Elizabeth Dyer made a face, placed the magazine down on its spread-out feature on the latest breakup of the 2010 Bachelor, got up from her desk chair, and strode toward her door.

"Jimmy?" she called out as she pulled it open. "Claude?" Jimmy Stearns was the mortuary assistant, along with his partner, Claude Roke. Even in Northam, with its cratered economy, Claude represented the last scrapings of the barrel. He was a slob and a drunk who owed his job to the fact that his great-uncle was a county commissioner, and one in favor of nepotism even for the grungiest of his relatives.

But Jimmy Stearns, tall, with sad blue eyes and a pathological shyness, she liked. He was considerate. And he did as he was told.

Claude and Jimmy had taken the van out on a run forty minutes ago, and Elizabeth didn't expect them back for another half hour. She hadn't heard the van pull up.

She yanked the door open. The room appeared to be normal. The metal shone blue in the emergency lighting that always kept the place half lit unless she hit the main switches. The body lockers were to the left, twenty of them, rarely all filled except during natural disasters or the last flu epidemic.

Then she noticed one of them was ajar.

From where she stood, Elizabeth could see an extra inch of black space between the locker door and the steel housing. Elizabeth began to walk over, the tapping of her feet echoing under the thick arched ceiling.

She came up to the locker. Number 12B. A faint exhalation

came from the one-inch gap between the opened door and the locker frame, air from the interior cooling system that kept the bodies from putrefying. The lockers were kept at a steady 35.6 degrees at all times, the smell of decomposition wafted away by the air purifiers connected to steel pipes running up the side of the building and venting above the roof. You rarely smelled death in the morgue, unless there was a body on the examining table. You could have twenty bodies in the lockers after a casino bus accident out on 95 and still have a very nice wine-and-cheese party in here. If she had anyone to invite, that is . . .

The lights above her flickered once, then again. She looked up and saw that one of the fluorescents in the fixture above her was dying. She'd have to get Jimmy to replace it. The blinking threw the tables and the saws and utensils into grotesque shadows, ballooning and then shrinking back. There was only one other light on, near the big stainless steel sinks next to her office door.

Elizabeth Dyer liked the dead, *preferred* them to most living people. But right now, she began to feel uneasy.

The light suddenly sputtered out and the shadows expanded. Elizabeth spotted something out of the corner of her eye, just over her shoulder. Her heart went cold. The air continued hissing out of the open locker; it was as if someone were standing behind her, moving along as she walked. She felt dread course through her, and her heart began to beat violently.

"Who's there?" she said in a low voice.

The light flicked back to life, and Elizabeth turned, her hand rising up to push the thing away.

A black plastic coat hung on one of the poles next to the examination table.

Claude. She was going to ream him several new orifices. He was supposed to collect the examination coats at the end of each day, but this one he'd left hanging on its hook. The lazy bastard.

Her heartbeat slowly returned to normal.

But how did the locker get open?

She stared for a moment at 12B, the whisper of wind coming through the gap.

She was reaching to pull it open fully when she heard the van's engine growling near the middle window. She looked up and saw a shadow fall across the glass, and then the engine cut and two male voices struck up a conversation.

They were back. Claude and Jimmy.

Their voices gave her a little jolt of adrenaline. Afraid in her own workplace? Seeing ghosts in the corners? She didn't want them seeing her spooked. She shoved 12B completely shut, the *chunk* sound ringing in the room and hanging there.

Elizabeth strode back to her office and shut the door. She sat down at her desk and picked up *Us* magazine again. Despite her dim view of humanity, despite her loneliness and the fact that she had no friends who she could call and gossip about what Catherine Zeta-Jones was wearing—a green-and-black suit that she thought was *hideous*—she liked to save the beautiful pictures in the front of the magazine for last. It was like a little journey she took every week, from the public humiliations of the back pages through the ads for lonely people who sought salvation in a celebrity magazine, through the drug binges and sad dramas of the middle, until you finally stopped reading and just looked at gorgeous women splashing through the surf in St. Barts or the South of France.

Elizabeth Dyer liked to end there. Gave you some hope.

––––––––

Jimmy Stearns, the morgue assistant, knocked sharply on Elizabeth Dyer's door and watched a shape—warped by the frosted, uneven glass—rise from the desk.

Elizabeth pulled the door open.

"Everything okay?" Jimmy said.

"Yes, Jimmy. Thank you."

"Claude heard a loud noise, like a door slamming."

Elizabeth's thin lips worked. "Everything's fine," she snapped. "Why don't you tell Claude to worry about his duties? Like taking care of that coat."

Jimmy followed the woman's spindly finger and spotted the coat. "I'll get it."

"No, Jimmy, it's Claude's job. Please let him do it."

"I'd rather just get it done," he said quietly. "Anyway, we got the body from the old folks' home. Dr. Hobart's in the parking lot. He's going to do the autopsy on Walter Prescott now. He asked if the body was ready."

"Prescott? Now?"

Jimmy shrugged. "That's what the man said."

Elizabeth pushed past him, bunching up her cardigan sweater as if she were cold. She pulled out a locker, and there was the body of Walter Prescott, still in the clothes he'd been brought in with. Jimmy brought one of the rolling metal stretchers over and positioned it next to the locker.

"Can you grab his feet?"

"Sure thing," Jimmy said.

Jimmy took hold of the bare ankles, lifting the man and setting him on the table. He could feel the rigor mortis getting ahold of the bones. The knees were beginning to lock. Made Jimmy's job easier, but he still couldn't get used to it. Some nights he woke up in his apartment in the Shan, and for that first second of consciousness, he'd be convinced his knees and elbows were frozen in place and he started to inhale for a good bloodcurdling scream before his elbows released and out came a big yelp of relief instead. But one of these days, he was convinced, his limbs would stay locked and he'd have a coronary right in his own damn bed.

They hefted the body over to the stretcher, then rolled it to the first examination table and lifted again. Jimmy moved the stretcher away, and Elizabeth began to strip the body down. As Jimmy steered the stretcher to the far corner, he saw Dr. Hobart come through the door, all brisk and businesslike. He marched right over to the examining table and looked down at the body of Walter Prescott.

"The police want this one quick."

Elizabeth blushed. "I'll have him ready in five minutes," she said.

Jimmy watched. He was beginning to suspect Elizabeth had a secret crush on fat old Dr. Hobart. She acted like a Waltham undergrad whenever he was around. Anything he wanted, he got, and lickety-split, too.

"Why they want him so fast, Doc?" Jimmy said, leaning against the metal stretcher.

Dr. Hobart looked over. "I'm sorry?"

"I saw them cut him down from the tree the other night. Suicide, clear as day. But you said they want the report quick. They think someone strung the old boy up?"

"Now why would you say that?" Elizabeth, now carrying a pair of dissecting scissors in her hand, was glaring at him.

Dr. Hobart reached out a gloved hand and touched her shoulder. "That's all right, Elizabeth."

Jimmy looked down. "It's just that people talk, Doc, you know that. After the Margaret Post thing, I got strangers coming up to me, talking about things they heard, weird things happening around town."

"Mm-hmm," Dr. Hobart said, nodding.

"All I'm saying is that hangers and jumpers don't usually get special treatment. Wondering if there's something else going on."

Dr. Hobart smiled. "Nothing whatsoever. The Prescotts are an old family. They are—or they were—an important one."

"Until Chase, you mean," Jimmy said, but without malice.

"Well, that's neither here nor there. But there's nothing un-usual about the case. At least not yet."

Jimmy frowned.

Dr. Hobart bent over the body, the light catching the gold frames of his glasses as he examined the corpse. Elizabeth began to cut the man's clothes away with the autopsy scissors.

"And Mr. Stearns?" Hobart remarked.

"Yeah?"

"Please don't go out on the streets broadcasting any . . . *theories*. We don't want to get people riled up over nothing."

"Just like you say."

"Bag these up, please?" Elizabeth said. She'd finished undressing the body and was holding Prescott's clothes up between her thumb and index finger. Jimmy walked over and took the collar of the jacket and held it firm between his index finger and thumb, then went toward the left corner where they kept the clear evidence bags.

Dr. Hobart was murmuring something to Elizabeth. Jimmy heard the words "Margaret Post," he was almost sure.

Jimmy snatched up the bag quick and stuffed the clothes in, pretending to be absorbed in his work. He wandered back toward the examination table.

". . . the knife marks."

He passed Elizabeth and headed toward the little evidence locker where they kept personal articles for the next of kin. So the police *did* have some suspicions about old Prescott. He'd seen the little cuts in the back of Prescott's shirt, the ones that looked like someone had been poking him hard with a knife. Maybe someone had put Walter up on that cooler and made him put his head into that noose.

Was the old man's death related to Margaret Post's somehow? Were they going to compare the bodies?

Jimmy got out a white label with adhesive on the back, peeled

off the sticking paper, and stuck the label on the plastic bag holding Prescott's clothes. He searched his pocket for a pen. He saw
Elizabeth move toward the body lockers while Dr. Hobart was
scrubbing up at the sink, getting ready for the autopsy, his sport
coat laid across the back of one of the office chairs.

Jimmy swore and bent down to see if there was a pen in one
of the desk drawers. He heard Dr. Hobart run the water, which
made a loud thrumming sound on the metal floor of the sink.
Jimmy was rooting through the top drawer, which was filled with
papers and spare boxes of staples, when he heard Elizabeth make
a sound. An odd little scream.

Jimmy swiveled around. She was now standing on the other
side of a locker she'd pulled out.

"What is it?" Hobart said, and the water stopped.

"Sh-sh-sh-she's . . ."

Jimmy felt uneasy. He'd never heard her stutter before.

"Yes?" Hobart said.

Elizabeth bent her head. "She's gone."

"*Gone?*"

Dr. Hobart hurried over. Jimmy stared, his mouth agape.

"What do you mean, gone? Her family still hasn't claimed the
body."

Dr. Hobart came up to the locker, 12B, pulled it out another
six inches. Even from where he was standing, Jimmy could see it
was empty. Elizabeth looked at the doctor in confusion, wringing
her hands.

"Check the other lockers. Mr. Stearns, lend her a hand."

Jimmy dropped the bag on the floor. "Sure thing."

He walked to the end and began pulling open lockers. There
were only two other corpses in them that he knew about: a drunk
driver and a heart attack victim, both older women. He found the
heart attack on the second pull, the drunk driver—God, what the
dashboard had done to her face—in the fourth.

Elizabeth was at the other end, working almost frantically. The lockers went *hooooosh* and then *chunk* as they pulled out and pushed back. *Hooosssh, chunk*, like a piston that needed oil.

He pulled a bottom-row locker and stepped back as Margaret Post came rolling into view, the black thread around her throat where Dr. Hobart had sewn her up.

He coughed. "Hey, here she is," he said.

Elizabeth came running over. She checked the locker number: 6C. Her mouth worked like a fish out of the water, and the back of her neck was as pale as alabaster.

Her face tilted up toward him. "That bastard. Has Claude been having fun with me?" she said.

Jimmy looked at her, startled. "Claude? What are you talking about?"

Elizabeth Dyer's right eye was twitching, and she looked like she was ready to scream. "I think he's a low-down, terrible, *terrible* man."

"Ma'am, Claude never—"

"Elizabeth!" Dr. Hobart touched Elizabeth on the arm, and Jimmy saw her color change just a bit.

"Somebody moved her. I heard them. Just before Jimmy came in. Playing tricks on me."

"I don't think Claude would do that. I really don't," said Jimmy.

Dr. Hobart gave him a nod. He took Elizabeth gently by the arm and led her back toward the office.

Jimmy watched them go. It worried him to see Elizabeth all roused up. Elizabeth's door opened and closed, and he heard murmuring from behind the frosted glass.

Jimmy then gazed down at the corpse laid out on the gurney.

His left eyelid spasmed. There was something wrong with Margaret's face. The skin had a luster that other bodies didn't have. He was an amateur expert on the skin tones of dead people, and this one didn't look like quite right. Her face looked . . . moist, like waxed fruit. Not dry and gray, like it should have been after two days. She honestly appeared to have just taken her dying breath the second before he'd pulled the locker.

Margaret's face was eggshell blue above the light blue plastic "modesty sheet" that covered her body, the eyes closed, the hair greasy. Her plump arms lay by her side, the red scratches that traced across the inner flesh near the elbow turned to black lines. He couldn't smell anything off her, not even a whiff of decomposition.

Jimmy came around the front of the locker and moved his head slowly so that his face was lined up with Margaret's.

People were saying she'd been cut up like a Christmas ham. He had to see. He had to tell Sam and them over at the coffee shop what the real deal was.

He pulled down the thin coat of plastic.

Jimmy's face turned from boyish mischief to a look of retching horror. He said "Oh" once and looked away. Finally, he forced his eyes back and they drifted down. His eyes caught a glimpse of fresh scars—stitched with black thread—across her stomach.

Jimmy whipped his head to the left. He let the plastic fall back. He felt like throwing up now. Like this morning's breakfast was coming back up the sides of his throat, changed to acid.

He took deep breaths of the cool, disinfected air that burned his throat.

"Jesus Christ," he said to himself. "Jesus H. Christ."

CHAPTER TWENTY-TWO

John Bailey followed Nat into his apartment. It was Tuesday night and they were both dog-tired. Nat was gray-skinned, his usual ironic smile replaced by a tight frown across his lips. His hazel eyes looked haunted.

They'd spent the last two days together investigating the suicide of Walter Prescott, if it was a suicide. Nat had traded some shifts at the hospital, and the two of them had been at it like a pair of longshoremen. Sunday night, after his conversation with Becca, Nat had given John a condensed version: the chopped-up door, Becca's dreams of a French-speaking man. John had gone up to her room after Nat and asked to speak to her alone, but she'd gone practically mute as soon as Nat had left the room. Bent over at the waist, gripping her arms across her chest, she would only shake her head yes or no. She seemed drained, almost lifeless.

John had studied the gouges on the door, photographed them, and then they'd searched the house for something that could have made those marks in the wood. Nothing.

Monday, they'd checked on the old man's medical history and knocked on neighbors' doors to try and come up with a chronology or a motive. Today, they'd gone back for the people who hadn't been home the day before. Nobody had seen or heard anything, and their only conclusion was that Walter Prescott had not been a very popular man in his neighborhood. Nat had gone in to the hospital for a few hours, and John had gone through his notes and made a number of calls that had produced precisely nothing.

They stood around debating the relevant questions: Who had been trying to break down Becca's door? Was it Walter Prescott or someone else? Had Walter been abusing Becca? Or did Walter discover someone trying to get into Becca's room? Was he then murdered by the mystery assailant?

They were no closer to any answers. In fact, the very idea that answers existed to the death of Walter Prescott seemed to be retreating from the realms of possibility.

"I'm going to have to find you a tin badge," John said as he sat heavily on Nat's streamlined leather couch.

Nat looked up in surprise. "What do you mean?"

John slumped back. He took the remote from the arm and absently snapped on the TV.

"Five minutes ago, I got a text from Dr. Hobart."

"Saying what?"

"They found stab marks on Prescott's back. And it looks like the same type of weapon was used in both . . . situations. Margaret and Walter."

Nat came over and sat next to him. "I didn't see any stab marks."

"His arms were blocking the wounds. I didn't want to untie his wrists, so we didn't see them. Hobart confirmed it."

Nat rubbed his eyes with his thumb and index finger. "Same kind of knife?"

John shook his head. "Not a knife. Bayonet."

"How does he know that?"

"Something about 'evidence of a blood gutter,' whatever the hell that is. And get this. The stabbing wounds to Margaret Post—as opposed to the cutting ones, I guess—showed the same thing: the weapon had a deep indent in the side of the blade. On Margaret, the killer also pressed the blade against her skin, and the impression showed this blood gutter. Knives typically don't have them. Bayonets do."

"There was a security camera that recorded some footage on the night Margaret was murdered, right?"

John sighed. "Yeah."

"I'm guessing no maniac carrying a big-ass bayonet is visible on the tape?"

"Correct."

"So what *could* you see on it?"

John frowned. "A shadow."

"A shadow?"

"Yeah. It just swallowed her up."

Nat rubbed his forehead. "Swallowed her up. Jesus, John."

"It swallowed her up, Nat! It got larger and then . . ."

"She wasn't killed by a damn shadow."

"I know."

"She was killed by someone with a knife or a bayonet and four feet of good rope."

John said nothing. But he knew what was coming. *Tell me about the crime scene. Tell me about the body.* He really didn't want to think about it.

It was the second reel in the double feature of Margaret Post's death. The first one was his first look at the body hanging on the ash tree. The second one was the surveillance film, and that one ran in his brain whenever he lay down on his bed at night.

Nat was playing amateur investigator. People got into that.

"The crime scene and the video told us nothing, okay?" John said. "The papers have been clamoring for a look at it, but are their readers going to identify a shadow and tell us who the killer is? No. So we denied their request. Nothing in that tape will lead us to the killer. Nothing *on* that tape made any goddamned sense. So let's focus on Prescott."

"Okay, okay." Nat moved his index finger to his temple and

rubbed hard. "So . . . maybe then someone was jabbing Walter in the back as he got ready to hang himself? Well . . . it then explains the rope around his wrists. Coercion."

"I'd call it more than jabbing," John said. "I checked with Hobart and he says the wounds went an inch deep. I don't think it's a matter of Prescott not wanting to step up on that crate."

Nat considered this.

"You think Becca saw anything?" John said hopefully.

Nat blinked rapidly a couple of times. "No. I don't think so. I don't get the feeling she's protecting anyone. She wants to know what happened as much as we do."

John looked over at his friend and rested his hand on Nat's shoulder. "We're going to need you on this."

Because of Becca, of course. In a way, Nat approved of her refusal to talk to the cops. Solving Walter's murder wasn't a psychiatric priority; saving his daughter was. She was as fragile and as complex a case, a *person*, as any he'd ever encountered. And, as much as he loved John, his friend was fairly ham-handed when it came to women, especially high-strung women, not to mention nineteen-year-olds suffering from Cotard delusion and God knew what else. If John insisted on questioning her further, he might send the girl scuttling back into silence. *I'll talk to you*, Becca had said to Nat before John had left the room. *I'll only talk to you.*

When Nat had heard those words, a warmth had spread across his chest. The look of fragility and defiance in those brown eyes . . . he had to admit, it had moved him.

Now Nat took two Stellas from the fridge, popped the caps, and handed one to John. "I need to know about Margaret Post. Everything," Nat said.

John flicked the channel selector. "Where's ESPN?"

"576."

John frowned in complete concentration.

"John?"

John grunted.

"What happened to Margaret?"

John slowly put down the remote. He watched two ex-football players on *SportsCenter* talking about an upcoming AFC divisional championship. Finally he looked over at Nat. "What do you wanna know?"

Nat shrugged. "How was she killed?"

"Knife. Or could be a bayonet, I suppose. Slit her throat."

"That's it?"

John bent his head forward and rubbed the back of his neck. "No," he said finally.

"What else, then?"

"How does this help us find out what's going on?"

"Damned if I know."

John stared at the screen, stone-faced. "Whoever did it removed things."

Removed things. Nat felt something run through him, a suppressed hysterical laugh, followed by a wave of dread. It was almost as if he'd expected John to say that.

"Organs?"

"Yep."

"Which ones?"

John looked over. "Which *ones*? Does it matter?"

"I guess not."

John sighed. "You got any pretzels in here?"

Nat gestured with his hand in the direction of the cupboard. John launched himself from the couch and came back a minute later with a handful of mustard-flavored mini-pretzels on a napkin.

"Want some?"

Nat shook his head and took a gulp of his Stella. The fresh cold beer ran down his throat, seeming to revive him, and he immediately took a longer pull.

John smacked his lips with gusto and held the bottle out to look at the label.

"Fancy shit you've got here. But not bad." He looked at Nat. His eyes were full of warning. He took a deep breath. "Liver. Both kidneys. And the heart."

"Did he sew her back up?"

He heard John stop drinking the beer suddenly and heard the Stella sloshing in the bottle. "How'd you know that?"

"It was a guess."

"Yeah. That freaked me out worse than anything. Why do you spend the time fixing her back up, as if she's going to jump back up and *not notice* that you've just removed her fucking heart? And to take that time, right off a major road? It was a crazy risk."

Nat stared at the moon in the loft window. "Jack the Ripper took some organs, but he didn't stitch his victims back together. What about some kind of cult?"

"We're looking into it. I'm praying we don't have some little Satanists running around."

"That would suck for you."

John laughed. "Yeah, right?"

"You don't think Becca could have had anything to do with Walter, do you?"

The answer came after a three-beat pause. "That I don't know."

The words hung there between them.

John gestured toward Nat with the beer bottle. "Do me a favor. If she talks to you, ask the girl if she'd seen anyone around. If her father had any visitors."

"That might be tough, old man. She doesn't believe Prescott was her father. She'd blocked him out of her life."

He'd already explained the Cotard delusion theory to John on the way back from the Shan. John had seemed to absorb the basic points, but not the subtleties.

Nat looked out at Grant's Hill. "Gotta say, there was something strange going on at that house that I have to understand. Something beyond pathology. Something . . ."

"Evil?" John said, widening his eyes with humor.

"Yeah. As corny as it sounds."

He watched shadows flooding over the hill's summit as the sun sank in the west. He looked at John.

"My first duty is Becca, John. But I'll do whatever I can."

"All I'm asking, bro. All I am asking."

CHAPTER TWENTY-THREE

The Toyota coughed roughly and then purred to life. Chuck Godwin reminded himself to call the mechanic's to see when the Volvo would be ready. The Toyota was serviceable, but he missed the block-like solidity of his Swedish car.

He was parked down the block from Mary Reddington's house, and he was late getting home. Mary had been especially randy after their decades-long drought, answering the door in an old silk bathrobe that she'd parted to reveal plum-colored panties and a matching lacy bra, rich against her pale, freckled skin. They were both working off years and years of stored-up sexual drive.

Thinking of some time away with Mary—Barbados, or all the way to Hawaii?—Chuck pulled the gearshift into drive and gave the car some gas. He did a U-turn and headed toward Willow.

Barbados would be good. Mary would adore the surprise. And he could tell Stephanie he had to meet a skittish client who couldn't come back to the country. Paternity issues. Why not?

He drove down Willow Street. Dusk was stealing over the city, and the light was turning a pearly gray. He could see the red light at the foot of the hill on Wellesley Avenue, glowing a hundred yards ahead like a buoy on a fog-shrouded sea. But there was something in the road just beyond it he couldn't make out. Chuck hit the wipers, and they pushed aside the icy raindrops on the windshield with a loud, rhythmic squeaking.

For the first time, the thought of leaving Stephanie completely and spending his remaining years with Mary sailed cleanly into his thoughts. Why live a lie? Why waste whatever time he had left? His hands were still warm from the touch of Mary's flesh. He felt swaddled in the heat of their last moments together.

What would the financial implications of a divorce be? How much would it cost him? The house, surely, and half his Fidelity account, but he had two accounts under his dead son's name in a private bank in Boston that should tide him over. Just thinking about doing it made his whole body feel lighter.

He was coming up on the intersection. The thing in the road beyond the stoplight was a car, an old cream-colored Mercedes-Benz, that appeared to have stalled out. It looked like Betty Whitmore's car, the one she drove to church and to the supermarket at about 12 mph. *Those old diesels*, he thought to himself in annoyance. *Why do people drive them in winter when they're always freezing up?* Because if it was Betty or one of his neighbors, he'd have to stop and try to help, costing him more time. He couldn't just shoot by the stalled car on his way home, as much as he wanted to.

When Chuck was twenty yards away, he heard something whine on the hill to his left. Probably a plow, he thought. He glanced up but only saw headlights cresting the top of the hill and shining on the frost-covered tarmac as it headed down.

He eased his foot onto the brake until the Toyota bumper was practically touching the cream-colored Mercedes. He flashed his lights. The car didn't move.

Chuck rolled the window down and craned his head into the frigid night air.

"Betty?" he cried.

Chuck honked the horn.

"Come on, you old biddy, move it," he muttered. Exasperated, he put the car into park and reached down to unbuckle his seat belt.

Suddenly, he heard an engine rev high to his left and he

snapped his head over in horror. Two bright lights were bearing down on him from the hill road at an insane speed.

"Wh—" Chuck cried, pivoting away from the seat belt, his hand clawing for the door handle. He screamed as the lights grew bright and merged in his vision just before the vehicle slammed into his door with a concussive blast. The window blew out and the Toyota shot away, tumbling sideways, spraying antifreeze and shards of glass down Wellesley Avenue. The car completed three flips before the roof slammed into an oak tree bordering the street, and a shower of snow came down on its crumpled form as it rocked and then went still. Something whirred loudly in the engine block, the noise peaking and then beginning to fade. The gnarled roots of the oak were already speckled with blood, which glowed black in the moonlight.

Across from the oak tree was a gas station, closed for the evening. But lights went on in the low-slung house at the opposite corner.

The vehicle that had slammed into the Toyota was not a snowplow but an old Land Rover, blue. Its front end was crumpled, and the bumper was lying in the intersection of Wellesley and Willow in a V-shape. The engine was making a low grinding noise and steam drifted from its buckled hood. With no air bags in sight, a body was crushed against the driving wheel, its right shoulder brokenly sticking up.

The whirring from the Toyota stopped, but a green liquid was flowing from the engine and hissing when it hit the snow.

A door now slammed in the house opposite, and a man stood on the porch, staring at the crash, a phone in one hand and the other clutching a heavy coat around his belly. His voice rose a notch, and he pointed at the wreck as if the person on the other end could somehow see it.

Suddenly, the figure at the Land Rover's wheel began to move. It seemed to pull its impaled chest and limbs away from the steering wheel. As if it were testing the bones in its neck, it wrenched its head left, then right. It slumped back into the driver's seat. Thirty seconds later, the driver's door made a wrenching sound and popped open.

The man on the porch stopped speaking, and he held his hand out, as if to tell the Toyota's driver—fifty yards away, still slumped against the blood-spattered seat—not to move, that an ambulance was on its way. The man turned back into the house. He was yelling into the phone for the ambulance to hurry.

When he was fully inside, an elderly male figure slowly stepped out of the Land Rover. Walter Prescott was dressed in what looked like a black plastic raincoat, his broken shoulder still stuck up, his left leg dragging as he moved toward the stalled cream-colored Mercedes. His hair was matted and askew, his spectral face crumpled in on the left side; his lips had been smashed against his teeth and were torn jaggedly in several places. But there was no blood on his face or on the black poncho. Prescott went around the back of the old diesel, pulled open the door, and stepped into the driver's seat.

The Benz roared to life, then shifted into drive and moved off toward the Shan.

Behind him, Chuck Godwin was dead in the Toyota, his face awash in a combination of wiper fluid and arterial blood that was quickly drying in the frigid air.

CHAPTER TWENTY-FOUR

John Bailey put down the phone and looked at the notes he'd made. If it was humanly possible, he now disliked the Margaret Post case more than he had five minutes ago. That was before he'd gotten on the phone with the military souvenirs guy. This was now Wednesday, a full week after the murder, and the case was beginning to eat at him.

He eyed the top of the page. *Marcus Wilbur.* Mr. Wilbur of Bethesda, Maryland, was the foremost expert on bayonets in the United States of America, apparently. One person who'd referred him to Marcus had actually called him "Mr. Bayonet."

John sometimes wondered why he'd become a cop. It led him down to levels of human behavior that he had less and less interest in exploring. Forget exploring, *knowing about.* Not just the kiddie-porn freaks that he'd nabbed as part of Operation Protect Our Children a few years ago. The first time he'd gone swimming in his neighbor's pool after those arrests, he'd hesitated. He'd hesitated to pick up his neighbor's little girl, four-year-old Berenice, because he'd instantly thought of those grub worms he'd encountered during the sweep.

Now he knew there was a guy whose whole life was bayonets. And he'd had trouble getting Marcus Wilbur off the phone. Marcus was *fascinated* to know that a killer was using a bayonet with an inch-and-a-half-wide blade to kill women and to force old men to hang themselves in their backyards.

What John had learned from Mr. Bayonet was this: the

weapon used in Walter Prescott's killing—and perhaps Margaret Post's, too—was probably an antique. Mr. Bayonet had told him that bayonets did indeed have blood gutters, also called fullers or blood grooves, as Dr. Hobart had mentioned. John had tried to stop Marcus Wilbur from explaining the structure of a bayonet, because he had a vision of the bayonet entering Margaret's chest just above the nipple and the thin gutter filling with her blood and then spilling over onto the broad shiny part of the blade. A bayonet with a blood groove was just as strong as one without one, Mr. Bayonet explained, but 25 percent lighter. When John Bailey didn't immediately express astonishment, Mr. Bayonet had prompted him: "Isn't that remarkable?"

John had wanted to say, *In what world is that remarkable? Didn't you just hear me describe the wounds to an innocent twenty-one-year-old girl, you sicko?* Like his fellow cop Barney Waverly said, *It's not the dead that are the problem, man. It's the living.*

There was more. The Japanese were fucking blood groove *crazy*, according to Marcus Wilbur. They had many varieties of them on their weapons, and they named the top of the blood groove the *hi* (pronounced *bi*, said Mr. Bayonet with a vigorous little grunt) and the bottom the *tome*. One example was the *kaki-nagashi*, where the blood groove tapers . . .

John had roared at him, "Just tell me about the fucking bayonet, okay?!"

Mr. Bayonet had gone quiet and asked: "What do you want to know?"

"Let's start with where it was made."

Marcus asked for the measurements of the blade incisions. John Bailey gave them.

"The blade was straight?" said the voice on the other end.

"What do you mean, straight?" John had said, cupping his forehead in his right palm.

"The edge was straight, not serrated? It's just that during

World War II, the Germans used a sawtooth blade that infuriated the American—"

"Yes. For fuck's sake, yes."

Silence.

"Well, then. It's probably American. Remember I said *probably*."

And so now he knew that the blade that had pierced Margaret Post's flesh and cut her chest from the dimple in her throat above the breastbone down to the belly button in a clean arc, laying her intestines and chest cavity open to the night air, and then proceeded to nick the large arteries attached to her heart before going on to push the lungs aside so the person wielding it could get to the kidneys, probing and cutting Margaret Post's innards . . . He'd listened to Dr. Hobart describing what happened, but he'd blocked it out at the end. Well, it was a bayonet, a product of our great steelmaking industries, made in the good ol' US of A.

And it was probably old, Mr. Bayonet went on to say, undaunted by John's curses. Something about the dimensions of the gutter . . .

John Bailey stood up now and headed down the badly lit hallway that led to the locker rooms. He was going to spend some time deciding which soda to buy instead of thinking about blood grooves. Mountain Dew or Dr Pepper? He reached the soda machine glowing in the darkened hallway and began to debate the merits of each of them. Mountain Dew had a kick to it, good for getting the old blood flowing. Then again, he hadn't had Dr Pepper in a while, not since he'd eaten that spicy Italian grinder for lunch at the station last week. That was a damn good sandwich, too.

Good, John. Keep it up.

Dark thoughts make bad cops. That's what Marty O'Farrell had told him his first day on the job. Meaning, don't take all the awful things you see to heart. *Dark thoughts, they make a home inside your brain,* Marty said. *You invite them in one too many times and you can't get them to leave. Stubborn fuckers. Then they start controlling your thoughts, your alcohol intake.*

It was good advice. He'd found it to be true.

Maybe he'd call Marty. Talk the Patriots' passing game or something. Anything but fucking bayonets.

CHAPTER TWENTY-FIVE

Nat strode toward the city hall, carrying his laptop in one hand and a flashlight in another. More psychiatric outreach tonight—two more sessions and he'd have enough for Buenos Aires. He'd been spending an inordinate amount of time on Flickr lately, looking at people's vacation pictures, imagining himself at Punta del Este, the Uruguayan beach near Buenos Aires that his Argentinian friends were telling him to visit. Drinking the cocktail known as El Pato while he waited for his steak to be seared and served to him with thick-cut fries. The pictures calmed him. There were other places besides Northam, other lives being lived out there beyond Grant's Hill.

The weather was closing in again, as it seemed to do every evening lately. Black-shadowed storm clouds spilled over the foothills to his left, and mist was moving up the valley to his right from below, where the Raitliff Woods began. It was going to be another cold night in the clinic. This time, he hoped for no visitors at all. He would surf the web, checking out restaurants in Buenos Aires, confirm his flight reservations for next month, book one of those hop-on, hop-off bus tours in advance. *Do those things sell out?* he wondered, and the small question seemed to confirm that, yes, he really was going to get on a plane to Argentina in the near future. So tonight he would be calm, responsible, anonymous.

Nat didn't want to do any more community outreach. He was fully tasked with Becca Prescott, thank you, and the outbreak of . . . He didn't even have a name for it. The murder hysteria. In the face of what was happening, he felt an urgent and growing need to keep his routines as normal as possible.

He was beginning to find Northam oppressive. He'd woken up this morning and been breathing as if he'd been running a half marathon, the sweat running over his rib cage in little trickles. The sheets were wet. Some oppressive weight that had been pushing down on his chest had stayed there until his second cup of coffee. Three days after Walter Prescott's death, the whole business was getting to him.

What had he been dreaming of? He couldn't remember. Just heat. Heat and fear.

Nat came around the corner of city hall and saw someone waiting for him. His heart jumped as he stopped dead in his tracks. The figure was leaning toward the window of the door, looking in. It put a hand over its eyes and shifted around, trying to see down the hallway.

Nat took a breath and resumed walking, slower now.

The person waiting at the door heard his footsteps and turned toward him.

When he came closer, he saw that it was a woman. A gaunt, elderly face with too much makeup on coldly regarded him.

"Are you the psychiatrist?"

It was like an accusation. He came up to her, the steam of his breath hanging in the air between them.

"Yes. I'm Dr. Thayer."

Fussy was the thought that crossed his mind. She looked petulant, standing there, and impatient. He felt an instant dislike for her.

"I need to see you."

"Okay," he said, "come on in." His voice sounded fake: wholesome, falsely upbeat. *She's just having trouble sleeping and wants some pills*, Nat thought. *She wants to talk about an affair she had that she never told her husband about. She's lonely; she's constipated and misunderstood what the clinic was for. Normal matters of the human heart and maybe the digestive system.*

Nothing weird.

He took out his key chain and found the key for the hall door. It flashed dimly in the moonlight as he turned it to make sure it was the right one, then inserted it into the lock. Nat pushed the door open and held it for the woman, who was, he could now see, dressed in a trench coat. She scuttled forward, the corners of her mouth pulled down as if attached to weights. He walked past her, letting the door slam shut behind him, and headed down the stairway. "This way," he said. The woman—the silent, dour Yankee, the real article—followed Nat into the office.

"Have a seat," he said, flicking the light switch up. He laid his laptop on the desk and propped the flashlight in the corner next to his office chair. He took off his coat and placed it on the back of the chair.

The woman had already sat down and was watching him, her eyes gray.

"My name is Stephanie Godwin," she said.

"Okay, Mrs. Godwin. What brings you here tonight?"

No games. Play it right down the middle. But then the sudden feeling came over him: *Nothing will ever end well again.*

Nat studied her as she fidgeted in the seat.

"I saw him."

His flesh pebbled under his oxford shirt. *Shit, not this again.*

Nat felt the urge to throw her out of the office, physically force her down the hallway and stairs and eject her from the building into the night air before she could speak another word.

"Saw whom?" But he knew. He *knew* . . .

Her face was a mask, dead flesh, but her eyes were burning. "Chuck. My husband."

"Okay."

"You didn't hear?"

"Hear what?"

"He was killed in a car accident yesterday."

Sure he had, though. Local news. An accident over on Wellesley Avenue. Hit-and-run.

"I'm sorry to hear that. And you . . . saw him?"

Her eyes were boring into his. "Yes. Walking into the Raitliff Woods tonight around dusk."

Nat sat back in his chair. His body felt suddenly cold and lifeless. The lines they were speaking had been written long ago and had to be said. But he wanted to stave off the ending.

"Your husband just died yesterday, Mrs. Godwin, and you think you saw him—"

"No, I don't *think*," she said, her voice quivering. "I'm not senile, I don't have dementia, and I'm not drunk! My mind is very sharp. I saw what I saw."

Mrs. Godwin tilted her face up at him, as if to say, *Deny it.*

"Of course not," Nat said, dropping his eyes to the desk. "How did you sleep last night?"

"Terrible. The dreams." She pursed her mouth and shook her head.

"Tell me about the dreams."

She paused. "What I saw wasn't a dream, Dr. Thayer. Not an illusion or a wraith. It was Charles . . . Enright . . . Godwin, my husband. Do you hear me?!"

Her voice was beginning to screech.

"Did you identify your husband's body at the morgue?"

"Yes. He was supposed to have been brought to McKinley Funeral Home this morning. But I called them and the body wasn't at the morgue when they went to pick him up. They thought I'd gone to another mortician's." She was now leaning over the desk. "I did no such thing. I told Mr. McKinley, the son, when he called me.

The McKinleys are the funeral directors for the Godwins, and they know that. Something else is going on."

Nat closed his eyes. "What did the morgue say?"

Silence. He looked up. "You did call them?"

Mrs. Godwin shook her head slightly. "No. I was afraid to."

Nat massaged his forehead. He stood and went to the window. The yellow cone of light, the streetlight shaking in the wind. It was like the night with Walter Prescott, the same night over and over again.

"Mrs. Godwin, grief is one of the most powerful emotions we know of. We can desire to see our loved ones after they pass. It's very . . . human. And common. But we both know that your husband is dead. And the dead don't just . . . rise up."

"What if he *didn't* die?"

Nat made an impatient sound. "I'm not sure I'm the right person to be having this conversation. I—"

"Doctors make mistakes, don't they? I read about people waking up in their . . ."

"In their coffins. That's very rare."

"But it happens." She paused suddenly and took a deep shaky breath. Her eyes swam with tears. "I think he woke up down in that morgue. And came looking for me."

She smiled, and for a moment he saw the face of a young woman flitting behind the dry, chapped skin of Mrs. Godwin.

He looked down. Something told him, *Go on. This is your world now. Deal with it.*

"Did you approach him?"

"Yes. I ran out in my housecoat. I crossed Village Road and ran after him. I could feel the cold mud splash up. He was walking down the path that the rabbits use."

"You called to him?"

"Yes."

He could imagine that. The fear in her voice turning to disbelief. *It can't be* becoming *Maybe.* The whispered prayer that her husband was really alive.

"Did he turn around?"

She shook her head no.

"What did he do?"

"Walked. As if he was drawn to something. I ran up ahead and . . . and . . ."

"What?"

"I reached out for his arm and grabbed it. He . . . he stopped. And he turned to look at me."

She pulled open her handbag and snatched a handkerchief out of it. She was making a whimpering noise as she pressed the piece of gaudy silk to her lips. Mrs. Godwin began to rock back and forth.

"Mrs. Godwin?"

"He wasn't . . ."

"Yes?"

She shook her head as she rocked.

"He wasn't what?"

"Alive." Her eyes were wide and terrified. "Not in the way you and I know. Then I thought of the coming of our Lord Jesus Christ."

"Revelations, you mean."

"Yes. Are you saved, Dr. Thayer?"

"No," he said, now annoyed. "I'm not. So, what happened next?"

"His eyes were black. The pupils and the whole eyes were *black.*"

A pipe banged in the subterranean depths of the basement.

"It was dark. Are you sure you could tell?"

"Dr. Thayer, we were husband and wife for forty-two and a half years. Are you saying I couldn't see Chuck's own eyes?"

Nat frowned. "I'm merely suggesting that it was dark."

"*It was him!*" she screamed suddenly.

Nat took a deep breath. Her scream echoed out into the hallway and came back. *I know it was him*, he thought.

Right now, he didn't want Mrs. Godwin in his office. He didn't want to think about her problem. He only had the strength right now to battle for Becca Prescott. *What am I supposed to do for this damn woman anyway?*

Mrs. Godwin placed her bag on the floor next to her, as if she would stay awhile. He looked at her fearfully.

"I said to him," she began, " 'Chuck, where have you been?' He looked at me as if he'd never seen me before. His face was . . . set. There were bruises on his forehead, two deep cuts in his right cheek. But his face had no . . . expression . . ."

Nat hesitated before he spoke again. "I believe you saw your husband. I do. But I don't know how to help you."

Mrs. Godwin looked at him, and a fresh wave of terror crossed her face. "Can there be any other explanation?"

"I think we've covered them all."

"But I was thinking, what if Revelations was wrong?"

"Wrong how?"

She stared into the hands sitting in her lap.

"Mrs. Godwin?"

"What if the dead do come back, but under someone else's power, Dr. Thayer? What if the last days are here but Jesus isn't in control?"

Nat's eyes went wide. That thought had never occurred to him. Yes, what if? He felt dizzy.

"Then I think we're all in a lot of trouble," he said finally.

"I believe that we are."

Nat looked up. Mrs. Godwin's eyes were filled with that panic you see in old people when their mind begins to go, when the world they knew disappears seemingly overnight and is replaced by something darker and altogether new.

———————

Stephanie Godwin left a few minutes later, with Nat having recommended a visit to her priest at the Anglican church. This had seemed to calm her. Nat walked her to the door, murmured good night, and then walked up to the main level and its long dark hallway, to pace and think.

To the sound of the water fountain motor surging on and then quitting, Nat walked up and down the hallway, gleams of moonlight on the old tiled floor. His mind was foggy, stubbornly so. All that came to him was a black-and-white image, drifting into hazy view at the back of his mind before flitting out of sight. The same one from the other night.

What the hell was it? Some memory of a painting? A photograph maybe? Was it something he'd drawn as a boy? The image felt familiar, and old, but he couldn't place it.

And what was its connection to the walking dead and Mrs. Godwin?

Nat bit his bottom lip and continued back and forth up the hallway, his heels clicking loudly, rhythmically, on the waxed floor, until his shift at the outreach clinic was over.

No one else came to call that night.

CHAPTER TWENTY-SIX

The pale brick steps of St. Adolphus School were teeming with kids. John Bailey pulled into the circular driveway twenty feet away behind an old green Suburban and began scanning the smaller children for Charlie. Every day when he picked the boy up, he hoped he'd find him interacting with some other kid, their heads bent over a Transformer or something. An ally, a pal. Someone to share secrets with.

Kids find each other, he thought. *Someone will find Charlie and see what's inside of him. So what if he doesn't talk? Half of what kids do, you don't even need to talk.*

He scanned the roiling mass of schoolboys wrestling and talking and bumping into girls, and there was no Charlie. His gaze went to the right, to the stone banisters flanking the steps, where the older kids were hanging out, too cool to actually watch for their parents' cars. Nothing. Finally, he arched his neck and looked all the way back.

There. Charlie was sitting alone, near the far banister, staring at the ground. John frowned. *God,* he thought, *can't he at least make an effort?* He hit the horn, two short bursts, and Charlie's head came up. John gave him a bright smile, though he didn't feel it, and the boy came walking over, his shoulders stooped.

Charlie opened the back door, and freezing air came rushing into the car.

"Hey, buddy," John called. "Jump up here with me."

Charlie looked at him, then closed the back door and opened the front passenger one. He bundled into the seat and buckled himself in. John sat there, nodding.

"How was school?"

Charlie made a sign with his hand, one of the few they had. The hand tilting left and right. So-so.

"Okay. Do anything fun?"

Charlie shook his head.

"Can I see your folder?"

The school put all his homework and notes to the parents in the same creased yellow-and-black folder every day. Charlie bit his lip, then pulled his backpack from between his feet, unzipped the top, and handed the folder over.

John opened it.

"Sight words today, huh?"

Charlie nodded.

"Okay, we'll go over those later." He put the list of words in the facing compartment. "Whoa. What's this?"

John was staring at a drawing of a black face with orange eyes. It seemed . . . too grown-up. A devil. And those eyes . . . John felt a flutter of worry.

"Huh, buddy?"

Charlie pulled his notebook from his side pocket and began to write.

DRAWING WE DID ON MONDAY

"Yeah, I can see it's a drawing. Why did Ms. Sena send it home?"

A blue Subaru moved off from in front of John's car and a Toyota took its place. Charlie was writing.

DON'T KNOW

The woman in the blue Subaru honked her horn. John saw the steps emptying out.

"Okay. So who's it supposed to be?"

A FRIEND

"No shi— Sorry, I mean, really? *This* guy is your friend?"

The boy nodded.

"Wow. I'd be a little scared of him."

Charlie looked at him, something strange in his eyes.

"Um, not because he's black," John said quickly. *Damn, you had to be so careful with kids.* "You know . . . of course, that's fine. But I mean . . . who is he?"

Charlie pointed to the drawing. John had to shift around to see the words at the bottom.

THE MAGICIAN

Maybe he was a new comic supervillain, John thought. He couldn't keep up with them anymore.

"Where'd he come from?"

Charlie didn't move, just watched the kids jumping and yelling through the corner of the windshield.

"Charlie?"

The boy sighed, then bent to the notebook.

HE WAS AN EXSILE. HE WAS FORCED TO LEAVE HIS HOME.

"Oh," John said, stumped. *And what the fuck do I say now?* "And he . . . comes to visit you sometimes?"

Charlie's eyes, so brown and deep, blinked at him. This seemed to indicate *yes.*

"Right, right. And is he a good guy or a bad guy?"

More writing.

DON'T KNOW YET.

"Okay, okay. It's just a picture, right? Using your imagination. I guess that's good."

Charlie nodded. John stared at him for three more beats, then started the car. He waited for a woman with her hand linked to a squalling five-year-old to clear his bumper before pulling out of the St. Adolphus driveway.

As he sped up, heading for home, he looked over at his boy, slumped in his seat.

Charlie reached for the radio dial. He looked out the passenger window as the pop songs played.

CHAPTER TWENTY-SEVEN

Nat called in sick to Mass Memorial the next morning. He felt off, and there was too much to do with Becca.

He needed to establish a baseline on the Prescott case. Something definite.

Nat found his cell phone plugged into a wall charger—he had no memory of putting it there, he'd been so tired the night before—and found John's number.

"Hey."

"What's going on?" said John.

"Listen, I'm going to ask you something, and it's crazy, but don't give me an argument, okay?"

He heard John sigh on the other end. "You know what? Less and less seems crazy to me these days, buddy. Hit me."

"I need to get into the morgue."

Silence on the other end. "I'm coming over," John said and hung up.

Nat hung up, walked over to his fridge, and poured himself a glass of orange juice. He leaned against the counter and drank the juice, his eyes staring at the pale green backsplash that glowed under his undercabinet lights. His eyes were unfocused.

What the hell, Nat thought. *How did a suddenly announced desire to go on a tour of the Northam morgue become just a regular thing? What's next, midnight picnics at the cemetery?*

Nat heard a car honk. He looked out the window. There was John, sitting in a beat-up black Crown Vic, a department car.

Nat pulled on his coat and boots and locked the condo as he left. When he got in the car, he slapped John on the shoulder in greeting. John looked over at him. "Hey, bud."

Nat nodded. Now that he was in the car, he found the words he was about to speak ridiculous. *Let me see the corpse of Chuck Godwin. I want to make sure he isn't out wandering the streets.*

John put the car in reverse.

"Where we going?" Nat said.

"You said the morgue, right? Well, then, it's the morgue."

Nat gave John a sharp look. "What the fuck is going on that I don't know about?"

"You asked me—"

"No, it's not you. What I mean is, why would I feel compelled to go to the morgue? Jesus, John, what's happening?"

A fold of flesh under John's right eye twitched. "I got a wacky report awhile back," he said.

"'Wacky'? The hell's that mean?"

"I don't want to talk about it."

"About someone who should be dead?"

John grimaced.

"All right," Nat said. "Who's yours?"

John frowned. "Margaret Post."

Nat sucked in a breath, then let it out, staring at the pedestrians in the window as John drove downtown. Normal people leading their normal lives with normal everyday problems. Just a touch of seasonal depression around here, that's all this was.

"Don't you want to know who mine is?" Nat finally said.

"Yeah, not really. But I guess I have to ask."

"Chuck Godwin."

John swerved to avoid a pothole. "The guy from the car accident?"

"Yeah."

John shot him a quick glance. "I feel like I just went a little insane right there, just a little bit."

"How did you hear about . . . God—" He stopped, massaging his forehead with his free hand. "You know what? I don't even want to know. Let's just go over there and make sure they're where they're supposed to be."

John flipped the siren switch and blew through three red lights on the way to State Street. They pulled up to the county building, and John threw the Vic into park. He shut off the engine and took a pack of Big Red gum with two sticks left out of his shirt pocket and offered one to Nat. Nat shook his head.

"You're right that something's off," John said. "I've been feeling it all week. You ever get the feeling that everyone else is in on some joke, that they're walking around with their lips pressed tight, but no one wants to tell you?"

Nat stared out the grimy window. He stared at the people passing on the street. A black woman with dreads was walking toward them—must be a Wartham student, Nat thought—hugging her long down coat to her and puffing out large clouds of steam. Her eyes flicked to him as she passed, and Nat stared at her. She looked away quickly and he saw her in the side-view mirror increase her pace.

"I don't know," Nat said slowly. "There is such a thing as mass psychosis. These things are like chemicals in the water. They travel underground, unseen. One person says something innocent at an office on a Wednesday morning, and in three hours it's reached the other side of town and someone susceptible starts imagining there's something weird going on. And with e-mail, texting . . ." His voice faded away. *I'm not even convincing myself,* he thought. "One way to find out."

They both got out.

At the morgue door, John rang the bell and a buzzer sounded

loudly in the room beyond. The stainless steel doors were set flush into the wall, separated only by a thin steel molding. Nat thought they looked like the doors on a nuclear silo.

A thin, nervous-looking woman opened the door two inches and looked at them. There was annoyance on her face.

"Hi. I'm Detective Bailey. I called ahead?"

The woman looked him up and down.

"Can I see some ID?" she said.

John stiffened and gave her an extra two seconds of staring time, then pursed his lips and reached inside his blazer. He came out with a worn leather document holder and flipped it open. Nat saw a quick flash of silver.

The woman studied the photo and looked at John, then went back to the picture.

"Are you keeping JFK in there or something?" Nat said.

The woman's watery eyes swung to him.

"This facility is for authorized personnel only. Who are you?"

"He's with me," John said, a little louder than before. "We need to check two bodies."

The woman pursed her lips before stepping back and let the door slam shut. John looked at Nat, his look saying, *Do you see what I have to put up with all day?* He pushed the door open.

Elizabeth was walking back toward her office, her hands clasped and bloodless by her side.

"Excuse me," John said.

The woman stopped.

"Margaret Post?"

"She was put ba—" Elizabeth said, turning. "I mean . . . She's in 12B."

John looked at her quizzically. "Aren't you going to open it for us?"

Elizabeth swiveled. "I have a call waiting for me."

John's face was slowly going beet red. "Where's the other one? Godwin?"

"8A. You'll find gloves over there."

——————

John began looking for 12B. There was tiny black lettering near the top right corner of the lockers, but the glare of the fluorescents made them difficult to read.

"Why is Margaret Post still here?" Nat said.

"Her parents are missionaries," John said, bending over to check a number. "They were working in, um, was it Brazil? I don't know, some South American country, way back in the bush, preaching the Pentecostal Bible to the natives. Took them awhile to get their affairs organized and get back to the States. They're flying in today, I think. They still keep a house here."

Nat pointed to the right. "It's down here, genius."

John straightened up and followed him.

"The Posts are from here?" said Nat.

"Originally? Yeah."

"From Northam?"

"Yep, from the Shan."

Nat found 12B, a middle locker in the stacks of three. He gripped the handle. "I thought she was from somewhere else."

"She was born down there in Brazil or wherever the fuck. But the parents were originally local. Hang on . . . she might not smell so good."

"Man, so long as she's laid out here, I don't care if she reeks like the Cryptkeeper."

Nat pulled the locker. It came sliding out with a screech.

John looked at Nat. The locker was empty, the metal clean and shining in the overhead fluorescents. Nat felt little darts of adrenaline shoot through his bloodstream.

"She did say 12B, right?" he said.

John called, "Hello . . . ? You believe that shit?" Nat could hear a thin note of worry in his voice.

He felt the same thing in his chest, needles of doubt growing colder and colder.

Things began to move in a swirl. Nat didn't wait for Elizabeth Dyer, but walked down to the center of the lockers, his shoes clicking fast on the linoleum. John went past him and pounded his fist on Elizabeth Dyer's door. Nat saw him moving, his jaw tight, as he looked for 8A. Out of the corner of his eye, Nat saw the door crack open an inch or two.

"Hey, you said 12B for Post," John said, exasperated, to someone on the other side.

The morgue attendant pulled her door open. From the corner of his eye, Nat saw the pale white sheet of her face.

"That's right," she said, her voice high. She was staring at the empty locker.

Nat found 8A. He grimaced as he pulled on the stainless steel handle. The drawer refused to budge.

"Well, she's fucking missing," John said.

Nat swore at the locker handle and pulled again. Nothing.

John came up behind him and wrapped his thick, muscular hand over Nat's sinewy fingers and they both pulled. The metal handle didn't move.

"What the fuck is going on in here?!" John barked at the attendant.

She was moving past them now. She began pulling other lockers, then pushing them back. *Shooo. Clank. Shooo. Clank.* They were empty. No Margaret.

Nat and John looked at each other, and Nat braced his foot against the locker's base. "Now," he said, his voice tight. They hauled back, and suddenly the locker came away with a rasping sound. Nat and John both let go and jumped back, John staggering all the way to the nearest examination table, which he bumped hard with his hip, rattling it in its floor screws. The locker slid all the way out on its own momentum and jumped when it hit the end of its runner.

"Fuck me," said John.

The locker was empty.

John's eyes seemed to fill with a cold fear.

Nat was trying to control his breathing. His thoughts flipped back to the talk with Dr. Jennifer Greene back at the hospital. What had she called Cotard patients?

Walkers.

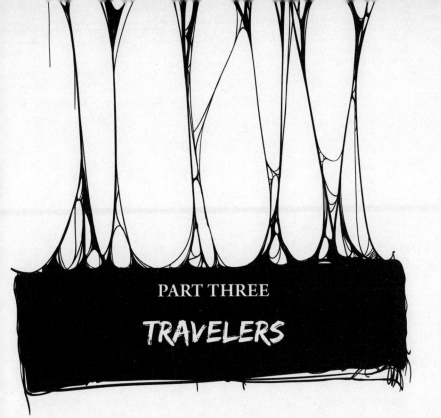

PART THREE

TRAVELERS

CHAPTER TWENTY-EIGHT

Nat Thayer sat at his desk and stared at his computer screen. It was Friday afternoon, the day after his visit to the morgue, and what he was about to do seemed not only insane to him, but somehow . . . a betrayal. Not only because of what he was considering, but *where* he was considering doing it. In his office at a pristine psychiatric hospital in Massachusetts, a temple to the scientific spirit. And he was about to desecrate it.

Is this really what it's come to? he thought. *I'm surrounded by some of the best scientific minds in the Northeast, and I'm about to do an Internet search for zombies.*

Yes, he decided, this was what it had come to. The missing bodies at the morgue were the final straw. Something was happening that was beyond his experience.

He smiled, but the laughter didn't come. Suddenly uncertain, he stood up and paced over to the window that overlooked the hospital atrium and the Shan to the west. His eyes moved past the traffic turning into the hospital in the direction of Endicott Street and Becca's house. He hadn't been able to get her off his mind. With any other patient . . .

As he debated his next move, Nat tapped absently on the glass. *Becca, are you there?* he thought idly. *Are you . . . all right?*

Nat wasn't really afraid of being made a laughingstock. His geeky high school years had cured him of most social anxieties. He'd been purified in the scorching fires of Northam High.

But this?

Get on with it, he thought. He sat in his office chair, his fingers reaching for the keyboard. He tapped in *zombie expert* and hit *Search*.

He spent the next hour and a half reading. He skimmed two pages of the original results and found them full of cranks, Amazon.com listings for *World War Z*, and reviews of films on the undead. *I may be the only person in America,* he thought to himself, *looking for usable information on actual zombies. Goddamn fanboys.*

Finally, he modified the search to *zombie academic* and began slowly reading through the links. He found a paper by a Professor Helen Zimmerman of anthropology at North Carolina State: "Culturally Undead: The Roots of Zombie Belief in Bantu Animist Communities." He clicked on it and read in silence for five minutes before sighing and hitting the back button. The piece was gibberish to him, and had induced flashbacks to the lit classes of his undergraduate days.

The link below was a first-person account by Helen Zimmerman on investigating zombies. "Ah, now that's more like it," Nat said aloud.

CHAPTER TWENTY-NINE

Ramona Best took the green can of Comet cleaner and shook out some powder onto the old white T-shirt she was using as a rag. It had been one of the shirts she'd left behind when she'd gone to Wartham, a track jersey from her freshman year at Roosevelt High. Her boobs had grown enough since then that wearing the T-shirt now risked turning the catcalls of the boys on the corners into outright propositions. You couldn't be so sexy that they jumped down from the mailboxes or the stoops and started following you, talking *Hey, can I walk you home?* or *You bustin' that top* out! The shirt now took her over that fine line, so she'd sacrificed it to the task at hand.

The chrome in the kitchen was all that was left to be done. She worked with the lights out, following the gleam of late afternoon sunlight around the chrome where it met the green stone backsplash. She didn't need the lights; she had the path of the chrome memorized. This is where she'd done her homework when her mother was out working as a nurse's assistant at Jamaica Hospital, the 7 p.m.–to–7 a.m. shift, before she passed away five years ago. Her mom had never saved enough money to renovate the kitchen, so it was still circa 1974, all linoleum and fake granite and as much chrome as a big-finned Cadillac Eldorado.

Ramona took the Comet, cut it with a little water from the tap, and leaned over behind the faucet and started scrubbing there. She could feel the granules of the cleaner grating underneath the cotton, and the smell nearly made her dizzy. It was a smell she remembered from childhood; every Wednesday, it had been her job to get the kitchen "army clean" by the time her mom got home from work. Now Ramona dug the cloth into the base of the fountain and found release through the ache in her biceps. She didn't want to think about Mama right now.

Ramona leaned into it, making little circles as she slowly half stepped along the counter. When she was done, she went back with a clean end of the T-shirt and wiped off the milky residue that lay on the chrome. Then she put the Comet and the T-shirt under the counter, next to the garbage bags and the cat litter for her aunt Zuela's cat, Jasper. She wiped her brow and felt the need to sleep rise behind her eyes like a dark wave. But instead of heading upstairs to her bedroom, she went to the fridge. The light spilled out onto the dark floor, and she took out the Diet Coke Lime that she'd bought on the way down from Massachusetts, knowing her aunt wouldn't buy the stuff. *Sugar won't hurt you, Mona*, Zuela would say. Imagining her aunt's disdain, Ramona huffed. *Yes, it will.* Wartham hadn't made her anorexic by any means—she still ate what she wanted—but being up there with all those skinny white girls did tend to focus the mind on calories and all related matters.

She went to the dining room table and sat. She took a sip of the soda and laid her head on the crinkly red-and-white-checked tablecloth. This, too, was the same as her childhood—or a replacement that smelled and felt the same. The refrigerator was a big, old GE, and when its motor kicked in, it flooded the room with a low hum that Ramona loved. It was like hearing her mama's heartbeat. Here is where she'd spent half her childhood. The curtains had always been open then as her mother cooked one of her West Indian specialties, and she could watch the neighbors hang their laundry on their backyard lines. Or, at night, listen to the Brambles, the Jamaican family next door, laugh and play their lover's rock records, old Desmond Dekker and Peter Tosh tunes. The window had been her jukebox and her air conditioner, too.

But as the afternoon light turned dusky, the window and the curtains were closed tight.

Right now, she didn't want to see out. And she didn't want outside coming in.

CHAPTER THIRTY

Nat had landed on a site called sacpasse.net, which seemed at a glance to be dedicated to essays on Haitian culture. A lot of first-person reports on Haitian food, the Creole language, compas music. The piece he'd clicked on was by Professor Helen Zimmerman, and it looked to be a travelogue about her search for the true origins of voodoo practices, particularly relating to the idea of the undead. The first thing Nat noticed was that she refused to use the word *zombie* throughout the piece and instead substituted the term *nzombe*. *Is that African?* Nat wondered. *Swahili, maybe? Are we talking about the same thing?* He shook his head and started reading.

I spent five years tracking the nzombe *phenomenon all through West Africa.*

I even drew maps: purple for deepest belief, orange for moderate, and so on. And I found the heart of the nzombe *tradition was in a thin strip of territory that didn't, of course, correspond to any of the modern states that had been superimposed on the area during colonialism, but that ran generally north to south from Senegal to Liberia. This was where the belief had been born, where it was oldest and most rooted in the lives of the people. The Nzombe Belt, some people called it.*

I have no idea how this belief began. Perhaps it was a response to the epidemics that swept through the bush villages back in prehistory. Perhaps some of those illnesses reduced the sufferers to a waking death—comatose, in other words—and the first sorcerers

were those village men who were able, by hook or by crook, to bring
them back to life, or to appear to. Clearly it had a great deal to do
with the spirit life of the people, who saw life and death in many
living things, and in some things that did not live. Spirit in those
parts of Africa isn't a black-and-white affair, if you'll pardon the
pun. It's a permeable frontier. People go through and come back.
Their spirits haunt the places they died, or haunt the people who
caused their deaths. The soul exists in a continuum that the real,
physical world only connects to here and there. Death is not really
death, not as we understand it.

This was hardly groundbreaking news. But what I found was
that the ability to bring the dead back to life, to create nzombes,
was different from the other parts of the people's belief systems.
The sorcerer was the key to the whole tradition. And here's where
I made two discoveries, both confirmed by several oral traditions
from discrete parts of the belt.

The first is that sorcerers, good sorcerers, are born, not made.
They're incredibly rare. The idea that any village medicine man
can create a nzombe would be laughable to any true believer.
It's a talent, and in order to perform the highest work of the
tradition—raising the dead—you need to be a genius. I came to
think of it this way. I brought three things into the bush with me:
antimalaria tablets, a beat-up Sony tape recorder to document my
interviews, and Mozart cassettes to play on it during the nights
when I wasn't transcribing. And I began to think of the great West
African sorcerers as rarities on the order of Mozart. They were the
flower of thousands of years of genetics and belief. They were able
to harness the spirits in ways others were unable to.

You can wait many generations for a sorcerer who can create a
nzombe. And there are many limitations on what he can do. He
has to be close to his victim—physically close. You can't control
a nzombe from five hundred miles away. And that control is
extremely difficult. The women I interviewed—and later the men,

when I had been there too long to ignore them anymore—were adamant about this. They insisted that the human spirit isn't so easily mastered. There are times when the nzombe becomes aware of his own strangeness in the world, when he breaks free from the thought stream of his master. When he wanders, searching for an answer to what has become of him or her.

He senses he is among the dead, but he cannot break free. He wanders back and forth across the line of consciousness and individual action, until the master reasserts control. That was the second thing I took from Africa.

The rest was taught to me by a man named Tshompa, a Guinean healer in his forties who I'd been told by reliable contacts was a sorcerer. I met him one day in 2001 in Conakry. I had sent word through an intermediary that I wanted to talk about nzombes. After many false starts and refusals on Tshompa's part, I offered to bring him a bottle of his favorite whiskey: Johnnie Walker Green Label, which was practically unobtainable in Guinea at that time.

When he first walked into the house where I was meeting him—a shack off the main road in Conakry roofed with sheets of tin—I immediately felt a presence. The air seemed to hum, as if I were standing beneath one of those huge overhead power lines. Brimming with something powerful.

He appeared younger than I'd expected. Small eyeballs behind thick eyelids, a sloping forehead, balding with tufts of hair cut close to the scalp. Wide mouth, lined all around with a small gutter, an indentation, which gave every movement of his mouth, every expression, a subtle power.

I will recount here from my notes the essence of that conversation. "Tell me about the nzombes," I began. He'd looked at me with contempt. I took the bottle of Johnnie Walker out of my bag and offered it to him.

"What do you want to know?" he'd said with mocking courtesy in his surprisingly good English.

"Everything."

He'd snorted with laughter as he held the bottle in his hands.

"I've read something about your zombies," he said, his eyes blooming and his lips opening wide as he pronounced zom-beez, *in cartoonish disgust. Then he made the African sound of dismissal inside his mouth. Tssssshhh.*

"What was wrong about what you read?"

"Everything!" he roared. He twisted the cap on the Johnnie Walker, took a dirty glass, and poured some whiskey into it. As he drank, his eyes studied me. "This at least you can do right, you murungu. *Making whiskey. Ha-ha."*

"Tell me about nzombes."

"In this book I read, a murungu *book, it said the sorcerer creates the* nzombe *to work for him. To plow the fields, to plant his beets! Is this true?"*

I nodded. "I've read those books, too."

Tshompa laughed sourly. "To work in his fields! Is that all an African can do? I can get a worker in Kasama for one dollar a day. One dollar! You think a sorcerer would exert himself for that price? Tsssshhh. You think even our great men are nothing more than animals."

"I'm not sure what you read, but that isn't all—"

"You are another slanderer. Perhaps I will show you what being a nzombe *is, ha? Just a touch?"*

"I came here for information, not to be insulted."

"You can learn nothing," he said dismissively.

"Perhaps there's nothing to know."

"What?!" the man said, angrily.

"You talk about everything the sorcerer doesn't do, but nothing he does. Perhaps you don't know. I can't tell you how many pishers I've met. Have I wasted good whiskey on you?"

"Ah?" he said, turning his head as if he were hard of hearing. "What is this pisher?"

"Charlatan. Faker."

The eyes now. And I felt as if the darkness behind him moved, as if shapes had been rearranged there.

"You insult me? Why do you ask about the nzombe?"

"Because I want to know."

"You are not worthy of this knowledge."

"Because I am murungu?"

He made a face. "You think only Africans can make a nzombe? Only the Haitians? We are the only ones who will admit to it."

"Murungu can make a nzombe?"

"Oh, yes. But he will do it his way. In secret."

"Tell me why you make your nzombes, if not to work for you."

"This"—I didn't catch the word the first time, but I wrote out pam-way in my notebook blindly, in the darkness—"is not possible to explain."

"What did you call it?"

"This pamwe. This . . . binding."

"Tell me."

"The nzombe, how can I tell you? It is the most difficult thing in the world. This is the first thing no one understands, not even these chickens—" He gestured outside, meaning the passersby, the poor peasants dressed in greasy, torn clothes. "Listen, murungu. Sorcery is a world bigger than this world. And sorcerers seek out the nzombe because it is the final thing in their world. The pinnacle, yes? A test of who is a master. You understand? They do this not because it is easy. Only because it is difficult."

He was staring at the ground.

"I will talk so you can understand. You Westerners, you love your houses. I've seen the pictures, eh, these enormous houses with the cars parked in front. So the human, you can say she is a house. A dark house you come to at night across a broad field, no stars shining. You can feel its size in the night. A great human, a . . . a . . . a significant person, is a big house. A mansion! And when you come *close, the lights lit up for holidays. Like the British used to have here, you understand, for their Christmas parties? This could be the soul of the poorest man in the village. When the sorcerer approaches his soul, he sees the dimensions. And the richest man—"* Tshompa spit. *"He could be a hut, a simple dwelling. Unworthy of the sorcerer. He will pass him by."* Laughter, sinister in the gloom.

"Unless he has use for him."

"Perhaps." Tshompa stared at the ground and hugged his arms to his chest. *"The second thing you must understand is that a door must be left open. Why does the sorcerer sometimes strike at the moment of death? Because it is then the door has been left open! Why do the gullible fall? Because their defenses are weak. He needs this, because the work of entering another soul is not easy. So! Say a man is sick, getting close to his death. Well, then, a small door opens. Juuuuust a crack. The sorcerer slips in. He doesn't want a dead man—a sorcerer already knows death, he practices death! It's* life *he wants. Entrance, entrance into another's life. To bind with another soul in order to have that soul and walk in new worlds.* Pamwe. *The binding. This is what gives him new life."*

He stopped for a moment, considering what he'd said. *"But sometimes in life, this door is left open. You understand?"*

"How?"

"Ah. Sometimes the person wants it, wants to become a nzombe. *You don't believe, I see, but it's true. Maybe they are curious about the other side of the world, or maybe the sorcerer whispers a story in their ear, tells them the things that will come to them if they allow the binding."*

"So a living person can become a nzombe?*"*

"Of course! But someone who already has this open window. Perhaps it is in their past, an ancestor who played with the sorcerers, no? Or there is a wish to come over to the other side, and then they are trapped."

"By 'the other side,'" I said, "you mean death?"

"Death and everything beyond death."

I took a minute to take that in, but Tshompa barely noticed.

"They are curious!" he said with a guttural laugh. "They want to know! And, how do you say, curiosity, it killed the cat."

He paused. I saw the bottle of whiskey twist and lift, the green-and-gold Johnnie Walker label flashing in the semidarkness, and heard the tink of bottleneck on glass edge. He slurped.

Tshompa held the glass in his right hand, his left arm across his chest, held tight. He looked down at the ground, contemplating.

"So! The sorcerer goes inside. He is like a . . . What do you call it?"

"A thief."

"No!"

"A trespasser."

"Yes. Okay. And it is something I can't really describe to you. Poor murungu, your English does not have the words I need."

"Try, Tshompa. And before you finish my bottle."

"Ha. Mean woman."

Tshompa stared at me.

"You bind with another soul," I prompted.

"Yesssss. You can smell what her mother cooked for her when she was a baby, you can smell it in your own nostrils, do you understand? Memories she cannot have anymore, memories she has forgotten for years. You walk and you walk and you hear and see everything. The evil things in her heart, the evil things she has done, the deaths she wishes on those around her, like black powder smoke curling up, enough to choke you. And any one of these things, you can make her remember, you can make real to her again. Imagine a house with two million rooms. Some sorcerers have become lost in their own nzombes! They are trapped in their own bindings. Do you understand? It is dangerous. It is travel to another world. And what you can set in motion in this world!"

"So you don't control the nzombe? You aren't pulling the levers."

Another snort. "Murungu, you are so crude. You think this because you believe Africans are beasts. We walk around with our mouths open like AAAAHHHHH." He stood, his arms in front of him, his mouth open and his head tilted to the side. "AHHHHH!" he cried, louder. Then he gave me a sharp look and sat back in his chair. "A poor sorcerer has only a little control. It's like a young boy getting into his father's car and touching the gas pedal and—" Tshompa shot back in his chair, his arms coming up to shield his eyes. "It wants to go. And it goes. But you have pointed the way. You have found the evil thing that will make the nzombe yours. But a great sorcerer? Ahhhh. This . . ." He wagged his finger, head twisting toward the ground. "This is something."

"You're saying a great man can control the nzombe completely?"

He looked at me disapprovingly. "What is 'completely'? Even the great men are still men, huh? So the host may escape the sorceror's mind for a moment or two and come back to himself. But the sorcerer will capture him again."

"And what happens when the nzombe dies? Does the sorcerer die, too?"

Tshompa shook his head. "The great ones, they leap from nzombe to nzombe. We call them travelers."

It took me a minute to absorb this. "These travelers . . . they inhabit different bodies over time?"

"Yes."

"And what do they do in their new bodies?"

"Do?" Tshompa snorted. "The ones I have heard of, they have a mission beyond merely living. They seek revenge for crimes committed against them. Old enemies disappear, and their children and grandchildren suffer strange accidents."

I got the feeling Tshompa was becoming impatient with the subject, but I pressed on. "So this is about vengeance?"

"It can be. Or the traveler, he simply wishes to defeat death, to become the only human creature to escape death. This is what I have heard. But for myself I cannot say."

"Why not?"

"This is the great mystery, eh? No, the great joke."

"I don't get the joke."

He stared at me; then his eyes dropped. His voice was quieter now. *"Because for some reason, the evil ones make the best travelers, the only travelers. Look at me. I am not bad enough. I have only peeked in the doorway of a few houses. Eh?"*

He brought the glass up for another sip, gulping back the last two fingers of whiskey. He coughed, then looked at me levelly.

"The world doesn't want good sorcerers doing this. It saves the power for the dark men."

———

With the sound of sleet tapping on the picture window of the condo, Nat slowly read through the rest of the piece. Tshompa went on to say that salt can protect you from the lower-order *nzombes*, but that little else works. And that in order to kill a *nzombe*, you have to surprise the host body. You have to surprise it and kill it before the sorcerer can bind with another. When the host dies, the traveler inside him goes, too. If you're quick enough. And when the traveler dies, his *nzombes* go back to their former state. If he raised it from the dead, the *nzombe* dies again. If he possessed a living person, the person simply wakes up as if after a long sleep.

That was it.

Nat closed the laptop and stretched. How much to believe? he wondered. How much of this could be true?

He tried to keep Becca Prescott's face out of his mind as he thought about what he'd just read.

CHAPTER THIRTY-ONE

The next morning, it was snowing and the flakes bloomed briefly in the headlights, the storm clouds above casting a black pall over the city. Nat hurried to his Saab and then steered the car down Minotaur, heading toward State. He kept his face composed, the muscles under the cheeks taut. He wanted to check on Becca, to see if reading the account of the *nzombe* hunter changed anything, made him notice new details about her.

Nat drove through the streets of east Northam. A man with a newspaper held over his head hurried down the slick sidewalk. Passing cars threw sheets of freezing water that slapped hard against the windshield.

He reached the city square and turned left on State. He stopped at a red light and watched the pedestrians cross. The light glimmered crimson through the sleet-dappled windshield, then green. Nat hit the gas. But twenty feet from the intersection, he caught a glimpse of a pale face above a dark green slicker, made a noise in his throat, and quickly swerved into a parking space by the curb. The driver behind him honked, and the smear of the horn grew and then faded as the car roared past him and down State.

That was just her, he thought. It was Becca, her profile unmistakable underneath a tan waterproof hat. She'd just crossed State, going toward the old town square. The sight of her out here, outside of her room in the Shan, had sent a shock through his chest.

Nat opened the door, and pelting ice struck his face like little daggers. He ducked and ran around to the sidewalk, cold water splashing above his ankle and giving his heart an electric shock.

Becca had already disappeared in the small park that lay between State and the old town square.

Nat raced ahead, his feet sinking into the snow-covered grass, crossing the little park diagonally. A statue—a rotund figure in a military coat pointing his sword vigorously back the way they'd come—loomed above. He crossed the little park and took the lane on the other side. At the corner, he stood stock-still.

He saw the figure in the dark green turning at the end of Cross Avenue. He strode off after her, crossing the street without looking. A passing car had to brake suddenly, and its horn blared in his ears. Cold rain streamed down the back of his raincoat.

Nat reached the corner of Cross and made a sharp right onto Williams. The rain was clattering on the slate roofs of the houses nearby. The houses were old Victorians, of course. There was no one moving on the street, just a few glowing windows in the homes.

He looked again, and now he saw the girl, a dark blot of a figure thirty feet ahead. She was standing on a sidewalk in front of a run-down Victorian with weeds spilling out through the iron railings of its front fence. Nat could see only the long coat, black boots, and those details of her face not obscured by the upturned collar and the rain hat.

A wave of weakness went through him. Whose house was it? He'd never spent much time in this part of the city. He didn't know anyone who lived here.

He watched as Becca Prescott took a step forward and opened the metal gate. She moved ahead as if she were walking across a frozen pond in late winter, wary the ice would give way.

Nat stared. Wet strands of dark hair were plastered across his forehead, and the skin under his eyes was wet with rain. But he didn't seem to notice the rain or cold.

Becca was walking down the front path toward the house, but suddenly the white glimmer of her face disappeared. A low hedge on the side of the yard obstructed his vision.

The number. The old family homes in this part of town had the house numbers engraved on the porch steps. He would have to find the number without losing her.

Now Becca reappeared, and she came out of the gate but didn't turn to fasten the latch. The metal gate swung in the wind as the figure turned left down the street. The thin profile of her coat was quickly lost in the darkness and slanting rain.

He hurried after her, glancing left as he came to the house and hurried by.

52 Garmin. He repeated it to himself.

He followed Becca Prescott for another three blocks. She would appear under a streetlight like a miniature float in the Macy's Thanksgiving Day Parade, but one filled with menace and strange intentions. Then her figure would be snuffed out by the blackness and she would appear again ten yards ahead. Nat felt a fresh rush of dread every time she bloomed into view.

Nat moved on to Hicks Street and saw nothing at first. Then he spotted Becca up ahead, near the end of the block, still, her back to him. Her head was raised up, as if she were listening. Then she turned left, her ghostly face appearing briefly in profile.

He watched her black shape move across the lawn, head down, in that strange floating gait. He began to run.

The field was an empty lot between two Tudor homes, overgrown with black weeds and pricker bushes. There was a path beaten down there that appeared to Nat as a trace of brown in the dark grass. He followed it. The wind picked up and the long grass soughed.

Can this really all be happening? he thought. But he knew it was just a reflex, an expression of bewilderment. Of course it was happening.

There was a stand of trees in his way, black-branched in the gray sunlight. Becca was nowhere to be seen. Nat brought up his arms and began to push his way through the tree limbs and vines. His feet sank into the mud as he struggled through, turning and twisting, looking for an opening not blocked by the thick foliage, dripping with cold rain. Strips of wood snapped and for a moment he thought he was going to be entangled in the tree, that he was being wrapped in strong green coils that he couldn't escape. A thorn raked painfully across his cheek. He felt a drop of blood bloom at the corner of the cut. He swore violently and swept the vine back with his arm, then bent at the waist and crouched down. A smell of pungent decay swept into his nostrils: the sickly sweet smell of mold and tree rot. *How are these vines so strong in wintertime?* he thought.

The little copse of trees smelled almost like . . . jungle. Hot, ancient, alive.

Nat floundered in the gloom, touching thick branches. What felt like a frond leaf, stinking of mold, brushed against his face, and he recoiled. He looked around wildly.

He saw the sun through a curtain of webbed black, and he pushed toward it, turning his back as he crashed through the bush. The vines tensed and then broke, and he was out of the foliage. His foot caught a hard root, and he fell. Nat cried out as his hands sank into mud.

The gray sky was now above him. The mass of foliage he'd passed through appeared as a black hump, with the streetlights of central Northam beyond. He wiped his hands on his jeans, then crouched and slowly stood.

Becca was thirty feet away, standing in the middle of the field that backed the copse of trees. She was facing to his right, and he saw her in sharp profile, even down to the red of her lips. The rain was slackening, and a break in the clouds allowed sunlight to pour down on her as if it were a pale spotlight.

Nat caught his breath. He wanted to approach, but he was afraid of breaking the trance.

Becca was staring at something in the distance. Her hat was now off, and stray tendrils of her hair were flying out behind her. She appeared to be leaning forward, and her hands were gripped at her side, and even from here Nat could see the bone-white knuckles. She appeared to be glaring with unconcealed hatred at something off to the right.

Puzzled, Nat slowly followed her gaze. Opposite the field they were standing in was a building on a small hillock. It was two stories high, squat and heavy, clad in gray limestone. Its odd horizontal windows were dark. The Northam Museum.

Nat had expected some ruin, a burned-down shell of a building, a Victorian pile where a family had been murdered a hundred years ago. Northam was old, as the locals never got tired of saying, and there were more than a few houses like that in the city. But this place was familiar to him. He looked at her, bewildered.

The wind picked up, and a gale raced over the meadow, shrieking in his ears.

Why is she here? You're making a mistake! he wanted to shout. *Nothing horrible happened here. There is nothing buried here. It's a harmless museum. I even know the old prick who runs it—his name is Atkins—from his upstairs bedroom!*

He cried out. "Becca!"

As he watched, Becca seemed to go limp and lose her balance. She put her hands to her knees and then pitched forward, turning away from him as she sank to the ground.

Nat went to her, his feet slipping in the mud. He also stumbled, and his bare hands slapped at the grass and the dark clay beneath it as he struggled to stay upright. Nat steadied himself, then came up straight and started running toward the dark shape on the ground. The wind was whipping the rain slicker around her, strands of hair twisted in the swirling gusts. The burning energy that had seemed to stand Becca up straight was gone.

Nat was a few feet away when he slid to her side and reached for her. "Becca," he said. He cupped her face in his hands and thought, *Too cold, too cold.* Her body was slack, and he reached across and braced her shoulders, pulling her up.

Her head rolled onto her shoulder and her hat fell back to the ground. He saw that under the dark green slicker she wore a black turtleneck. The cotton was folded once over her thin throat and held tightly to it. He wanted to reach and touch her jugular, but he couldn't even seen the pale violet line of a vein in the flesh.

Don't do that, he said to himself. *What if there is no pulse there? What if there is no pulse but her eyes still open? Then Becca will be dead, or undead, and you will live in a different world.*

The scratchy voice from the child's record floated into his mind. *The black velvet band fell to the floor. And . . . off . . . came . . . her . . . head.*

"Becca!" he yelled, and he took his hand and slapped her face. The eyelashes were a dark, unmoving line against the pale eyelids. The wind blew her hair into his eyes, and he arched his neck back to get away from it. Becca was still out. He shook her violently. "Damn it, Becca. Wake up."

He felt the bones move beneath the thin layer of flesh. Another memory of childhood—bats in a heavy canvas baseball bag at the Pruitt diamond. What living thing felt like this?

Becca's head lolled back lifelessly, and Nat grimaced. "Goddamn it!" he cried, and let it fall back, laying her gently on the ground. He began tapping his pockets and felt the shape of his cell phone in his right jeans pocket. He reached for it, swore as his fingers fumbled against the cold glass, then brought it up.

"Just give me a bar," he whispered.

The screen loomed up, and Nat saw that he had three bars. He was about to dial 911 when he looked down and saw Becca's mouth move. He leaned over and brought his lips down to her ear.

"Becca, can you hear me?"

She mumbled something, but the words were blurred and shapeless, as if she were talking underwater.

Nat crouched over her, his ear near her moving lips, but he couldn't make out anything. He rubbed her cheek and saw some color returning to her face, crimson leaking slowly into the flesh.

Her eyes came open, and Nat saw that it was Becca's gaze, the composed look in her eyes that he recognized.

"Dr. Thayer?"

"Yes," he said, "it's me." He felt a rickety smile across his lips. Why did this girl make him feel like a fumbling schoolboy?

She reached up and he took her hand—*Too cold, Jesus*—and lifted her into a sitting position. She looked down at the rain slicker, spotted her nylon hat on the ground, and picked it up. She reached for her hair, tendrils of which had come out of the bun and were now blowing in the gusting wind. She tried to secure them with a rubber band brought up from her pocket, but gave up. Finally, her eyes looked past him to the field beyond. When her eyes came to the museum, they registered nothing except confusion. The hatred was gone.

"Where am I?"

"You mean you don't know?"

"No. I . . . I . . ."

He felt her move, as if to get up. Nat reached across her shoulders and slowly began to stand, pulling her up as he went. Now that she was talking, he felt how the coldness of the ground had deadened his legs. "Are you okay?"

She stood up uncertainly. "Yes."

"You're not too far from the old town square."

"I know where I am now. I must have gotten lost."

He stared at her. *Are you really going to pretend you were out for a stroll and took a wrong turn?*

"Becca, what do you remember about the past hour?"

Her eyes swiveled to his. "I remember everything. I wanted to get some fresh air." She looked around. "It started to rain. And I got lost."

Nat said nothing, but their eyes locked and she looked angry. *This has happened before,* he thought. *She wakes up in strange places, but she doesn't want to know why.*

"You were following me . . . ?" she said, and something about how she said it made him laugh.

"Not really. I was trying to *catch* you. There's a difference."

"Why?" she said, and began to walk.

Without waiting for an answer, she strode away, heading toward one of the old Victorians they had passed.

"I wanted to see you," he said, catching up.

She was up ahead, her long hair flowing out behind the turned-up collar. She looked back at him, suspicion in the widely spaced brown eyes. The ground was making sucking noises as their feet pulled out of the mud.

For a moment, the notion that she would be furious and refuse to see him anymore had crossed his mind, and he found himself fearing it. Seeing her walking—no, driven—through the streets, a haunted marionette, had touched him. Unnerved him. What else was at work in her was beyond his experience, but now he believed it did exist.

"I thought we agreed I could help you," Nat said.

They reached the street, and with the end of the rain, a little life had returned to the neighborhood. An elderly couple was coming down the stairs of their house, the man holding a madras-patterned umbrella. A burly Dodge pickup came rolling past, its wheels making a sizzling noise on the wet tarmac.

"Help me do what?" Becca said as they turned onto Garmin.

"Find out why you feel the way you do."

He was walking next to her now on the pebbled sidewalk. He could hear the swish of her slicker and found that her strides were smaller than his. She was walking normally again.

"I know what's wrong with me."

She's nineteen, he thought. *She's a teenager. I have to remember that.*

"Your father . . ." He felt her tense. "He's gone. You have no one else here."

She said nothing. When they reached State Street, he led her to his car, and she came, though not eagerly.

"Come on, I'll take you home."

She got in, and soon they were heading back to Endicott Street. In the ride back to the Shan, he could feel her intently looking at him. But every time he smiled at her, Becca would glance away and he would see that profile marked by the flattened part of her nose that looked almost broken.

When he pulled up to the house, she stared ahead, not looking at him.

"I want to ask you a question," she said, her voice low.

Nat felt uneasy. To lose her . . .

"Okay," he said.

Finally, she looked at him and her eyes were filled with an urgency. "How did your parents die?"

His eyes went wide. "How did you know—"

She shook her head, as if to block out his words. "Please just answer the question."

Nat stared at her, confused. "They died in a car accident, Becca."

She looked straight ahead again, and her gaze was fogged over, as if she were trying to re-create the accident, to see it. "What happened?" she said.

"They were driving home from my mother's parents in Virginia. They'd been visiting just before the holidays while I was off on a school trip to DC. They were ten miles away when the car went off the road. Why are you asking me this?"

She turned back, her head bobbing quickly. It was as if she were hearing some other explanation in his voice.

"It was an *accident*, Becca."

Her expression was inexplicable. Pain and . . . *wanting something*. Her eyes brimmed with tears.

"I know you're worried about me, Dr. Thayer. And that means a great deal to me. But what you don't know is that I worry about you, too."

"You do?" he said. He was surprised by how happy he was to hear that. "I had no idea."

Her eyes were on his. Nat wanted badly to kiss her, but the last vestiges of professional training held him back.

"I do," she said, her voice low.

He took her hand and squeezed it, and a smile appeared at the edges of her lips. Her eyes closed briefly.

"Please be careful," she said, and she was out the door before he could respond.

CHAPTER THIRTY-TWO

Charlie was in his room, looking at his Captain America book. He'd heard the *Jeopardy!* music from the living room, so he knew Mrs. Finlay was in there watching it. She had trouble with the questions, but she loved Alex Trebek, so she never missed a show.

He turned a page. This was *The Courageous Captain America*, his official favorite book. He turned back to the first page and lingered over the words. *America had always been the land of opportunity. People came from all over—*

"Cleopatra," Mrs. Finlay barked suddenly.

Charlie looked up.

"No, I'm sorry, the answer is," Alex Trebek said, " 'Who was Queen Elizabeth the Second?' "

Mrs. Finlay made a disgusted sound.

A train hooted in the distance. Charlie turned to the window. Set low in the wall, it looked out on a big backyard filled with trees, now throwing long shadows in the evening light. Beyond the trees, there were the playing fields of Bishop Carroll. In seven years, he'd be out there in the spring, playing lacrosse. There was no talking in lacrosse, that he'd seen anyway, and it was invented by the Indians, and he liked Indians.

Charlie picked up his Captain America book and walked across the worn carpet, stiff-legged. Waiting for him, propped against an old Nike box, was Buzz Lightyear, the king of Planet Earth of the future.

Charlie.

The voice had come from inside his head, but far away inside it. Charlie looked up, startled. No one had ever talked to him inside his head before. Not even his daddy. Only the Magician, who'd visited twice.

The window shades were pulled all the way up and he could see leaves blowing over the white snow in the backyard. The trees shook their branches in the wind back and forth. Who would be in the backyard? The Kittinger boys next door had stopped sneaking over to throw rocks at his window, ever since his father found out what they were doing and went over to have a talk with Mr. Kittinger. He never even saw the boys in *their* backyard for six months after that.

Charlie?

The voice was closer now. Charlie squinted his eyes, and suddenly his heart skipped a beat. There was something out there, in the back corner of the yard. One of the tree trunks had gotten thicker at the bottom. There was something extra on it. No, standing next to it. Not moving, pretending to be part of the tree trunk.

Charlie scuttled back against the back wall across from the window. The open doorway was three feet away to his left. Should he get Mrs. Finlay to come in here with him? Or should he go out there and sit and watch *Jeopardy!* with her? Charlie turned and through his doorway saw the circle of light from Mrs. Finlay's reading lamp on the living room carpet. He could be there in three seconds.

Charlie turned back. The dark shape was gone, but now, four trees closer, he could make out someone standing in the snow. It was a girl. She was wearing a hood that made a teepee shape over her head.

His stomach grew cold. He looked again at the glow of light from the living room, but his eyes came back to the girl. What did she want? And how could she talk inside his head?

What do you want? he said, without moving his lips.

He could hear the girl's voice. Raggedy, as if there were something wrong with her breathing, as if she had something caught in her throat.

Please help me, Charlie.

The girl stepped behind a tree and disappeared. Charlie searched the window frame frantically. *Maybe she's hiding,* he thought. He started to crawl toward the windows, his fingers scraping across the nub of the carpet. As he passed a Captain America figure sprawled on the rug, he picked him up in his right hand and carried him along. The room suddenly seemed huge and the window far away. He was small and down low, like an ant crawling on the floor.

He heard breathing in his head. Ragged breathing.

Help you do what? he thought.

"Rhett Butlah," he heard Mrs. Finlay say, but she seemed far away now. He couldn't hear Alex Trebek's answer. His ears filled with a low staticky sound.

He reached the window and propped Captain America up against the wall beneath it. He put one hand up on the white paint of the little window shelf under the glass pane. Then the other. He lifted his head up and brought his nose up and peeked from just above his hands. Where did she go?

His eyes shifted all the way left, but all he could see were the blue-gray shadows of the trees on the snow and the green shape of the Kittingers' garage and the front end of Mr. Kittinger's Mustang through the chain-link fence. His eyes came around slowly to the right, scanning, pausing, and scanning again. There was the bird feeder on the pole that his daddy had put up. The tool shed with its two big Xs on the doors. Hanging on a wire, an old sack full of clothespins that his mommy . . .

Suddenly, he felt her. His eyes froze, then shifted slowly all the way right.

Please, please, don't let it . . .

The girl was standing right outside the window. Her skin was blue, and her eyes were looking at Charlie with some awful expression, as if there were someone standing right behind him with a . . .

Charlie swept his head around. Nothing but his own room, empty. He was panting now, his heart racing.

He turned back to the girl. Her mouth was open, and she was pressing her fingers against the glass, as if she wanted to come in. The fingers were pale as French fries when they go in the oven. Charlie's heart leapt and froze at the same moment. His eyes were riveted on her pale neck.

The throat. There was something wrong with it. It was ragged and black with dried blood.

That's why you can't breathe good, he thought.

Yes.

Somebody hurt you?

Her breathing.

Come with me.

Charlie stared at her. The glass seemed to disappear, and it was as if he were out there in the cold, standing next to her, the freezing wind blowing right through his jammies and goose-bumping his skin.

The *Jeopardy!* music rang in his ears, just the faintest trace. Mrs. Finlay's voice came to him from far away, but he couldn't tell what she was saying through the wall of static.

The girl stared at him, the eyes round and horrible, glistening. Why could he feel her terrible breath on his face?

Watch, Charlie.

She closed her eyes. Her head sank down, the greasy hair hanging at both sides. Charlie's eyes were bugging out, but he knew she wanted to show him something. He tried to turn toward the door, but his head wouldn't move now. The muscles were frozen like when he fell asleep in his daddy's chair.

Are you . . . watching?

Charlie let out a whimper and shut his eyes slowly, the light flooding out until there was nothing left.

He was in a basement, lit by a naked bulb. Clanging behind him. Like something walking. The basement was filled with old broken furniture and a box that said *Morgan's Apples* and an old-fashioned thing that heated up water and it was dark and cold.

I don't like it here, he said to himself.

A fat teenager walked straight past him, carrying a wooden box. He blotted out the light from the bulb, and then he was past it, a few feet in front of Charlie. He set the box on the ground, then stepped up on it. Charlie saw something dangling above the boy's head that brushed gently against his hair. Was it a vine, one that was growing on the inside of a house, and how could that be? Charlie couldn't see the boy's face, but he felt that he knew him. The boy moved and the thing above him . . . It was a rope, tied to one of the beams above, a rope with a little circle at the bottom of it.

Too sccaaaaarrrry.

The boy began to chant something. Charlie listened, but the words were strange and not even English. The boy took the rope and looped it slowly over his head. It fell onto his back with a little thump, and the coil was thick as a snake. The boy began to pull the rope from the other side, like Charlie's daddy putting on a necktie and pulling it tighter and tighter around his neck. He was chanting those strange words. When the rope was as tight as it would go, puckering the skin on the back of his neck, the boy leaned forward.

Don't do that, pleeeeeaaase.

Something was going to happen. It was going to happen soon and Charlie tried to open his eyes but they wouldn't go and then the boy fell and the rope caught him with a jerk, making a ripping noise against his neck.

He swung there, turning, and Charlie couldn't close his eyes and now he didn't want to see the boy's face but here it came, around and back and around again, and his tongue was sticking out and the eyes were staring at Charlie.

Uncle Matt. Uncle Matt from the photo in the hallway.

The basement disappeared, and now it was a young blond woman, her back to him, wearing a red dress and black shoes with tall heels that his mommy always said were hard to walk on. She was sitting at a desk with a mirror propped on the back edge and things spread across it in a mess in front of her, as if she'd been pulling things out of the desk drawers looking for something. Yes, that was it, because two of the drawers were hanging open. The girl took a thick silver thing and held it up. It was a penknife like the one Mr. Roy, the janitor at school, had on his key chain. She slowly opened the blade, which winked in the light from the table lamp.

Please make it stop, I want it to . . .

The woman looked into the mirror and reached up with the knife. She turned the blade to the flat side and slid it along her neck like she was hot and the steel was cool on her skin and her eyes were wide now, like she was surprised, and her lips were saying something over and over. Then the blade turned and—*Oh, no, please no*—went into her neck, and Charlie watched as it sliced down and a spout of blood went rushing at the mirror.

No, please make it—

Aunt Stephanie, who was supposed to live in Georgia with the peaches.

A young boy, his own age, asleep and being carried from a car, its engine rumbling. The vehicle was old and heavy, the road covered with ice. Charlie couldn't see who was carrying the boy, but he whimpered in his sleep and they were walking across the road and it was icy so they should watch out. There was a railing coming up; he could see it now and past it, all black and scary.

The woman carried the boy toward the railing, then stopped a few feet away, as if listening. Charlie watched the side of her face and it was the right side and the eye was black and staring, and suddenly he knew: this was Middy. Bad old Middy. Charlie's heart seemed to thud against his rib cage so loud that surely Mrs. Finlay would come and he was very afraid now and wanted to wake up oh so much.

The wind howled and little funnels of snow came racing down out of the black and past the railing. Middy opened her mouth and made a horrible sound, like when you step on a dog's foot by accident. Then she shook her head and rushed toward the railing, the boy limp in her arms, his bare feet hanging down over her limbs, and they must be very cold. Why didn't she give him some socks? Why did she have him out so late—

Middy stumbled to the railing and she threw the boy into the funnels of snow, pushing him out from her chest as if he were hurting her, and the boy screamed once loud and scared as he went down, down, down into the darkness.

Middy turned and ran back to the car. She opened the driver's side door, and Charlie saw a jumble of nightclothes, feet, and uncombed hair. There were more children, stacked like firewood on the backseat. But she bent down and reached into the car, and her big behind shook like a dog's as she tried to pull the top body off the others, and Charlie tried to look away but the muscles in his neck were still stuck. And as Middy was fumbling in the backseat, pawing at the kids there, his eyes locked on the face of one of them—a girl, with a green nightgown with red flowers on it, almost like Christmas—because the girl was waking up, and Charlie watched as she wiped her eyes and then she saw Middy and the bridge railings and the girl's mouth opened wide and she began to scream and Charlie screamed, too:

Middy, pppppleeeeeeaaaaasse!

Suddenly, Middy and the road and the bridge vanished and

Charlie's eyes snapped open and he was kneeling on the floor. The light above his head was on. His hands were trembling as he reached up to rub his face.

"Charlie?" came a voice from behind him, far away. It was Mrs. Finlay. "Are you all right?"

Charlie looked at the window, showing only the inside of the room and his reflection, pale, mouth open. The girl was gone. He could feel it.

Mrs. Finlay was pulling on his arm. He didn't want to get up. Middy was in the hallway, and Charlie now knew what she'd done.

CHAPTER THIRTY-THREE

Ramona Best was asleep on the living room couch. She was dreaming. Her lips were moving, and a whine of protest slipped out from between her lips.

From the kitchen came the sound of the back door rattling on its hinges.

Ramona slept on, her eyes moving rapidly back and forth beneath the lids.

The door shuddered. A shadow blocked the light underneath it, and the handle jiggled. Something was slipped into the key of the lock, and the shadow shifted.

Ramona sat up with a start. She looked to the window and began to edge cautiously up from the chair. Then she heard a lock turning and her eyes went to the doorway to the kitchen.

The back door rattled, sharper this time. Ramona froze and drew a breath deep into her lungs.

Zuela. It had to be Zuela.

She walked quickly to the kitchen and up to the door.

"Who is it?" she said.

The voice came back instantly. "Michael fucking Jackson. Open the door, girl."

Ramona closed her eyes, then turned the dead bolt and opened the door. Zuela came striding in. She was tall and regal, dressed in a thick Saks Fifth Avenue overcoat that she'd bought at T.J. Maxx in one of the great coups of her life. Her long and handsome face was done up, but lined with exhaustion behind the makeup. She had a broad beak of a nose, full lips, and luminous brown eyes.

Zuela worked on the perfume counter of Saks Fifth Avenue, selling lotion and scents to rich American women and bargain-shopping Europeans. She shook her head at Ramona.

"You still up?"

Zuela flicked on the overhead light, then went to the kitchen counter and hoisted a plastic bag—it looked to be full of green plantains—up on the newly washed linoleum counter.

"Yep," Ramona said.

"Mona! Why are you sitting here in the dark?"

Ramona shrugged. "I was in the living room."

"Mm-hmm."

Zuela went to the fridge and reached for one of the three bottles of wine—two red, one white—that stood next to it. She took down a wineglass and poured herself a full glass of red, the merlot chugging at the neck as she tilted it down. When it was nearly full to the brim, she set it down, put the cork back in, then came down and sat across from Ramona at the kitchen table.

"You enjoying your break?"

Ramona said nothing. She'd told Zuela that Wartham observed something she called Founder's Day, a long weekend when they honored the Puritans who'd signed the deed creating the college on an old Shawnee settlement. Zuela didn't use the Internet, and she was a little in awe of Wartham College, which she'd seen exactly once, when she dropped Ramona off, idling in the Altima amid the gleaming Range Rovers and Mercedes coupes that ferried the other girls to school for freshman orientation.

I'll come back for your graduation, she'd said then. *And you better make sure you're up there on the stage with* aaaallllllll *these white bitches.*

Ramona could feel Zuela's eyes boring into her now.

"It's Saturday night, Ramona," Zuela said.

"I know that."

"When's this Founder's Day thing over with?"

Ramona shot her a *stay out of my business* look. "It went on all week," she said.

"A day that goes on all week? My, my, those white folk can do anything up there, can't they?"

Ramona glared at her. "Have I ever had a problem at Wartham?"

Zuela took a sip of wine, then shook her head slowly.

"Have I ever brought home one report with anything lower than a B-minus?"

"Unh-uh."

"Then mind your affairs, thank you."

Zuela's eyes were heavy. "You haven't left the house once since you got back. You haven't called Girl or nobody. You're up half the night—I can hear you watching TV on that computer. And if the circles under your eyes get any darker, they're going to start calling you Raccoona."

Ramona frowned.

"What happened, Ramona? Are you in some kind of trouble?"

Ramona shook her head. "I told you to mind your business."

"Honey, listen to me. You're one semester away from graduating. First in your family. Baby, please don't tell me you got messed up with some boy up there . . ."

Ramona sucked her teeth. It was just like Zuela to think the worst thing that could happen to a twenty-first-century college woman was to get herself pregnant. The woman was trapped in some 1950s idea of coeds and rampaging college quarterbacks. She had no idea. No one around here did.

She opened her mouth to reply, but Zuela held up a finger.

"Don't get fresh," Zuela said.

"My grades are fine. I will graduate. Can you just leave me alone?"

Zuela exhaled. "Tell me what's wrong then. Are you involved with one of those girls?"

Ramona rolled her eyes. The second worst thing that could happen to her in Zuela's eyes would be a lesbian affair. "No, Zuela."

Zuela gave her a hooded, doubtful look. "What then?"

Ramona caught her aunt's gaze and held it. Zuela's eyebrows went up, and she took another draw on the merlot.

Should I or shouldn't I? Ramona thought. She wanted badly to tell someone, just to speak the words out loud and see how they sounded. Zuela was crafty and practical, but prone to becoming excited. Ramona didn't know if it was worth the risk.

Finally, Ramona spoke.

"Zuela?" she said, softening her tone.

"Yes, baby?"

"Have you ever seen someone who died?"

Zuela's eyes had been mellowed by the wine. A smile spread across her face. "Shoooo. Seen someone who died? I've been to a million wakes."

Ramona rolled her eyes. "See someone in your dreams, Zuela. Someone who's passed."

Zuela made a *tch* noise. "Well, of course, Mona. I dream about your mother all the time."

"What does she do?"

"Do?"

"Is she trying to . . . tell you something?"

"*Tell* me something? Like what?"

"Like anything. Like warning you or . . . asking for help."

Zuela clucked, swirling the wine in her glass. "No, baby. They're just memories, things we did together. Why? Who's coming to you?"

Ramona ran her fingernail along the chrome edge of the table where it met the top. "A student. A friend of mine. She was murdered."

Zuela drew in a breath. "And she's coming to see you in dreams?"

"Yes," Ramona said, blinking. She couldn't hold it in any longer. Zuela's eyes were getting bigger as she watched Ramona, and a look of fear twitched across her face. "And I think . . . outside my dreams, too."

Ramona looked over and saw that questions of pregnancy and lesbian affairs had been wiped clean away from Zuela's mind.

"You're serious?"

"Yes."

Zuela's face was now contorted into a kind of avid horror. "Well, you better tell her to stay away from you."

Don't you think I tried that? Ramona thought. *Why do you think I haven't slept in three nights?*

"I can't control—"

Zuela's hand closed over Ramona's wrist with shocking strength. "You don't mess around with this stuff. If this is really happening, you . . . tell . . . her . . . to go away. Do you hear me, Ramona?"

Ramona looked at her. She felt something give way in her. "What if she won't?" she whispered.

Zuela shot up straight out of the chair. "What does this friend of yours tell you in these dreams?" she asked loudly.

"She asks me to help her. I . . . I don't think she knows that she's dead." She looked up at Zuela. "Other times, she's different."

"Different how?"

Ramona closed her eyes. The sleep man was coming for her. She couldn't hold out any longer. Her head felt as heavy as a boulder.

"Ramona!"

Ramona snapped her head up and focused on Zuela. "Her eyes are black. And I can feel . . ."

"What?"

"That she wants me dead, too."

Zuela reached down and put both her palms on the flat of the table. Her eyes were closed suddenly, the lids trembling. Her lips seemed to mumble something. She looked as if she were ready to collapse.

Oh God, why did I tell her? Ramona thought.

Zuela seemed to be gathering her strength. The cords on her wrists stood out as her body weight pressed onto them. Finally, she opened her eyes. "Hold on. You hold on right there," she said in a husky voice.

Zuela turned and dashed out of the room. Ramona watched her go, a question on her lips. She heard a closet door slam, and thirty seconds later Zuela was back, holding a thick, fraying paperback book in her hand. "Maybe it's in here, Ramona. Maybe it says something." There was a look of crazy hopefulness in her eyes.

Ramona read the title: *The Dream Book.* The old paperback that had told them that cousin Stacy was going to have twins that time she dreamt of seeing a waterfall, and that Marcella shouldn't take the plane to France, the one that nearly crashed. It was like a second Bible in the Best family.

Ramona slumped back in her chair. She stared at Zuela, her lids half lowered. "*The Dream Book*? Are you *kidding* me, Zuela? This is not going to be in there. They don't have a section on the undead. Do you understand me? I saw her when she was supposed to be *dead* . . ."

The vision of Margaret Post beckoning her on the quad came back to Ramona and her throat closed. She felt as if she couldn't breathe.

Zuela, meanwhile, was hyperventilating. "Your great-aunt Madame Susu saw the dead after they passed on."

Ramona had heard about Madame Susu.

"They found Susu hanging from the mulberry tree in their backyard," Zuela continued.

"She was an alcoholic," Ramona said.

Zuela looked so fearful that Ramona got up suddenly and put her arm around her.

"She drank to get those things out of her head, Mona. But they made her make that noose and they made her put her head through it."

"What are you talking about?"

Zuela was shivering through her print dress. "Susu couldn't tie a noose. She was a homebody. The knot on the thing was some kind of sailor's knot. No one in the family had ever seen her tie anything like that."

"Did you tell that to the police? What did they say?"

"Of course we told the police," Zuela said. "But they didn't do a damn thing."

Ramona stepped back and looked her aunt full in the face. "Why didn't you ever tell me that?"

"For what, Ramona? For what possible reason would I tell you that?"

Ramona stood there on the kitchen linoleum, her arms around her aunt. She felt hope draining away, out of the room, and darkness replacing it.

CHAPTER THIRTY-FOUR

Nat met John Bailey at the Coat and Arms, a faded tavern just off State Street. There were four or five guys at the bar, a few wearing tan Carhartt jackets speckled here and there with amoeba-shaped blobs of cement. Nat nodded at the bartender—he recognized him, Frank Riordan, a typical Northam wastrel from high school—then walked along the long rib-high gleam of the bar. John, down near the end, leaned back, raising his hand.

The Bruins were on the two TVs at each end of the bar—not even flat screens, as the Coat and Arms was a hole-in-the-wall that time had passed by. Nat caught the score—3-1, Rangers—as he sat down. Groans echoed from the back of the place as a Rangers forward broke toward the Boston goal alone.

"I'll have a Stella, Frank," Nat said.

John gave him a look. John only drank domestic in bars—in this case, Pabst Blue Ribbon. A point of pride and cheapness.

"And I now call the meeting of the Northam Zombie Club to order," Nat said in a low voice. "Hear, hear. First order of business: getting sideways."

He'd called John before and told him the basics of the *nzombe* paper by Professor Zimmerman, summarizing the basic points. John's reaction had been one of disbelief tinged by unease. Now his friend looked quickly down the bar. Frank was pouring the Stella at the other end. The nearest drinker was a no-necked off-duty cop (Nat could see the gun under the hem of his stiff leather jacket) three stools away. John's paranoia seemed to fade, and he gave Nat a smile.

"How's Charlie?" Nat said.

John made a face. "Okay. The boy keeps to himself these days."

"What about the morgue?"

"They turned the place upside down. No bodies yet. We're trying to get them to keep it quiet, but how long can that last? Two bodies go missing, people are going to talk."

"Maybe they can paint it as incompetence."

"Maybe."

"But hey," John said, "look at the bright side. Since this thing started? At least we're seeing a lot more of each other."

"Yeah," Nat said. "Silver linings, pal."

Nat began to laugh and John took it up. Soon they were giggling like two maniacs. John slapped Nat on the back.

Frank came up with the drink, looking at them quizzically. Nat couldn't speak, the laughter now edged with craziness. He motioned for Frank to put the beer down and tossed a ten-dollar bill at him.

"You guys get started a little earlier today?" Frank said, leaning on the bar.

"Yeah," John said. "Yeah, Frank. You see, we're here to remember . . ."

Frank grimaced.

". . . some people who recently passed," Nat finished.

They both cracked up.

"An Irish wake, huh?" Frank said.

"Something like that," John said.

Frank knocked on the bar with his knuckles. "Sorry for your troubles, boys."

"Oh, you don't know the half of it," Nat said, and heard John break out again.

Frank drifted away, frowning at Nat. Nat only nodded back at him, a manic smile remaining on his face.

John gave him a look. Nat shook his head, and they both began to breathe out the last of the hysterical laughter.

"I needed that," Nat said.

"Fuckin' A right."

They sat there and watched the rest of the Bruins' third period, saying nothing. It was good to sit here, like old times, Nat thought. It was good to pretend. Why had he been so hard on his delusional patients all those years? Pretending was highly effective. Those missing bodies and the gutted coed outside the Wartham walls? Never happened. Figments of his imagination.

Just forget them. It was wonderful. But it couldn't last.

"What are we gonna do, Nat?"

Nat moved his Stella a few inches across the bar. "Do you want to tell your boss?" he said finally.

John's eyes boggled. "Well, that's the thing, isn't it? Tell them *what*? That a ring of zombies is stealing bodies and killing people all over town? I'm not sure even I believe that. I'm not sure what I believe is happening out there."

Of course, if Nat went to his own boss, Dr. Albini, and said the same thing, he'd be under review immediately. No talk of zombies and the undead could enter the pristine halls of Mass Memorial or the entire enterprise would collapse. The administration would bury him so deep that he'd never practice again.

And so what if Becca Prescott was slowly losing her mind at the same time that a murderer was on the prowl and a few bodies had gone missing from the morgue? What did it really add up to?

John leaned back. "Maybe someone wants us to believe that something strange, something . . . occult is happening. Have you thought of that? Maybe someone *wants* it to look like zombies."

"Do you really believe that?"

John shook his head.

"I think we have to tell someone," Nat said. "We have a responsibility."

John shot him a dubious look. "You don't work for the city, Nat. Say I went to Trotter"—James Trotter, Northam's chief of police—"and laid it out for him. We're talking about Northam, Mass., here. You think the town fathers are going to be up for an investigation into the undead? With the tourist season coming up in a few months? And can you *imagine* that phone call to the president of Wartham? 'Hey, Wingate, yeah, James Trotter here, we're putting together a press release letting people know that fucking *zombies* are wandering all over the city and that one of them probably killed your student. Sorry about all that.' Not hardly, I don't think. Wartham pays half the tax revenue in Northam, John, and they sell themselves as a safe little college in the Berkshires. The Internet and the *Globe* are already all over the story, and this would make things a hundred times worse. It's not going to happen."

"If there are more bodies, it'll happen," Nat said. "Serial killer or whatever, the town will have to decide which way it wants to play it . . ."

"It's only a serial killer if he uses the same methods. We only have one dead girl here so far. Prescott hung himself. Godwin was killed in a car accident. That's not enough to go to anyone with."

John looked at him, and there were dark circles under his eyes. His eyes looked sick, and they caught Nat's and stayed there.

"There's one more thing," John said.

"What?"

"Charlie."

"What about him?"

"If I go public and say zombies have come to Northam, Leah will go straight to a judge and say I'm wrong in the head. They'll give her Charlie. And that would be . . . that would be the end for me."

"You're right." Nat felt like the thing, the evil thing, was in the room, hanging like dank humidity in the air. There was no hiding from it. It was part of their lives now.

The horn sounded to end the game. Boston had lost. Two drinkers filed out the door, waving at Frank the bartender.

"So, you been over to Becca's house?" John said.

Nat looked down at the bar. "Yeah."

John took in some of his Pabst Blue Ribbon, held it in his mouth contemplatively, then swallowed. "You're spending some time with this girl, huh?"

"Yeah, I guess."

John looked at him, his eyes unreadable in the gloom of the bar. Suddenly, he let out a short gust of laughter. "Frank!" he called out suddenly.

Nat looked at him. "What are you up to?"

Frank came loping down the rubber mats behind the bar, then raised his chin at John.

"Two shots, my man," John said. "Your finest tequila."

Frank frowned, which was his way of showing he was impressed, then turned to his rack and studied it. He tapped his front teeth with his index finger, then chose a square bottle and brought it back to them.

"You guys are doing it right," Frank said. "Respect."

"Damn right," Nat said. "And one for you."

John snickered. "Yeah, let's do it."

Frank slid three shot glasses onto the bar and poured the tequila in. All three of them picked up the glasses, held them in the light, judging the color of the amber liquid.

"Eighty-five bucks a bottle," Frank said. "Now who are we toasting?"

Nat looked at John. "I don't know. Who are we toasting?"

"You, brother," John said. He turned to Frank. "My friend has fallen in love."

Frank made a face at Nat—like, *Salut*—and the three men brought the shot glasses to their lips and tilted them back.

Nat slammed his shot glass down on the bar. "Another."

They did another.

Frank tapped the bar. "That last one was on me, gentlemen." He put the tequila bottle back up on the rack and wandered down toward the other end of the bar, where a man in a green down jacket had his hand raised for another drink.

Nat felt the buzz surging up his spinal column, dividing into two, then seeping warmly into his brain.

"What was that all about?"

The corner of John's lips started to curl. "I was just thinking . . ."

"I warned you about that."

John shrugged. "I know, I know. But what I was thinking was, you finally took the fucking plunge, buddy. Fell in love and all that, the whole shebang."

"We're not dating, dude," Nat said. "She's nineteen."

John pulled back, spread his arms wide. "Hell, I know. But you're crazy for her, and that's my point. Don't you see it?"

"No!" Nat said. "No, I don't!"

"It's beautiful. Sick but beautiful."

Okay, we're drunk, Nat thought. *We are scudded for sure.* "I don't see it," he said fuzzily.

John leaned in and whispered, "You fucked me again, Thayer."

"How?" Nat said, bewildered. He looked around the bar, raising his arms up in an appeal. "Somebody tell me how!"

John's voice was lower, right in his ear. "For your first love affair, you chose a dead girl." John leaned back. "You see what I'm saying? I mean, *how long can it last?*"

Nat's friend was watching him, his lips twitching, a kind of madness in his eyes.

Nat thought about it. Something tickled his throat, and a spurt of laughter escaped his lips. Then another.

"You know what?" he said, his hand over his mouth.

"What?"

Nat dropped the hand. "I think you're right."

The hysteria came back up his throat. John opened his mouth wide and lost it, too. They were roaring now, pounding the bar, and out of the corner of his eyes, Nat saw the off-duty cop turn slowly to stare at them. He didn't care. The people here were just dummies, phantoms, backdrop. John slapped him on the back, forming the words *a dead girl* with his lips, and a fresh gust of horse laughter ripped through them.

But as Nat heard himself, he realized their laughter was different now. He looked down the bar and saw Frank looking at them strangely. His hand stopped polishing a glass, hanging there in midair with the cloth still grasped lightly in his fingers.

Their laughter bounced off the mirror behind the bar and the dark-stained oak walls shining red in the filthy lights and came back to Nat. And it sounded mad, convulsive, *sinister*.

This is how people sound in the fucking Iso cell at Mass Memorial, he thought. *What is happening here?*

CHAPTER THIRTY-FIVE

*B*ack in my old bedroom, Ramona thought. She could hear music coming from Zuela's part of the house. Her aunt watched those crazy Nigerian DVDs that people sold on the street. Nollywood love stories. They were low-budget crap and the stories were just absurd, but Zuela swore by them.

Her eyes began to feel heavy, and Ramona laid her cheek on the pillow. *I'll just close my eyes for one minute,* she thought. *What harm can there be in that? No harm at all.*

Ramona felt herself immediately slip into a dream. It was as if it had been waiting for her, patiently waiting behind her eyes to whisk her away. A movie on pause. A movie she'd never seen before.

She was floating. Below her were the headlights of cars. She knew the highway was 95 and that she was floating north.

It was all so real. Every detail—the cool wind on her face, the distant honking of cars—as real as life itself. She could smell, faintly, car exhaust and brackish salt water at the same time. She moved effortlessly and picked out the faint line of waves breaking. She was heading back to Massachusetts. Back to Northam.

Please don't show me Margaret, she thought. *I don't want to see her.*

Soon she recognized the mountains that surrounded this corner of Massachusetts, seen from above now as if lit by a full moon, the little towns ringed around their feet looking lonely against the massive black bulk of the Berkshires. The hills had always been friendly, but now they sucked in the light and they seemed ready to roll over on the towns and crush them beneath rocks and darkness.

Ramona saw the glow of Northam—she knew it from the town square and the stores along State Street—and began to descend. A swell of homesickness. *Shit, I miss it, I really do.*

But though she felt awake, she couldn't end the dream. She began to panic, thinking that if she couldn't escape, then this was really happening to her.

She drifted down farther and saw the walls of Wartham, a brick-red line snaking in a rough circle. *No, no. Go past it.*

And she did. She breathed easier as she soared past, and then the roads disappeared and beneath her were acres of tall pine. She realized she was floating over the Raitliff Woods.

A thin icicle of fear seemed to slice through her chest. She'd only been here once, and that was during a hike freshman year. Hiking was something that white people did, she'd realized then, white people from cities who came to colleges near the great outdoors and wanted to feel like they were Henry David Thoreau. But black people from the city don't ever want to see the woods, especially not with a bunch of crackers they didn't know. The woods were for lynchings and secret meetings, for hillbillies with eager axes.

Now that feeling came back to her. Entrapment. Her breathing sped up, and her pulse throbbed in her ears. She was drawing lower, and the branches of the trees were reaching up to take her in. A spasm of fear went through Ramona's body, and she cried out, *Nooooo!* But now she was in a dream, because the voice that she heard in her ears was the ugly moan of a nightmare.

The wind whispered in her ears. She passed the outstretched branch of an evil-looking tree, and she was above a clearing. A rectangular clearing that looked like it had been cut out of the woods a long time ago. A place you could only find from the air unless you stumbled on it while walking. She heard the grass sigh and swish underneath her, a wind seemed to be driving it back and forth. And then she saw the figures.

There were three people in the middle of the clearing. They were standing together, holding hands, heads bowed in the light pouring down from an unseen moon. They were in a trance, unmoving. Their bone-white hands touched, laced into one another. Two of them wore black, and their clothes fluttered in the wind.

Ramona could hear whispering. They were whispering to one another.

One of the heads turned up. It was Margaret, poor Margaret with her pale skin. But in the dream, her eyes were black now and searching. Searching for Ramona.

Ramona sensed danger building like static in her ears. Margaret's face wasn't sad and beseeching, *Help me*. It was hard, the eyes washed by a dark sheen.

This wasn't lost Margaret asking Ramona to help her. No, something was different. This was bad Margaret.

Don't let her see me, Ramona thought. She writhed, trying to pull her body away from the sky above the clearing. She felt that if Margaret's gaze fell on her, she would plummet to the earth, into the middle of their circle, and then the three figures would fall on her.

The other two were men: a tall, gray-haired old man who looked like an actor who played kindly grandfathers on TV and a bald man with bulging, yellowish eyes. But she went back immediately to Margaret.

The dead girl's eyes seemed to search the air above her, as if she sensed Ramona up there, but then Margaret turned her gaze toward the earth. And the whispering began again, like rat claws scurrying in the attic. *Tchhh-tchhh-tchhh.*

As much as she wanted to tear herself away, Ramona suddenly felt the need to know what they were saying. *Are they talking about me?* she thought. *Are they making plans?*

The wind ruffled in her ears.

Her eyes went to Margaret, and she watched the words form on her mouth. All she could hear was the moaning of the wind, but as she watched, she realized they were repeating a few words, over and over. The bluish lips seemed to loom up in her vision.

Ramona followed the words, which seemed to echo in her own head.

The the the the . . .

Ramona couldn't decipher the next words. She waited for the chant to return to the beginning, as her bones seemed to turn to ice.

I want to go now. But I can't. I can't turn away.

She watched the lips.

The . . . cut . . .

The wind shrieked. Margaret chanted louder now. Ramona could feel it. She watched the lips in terror.

The cut throat . . .

Please don't say that, Ramona thought. *Plea—*

. . . is silent.

Ramona looked at the bald man.

The cut throat . . .

Now the old man.

. . . is silent.

She took in the old man's whole face, the swelling bruise on the left eye, the purplish discoloration of his skin.

Alive and not alive.

The cut throat . . .

Ramona couldn't take it. She squeezed her eyes shut. But the words echoed in her head.

. . . issilentissilentissilent.

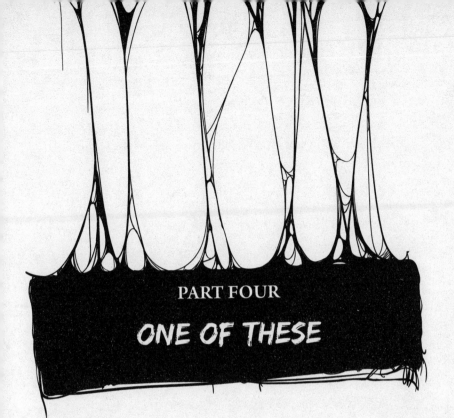

PART FOUR

ONE OF THESE

CHAPTER THIRTY-SIX

It started with Margaret Post," Nat said to John.

They were holed up in John's cubicle at department headquarters, hung over from the night before. They'd already studied the autopsy photos of William Prescott for twenty minutes, and had spent the last thirty trying to chart a course of action. The office was mostly deserted, with only a uniformed cop wandering in once in a while on the way to the lockers.

"Maybe we should begin with her," Nat continued. "So I want you to tell me about the damn security tape."

"For fuck's sake, Nat."

"Just tell me. Nothing will surprise me at this point, believe me."

John had watched the tape so many times that the details were sharp in his mind.

"We can go down to the evidence room and look at it. It's on a disc . . ."

"Just tell me. I want to hear it from you."

John took a sip of his Dr Pepper.

The camera faced west along Hanover Road, he explained to Nat, the street that ran parallel to Wartham's curving stone wall on the west side of town. Anyone approaching from the west, the direction of downtown and the Shan, would have to come along Hanover, then make a sharp right into the college entrance, where the security guard sat all night in his little lighted box. You could even see the glow from the sentry box on the lower left edge of the black-and-white film. The entrance itself wasn't visible: the camera was placed on a pole to the left of the entrance and had recorded the minutes leading up to Margaret's death.

Margaret first appeared in the video in the soft wash of a streetlight at 12:50:24 a.m., the time appearing in the lower left of the video image. She was walking along Hanover Road, the bushes that fronted the wall to her right, the street a few feet to her left.

Margaret approached the college entrance. She was moving briskly, her hands in her pockets, and even in black-and-white, her face was deathly white.

She'd seen something out there, John had thought the first time he saw it. *And she's trying, trying very hard, not to run.* In her hunched shoulders and the way her head and shoulders seemed to be drawn in to her body, expecting a blow from behind, John could feel a barely controlled terror.

"Why didn't you run, Margaret?" he'd whispered as he watched that first time.

She moved, head down, closer to the camera. She glanced left across the street, and John could sense the panic in her throat. She knew she was being followed.

But then, inexplicably, her pace slackened. It was as if she'd started sleepwalking. Her legs began to slow and her eyes slowly closed, as if she were climbing the last few steps to the summit of a mountain and her lungs were about to burst.

What are you doing? What's holding you back? thought John for the twentieth time as he told Nat the story. *Run, goddamn it, just run for the fucking entrance. The guard is twenty yards away. If you scream, he will hear you and come running. He has a can of mace issued by the college and a Louisville Slugger that the dean of students doesn't even know about leaning up against the wall of his little white sentry box. I've held that Louisville Slugger in my hand. It would have bought you sixty seconds, all you needed . . .*

Why didn't you scream?

Finally, Margaret was standing stock-still. The numbers to the left ran on and on, 12:51, then 52. And still Margaret stood as if some force field had her in its grip.

At 12:52:11, the shadow along the wall began to swell. There were shrubs there, underneath the tall pines that soared above the level of Wartham's stone wall, and it was hard to tell where the bushes ended and the shadow began. But you could just feel the image there growing darker and bigger, creeping along the wall, but without being able to see the shape throwing it.

Margaret's face was twitching, the eyes unblinking, but it looked like there was a tic near her right eye. She knew. John had read about rabbits that became so transfixed with terror that they stared helplessly at the fox, watching their murderer approach inch by inch, their bodies shaking with a fear so profound that it paralyzed them. Margaret had the same look. Her eyes were wide open but unfocused.

Now, 12:53:02, the chanting began. Margaret's lips opened and closed mechanically. She appeared to be repeating something. A cold tremor ran up his spine every time he watched the tape.

When he had the lab blow the footage up to the greatest possible magnification before it collapsed into a bunch of shifting pixels, the mouth became a huge hole, opening and closing. It was forming a few words. But which ones? He'd had a lip-reader from Boston come in and look at the tape, but she'd given up after three hours. The image of her mouth was too grainy at high magnification and too far away at the lower ones. What was Margaret saying to herself as her killer crept slowly along the wall and she could feel her skin pucker and her heart race with pure fear? Was she chanting something to protect herself?

Or was she begging for her life?

Please? Pleasepleaseplease?

The shadow grew larger, lengthening against the wall, and Margaret slowly swiveled to face it. 12:53:45. Now her face was turned away from the camera, and all John could see were her shoulders slowly inching higher. Her hands came forward as if to push the black shadow away, to keep it off her.

Turn and run, Margaret. Now.

This is your last chance. Just tear your eyes away from whatever thing is in that shadow and run.

This was the moment that haunted him.

Instead of running, she began to walk toward it.

All John could compare it to was a girl being pulled on an invisible rope into some dark cave where she knows a monster awaits. Okay, so there was no actual rope, but even with her back turned, something inside Margaret was resisting as her body staggered forward. It slowly pulled her toward her own death. Later, he found the toes of her leather shoes were scraped, as if she'd been physically dragged along the sidewalk.

John finished the story with that detail.

The sound of a metal door slamming from the locker room. Nat's eyes were lost in thought.

CHAPTER THIRTY-SEVEN

Jimmy Stearns made his way down the sidewalk that curled toward the county building up on the left. He could see the gray stone of the place, glowing under yellow lights.

Jimmy wanted to be back at home, watching *History's Mysteries*, his favorite show. He wished he were sitting in his old recliner with his favorite meal: cold slices of ham and hot mac and cheese. But he'd forgotten his paycheck in his work pants and he needed to settle the electric bill. With only thirty-four dollars in his checking account, he had to make a deposit, or the lights—and the TV—would stop working. If he deposited the check into his bank's ATM, it would be credited to his account immediately.

He'd had to go back to the morgue. He didn't like to go in late at night. It embarrassed him. What if Dr. Hobart was there working on a body? He felt like a trespasser, even though he had every right to claim his check.

He rubbed his hands together as he made the turn onto the stone pathway that led to the building. He paused for a second. Should he just wait until tomorrow? But the thought of sitting alone in his room if the lights went out, well, that scared him. He would be like one of those corpses down in the lockers, staring at the black ceiling above him.

No, he couldn't do that.

As he got closer, Jimmy noticed a light was on in the third window. That was Elizabeth Dyer's office. A smile appeared on Jimmy's face, and he thought about the Christmas party and how he'd nearly gotten the nerve up to ask her to dance to that Bon Jovi song. Next time he would.

He walked toward the morgue door, watching the warm light glow in Elizabeth's office.

A mist was sweeping over the Shan as Nat parked in front of the Prescott house. He'd left John behind in his cubicle to come talk to Becca. The Saab windshield was covered in dew that appeared as soon as he shut the wipers off. Within ten seconds, the windows were covered in tiny droplets, the cold from them frosting the glass so that Nat couldn't see out any of them. The only sound was the soft whoosh of the water hitting the metal and glass and the mist storm moving west toward the city.

He glanced out the passenger-side window. The house was just a dark blur in the window, its shape melted, moving as the mist pressed against the window and droplets ran down the glass. Its outline kept shifting murkily, the roofline tilting up, the lines of the porch flexing in and out with the running water, but its dark mass remained.

He was willing himself to get out of the Saab when something in the night sky caught his eye through the windshield. He gripped the leather of the steering wheel and pulled himself forward. Something was glowing off in the distance, but not in the sky. It was on a rise, deep in the Raitliff Woods, maybe two miles away. Glowing deep orange and red, with a smudge of gray-brown smoke hanging above it.

Someone made a fire in the forest, he thought. *I've never seen that before.* He stared, fascinated, at the fire surrounded by banks of dark trees that smudged together into one dark gray wall.

Strange, Nat thought. *Hunters?*

He got out and slammed the door. The house was solid again, its dark blacks and greens now shiny and hard in the rain, its edges sharp, its gutters dripping. It stood as cold as a tomb. Nat climbed the steps.

He felt the knob; the door was open. He pushed and the door fell back, soundlessly. The light inside the entrance hall was gray, as if the mist had penetrated through the window. He took a breath, steeling himself, and walked directly to the stairway, turning left and quickly heading up. He made the landing, turned, and stepped fast up the remaining eight stairs. Then he was on the second floor, his hand on the cool banister. The hallway was dark. He didn't believe anymore that there were lights up here, except for the one at her door.

"Becca?" he called out. No response. The house seemed to drink up the sound of his voice, returning no echo.

He walked down the hall, hearing the sound of his heels striking the floor as darkness rose up on both sides. He'd counted last time: fourteen steps to make it to her door. Why hadn't he brought a flashlight? His steps echoed. He counted eight, ten, twelve—he reached out and felt the fur of the mounted head he'd never seen.

Nat breathed out. But somehow he felt the house had let him arrive at the door without any incidents. Stupid. He had to stop thinking this way, giving the house this power.

Nat knocked on the Becca's mangled bedroom door. The outside locks were undone and Becca must have been waiting for him because the inside ones snapped immediately and the door edged open. Her profile glowed in the beams of a light to her left. She was staring at him. His heart beat loudly in his ears.

She was lovely, her brown eyes and that half-flattened nose. She was wearing a thin ivory blouse and jeans.

"Hi, Becca."

Becca turned and walked away without answering, leaving the door ajar. He pushed his way in and found the room just as he'd remembered it: the books untouched, the colored bottles of perfume each at the same angle to one another, the dappling sound of water droplets thrown against the glass window. There was a feeling of sanctuary here. Not only for Becca but for him, too.

Becca's eyes were ringed underneath by dark circles. When she sat and turned to look at him, he could read them clearly. *Why do you keep coming here?* they said.

"I wanted to see you," he said.

She turned toward the window. She was looking out, down at the yard.

Nat sat in the room's only chair. "I wanted to tell you that I believe you."

He dropped his head and stared at his hands, but he could feel her gaze turned on him.

"You believe . . . what?"

"Everything. I believe that you are . . . under the power of someone else."

"That I died?"

"*No!*" His voice caught. "No. I've read up on this."

She looked, of all things, amused. "You read up on this?"

"Yes."

She turned back to the window. "And?"

"I want to know about him."

"Who?"

"The man who tried to kill you." He couldn't say anything more. He felt as though he didn't really need to speak. Everything between them was known somehow. "Is he . . . here now?"

"Here?" she said. "He's always here. Nearby. But now he's roaming somewhere else."

"You can feel that?"

She glanced at her hands and nodded.

"Do you know who he is?"

"Dr. Thayer," she said, a smile curling the corner of her lips. "Nat."

"Nat."

"Why are you laughing?"

"You're so eager. You think that by knowing his name you can get rid of him?"

You should be laughing because I'm a trained psychiatrist, Nat thought to himself, *and I've just admitted to you that I think you're full-on possessed. That is not a normal diagnosis; that is a sign of an unbalanced mind. Laugh for that.*

"Maybe," he said.

"No. Not maybe."

"Leave that to me. Who is he?"

Her throat worked. "I've only seen him in dreams."

"Then tell me about the dreams."

Becca closed her eyes, as if the dreams were too painful to go back to. Her fingers began to interlace and then unlace in her lap, a nervous tic he hadn't seen before. He waited.

"In the dream I was in some hot country," she said finally, her voice strained. "I could feel my clothes on me, though I never looked down to see them. I wasn't able to do what I wanted, to look at what I wanted. It was as if . . . as if I was being carried along, remembering something that had already happened and I couldn't change it. But I was wearing khaki, which was sticking to my neck and my back, with drops of sweat running over my spine. Hot. Almost unbearable. I was wandering through forests, thick. I was far from home and felt anxious. I was searching for something, something I must find or . . . or else."

"Okay. Go on."

"I began to feel another heat pressing through the forest. Not a natural heat, not the humidity that you get in a jungle, or so I've read . . . but something that pressed against my face and began to turn it red. In the distance I could hear something crackling. Like sticks being broken, or popping open themselves. As I got closer, the noise grew louder.

"Then . . . It's hard to describe. The jungle trees just dissolved in front of my eyes and I was suddenly standing in a yard. In front of me was a small house, a hut really, but I remember every board as if I'd seen them for years. It was made up of slats, painted white with green trim around the windows. There were white curtains, nice ones, you know, unexpectedly nice for the house, hung in the windows. I had the impression—could I smell them?—that they were freshly washed. The house was well kept. *This is a well-kept house*, I thought to myself.

"And then, fire. I felt the heat on the left side of my face. Something burning the skin there, as if I'd stepped too close to a campfire. I was about to turn and look when something in my head said, *Don't look, don't turn.* That voice was not part of me; it came from outside."

She stopped.

"The voice was him?"

Becca nodded, her pale throat working. "I was thinking in the dream, too. I told myself, *I'm not afraid.* And then I saw the house. And I *was* afraid. To the left was a man dressed in khaki. His eyes were the eyes of sickness, black, with no pupils or whites, just insect eyes. They were looking at the house, and as I watched him the crackling of the fire rose in my ears."

Nat said nothing.

"Suddenly, I knew what the man was looking at. There was someone inside the house. The man had put him in there and he was burning."

Becca spoke faster now.

"I heard a scream and turned back to the house, and the clean white drapes whipped back silently as if a hurricane had blown its first puff of wind and then the window . . . just . . . vomited out a thick belch of smoke. It was black and gray and black, like a tornado twisting and roiling, and it was so *thick*."

Becca coughed, bending at the waist. Nat watched her, fascinated.

"Go on," Nat said.

She shook her head.

"Becca, you have to."

"I don't want to remember." Tears formed in her eyes, and he could see she was grinding her teeth, as if she were in pain.

"Please."

She shook her head again, took a deep breath.

"Then I heard someone scream. The person in the house was screaming. I turned back to the man, and his mouth was open. And in my ears, the voice saying, *DO YOU HEAR THAT?*"

Becca clapped her hands to her ears, and her face contorted in pain.

"I sank to my knees onto the packed-down earth of the yard. I remember that, the feel of it under my knees. The man's head was thrown back in a terrible contortion and for a moment I imagined that his neck was broken but it seemed to be vomiting the smoke that was now pouring out of the house and he heard the dark roar of the flames deep inside. My skin was burning up.

"I wanted to save the man who was screaming inside. I staggered up to my feet and tried to walk around the front of the house. The door blew open and I felt the air suck by me and into the house and the flames inside blew up like gasoline had been thrown on it. I . . . I saw that black holes were beginning to appear in my khaki clothes, like holes were being burned right through. I screamed as the fire leapt to my body and bit into my chest as I reached the first step, then the second. I felt my hair beginning to combust and the air I breathed in was . . . it was made of flame."

Her hands were shaking violently in her lap.

"Go on, Becca," Nat urged.

"And then I saw something that made me stop. The inside of

the house was a charnel, burned to charcoal along the boards and the floor. There was a table that seemed to stand on legs made of ashes and on top of the table stood . . . a man. The whole body was engulfed in flames, and I saw something spatter down onto the table and sizzle, like a piece of butter in a hot pan. I realized it was flesh, human flesh."

Becca's face twisted in disgust.

"The flames were going through me now, right through my body. There was a wooden beam, which ran from one end of the room to the other. And on the rafter there was something hanging visible just above the flames. *Why did they leave a cut of meat to cure?* I thought to myself. *This isn't a smokehouse*, I thought. *This is a house for people to live.*

"My hair caught fire, and the roots of my hair brought the flames down into my skull. The fire was eating me up, eating into my clothes, eating my skin, and I could feel each little patch of my flesh melting."

She looked at him, and there were tears in her eyes. She paused, and with her left hand wiped them away. She shook her head. Her nose was growing red with the crying.

"And that's *all* I remember. I either passed out, or I died. In the dream, I died, too, just like in real life."

CHAPTER THIRTY-EIGHT

Jimmy Stearns walked quickly around the side of the two-story county building all the way to the morgue door. He arrived out of breath and braced himself against the stone building as he reached for the handle. It was locked. He reached into his left pocket, found only lint and a pack of Life Savers, then switched to his right and pulled out his work keys. He found the right one almost immediately, slotted it into the keyhole, and pushed into the space.

The hallway was lit by sconces on the right and left. Turning, he saw there was nobody out there in the dusk along the path or up on the road, lit by the circular glow of the street lamps. He shut the door, flicked the bolt. The ringing noise of the bolt slamming into the lock hung in the air as he moved down the hallway.

He opened the door to the morgue proper, what they called the cooler, and felt a rush of formaldehyde-laced air push past him. He took a breath and coughed. He hated the smell. He just wanted to get his check and forget about this place for the night.

The room was blue-gray, with the white tiles winking here and there, with streaks of moonlight and the instruments sending out the odd gleam. The examining tables were empty, of course; they had to be washed down and cleaned at the end of every day, all the fluids swirling down the drains. The janitors did that; Jimmy wasn't responsible.

There was no sound and little light, only the bright yellow line under Elizabeth's door.

Jimmy thought he would talk to Elizabeth. Surely she'd heard the lock in the door. She'd be scared, all alone here at night.

He approached the door. The frosted glass pane was rippled as well, so everything on the other side was distorted and opaque. He saw the light from her desk was on, not the overhead.

A humming sound, then nothing. Did something move in the right corner of the window? He couldn't tell.

He felt the knob. The brass turned easily in his hand, and he quietly pushed the door inward, the rippled window sending all kinds of weird shapes to his eye. But nothing could have prepared him for what he saw once the door went moving on its own energy.

It wasn't a package of scrubs on the desk. It was Elizabeth Dyer. She was laid out, faceup, on the broad wood desktop, and someone had hacked her throat apart.

Jimmy went still. Elizabeth Dyer's face was paler than he'd ever seen it, the eyes closed, and its muscles were fixed in a look of absolute dread. The lips were pulled back as if in the next moment she would wake up and scream. Her blouse had been torn open to below the breastbone, and he could see the no-nonsense flesh-colored bra. Her legs were straddled over the end of the desk, and one of her black shoes was off, the second toe sticking up through a hole in her panty hose. Her throat glistened red. Blood pooled on the floor, and there was one arcing smear two yards from his right foot.

Jimmy gaped, and a strange thought entered his mind. It was as if he'd come by five minutes earlier and had killed Elizabeth but lost the memory of it and was now witnessing the result of his own work, returning to the scene of the crime. He felt a panic rise in his throat. *Did I do this and black out?* His head spun, and he reached for the door knob to steady himself.

I didn't do this, he said to himself. *I'm just a guilt-feeling creature who takes too much to heart.* He checked his hands. No blood. Of course not.

He took a few spasmodic breaths. Then he looked up in wonder, again studying the body.

Oh Lord, he thought. *Not Elizabeth.*

He thought of calling 911. Or building security. Or running out to the street and flagging down a cop. Anything to settle his nerves. He took a step, pulling the brass knob behind him. Suddenly, he stopped, hand still on the cool metal. He listened into the room. Nothing stirred. He could hear the industrial ventilating system kick in and begin to suck the air out of the room, but no footsteps of a killer.

Jimmy looked at Elizabeth again. His gaze roamed over her body. His eyes dropped to the desktop, and suddenly he saw a wink of light near her elbow. He stepped closer. It was a scalpel, one from the examining table's stock, sitting on the desk right next to her elbow. The murder weapon. The tip still had a smear of blood on it, just thickening now as the cool air brought its temperature down.

His eyes went back to Lizzie, to her neck. Then they drifted down to her bra.

She's gone, he thought. *Soon I'll never see her again.* He drew his lips tight against his teeth.

I can get the cops later, he thought. *There's just a few minutes now for us.* He took two more steps and was next to the body. He would just take a look at her, up close.

He breathed out and in again. His hand, seemingly of its own accord, reached out and cupped her left breast.

Jimmy made a sound in his throat and walked back to the door, pushed it shut, then moved quickly to the far side of the desk. As he approached, his eyes never left the dead woman's face, which rotated in the golden light of the lamp as he went around. He stood where she'd been sitting. Her chair was tipped back on the floor a few feet from the edge of the desk.

Jimmy looked down at Elizabeth. She was wearing a knee-length black skirt. It was hiked up slightly from the struggle she'd been in before she died. Little specks of blood dotted her flesh-colored panty hose.

Jimmy studied her midsection just between the round little breasts. Her bra had a clasp on the front. Above it, the red of her savaged neck gleamed in the overhead lamp.

Now he bent to her.

"Elizabeth?" he said quietly.

He reached his right hand up and brushed her hair back. It moved in a wave as he pushed his index finger through it. As he did, he had the oddest impression. It looked to him for just a second like the woman's right eyelid had twitched the tiniest bit.

Postdeath something or other, they called it. Dead bodies will twitch and burp for hours after death, he knew.

"I wonder who did it," he said, feeling strange talking to a corpse but quickly getting over it.

He glanced around the room again, the rows of metal shelving full of manila files, the water cooler to the right, the door that led to the lockers, then back down to Lizzie. He could still smell a trace of flowery scent on the air.

He reached down to the desk to steady himself and accidentally touched Lizzie's left hand. Smiling, he took the hand and pulled her lank arm up and placed it over her chest, where it flopped and landed with a soft thump. Jimmy took a deep breath.

He bent over her, studying her eyelids. What color were her eyes?

"Blue," he said. "Your eyes were blue."

He laughed softly to himself.

Suddenly, Jimmy grew still. He cocked his ear away from Lizzie's body.

He swore someone had just whispered something in the darkness. A scratchy, thin voice. Was it his imagination, or was the sound still hanging in the dark room? He felt a cold terror grip his stomach.

It was something like . . .

Let him . . .

It couldn't be. Nothing moved in the room. The aisles between the metal shelves were deep in shadow, but nothing stirred there. The air suddenly felt heavy, tense with expectation. Fear ran in Jimmy's veins like a surge of electricity.

"Mind is playing tricks on me," he said, laughing awkwardly.

He leaned down to give Lizzie a little kiss. He stopped just before touching her pale lips.

"You'd like that?" he whispered. "Would you like me to kiss you?"

Jimmy swayed a little over the recumbent corpse.

Then the whisper again.

. . . join us.

Suddenly he felt something grip the side of his shirt.

"Wh-what the he—"

He reared back. A voice boomed in the corner.

LET HIM JOIN US.

Elizabeth Dyer's eyelids opened lazily on two black orbs. Her right hand was gripping his shirt and pulling him into a tight embrace.

"God—!" he cried.

His heart was beating, and a shriek—his own—filled Jimmy's ears as he pulled away from the body that was rising up off the desk, but Elizabeth's grip was horribly strong. Panic closed his throat as he heard the clatter of her nails on the wood—the other hand, he knew, grasping for the scalpel. The blade winked as she brought it up, and he bellowed in terror, her face looming up to his, the mouth opening wide as if for a ravishing kiss.

Her eyes. Oh God, her eyes were so dark.

CHAPTER THIRTY-NINE

Charlie's eyes fluttered open. The room was dark. Something had woken him up; he listened for its echo. He hadn't heard the sound so much as he'd felt it through the air in his mouth, like the bubble there was a little container of quiet that had been . . . upset. Something had made the air in his mouth shake.

He listened. The faucet in the kitchen was dripping. *Drip, drop, drip . . .*

There, he heard it now. A dull bang that seemed to shiver up the walls of the house and shake them ever so slightly.

His eyes wide, Charlie reached his hand out in the dark to the wall by his bed. The paint was cool. The wall wasn't moving. Was the noise real? Was someone really trying to knock the house down?

Silence. The hiss of the heat from the vent. Charlie stared at the rug, and suddenly it seemed like a million miles away and scary and the cold light on it was like the light on the moon.

Toom. Charlie's hand came away from the wall as if it had been burned.

He'd felt it. Something was in the house.

Run to Daddy's room? It was so far away. The light shining on the rug was cold and unforgiving. Maybe the thing shaking the house would snatch him before he made it.

He put a bare foot out of his bed and hung it there. The toes tingled, but nothing grabbed them or bit him. After three seconds, it seemed the right amount of time for something to seize the toes if it was there, and Charlie dashed out of the bed, feet making thumping noises on the floor as he ran for his father's room.

Dark, snow through window, lamps and pictures, he saw them all in the corners of his eyes, but it was the gap of his father's door that he aimed at. Once you're in there . . .

He was through.

. . . you're safe.

He looked at Daddy's bed, and his throat closed with terror.

The room felt cold. The blankets on the bed were all pulled up and twisted, but his daddy was big and he wasn't in that bed.

Toom. A little louder. Charlie felt it in the skin of his bare feet on the wooden floor. The tiniest shiver.

It was coming from the basement.

Charlie hugged himself. He didn't want to go to the basement. He *couldn't* go. But now the thought: *What if the something has my daddy down there? What if it's shaking him? What if he needs help?*

Charlie scooted to the door and peeked around it down the long hallway. The basement door was a dark rectangle at the end of the hall. The sound came again, and he could feel it move through the air. *Too-oom.* The tiniest bit louder.

Charlie walked toward the basement door.

Dadddyyy!!! he wanted to scream as he ran for the door. He tore it open but couldn't move another inch. *What if it's chopping off Daddy's head? What if it's stomping his face and making it bloody?*

The dark rectangle of the doorway seemed to shiver with the sound. It was definitely down there. Was Daddy down there with it? Did it have his daddy?

He closed his eyes, then opened them. Who could he run for? The Kittingers? No, he didn't want to go outside. He could call his mommy, but she was a thousand miles away.

Charlie took a step toward the stairs and touched the doorway. He leaned into the darkness. There was no light down here, just the wooden stairs going down into blackness and the glow from the old heater thing in the corner, which threw an orange glow over the edges of things.

TOOOOM. A big one. Charlie stepped on the first stair and bent over, trying to listen for his father.

One step, two. Charlie was shaking. He didn't want to hear the noise again. But he knew it was coming and then it shivered the air again. The sound moved through him and he thought he would drop to the floor. It was coming from somewhere behind the stairs. Back where he couldn't see.

What was back there? Daddy's set of weights. An old exercise bike. And the laundry room.

Three steps. Four. There were only two left, then the cold concrete floor.

"Daddy?" he said to himself. "Who has you?"

The floor sent a shock of cold up his feet. His mouth was open now. He started to turn.

TOOOOOOMMMMM.

He came around the stairs slowly. The orange glow lit up the arms of the weight bench, but the bench was empty. No one was killing his daddy with one of the barbells. The sound was coming from the door to the laundry room.

A door Charlie had never thought of before, but now his eyes strained in the darkness toward it, hard to pick out on the blank wall.

TOOOMMM. Oh God, it was loud. The noise made the lock rattle. There was something in the room. Trying to get out.

Charlie turned. If he could dash back up the stairs, he could run to Mrs. Finlay's house three doors down in a minute. But she was old and weak. He couldn't leave Daddy alone.

Charlie began to walk past the weight bench. His foot knocked against something metal, and his lips curled over his teeth in a silent scream. He paused for a second, his eyebrows arched in pain.

Slowly, Charlie reached out a hand, and it shook as he approached the door knob to the laundry room. It was gold and black. He ducked his head down and crouched over, in case the door opened and something jumped out.

He touched the door knob.

TOOOOOOOMMMMMM. The door shook and rattled in his hand.

Charlie pulled as far away from the door as he could, turned his face away and put his hand on the knob. The door squealed as it came open. He was shaking, but he had to turn and look. Had to help . . .

Charlie swiveled his head, his mouth open in horror.

Standing in the doorway was his father. His forehead was bleeding, and his eyes, oh, they were dead.

His daddy was all alone in the room. There was no monster. Daddy was banging his head on the door. But why?

There was nothing in his eyes. He looked at Charlie.

Charlie was too scared to run to him—his father's face was like a mask, it didn't move, just the eye. Charlie reached his fingers out for his father's hand. He would lead his daddy upstairs, and they would lie in his bed and get warm.

His father's hand reached out and Charlie felt himself begin to cry. His father had been stuck in the room and now Charlie had saved him. He just wanted to be back in bed with Daddy holding him.

But the hand didn't reach for his hair, to rub it the way Daddy always did. It reached to the left and it grabbed the handle of the door, and with his head wobbling with terror, Charlie watched as his daddy, his eyes staring at the opposite wall, pulled the door of the laundry room shut, leaving Charlie outside.

TOOOM.

Charlie stared at the golden door knob as it shook in the door. His mouth worked, but only a thin whine of terror came out.

CHAPTER FORTY

Nat walked down the stairs of the Prescott house and got into the Saab. His face was grim and drawn. He drove through the Shan over to State Street and parked his car in front of the squat granite building off the old town square that Becca had stared at yesterday with such hatred in her eyes. He paid two dollars on the muni-meter for an hour's parking before he realized it was Sunday night and he'd just wasted his money.

He'd been inside this granite building a half dozen—no, a full dozen times—all during his school years. He'd tramped to the Northam Museum with his parents every Fourth of July weekend for the parties given to celebrate the double holiday that all Northam people took pride in. He could practically hear the speech of the museum's curator, Mr. Atkins, a cynical plain speaker whose only joy in life was the history of the small city. Atkins spoke before they served the punch and the chocolate chip cookies on the waxy red, white, and blue paper plates. *This city was founded the same year as our country, 1776, and we are here to celebrate the establishment not only of our national home but of our little community of Northam, too.* (Small applause.) Then some patriotic songs, ice cream, and, when the sun had sunk below the western hills, fireworks.

When he was twelve, Nat had felt up Joanna Christien in the backyard during one of those fireworks shows, and she'd pressed her hand on his swollen crotch with promises of more to come, and that was his best memory of July Fourth at the Northam Museum.

He hadn't been inside for twenty years. It wasn't the kind of place you brought visiting friends to unless they were amateur history buffs, and Nat didn't know any of those. Atkins was too hard-core for the casual visitor.

As he walked up the stone steps, he performed a little mental health self-check. *Are you, Nat Thayer, experiencing delusions? No. Paranoid much? No more than usual. Sleeping well? Not really, but that's not new.*

Everything okay at work? Well, there you have it. The line of inquiry he was pursuing with Becca's case was not a normal one. It was bizarre. And he was not particularly comfortable with bizarre. Exhibit A: he'd admitted to Becca that nonrational forces were at work in her case. It shocked him now to remember that. He was so far into the deep weeds that it was beginning to scare him.

But there is no rational explanation for what's happening here. If I work off the Diagnostic and Statistical Manual, *Becca could end up hanging from a tree. I have to at least pursue this supernatural shit. If only to prove it wrong.*

He pressed the bell. He wondered if Atkins was still here. Back in the '90s, it had been his show. He did the tours, wrote the pamphlets, assembled the exhibits, and acquired whatever artifacts the locals brought in. He was Mr. Northam himself.

The glass in the door flashed and the door opened.

"Who's that?"

There he was in the flesh. Wilbur Atkins, thin and tense with annoyance. The prescription in his frameless glasses was more intense, and the man's blue eyes were freakishly magnified.

"Mr. Atkins, it's Nat Thayer."

"Nathaniel's boy?"

"That's right."

Mr. Atkins stood regarding him in his glasses. "Need to use the bathroom? The Subway franchise across the square has a better one."

"I had a few questions about the city. I was wondering if I could pick your brain for a few minutes."

Atkins blew out his breath. "We don't open late on Sundays. Says so right here." Atkins angled his arm out of the doorway and pointed at the *Opening Hours* sign.

So why are you here? Nat thought. Then he remembered that the guy lived in a room upstairs.

"I just need to talk."

Atkins regarded him through his lenses.

As if you have a lot of better things to do, Nat thought. *Airing out the Revolutionary-era quilts or rearranging the tin soldiers in the Civil War case? You self-important old bastard.*

"Well, I suppose."

Atkins didn't ask him to come in, just left the door ajar and walked into the coolness of the dark space.

Nat followed him in and pulled the door shut. The glass in the windows made a vibrating noise, and then he was inside, following Atkins's footsteps toward a lighted room off to the left.

It was the Seagoing exhibit. The walls and ceilings were painted eggshell blue, as if you were sitting under the Atlantic Ocean, and the glass exhibit cases were filled with shells, huge fishing hooks, lobster traps, a wooden harpoon, a few doubloons—Nat's mind filled out the inventory even before his eyes swept briefly along the cases and spotted the artifacts. It had been his favorite room in the museum as a boy, a tiny thread connecting him with Henry Morgan, Caribbean pirates, Captain Kidd, and treasure. In the corner was a tall wooden ship's wheel. Nat frowned. He remembered it as being enormous, a gargantuan thing taller than himself, its handles as big as bananas. But now it looked small and quaint.

He noticed there was now a *Do Not Touch!* sign affixed to one of the spokes.

"I used to spin that thing," Nat said.

"That's why I had to put a sign on it," Atkins said shortly. "That came off the *Lady Contessa*, a frigate commanded by a Northam man for thirty years. Carried black powder to the Union forces that was used at Gettysburg, among other things. But it would be a pile of wooden boards if I let the likes of you touch it."

Nat rolled his eyes. Atkins was picking nearsightedly through some carvings laid out above the glass case of foreign coins. He brought one up to his eye and turned it in the light. It looked like a gargoyle, a half-human creature with a human head, leering eyes, and a tongue, but the body of a shark.

"Scrimshaw?" Nat said. He was slightly proud of remembering the name.

Atkins grunted.

Good, Nat thought. *That's the end of the formalities.*

"I wanted to ask you about West Africa."

"What about it?"

"Do you know of any connection between Northam and Africa? Any travelers there, missionaries . . ."

Atkins put down the carving, and his glasses caught a glint of light. "Slave traders?" Atkins said.

"Them, too."

"Why do you ask?"

"I'm interested, that's all."

Atkins gave him a *don't you bullshit me* smile. "Don't say? You woke up this morning with a sudden interest in the connection of the Atlantic slave trade to Northam?"

Atkins was enjoying this.

"You know, I get people in here asking questions about pirates from Northam and slavers, all kinds of things. Usually, they pretend that they've discovered a sudden interest in the history of western Massachusetts, but after a few minutes it's usually revealed"—Atkins smiled, revealing a set of black-flecked dentures—"that there's a question of inheritance. People wondering if their ancestors stashed some bags of gold away. Or gossip."

Atkins polished a rough spot on the gargoyle's left ear. "But that's not why you're here?"

"Exactly. Pure historical interest."

Atkins eyes looked like freshly peeled grapes, moist and quivering. "I don't think so."

"Is the information classified, Mr. Atkins? Are you working up a big slave-trading exhibit that's going to blow the socks off Northam?" Nat hated to take that tone, but the man was annoying.

Atkins said nothing. He picked up another piece of bonewhite carving and began cleaning it with a cloth. Nat waited him out. He knew the man couldn't resist talking history, no matter what he pretended.

"There is no history to speak of," the curator said finally, scratching at a grooved mouth in the scrimshaw. "The slave-trading families were in Boston and Salem."

"What about missionaries?"

"Maybe one or two."

"So no stories of, let's say, massacres, for instance."

"*Massacres?*"

"Yes. Massacres. Notorious crimes. I need to know about bad things that happened in Africa but started here."

This was Nat's working theory. If he accepted that there was some power at work in Northam, and that it had something to do with Becca's being guided or enchanted or whatever you wanted to call it, and it was implicated in Walter Prescott's death and Margaret Post's, too, there had to be a reason that this force had chosen this place. Even if the *nzombe* idea was bunk, something had obviously returned to Northam with evil intent. Murders of specific individuals were the result of deep negative emotions. A need for revenge. Why else would these things be happening if some dark act hadn't caused the city to become a target?

Atkins stood up, color rising in his face. "What the hell are you talking about?"

"I need to know if there were any locals involved in anything . . . Opium smuggling. Slave buying. Spreading disease, like Lord Jeffrey Amherst giving blankets infected with smallpox to the natives."

"That happened right here in Massachus—"

"I know where it happened. Hell, you told me the story yourself, during one of your tours."

Atkins's eyes watched Nat carefully.

"I want to know about stuff like that," Nat continued. "Very bad things committed by Northam people in Africa. I have no goddamn idea what I'm looking for, which is why I came here."

Nat slapped his hand down on the case. The rattling sound hung in the air as he stared at Atkins.

The old man looked away first and something in his face had altered. "West Africa?"

"That's right."

Atkins shook his head no, the thin jowls vibrating with the movement. "Nope, sorry, Dr. Thayer."

"Nothing? And you would know of such things?"

"I would."

Something in Atkins's manner struck Nat as off. He'd gone polite, or at least civil. *Or maybe I'm just paranoid*, he thought.

Nat blew out a breath.

"You mind if I take a look around?"

Atkins gave him a smile. "Be my guest."

Nat began strolling through the exhibit rooms, glancing into the tall glass cases. Something was bothering him, that same image that had been tugging at the back of his memory when he was doing outreach at city hall. A painting, a photo, something in a frame. Something stark, black-and-white. Powerful enough to lodge in his memory banks and stay back there twenty years. The lines of it were waving from the back of his mind, and a chill spread across the line of his shoulders.

What was it he remembered? A boyhood thing? Was it here in the rooms?

Fifteen minutes later, he stepped over the lintel into the refracted blue light of the Seagoing room and glared at Atkins. The old man glanced up at him. "Find what you were looking for?"

"No."

Atkins shrugged.

"I'll be leaving now," Nat said.

Atkins put the scrimshaw down and came padding after Nat. He took hold of the door after Nat had pulled it open.

"Dr. Thayer."

Nat stopped and turned. Atkins was grinning, oddly. "I really would like to know why you ask."

It was as if he wished to say something but only if the circumstances were right.

"It's not an inheritance," Nat said.

Mr. Atkins frowned. "I know that," he said, his voice with a flat edge.

Nat wanted to tell Atkins. Maybe it would shake something loose. But Becca . . . he couldn't.

"Just let me know if anything comes to you," he said, and walked down the stairs to the path.

CHAPTER FORTY-ONE

Nat was sitting at his desk at the hospital the next morning, his forehead propped in the palm of his right hand. His skin looked pale, ashy. A lock of unwashed black hair had fallen over his fingers. The sounds of the hospital—the alarm of IV pumps, the chattering of nurses, and the occasional bark of manic laughter or cry of psychic pain—babbled outside his door.

I have to sleep better, he said to himself. *I'm not thinking right.*

The glow of his MacBook reflected Nat's puzzled face. He had the Google home page open, but he'd completely forgotten what he was supposed to be searching for.

He was trying to remember something. Something he had to do.

What was it? It had to do with Becca, he remembered. Did he need to check on her history? No, something to do with numbers.

Numbers. What goddamn numbers?

"Got it," he said. Fifty-two: 52 Garmin Street. The darkened house that Becca had visited on her catatonic tour of Northam.

He searched for *White Pages*, then hit on *Address & Neighbors*. He entered the street address into the little box, typed in *Northam, MA* and hit *Find*.

The result came back quickly: *Mark and Elizabeth Post.*

Nat stared at the screen for a moment, then clicked the little red button and the page disappeared. *How much do you want to bet that Mark and Elizabeth were Margaret Post's parents?* He didn't even bother to look any further. He knew it was true.

The Posts were staying at their Northam home while they

filled out the paperwork for claiming their daughter's body, got her affairs in order, dealt with the college and their attorneys. And, no doubt, consulted with said attorneys on what was sure to be a monster lawsuit.

Nat hunched his shoulders as a ripple of sheer dread seemed to wash through him. Why had Becca gone to 52 Garmin Street while seemingly in a kind of trance? Why was she scouting the dead girl's house?

Should he be getting a second opinion on all this? Should he bring Dr. Greene in, let her talk to Becca, walk it around a bit? But what could he say? *By the way, there's the possibility that the girl has been hypnotized by, uh, you know, some outside force. Just thought I'd mention it?* Not only would they stare at him in shock and pity—as he himself would have only a couple weeks before—but they would immediately take Becca out of his care as well. They would diagnose her as delusional and possibly psychotic and put her on antidepressants and maybe a mood stabilizer. Lithium. Valproate. He knew exactly the course of treatment that would be followed. And it would mean Becca would sit in her room and talk very slowly about how her oatmeal was that morning.

If that didn't work, they'd consider electroconvulsive therapy. A few rounds of ECT to shock her brain waves back into neat little rows. What if they determined that she had chopped her own bedroom door to bits, and was growing fond of sharp instruments? Straight into a state hospital for three days, minimum. Chapter 123, section 12, of the General Laws of Massachusetts: "Emergency restraint and hospitalization of persons posing risk of serious harm by reason of mental illness." He'd used it on a few patients himself.

Wasn't it better to work the case himself? Bringing in a colleague would be to leave Becca alone, defenseless. That he couldn't do.

At least admit there were things here he couldn't completely explain. Begin there. That was the only way to fully protect her.

CHAPTER FORTY-TWO

Ramona was watching one of those *Real Housewives* shows. It was a morning marathon, and she'd lost track of which city she was watching now: Was it Orange County or Beverly Hills? The people were definitely vulgar and very tan either way.

The fridge powered on with its sudden, seizing noise, and Ramona settled deeper into Zuela's leather couch. The woman bought quality, Ramona thought. The phone rang every other day with *A1 Collections* on the caller ID or some other creditor looking for money, but that didn't stop Zuela. Her TV was Sony—Ramona had tried in vain to convince her that Panasonic now made better electronics, but you couldn't tell the woman anything. Sony had been king in the '90s, when her tastes seemed to have frozen in place, and so Sony it was. The couch was probably from Macy's. Her luggage was two pieces of leather Louis Vuitton. That was all she owned. Zuela could go to Russia in October and she'd fit every damn thing she needed in those two pieces. If it didn't fit, it didn't go.

Ramona's eyelids began to weigh down. The fridge was humming loudly, filling the room with its comforting tones. She channel surfed for a few minutes, settling on a blond man dressed like a New York dandy who appraised a vase for $8,000. Ramona whistled. But as the show moved on to a Civil War–era pistol supposedly carried by General Sherman, the sleep man began to whisper in her ear.

Just twenty minutes. We'll get up fresh and juicy for the essay.

Ramona began to drift off, catching her eyelids closing and forcing them back open. Was Margaret coming tonight? A ripple of fear coursed through her mind as her eyelids fluttered again and closed.

The dream again, the one of flying above the Raitliff Woods. The stars seemed to be farther away in the sky, and the mountains massed hugely to her left, the ridges of them covered with the little saw teeth of pine trees, just visible against the blue-black sky. The sound of rushing wind came into her ears and, yes, she was above that clearing in the woods again, but the air was colder and the night darker than before.

I didn't even have to travel, Ramona said to herself, still half conscious, slumped on Zuela's leather couch. Direct flight to Wartham tonight. But the sarcasm faded and she groaned slightly on the couch. She shivered, and her finger plucked at the green-and-yellow knit throw that lay across her legs. The air in her dream was a frigid stream. *Oh God, why does it have to be so cold?*

She didn't want to look down. Fear now, like a shiver in her blood. But the adrenaline that coursed through her veins wasn't enough to wake her up and only made the stars glimmer a little more brightly as she sank completely into the dream.

Margaret's down there. Don't. Make. Eye. Contact. Just observe.

But her neck muscles grew tired and suddenly her head slumped down and she was closer to the earth than she had been the night before. The clearing glowed, the grass a pale green. It seemed the ground was being swept by some white fire, or was that the moonlight?

Margaret's voice came to her from a long way off.

One of . . .

Ramona tried not to listen. *Oh God, you bitch, leave me alone. Just leave me ALONE.*

This wasn't the Margaret she'd known asking for help. This was evil Margaret. Taunting Margaret.

The clearing was surrounded by tall pines, throwing their thick shadows straight down, as if there were a powerful source of light just above Ramona. At first it was pitch black on that perimeter and Ramona's mind rebelled. There was nothing there. Nothing, *Margaret, shut up now. Just shut up.* Her eyes darted to the periphery of the clearing, the dark edge of the square.

But then shapes began to appear out of the blackness at the border, shapes that had been there all along, waiting—heads down, Ramona sensed. There were three of them. Margaret and two others, but not the old man and the bald man this time. Two others.

Margaret's voice droning, like static on a radio with the station coming closer. Syllables coming clear.

One of these—

NO! NO! Margaret, I don't want to know who they are.

But she couldn't stop it. A nimbus of light flickered around the first figure, and Ramona saw a tall black-haired man, handsome and thin, in his thirties maybe. His eyes were closed, but Ramona was sure she'd never seen him before. And then the light faded.

Ramona was mute, too afraid to talk now. *Show me the other two*, she said, because she knew that she had no power to resist, that the faces would be shown to her whether she willed it or not.

The second one came into view on the side of the clearing nearest the mountains, and with a start Ramona thought . . . *I think I know him.*

The light peaked, and suddenly it was the sad walrus face of that detective who had come to see her. What was his name? John Bailey. Down in the clearing he was wearing the same tan shirt and dark coat that he'd had on when he came to interview Ramona at Wartham. His head was bowed and his hair ruffled in the frigid air. He seemed to be swaying in the wind.

A thought flashed into Ramona's head, a thought so horrible that she at first tried to block it out. But it demanded entry. *What if I'm supplying these people? What if they are all coming out of my mind and I've doomed them? What if the next face in the clearing is the next person I think of and I bring them into this nightmare just because they entered my mind? That would mean . . .*

Oh God, don't let the next one be Zuela.

Because she knew that it wasn't good to be in the border of the clearing. The thin whine of horror that was screaming way in the back of her mind let her know that.

Do you even know who this is, Margaret? Ramona whispered to herself. *He's a detective. He's trying to help you, you stupid bitch.*

One of these is . . .

A light pulsed from just beneath her. Ramona tried to keep her eyes on Margaret, but a heavy magnet pulled them down. To the border opposite the detective. Someone was standing there, smaller than all the rest.

A little boy, not more than six or seven years old. His eyes were closed. He had a mop of brown hair, and his shoulders were slumped dejectedly.

A child? Oh, please no. I never saw that boy in my life. Margaret, who is he?

One of these is . . . The voice a little clearer, like your favorite radio station as you drove home from college, getting stronger and stronger and bringing back memories of high school dances. But she didn't want to hear the rest.

The little boy's eyes fluttered open.

A voice came into her head, a thin scream: *Please don't let him get me!*

Suddenly the light faded and the border was dark and the white fire danced over the grass. And the malignant power of the place seemed to rise like a metal hum in her ears.

One of these is next.

Ramona groaned. She felt the stream underneath her grow unbearably cold, and something tugged on the pad of her right index finger, a nubby fabric. She clutched at it, but the metal hum was calling her back. *Come see . . .*

She willed her finger forward, and it reached, the knuckle painful as it unclenched.

. . . which one.

A thread tickled the pad of her finger, and Ramona hooked it and pulled. The whine rose and blasted into her ears and she felt a blackness behind it. *Oh God, wake up. Ramona, open your goddamn eyes or you won't—*

Ramona yanked the fabric and suddenly she came awake. She was breathing hard, and looked around the room in the house in Roosevelt, her eyes wide with adrenalized fear. She was still sitting on the couch, and her finger had hooked the knit throw and pulled it up to her chest.

"What if I told you . . ."

The TV was still on, showing *Antiques Roadshow.* A painting stood on an easel, and a white-haired woman dressed in a red-and-black sweater was holding her hands up to her cheeks in anticipation.

". . . that I would appraise this one at twenty-five thousand . . ."

The fridge motor kicked off and the sound died away. Ramona pulled the throw up to her chin and took in a deep, rattling breath. She stared at the TV, her expression growing harder.

Goddamn you, Margaret, she thought. *You think you can scare me all the way from Massachusetts?*

Ramona's lips set in a hard line, and her eyes narrowed. *Look at me, scared of my own shadow. I might as well go down to the bodega and get some garlic and make a necklace, maybe spread some salt all through Zuela's house to protect us from the haunts.*

Suddenly, she threw off the yarn blanket and slapped the power button on the remote.

That little boy, she thought. *Something is looking for him, the thing that killed Margaret.*

She closed her eyes, and the lids were rimmed with tears that mixed with the mascara she'd put on that morning.

But it wasn't just the little boy. She'd had enough of Roosevelt, of reality TV, of Nollywood movies. Her future ran through Wartham College. There was no way around it. If she allowed herself to be scared off, she would never get her diploma and she would be another promising child of the ghetto who'd given up.

Ramona Best decided that it was quite enough, thank you. She was going back to Wartham. Tomorrow.

CHAPTER FORTY-THREE

Nat's eyes shut tightly. A cart was coming down the hall, unseen. It had a bad wheel, and the wheel was making a whirring, clattering noise that only grew louder as it approached his office. Nat frowned and got up to slam his door. Dr. Jennifer Greene walking by, a clipboard swinging in her left hand. Her eyebrow went up, and she swerved toward his office.

"Hey there."

Nat gave a wan smile and let the door stand open.

"Dr. Greene," he said, walking back to his chair.

"Dr. Thayer." Jennifer Greene slipped inside his office and leaned just to the left of the door. "Any progress with your Cotard girl?"

Nat glanced at the computer. "Actually, no. I wish I had more to report."

"Is she still insisting that her relatives are imposters?"

"Yep."

Greene's eyes narrowed. Nat tried to arrange his face into some kind of normative expression; he wanted to confide in her, but at the same time he feared exposing Becca.

"Well, that aside," Jennifer said finally, "you look like shit, my friend. Are you okay?"

For a moment, the urge to reveal all to his colleague flooded through Nat like a splash of sunshine through an unshuttered window.

"Nat?"

Just to say the words and make the whole thing normal, to make it an odd clinical experience that could be analyzed and categorized. That would lift a pressing weight off his shoulders.

"I, uh, I'm fine."

"Bullshit," she sang out.

"No, really, I am." Nat reached forward and hit a few strokes on the laptop keyboard. "Maybe in a couple of weeks when I get a better handle on what I've got, we can talk."

"You sure? It'd be your show all the way, you know. I'm just interested."

"I know. I know you are. Thanks."

Jennifer shrugged, lifted off the wall, and slipped out of the office with a wave.

Nat sat back at his desk. The cursor was blinking. Nat began to write.

I am in love with Becca Prescott.

He stared at this line and let it stand. After a minute's pause, he began typing again.

She's nineteen, recently orphaned, possibly psychotic, certainly depressed, and under my treatment. I have not informed my superiors at Mass Memorial about my consultations or opened a case file in her name. I realize this violates the oath I took as a doctor.

But, oddly enough, these aren't my main concerns. If Becca were an ordinary case, those would be my only concerns. I would have terminated the relationship long ago and formalized her treatment. But we're far past that now. There are worse possibilities than having my license revoked and my career ruined. Those things seem to matter less and less. I don't really care if they happen now.

Nat read what he'd written and frowned in annoyance. After so many years of cauterizing his emotions—no, denying their actual existence—he found it hard to express exactly what he was feeling. It was like writing a description of a country he'd never been to. He stabbed the keys in frustration.

What I want to know: Is this what love feels like, a kind of warm electricity that swarms in your chest when you think of the other person? Does love make your body feel light? Do you suddenly have the belief that you can feel what she feels, across distances, as if by telepathy? Or is this something else? It's ridiculous, but I'm being completely serious. Do you feel that you can anticipate her moods, to know what her face will look like when you enter a room? And to feel as if there is a part of you, a channel, a connection that stays open, like an exposed nerve, except when you're with her, when the circuit is completed and your energy flows in a closed loop that is rarely verbal or even describable?

I've never felt anything like this, and it's frightening, to be honest. Because there is another possibility besides a normal romantic relationship between two people, and that possibility is that Becca was murdered and was brought back to life as something else. This opens up a range of possibilities too terrible to contemplate. But I have to contemplate them. A crisis is coming. More people may die if I do not act. I need to know what I'm dealing with.

If Becca is inhabited, partly possessed or whatever the hell you want to call it, if this kind of thing exists and that's what I'm facing, then there is no guarantee that my thoughts and feelings haven't been—

Nat paused. *Affected? Infected?* What was the right term? A dark, fierce expression played across his face and he finally wrote *altered*, and then continued.

I haven't abandoned the idea that Becca is suffering from a psychiatric illness. She may very well be. But, at the moment, that is not the clearest danger to her health. The deaths of Margaret Post and Walter Prescott are evidence that there is a predator at work. The attempt to gain access to her room the other night is clear evidence that the predator wants to harm Becca. Perhaps her awareness of this intention has triggered or intensified an existing disorder inside Becca. To ignore the possibility of some kind of the supernatural is, in this very rare case, to do a disservice to my patient.

If we allow for this possibility, what can we say about it? It's intelligent. Tactical. (What else can you call Becca's visit to the house of the dead girl's parents?) It's aware of forces that endanger it. That would have to include me.

He stared at the last line, his eyes questioning and his forehead deeply set with worry wrinkles. Then he started again.

No, I cannot believe this. I cannot believe that what I feel has anything to do with evil. At the very least, I love Becca. But what about when she is being unduly influenced—in whatever way—by something that is evil? What then?

Two weeks ago, I would have given six or eight perfectly good reasons why human intelligence can't inhabit a different person. Cannot possibly influence the minds of others to the point of having them commit murder. We have many examples of people who thought this was true: cases of supposed demonic possession, schizophrenia, paranoia. Even the National Enquirer *has stories about aliens stealing people's brains.*

But what if, lost in all those ridiculous stories, there were those rare—or not so rare—cases of true possession? And we've been missing them all along, from Monsieur Cotard to the Vatican to the rest of us? The interview with the nzombe *professor said great sorcerers are born, not made, and born infrequently. Could it be that the true cases of* nzombes *have been hiding among the insane, camouflaged by a science that thought it knew everything but was missing a pattern in the most extreme cases?*

I can't believe I'm writing this, but it seems possible. How else can I explain what I've seen? When the discipline's answers are no longer adequate, you have to search elsewhere. And that's where I am, far past the frontiers of everything I've learned and dreading what comes next. There is the sensation of falling . . .

Maybe I'm losing my mind. That would be another possibility, and would in fact explain quite a lot. But John has seen what I've seen and he can't explain it either. How can a cop and a psychiatrist both lose touch with reality at the same time, on the same case? It's not logical.

Perhaps if I'd been in love before, I could compare the two states and detect any oddities. Do a comparative study. (But perhaps this thing knows this, and it is my "opening," my blind spot, that I've never felt so strongly about someone else and so will mistake his probings for something they aren't.) But I haven't.

It doesn't matter if the monster has Becca, watches over her, intends to do evil through her. I know what her eyes said. She is still in there somewhere, even if the thing controls most of her mind. I can't leave her as a hostage.

So, this is the present status: I have no idea what is happening. And I don't know what the traveler can do. I don't know if the sorcerer's spirit is really here in Northam. I am seeing only the appearances of things.

And yet I have to go forward. I have to save Becca.

Nat stared at what he'd written. The wobbly cart was coming back again, from the other direction this time, the noise of the wheel slowly building to a crescendo in the hallway. But he didn't hear it this time; his eyes were alight with the white glow of the screen.

He was thinking of his mother and father. An image of them at the beach, an old snapshot, had popped into his head out of nowhere. Their vacations to Cape Cod were the best memories he had of them as a family, the trips to Dennis Port in their old Volvo, his father checking the oil and filling up on the neon-green coolant before they left. And the cheap, out-of-the-way motels his mother favored, like the Cutlass or the Oyster, outdated places built during the '60s and packed with college kids or working-class families looking for an inexpensive place next to the beach. His father would rather have rented a house in one of the established towns or stayed at a four-star hotel. "Why does she like these shitholes?" he would mutter to Nat as his mother headed into the tiny office of one of the motels to announce their arrival.

It was as if his mother didn't want to meet anyone from Northam during their little summer getaways. She'd always had this aversion to social life. His parents' friends were his father's friends: Mr. Deutch and Uncle Pat (not a real uncle, just his father's frat brother) and the Seager twins. She never seemed to invite anyone to their home and was distant even with her own relatives. "Your mother," his father had once told him, "is the only self-made orphan in the world."

He thought of the accident that had killed his parents. The police explanation had always seemed odd to him. The driver behind their car that winter night twenty-two years ago had told the police that his father's Volvo had been driving normally for the few miles that he'd been behind it. Roads dry. No deer or darting animals spotted. But twenty minutes from Northam, he said, the car had suddenly veered to the right, clipped through the wire guardrail, and sailed off into the small valley where it had cratered, roof first, killing both his parents. No brake lights visible before the crash. No dead bucks or does to explain the swerve.

The cops came up with a working theory, based on interviews with family and friends. They thought that his mother, waking up after a long nap after visiting her mother's parents in Virginia, had reached for something to pull herself up straight in the seat. It happens, they'd told Nat. Passengers unthinkingly reach out and grab the steering wheel, and half asleep, not realizing what they're doing, they yank the thing toward them.

And off the road you go, straight into oblivion.

Nat stared at the glowing computer screen. He took a breath and copied the whole page, the text glowing under the blue. Then he clicked *Delete*.

CHAPTER FORTY-FOUR

John Bailey woke up on Monday morning, rubbing his eyes. The TV was still on and some infomercial was blaring. He sat up heavily, and his belly jiggled left and then right before finally settling in the middle and going still. God, he had to lose some weight.

He checked his cell phone: 7:45 a.m. Plenty of time to get himself ready for work. Mrs. Finlay would be here in forty-five minutes.

John grunted, got up off the bed, and went to his chest of drawers, low and dark beneath the plasma TV. He rooted around, grabbed some boxer briefs and a clean white T-shirt. As he walked toward the bathroom, he hooked a pair of jeans from a wooden chair near the doorway and added them to the ensemble. Finally, he took a fresh towel from the closet and headed to the shower.

Inside the bathroom, he peeled off his Pats shorts and stepped in, letting the hot water dig into the back of his neck for a good five minutes. He slopped some blue liquid soap onto a hand cloth and spread it around. He felt buzzed—anxious—and sleepy at the same time.

John killed the water, got out of the shower, toweled off, and quickly put on the clothes he'd brought with him. He just needed socks, shoes, and a dress shirt, and he'd be ready to go.

He was trying not to think ahead too far. It had become a habit lately. *Take every minute as it comes, just try to survive the day.*

What was that awful song his mother used to hum as she made him breakfast, something about taking one day at a time, Sweet Jesus? God, he'd wanted to strangle her every time she sang it, but he was beginning to see the wisdom in its lyrics.

Dressed in jeans and socks, John walked into the bedroom, dabbing the last droplets of shower water on his chest, and stopped instantly. Something was wrong. Something had changed since he'd been in here ten minutes ago. He turned at the waist, his right hand still holding the towel slung over his right shoulder. He checked every detail in the room. The TV was off, the window to the backyard still showing gray sky, the bedside lamp still . . .

His eyes settled on the gun safe underneath the night table on the right side of the bed.

The door was ajar.

"Charlie!" he called, jerking the towel to the floor and breaking into a run as he dashed into the hallway.

He made it to Charlie's door in six long strides. The room was empty, the toys neatly aligned against the far wall, with Charlie's Avengers slippers next to them.

He called the boy's name again as he fast-stepped down the hallway and then through the kitchen, heading for the basement stairs.

Just let me get my gun back and that's all I'll ask. Nothing ever—

He flicked on the light and jumped three stairs to the landing, ducking to scan the basement. The weights on his old bench gleamed innocently. But no Charlie. Nothing.

John swiveled, charged back up the stairs, and headed for the back door. He burst through it and ran into the yard.

"CHARLIE!" he bellowed. A few startled birds cried out and flew upward into a cloud-dimmed sky. Breathing heavily, a void spreading in his chest, John looked right and left and ran toward the back fence, calling the boy's name. The air was frigid and he was shaking and the ground was covered in snow and he didn't see any tracks heading toward Bishop Carroll.

Charlie had to be here somewhere. Had to be.

He screamed the name again, feeling that he was tumbling, tumbling, a black pit opening up in his chest.

The sound of bird wings. A clump of snow fell from a branch. His hearing was closing down. John could only hear his own frantic breathing, rasping above the beating of his heart.

Charlie. No. No, Charlie.

He saw something to his right. Behind a thick oak near the rickety wooden fence. A pair of knees, boy's knees in their brown corduroy pants. John's eyes went wide, but something inside him told him to go slow. He ducked forward and put his hands in front of him, then stepped toward the tree, angling around as he approached.

Charlie was kneeling in the snow, staring off at the playing fields behind the house. As if he were watching for something. His eyes were glassy and fearful.

"Charlie!" John said, relief flooding his body like strong drugs.

Charlie didn't hear him. He was bringing something up, in his hand, something big and black.

John screamed and the cry hung in the crisp cold air.

Charlie stopped, the barrel of the gun resting on his bottom lip. The lip bent out under the weight of the barrel. John could see the pink flesh and then the whites of Charlie's bottom teeth.

John felt all sensation leave him. His body seemed to consist of a force field of terror.

He held his hands out toward the boy, palms out.

"Hey, buddy," he said. "Give Daddy the gun, huh? Charl—"

He took one step toward the boy. Charlie stared at him. His eyes were empty and dark. The bared lower teeth made him look insane.

"Charlie?"

Another step.

Charlie took the gun into his mouth. Like you did the thermometer when you were sick.

"Charlie, *please*. Just give me the gun."

Howhowhow did he get the combination to the safe?

Two more steps. John's boots crunching in the snow, so loud he was afraid it would startle Charlie. The boy was only three feet away now, his feet still hidden by the thick trunk of the tree.

There was only one word in John's mind now. One word holding back a world of horror that pressed on the word from the other side.

Please, he thought. And then, *God, not this.*

John took one long step to where Charlie was kneeling and put his hand over the gun, his middle finger slipping behind the trigger. Then he eased it away out of Charlie's hands. The boy, his head bobbling as if he were entering the first stages of hypothermia, stared up, his eyes uncomprehending.

John placed the gun on the ground behind him, then took Charlie by the shoulders and pulled him in.

"Oh God, oh God, oh Lord God," he said.

Charlie was busy scanning the trees.

The morning shift at city hall, in the basement office, where it had all begun less than two weeks ago. Nat Thayer stared grimly at the green wall opposite his desk.

Tomorrow he would book the Buenos Aires trip. He'd had enough of Northam. *Do not visit us in winter,* he thought. It had never been truer than now.

Maybe the killer will show up tonight, Nat thought, eying the clock. *Let me not say that. Look what happened last time I asked for company and Walter Prescott rang the bell.* He thought of Becca Prescott, closed up in her room like a specimen in a box at a museum. Her life slowly passing, breathing out her youth in that fucking monstrosity of a house.

The thing that had been bothering him, taunting him, popped into the back of his mind again. A stark image, black-and-white—he'd seen it a hundred times but he couldn't place it. Was it from his school yearbook? Was it something from the Internet, an image burned into his frontal lobe?

Take a walk, he said to himself. *Get the blood flowing.*

Nat walked out into the hallway and moved left. The passage was cold and dark, the emergency lighting on. The town officials and office workers hadn't yet arrived for the workday. He climbed the stairs to the main floor of the city hall and began pacing the wood floors, up and down. Exit lights glimmered in the distance and the whirr of a water fountain motor catching and then shutting off.

A photo.

Creak.

An old one.

Nat stopped. He walked over to the wall. On it was framed a photo of a fat man in a beaver-skin top hat and a gold pince-nez, squinting. Nat glanced at the caption.

" 'Rutherford Wills,' " he said aloud, his voice echoing gently along the corridor. " 'Notary and Mayor, 1908 to 1912.' "

The water cooler hummed to life again, and Nat, who felt like he was on the verge of sleepwalking, moved toward the sound. He found the silvery surface of the fountain glinting next to the men's room and instantly bent down and pushed the button, taking a sip of cool water.

Up again, turn, walk.

A photo in black-and-white, *very* black-and-white.

He veered this time to his right, and studied the photo between the doors marked *County Clerk* and *Water Department*. This one was of a baseball team, *The Black-and-Yellows, State*

Champions, 1906. The men, half with mustaches, wore droopy wool uniforms and held their banana-fingered baseball mitts out in front of them, frowning in concentration. Nat went on.

Toward the end of the hallway, something huge and red hung on the wall. He went farther and passed beneath the exit light and saw the red thing was a metal box fixed on the wall. Inside was a fire hose, its surface coarse like a snakeskin, fixed to a brass nozzle, new and glowing in the red light. The thing stirred something else in his mind.

Fire.

Turn, walk.

Yes, fire. Flames everywhere.

Pace. Water fountain. Pass on.

The dream. Of course. Becca's dream of the house on fire, somewhere in a jungle. The painting in her room was probably related to the same nightmare. A man burning.

Stop, turn. Walk.

Slower now.

Nat stopped suddenly. The glass window of the sanitation department, *William Carlisle, Commissioner* stenciled in gold letters trimmed in black was to his left. On the door up ahead, he couldn't read the letters. But something in his head had told him to stop.

You're warm.

He took a step forward.

Warmer.

An image started to come to him, but blurry. Figures against a phosphorous-white sky, bony stick figures.

He took another step.

Hot.

Suddenly, Nat turned his head, knowing what he would find there. The photo seemed to bloom in his mind even before he set eyes on the black-framed thing on the wall, with its stark blacks and bleached whites. The photo of the hanging in the town square.

His eyes open and his heart pattering fast, Nat stepped up to it. Of course. The image seemed to merge with the one that rushed into his mind now, the one that had been lurking in shadows. Every line, every angle matched up.

It was the photo of a public execution. The gallows stood in the town square on a crisp fall day. A thin man, his figure impossibly black against the sunlight that threw the photo into stark relief. The edge of the city hall's cornice jutted into the top left of the picture, while the backs of the townspeople, the men in their dark wool coats and the women in billow-sleeved white blouses, formed a black border from which the gallows rose. The photographer had obviously been down among the spectators, as the camera was tilted up toward the hanging man. Whose neck was clearly broken.

Nat's eyes darted to the little placard at the bottom.

> The execution of Captain Thomas Markham, US Marine Reg. Two. June 14, 1920. Convicted of murder during the occupation of Haiti.

Nat stared in astonishment. Not West Africa. *Haiti.* An echo from his high school history class came back to him, and he remembered an occupation, American soldiers sent down for . . . He had no idea. But the Marines had gone in, that he remembered, and here was one of them, apparently a Northam man, being hanged for murder. But the murder of whom?

He brought his face closer to the photograph. *Who did you kill, Captain Markham? What did you get up to down in Haiti?* The white spaces of the photo seemed to throb, phosphorous and aglow in the darkness.

Nat reached up and rubbed his lips with his palm. *Easy, man. Take it easy.*

CHAPTER FORTY-FIVE

Charlie was swaddled up in his father's bed. There were wisps of things still in his head—the Magician's face, smiling and then scowling, and a feeling of heaviness in the back of his brain, as if a cloud were slowly moving away—but he felt fine now. Just a little cold. The grass outside had been cold like little icicles that bent.

Out in the backyard, before his daddy came, he'd been talking with the Magician. About many things, snowstorms and flying horses and red-striped monsters. Mostly about monsters. While they were talking about the ones they feared the most, the Magician had revealed to Charlie a rather big secret. There was a monster of sorts, a little goblin that lived inside his—Charlie's—mouth.

And do you know what? the Magician said. *That's the reason you can't talk like other boys. The goblin won't let you! He's quite mean. He's afraid if you tell someone about him, they'll come and pull him out.*

Well, that's terrible, Charlie said in his mind to the Magician. And he'd flushed with anger at the thought of a goblin blocking his words before anyone could hear them. He felt shock and happiness at once—he'd always wondered why he couldn't speak *really,* though his parents had tried to explain it to him.

It is, said the Magician. *Indeed it is.*

Charlie had moved his tongue around, trying but failing to feel the goblin in the back of his mouth. He told the Magician this.

Oh, you'll never catch him. He has a powder that made your tongue all numb back there. He's quite safe.

Charlie had thought about that.

Hold on. Does this mean you'd like to talk, Charlie?

Yes, I would. Very much!

Well, then, I'll tell you a little secret. Do you know what the goblin is scared of most in the whole wide world?

More than grown-ups finding him?

Yes, more than that.

What? he'd said in his mind. *Tell me.*

A gun.

He felt the gun in his hand then. He hadn't remembered taking it from his father's safe, but he must have. He could feel the little bumps along the handle, and he'd run his finger along it.

Show it to the bad little goblin and he'll get scared and run away, Charlie. Then you can talk all you like. You'll gab all day long!

He'd hesitated only a moment before opening his mouth. He'd raised the gun, so big it almost didn't fit over his bottom teeth, and worked it in past the tip of his tongue. The metal was oh so cold.

But I still can't talk, he'd said to the Magician. *Did I do something wrong?*

Oh, dear. The reply had come after a moment. *The goblin isn't scared enough. I'll tell you what, pull back on the trigger and scare him good, Charlie. He's a tough one. He won't go 'way unless you give him a real fright.*

He'd started to pull the trigger back, but his daddy had come to stop him then. *I'm getting rid of the bad goblin,* he'd wanted to tell his daddy. But of course he still couldn't speak, and his pad was nowhere close. Daddy had carried him inside to the bed, and worn out with the disappointment of not getting the goblin out, he'd fallen asleep.

But Charlie still wanted to talk. Maybe there were other ways to scare the goblin enough so that he'd leave. He would ask the Magician the next time he came.

Before he fell asleep, his daddy had talked to him about never touching his gun, never ever, no matter what, and told him the gun would be locked away in the safe from now on, but please, he should never even touch the safe. Charlie had nodded at all of it; his father looked like he was getting sick, like he'd eaten something that made him feel bad, and Charlie wanted to make him better.

Now, refreshed by his nap, he waited for his father to leave before he went out and talked to Mrs. Finlay. There were three door sounds that always followed one after the other: the door to the garage closing, the chunk of the car door, and then the screech of the automatic door as it went up its track and then back down. When he heard the last one go still, Charlie walked out to the living room.

HI, he wrote on the notebook. He walked up next to Mrs. Finlay, who had almost disappeared into the recliner she was so short, and tapped her on the shoulder.

"Hello, Charlie. How are you?"

He swiveled the notebook back and wrote with his favorite blue Sharpie, then turned the page toward the old woman.

FINE. CAN I PLAY A COMPUTER GAME UNTIL SCHOOL?

Mrs. Finlay frowned. When she did that, her whole face got wrinkly.

"What about inviting a friend over? Have a little playdate? Don't you have any friends, Charlie?"

Charlie thought quickly.

WELL, I CAN ASK ONE OF THEM ON THE COMPUTER.

"On the computer?"

SURE, Charlie wrote, feeling bad already for lying. But this was important.

Mrs. Finlay glanced at him uncertainly. The tip of her tongue appeared in the corner of her mouth.

"Well, okay. But no YouTube. I heard about that one. Just see if anyone wants to play."

Charlie scooted off to his father's room. His daddy's computer—the one with the Internet connection—was sitting in the corner on a rickety little desk. Charlie pulled the wooden chair closer and sat in front of the keyboard. He listened for any sounds of Mrs. Finlay's approach but all he could hear was *The Price Is Right*.

He logged in to the Gmail account his daddy had let him keep for writing his mother. He clicked on the latest message from her and hit *Reply*.

Mommy, **he wrote.** How are you? I'm fine, I got a B+ on my history test, the one I was worried about.

Mommy, Daddy acts strange sometimes. I don't want to get him in trouble but sometimes he sits in the car when he gets home and Mrs. Finlay goes home, but Daddy just sits in the garage staring straight ahead. The car is running and everything and I heard that's dangerous. One time the garage got smelly and I knocked on the window and Daddy didn't even hear me.

Do you think he's OK? Maybe he has too much stress. Or his head is hurting him.

Charlie stopped and stared up at the corner where the ceiling and two walls met. He hummed a song he'd heard on the radio that morning. He thought about telling his mommy about what had happened in the laundry room, but just thinking about it made his stomach all squirmy. The car stuff was normal strange, but the basement, that was different, like a horror movie. He wanted his mommy to tell him what to do, but not to get Daddy in trouble.

What should I do, Mommy? You can write me back and tell me. Please don't tell Daddy, he has enough to worry about. I think he just needs a rest.

I get lots of homework. Could I get an Xbox for my birthday? It's OK if you say no but please think about it. I am being good mostly and trying not to get Daddy stressed too much.

I love you.
Charlie

CHAPTER FORTY-SIX

Nat banged on the museum's front door. The windows up above were dark, the doorbell dead. He opened the screen door and pounded again.

He took two steps back and looked at the second-floor windows. Just then, a light came on in the left one, softened by a gauzy curtain.

Nat breathed in deeply.

A minute later, Mr. Atkins's face appeared in the window, ghostly, white-blue against the black. His hair was disheveled, and he appeared angry. He opened the door. "What do you think you're doing? It's—"

"It wasn't West Africa. It was Haiti."

Atkins stood unmoving in the doorway. His lips were pressed together.

"Aren't you going to say, 'What was Haiti?' Or did you know that I'd be back? You knew what I was looking for, but you said nothing."

Atkins sighed. "I have no idea what you're going on about. I want you to leave. Now, please."

Nat stepped up through the door, forcing Atkins back. He closed the door behind him.

"Yes, you do. You know exactly what I'm talking about. And I'm not leaving until you tell me everything."

"Dr. Thayer—"

Nat shook his head. "Everything, Mr. Atkins. I can't explain why, but someone's life depends on it."

Atkins stared, the eyes raw and huge behind his glasses. "Whose life?"

"A young woman named Becca Prescott."

Atkins seemed off balance. His lips repeated the name, but no sound emerged. He turned without a word and walked back into the museum.

They walked in darkness, the artifacts from the museum, so friendly and harmless during the sun-splashed days, now giving off evil little gleams of light. Dark, furrowed arrowheads in a glass case, two long and battered muskets crossed on the wall, a brace of elegant flintlock pistols laid out on a table. Atkins went to the far wall, flicked on a light, then walked back, stopping at a display table. He took something out of his pocket and bent down to the storage area underneath. He slipped a small key into the lock on the drawer and pulled it out.

He held a thin paperbound book in his hand.

"I'm presuming you're here about Captain Markham," Atkins said.

Nat stared.

"I couldn't be sure before," Atkins said. "I don't like to stir things up." He fluttered through the first few pages of the book.

"They brought Markham back to Northam," Nat said, "and charged him with murder."

"Yes. The trial was held here."

"Anyone else?"

"No."

Nat glanced around the room. A Union flag with bullet holes through three of the stripes hung above their heads. "Who did he kill?"

Atkins shoved the book at him, turning away slightly as if it were a sample of something toxic and possibly airborne. "You can read it for yourself."

Nat took the book in his hands. Its surface was rough, not slick and glossy like a modern paperback. It had a black spine, and the lettering on the front was in gold. *The Journal of Sergeant Nicholas Godwin, United States Marine Corps, Expedition to Haiti.*

He flipped open the first page. *Printed by the Grotto Press, Northampton, Mass., 1929.* There was an introduction by a Smith College professor of anthropology.

"What is it?"

"A journal. One of Markham's soldiers kept a diary of the . . . events."

Nat rubbed his fingers across the cover. "Let me ask you something else."

Atkins stood there, and Nat could feel the man tensed, expectant. *He wants the interview over. He wants to get away from me.* "What was this place?"

Atkins started. "What do you mean, this place?"

"The museum. Before it was a museum."

Atkins's lips curled into a fearful snarl. "Why, it was the old courthouse, of course. I said the trial was held *here*. There's a picture of the whole thing—"

"I saw it. I thought you meant the trial was held in Northam. You mean Markham was convicted and sentenced here, in this building?"

Atkins nodded.

Nat closed his eyes. That was why Becca had come here. Stared at the little building with such hatred. Because the traveler's first host had been hanged in this place—after the traveler escaped to another. And the men of the squadron were in the crowd with all their relatives. Atkins was staring at the book with distaste. His peeled-grape eyes swung up to meet Nat's. "Just bring the damn thing back when you're done."

PART FIVE

THE SQUADRON

CHAPTER FORTY-SEVEN

Excerpts from the Journal of Sergeant Nicholas Godwin, United States Marine Corps, Expedition to Haiti.

Port-au-Prince, September 26, 1919: Rain this morning, letting up just after eleven. The heat has become a constant presence after two weeks in this country, and one finally begins to get used to it. Private Bailey said that during the first few days, he felt he was going to choke because there was nowhere to get cool. No rivers to jump into, like back home, no promise of relief at night. We have been issued with tropical khakis, which keep our skin covered from the punishing sun but must be washed frequently to avoid smelling and infestation with the native bugs. We will have to have a laundry day in one of the local rivers soon, if we can find a clean one; we must risk the banana spiders and the tarantulas, which can grow to the size of footballs. As it is now, there is no need for the cacos to post sentries. You can smell us from thirty yards distant, if you don't hear us tramping along the country roads.

The men arrived in good spirits to the harbor here. But the Corps has been in Haiti for four years and the population has clearly had its fill of the occupation. We heard stories back in the barracks of the Haitians welcoming the first Marines with bottles of rum and dancing. That, clearly, is all over. The looks we get on the road range from the stone-faced to the malevolent. We will have to watch ourselves closely, although

the Haitians know that any attack on an American soldier
will end only in death.

The hardtack sent from Florida appears to have been
infested with maggots. Private Prescott discovered them while
dunking the offending biscuits in his coffee this morning.
We went through our supply and found two more infested.
Captain Markham stares at us and tells us, eat the hardtack
or go foraging. The men do not consider this an adequate
answer. We've tried drying some in the sun, but what the
Haitians don't steal becomes as hard as New Hampshire
granite. We will have to requisition another supply when we
reach Gonaïves.

At least we've been given a mission, as of yesterday
morning. The task of locating a caco leader, Bule Alexandre,
a politician of some sort who has turned against our presence
here and gone rebel, is our assignment. Captain Markham
gave us a talk this morning that was notable for its bluntness:
"Get Bule is our mission. Get Bule is our only mission. Don't
bother me with anything else, any nonsense from the Haitians
or requests for food or water. We will get Bule or die trying. Is
that understood?"

Captain Markham is neither popular nor unpopular
among the men as of now. We are all, of course, from
Northam and its vicinity and knew of each other growing up,
though Markham grew up several miles from us, which in
our parish of Massachusetts is equivalent to half a county. We
didn't know him well. He was assigned to us just before we
sailed from Baltimore, after the death of our beloved Captain
Croton from dysentery. Markham is certainly ambitious, as
we all discovered rather quickly, and Haiti has clearly become
his path to advancement. With no wars to fight, it is missions
like this that will make one's career in the Corps. I can't
expect that to motivate our regular soldiers, who would just

*as soon sunbathe on the canal banks and shoot the occasional
miscreant for target practice, but they will be driven forward.*

————————

*September 27th: We are headed north toward the last known
sighting of Bule in the city of Saint-Marc. As we tramped
from village to village today along the cow paths—Haitians
do not seem to know the meaning of paved roads, despite
the "corvée" law, which states that they must all contribute
labor to building them—we are met with blank faces. Our
interpreter, Joseph, asks at every crossroad and every market
town what the latest is on Bule. The name brings terrified
looks; the women often suck their teeth in dismay. And yet the
Haitians profess no knowledge of this man. They are pathetic
creatures, dressed mostly in oily homespun outfits that look
like muslin. They have a smell, different from ours. They smell
like the earth.*

    *Captain Markham is growing frustrated and has
instructed Joseph to let our hosts know that anyone found
hiding Bule will be treated with the utmost harshness.*

————————

*September 28th, evening. We are camped at a town near
La Chapelle, a regular hotbed of caco activity, according
to Joseph. The stares in the village are perhaps a bit harder
than on the road here. Otherwise everything is the same: the
same dusty roads, the same hordes of black faces attending
our every move, the same smell of burning sugarcane and
cow manure. One gets the impression along these roads that
the occupation is faring badly. We see scrawled messages in
which the name Rosalvo Bobo, no friend to the Americans, is*

prominent. *The poor hate us for the corvée laws; the rich hate us for stealing away the fat they skimmed from public works. The middle classes, generally speaking, do not exist.*

And as for Bule? The same responses. Non. Non, monsieur. Mwen pa konnen nonm sa a. *I must take care not to learn their massacred French here or I will be laughed at back in Northam when trying it out on Mrs. Futter, our neighbor who spent many years on the Left Bank.*

Weather is changeable, rain in the morning, burning hot by noon. My skin is turning the color of my father's good saddle. Private Ford's heatstroke seems to be better; in any case, Markham orders him to march.

The men are grumbling. They want to return to Port-au-Prince. Being out in the bush has separated us from the basic conveniences of life. We have not had letters from home since our arrival; the hardtack continues to house grub worms, and the local fare is nothing to be desired.

At dusk, we witnessed something interesting to all of us. We were coming up on a village—you can smell their cooking fires along the path before you come into the clearings—and heard what seemed to be rifle shots. A flat crack, then another. We all crouched immediately on hearing these reports, and Markham, in the lead, waved his arm to get us off the path and into the scrub trees that line the roads—gnarled nightmare things. We spaced ourselves appropriately; then on Markham's whistle (I could no longer see him), we advanced on the village, whose name I never learned.

From the fringe of the tree line, we saw what was making the sounds. A man with a whip—off-white, not a bullwhip surely—was prancing around and snapping it on the ground. It sounded like a pistol shot or a red penny firecracker on the Fourth of July. The villagers hadn't seen us or, believe it or not, smelled us. They were entranced by what was happening. (I saw a few bottles of rum being passed as well.) Markham, fascinated, held his finger to his lips and so we watched.

A man was apparently being "possessed." He was a tall, stocky, well-built young buck in a red shirt and brown half-pants, his feet bare. His face was covered with tan-colored dirt—later I assessed from rolling on the ground. A good fire was burning in the middle of the village, and the man was falling, rolling, turning, almost pitching into the flames, circling around it, before one or another of the villagers would pull him away with a yell. He seemed quite oblivious to his own well-being and jerked and twisted in the most remarkable fashion. The fire drew him like the proverbial moth.

"Saw a puppet show once," Private McIlhane whispered in my ear. "Damned if it didn't look just like that."

I quieted him, but my thoughts ran along the same lines. The man was being twitched hither and thither as if by an invisible hand. There was a woman watching, and I thought I saw her lips move once or twice, just as the poor puppet snapped his back and cried out.

Crack went the whip. The rum was passed and chugged. And the man went deeper into his frenzy.

For a moment, a chill ran right down my back. He was being pushed and pulled, babbling desperately as if he wanted to escape, as if he wanted relief from something. We craned our necks and peered from the tree line as the sparks flew from the fire from him brushing against the burning logs. Private Dyer whispered, "Wouldn't mind some of that liquor—" but Markham cut him off with an angry hiss.

It became clear that the woman I mentioned, her clothes a little better than the others, was the mistress of ceremonies. The bewitched man would come to her and clutch his hands, babbling, and she would wipe his forehead with a cloth and whisper to him. We'd been warned about voudoun, but here it was, in the flesh, and here was its apparent master. A village woman, of all things.

A little boy came wandering to the trees—going to relieve himself, perhaps—and we drew back. But it was too late. He spotted us and lit out like he was on fire. We came out of hiding and proceeded toward the assembly. One of the men tried to wave us off, screaming something, I would guess, about this being a religious ceremony, but Private Thayer clubbed him with the butt of his Springfield. There was a rush at us after that, but we leveled our rifles at the two dozen or so Haitians and they quieted down right smart. Except for one.

The man who was being "possessed" came at Private Ford with his eyes aflame and his babbling at a horrible volume. In his hand was a bottle, its end smashed on a rock, now dripping golden rum. Markham shot him at eight paces, but the man—so great was his intoxication with the voudoun spirit—walked through the bullet "as if it were flying dirt," as Thayer said later. Bailey fired another shot with the man's chest only two feet away from his bayonet, and the impact of this, a direct hit on the heart, sent a cascade of blood spurting to the ground and over Bailey's khaki pants. Thayer was caught on the shoulder with a large dollop. The man sank to the ground and quivered there, like a speared rat. As he died, he spat out some words at us.

Joseph, our translator, claimed not to have understood the man's last remark, but I suspect he was afraid to tell us the content.

The villagers were predictably outraged. They attacked us like a pack of wolves, darting forward only to shy away from the ends of our rifle barrels. The possessed man lay there, shaking and bleeding until finally he stopped. How he lived even ten seconds with his heart blown wide open I do not know.

Markham barked for us to take the woman into one of the houses. Thayer and Bailey grabbed her. She didn't resist, only looked on us with contempt.

"What are you going to do?" I asked Markham.

Markham usually brooked no questioning, but he was pleased with himself, I guess, so he deigned to answer this time. "She's the chief of these savages. I'm going to sweat her."

You could see he was taken with the whole thing. Markham has been asking villagers about the voudoun since we got here. He is beginning to believe that we are being practiced upon, that somehow the Haitians are disguising Bule by casting spells on us.

After Markham went into the house, it wasn't long after that we heard screams. Female screams, of course. The villagers were on the edge of the fire, and their eyes were wide. They were crying out, scuttling around and hugging each other. I dreaded the arrival of the dead man's family, for we would have had a hard time with them, but they never showed. I kept an eye on the body as the screams from the house continued.

"Fix bayonets!" I called out. The Marines have come through here many times since '15, so the Haitians knew what would happen if they charged. They spat at us, some of them, and I had to restrain Private Post and Private Ford, for we needed no more bloodshed.

The screaming from the house, though, I have to admit, was horrible even for us. I have no qualms about dealing harshly with the cacos, but this was a woman. No words were spoken, but the looks from the men were troubled. Except for Private Dyer and one or two others, who seemed to enjoy it.

As second in command, I never considered accompanying the captain into the house. My duty lay in guarding it. I know now that Markham is depraved and lacking in the most basic *human virtues. But he is still our fellow Marine, as well as our leader, and the thought of stopping him never entered our minds. The Haitians are unruly and obstinate, and the cacos kill us when they can. Many soldiers in Haiti have done the same, some perhaps worse.*

But we sensed something different about that "interview," as Markham would later call it. Perhaps it was the dark atmosphere of the ceremony that preceded it. But I suspect it was that woman's agonized, bone-chilling screams.

I had the sense she was calling to someone.

———————

October 1st: Something occurred last night that has shaken us all.

What little we can glean about the whereabouts of Bule place him last in Gonaïves, on the western coast, so we adjusted our route accordingly. Last night, we were sleeping outside a small city called Dessalines. We had pitched our tents and cooked our meals over open fires before retiring at eight. Sentries were posted, of course, although this is not known to be rebel territory. The night was still, the air barely moving, which is the particular curse of this country that seems not to be in the Caribbean but suspended over some Mesopotamian desert. At about 9:15, I heard a cry. It was Private John Prescott, who was second man on the watch. This exclamation was then followed by a shot. I was up in an instant and found my revolver already in my hand as I pulled back the tent flap. There I saw Prescott backing up, his gun pointed out at the trees, the bayonet blade catching the last glimmers of the fire.

"What is it?" I asked. I could see other heads poking out of the three other tents.

Prescott was deprived of speech. He backed up until I caught his shoulder roughly with my hand and stopped him.

"Marine, what is your report?" I demanded.

"It . . . it was him," Prescott said. His voice was quivering and low. I felt terror in his body; if I had not held him up, I believe he would have fainted.

Markham came out of his tent, his hair wild.

"Who?" he demanded.

"The man in the red shirt," Prescott said. "The man we killed."

"That's nonsense," I said. "These Haitians look—"

"It was him, as sure as I'm standing here."

"Where's Monk?" Markham said, referring to Private Monk, the first man on the watch. He hadn't appeared, despite the commotion.

Prescott gave Markham a haunted look.

"That's just it, Captain. That's why I fired my gun. The man in the red shirt was dragging him off. Monk's throat was . . ."

I was watching Markham's face, and the range of emotions that came across it is still present with me. First confusion, then a dawning horror—what we were all feeling, I believe, at that fateful moment—and then something I can no more describe than I can understand. I will call it fascination. I got the sense that he wanted to believe that the man in the red shirt was with us again. But the campfire was throwing flickering shadows across all of our faces, and I believe this last impression was a trick of the light. I forgot it almost immediately.

Since Markham stood rooted to the spot, I called for search parties to be assembled. Someone piled fresh timber on the fire, which roared to life, and we began to inspect the tree line. The first party took torches and set out, while a second one,

which I directed to head west, wasn't twenty paces away when
they called out.

"Here!" The man's voice—was it Dyer's?—was filled with
a screeching terror. I felt it myself. The woods were as dark
as ink, and the image of the man in the red shirt, arisen, was
with us.

I ran up. There was something lying on the ground. I called
for a torch and brought the flame down close to the earth and
saw a pool of red, viscous matter. I knew immediately that it
was blood. But gouts of it, sprayed in a radius of five or six
feet. The men stared at it in a kind of trance.

"This is where he took Monk," Prescott said.

We followed the blood trail with torches as we ran forward
into the forest. But it gave out after forty yards. I didn't say
anything, but I knew that the human body has only so much
blood and that it was more a case of Monk's veins being
emptied than any attempt at misdirection by the killer. He
didn't seek to hide his tracks. The opposite, in fact, was true.
In chasing after him, trying to avoid the red gouts on the dirt,
I had the distinct impression that the murderer would have
been well pleased had we caught up with him, as he made no
attempt to take the smaller animal paths that branched left
and right off the main path he was on.

When we returned, Prescott described the murderer in
detail. He'd caught sight of him as he passed by the flaming
torch that the sentries always gathered around. The man had
the same red shirt, the same brown half-pants, the same round
face smeared with pale dirt as the figure from the ceremony.
When I say that, after what we had seen, having been so long
from civilization and the company of other white men, we
believed Prescott from the beginning, perhaps you will not
credit it.

But we did. Especially Markham. He revealed to us

*that the woman in the village had told him, after much
"persuasion," that Bule was not only a political enemy of
the current administration and of the Americans, but also
a sorcerer "of the highest reputation." When Markham
sliced open the woman's cheeks and choked her with
a sash—he confessed these details blithely—she was
muttering incantations, calling Bule to help her. Joseph, the
interpreter, had fled in terror, but he'd translated a few of the
maledictions. They were calls for our deaths.*

*When Markham told us this, I watched him closely. I have
begun to suspect something is amiss. Markham has sent no
messengers back to our HQ updating them on the search for
Bule, as has been our standard practice when on these small
squadron missions. (We are without any Morse equipment
in the field.) He hasn't asked for reinforcements—as the
attack on Monk certainly warrants, under our orders—or
volunteered any information at all to the commanders back in
Port-au-Prince. We seem to be going deeper and deeper into
the Haitian firmament, losing our connection to the battalion.
And Markham seems not to mind it one whit.*

*"Sir, I think we need to send for reinforcements," I said
to Markham once we were back in camp and he and I were
conferring. "If Bule has followers who are willing to attack us,
he's clearly more dangerous than we imagined."*

*Markham sat on his camp chair, his lank hair falling over
his forehead as he stared at the campfire.*

"Do you believe this was the man we killed?" he asked.

*"It could have been a man dressed like him. For all we
know, it's a ritual here to dress in the dead man's clothes and
avenge him. Who knows what these people get themselves up
to? But I know that—"*

*"I believe," he said, looking at me with his piercing blue
eyes, "that it was."*

"Even more reason to get more men here. We can send ahead to Colonel Fine in Cap-Haïtien for reinforcements."

Markham's scorn was palpable. "If you lack the resolve to finish the mission, Godwin, please tell me at once."

I could have struck him then. It was beneath my dignity to respond.

"What about Monk?" I said finally. "Will you leave him to the savages?"

"What I will do is track Bule and kill him."

"If we are at the beginning of some kind of insurrection, we have to at least let command know. And someone must search for Monk. If you insist on going ahead, then send word—"

"So they can steal Bule away from me?" Markham said loudly. There was something in his eyes I do not pleasantly recall.

"Sir, if we pursue Monk's killer and another unit takes Bule, what is the loss to the Corps?"

Markham said to me, "I will have him. No one else."

I continued my arguments for a few moments more, but Markham was not to be moved. We marched out of camp early this morning, with Monk still unaccounted for.

———

October 2nd: Squalls of rain today, surprisingly cold. We are still heading toward Gonaïves, a notorious haunt for rebels. I estimate the city is eight days' march away. The men are looking forward to fresh provisions, sleeping in camp beds, and a temporary respite from this cursed mission.

No sign of Monk or his killer. The men, I feel, will revenge themselves on any Haitian if they are not given the real culprit.

October 4th: More strange occurrences. I can now attest to them myself. Last night was one of the oddest of my life, and I do not wish to experience the same again.

We had spent the day cleaning our equipment, mending our clothes, and resting. These things can only be neglected for so long: the brass on our Springfields needed polishing, the barrels needed the brush, and all of us needed to clean the dust off our uniforms. It was an industrious and tiring day, and by late dusk I was ready for my bedroll. I made sure the sentries were posted, both of them on four-hour shifts, and I crept into my tent, grateful for the eight hours of sleep ahead of me.

I nodded off almost immediately. But soon my dreams began to perturb me. I haven't had such insistent and bewildering visions since college, when I was an inveterate drinker. I tossed on my bedroll and the heat of the tent seemed suffocating, although in fact it was a cool night with a fair breeze. I remember a strange taste in my mouth—a strong copper taste that seemed to coat my teeth and tongue. I have not tasted such a thing before.

I do not know how long I lay there. Without a glance at the night sky, I couldn't tell if it was midnight or four a.m. Most of the visions fled from my mind, and all I can remember is a series of nightmarish faces, black faces, enormously large, the red veins in their eyes looming up at me.

But what I do remember is hearing a voice.

It came to me clearly, and its words were clear.

"Depart this place," it said. "Go and do not come back."

The voice seemed to be right outside my tent. I woke, wiping the sweat from my forehead, only to find myself blind in the dark.

The dream didn't dissipate. I felt a thing—a presence close to me is the only way I can describe it.

"Who are you?" I asked.

And then a sigh. It came from just outside my tent.

"Leave, Sergeant. Leave before . . ."

The voice sank away, as if the speaker had caught something in his throat, but I believe the rest of what he said was "I come for you."

I knew the voice. I had heard it daily for many months. It was indisputably that of Private Patrick Monk.

I was paralyzed with fear. The blackness of the tent seemed to choke me. I knew Monk was dead; I had seen his blood and no man could survive that. What spoke to me had to be a ghost, but then what was the thing that brushed against the side of my tent, rustling as it got up to leave?

———

October 7th: We have felt for the past few days that we are being tracked. We were aware in the past that our movements are often reported ahead—you cannot travel discreetly through Haiti, as the island is too small and too heavily populated—and that we rarely surprise anyone. But this is different. Our lead soldiers on patrol report that they hear movement in the trees off to the right and left as we move, mimicking our progress. Several attempts to locate this contingent of cacos, for that's what we assume it is, have been unsuccessful.

Captain Markham seems uninterested in pursuing any enemy shadowers. His time is used up with "interviewing" the local inhabitants as to the whereabouts of Bule. He has taken to talking to these natives alone in their huts. He is, I have to say, remarkably gifted with languages and has

picked up enough of the patois to make even the services of
our translator unnecessary. Sometimes screams and begging
moans proceed from the huts when he is at his "interviews,"
other times not. Twice we have found a corpse when the
questioning was terminated. One of their faces was bashed
in; the other had his nose slit up either side and an eyeball
removed, as well as a fatal stab wound.

It is hard medicine. Markham claimed afterward that
the two men attacked him while he was conducting the
interrogation, but I have my doubts. I am for severe pursuit
of Monk's killer, but I cannot condone the murder of innocent
men. I have remonstrated with Markham about this, but he
only repeats the story of being attacked.

Lately, however, some of the natives have been emerging
with nary a mark on them, and seem to have been pleased
with the interview. I suspect Markham is using our
discretionary funds, supposed to be used for buying flour and
such, to prospect for information. I have asked him about
these concerns as well, but Markham denies them. More and
more, the leadership and daily business of the squadron is
left to me, the captain now seeing himself as focused solely
on the hunt for Monk's killer and the tracking of Bule. Even
Markham's appearance is falling away from Corps standards;
his hair is growing longer, he has not shaven in a week,
and his adjutant reports that the captain wears the same
underclothes day after day without washing them.

I will bring this up with Colonel Fine when we reach Cap-
Haïtien.

───────────

October 9th: Markham killed another man today. We
came to one of the unnamed villages that dot the sides of the

mountains here on the road to Gonaïves, and he grabbed
a teenager off the street and instantly went with him to a
local house, throwing the inhabitants out from their midday
meal. They stood outside and listened in fear as a series of
increasingly horrible cries issued from their home. One tried to
enter, but Dyer was at the door, guarding it.

Markham forces our hand in these situations. Once
the Haitians spot any break in our ranks, any questioning
whatsoever of our commander, they will overwhelm us. We
can't intervene, and in truth only a few of us would. But
Markham grows stranger by the day.

As the interrogation continued, I was negotiating the
price of some peaches with a bare-chested man in a tattered
straw hat by the side of the road—his harvest spread across
the ditch there—when I heard an ungodly scream. The
locals were battering at the window to try and get a look
inside. Dyer had another mob at bayonet point. I ran to
help him, calling for reinforcements to push the crowd away
from the poor hut, when there came the sound of a heavy
blow from inside, as if a man had been thrown against one
of its wooden sides. The whole hut shivered, and the Haitian
women began to wail. I got to the door and rapped on it
before entering.

I found Markham straddling the man, who was clearly
near or past the threshold of death. His skull was crushed
in on the left side and blood oozed out, and from his nose as
well. Markham was unmoving, his hand on the man's throat,
feeling the pulse there. It was a macabre sight, and I cried out
to Markham to ask what in God's name he was doing.

He said nothing, just felt the pulse winding down.

"Leave me be," he said finally.

When he turned to face me, his eyes were unfixed. I backed
out of the foul-smelling place and took out my revolver.

"What is it, Sergeant?" Dyer asked me.

"The prisoner is being interrogated," I responded.

I heard Dyer mutter a prayer and then yelled at the natives, "Deplase tounen," or "move back" in their language. I have rarely seen people look at us with such hatred, but that is the order of the day.

The house emitted no sound, but I thought I heard muttering. Almost a kind of prayer as well, but I couldn't catch the word. What was Markham saying to a dead man?

The captain emerged a few minutes later.

"Did he tell you where Bule is?" I asked as he passed.

Markham said not a word.

October 11th: We are two days' march from Gonaïves, proceeding by foot in fine sunny weather. We were having breakfast this morning when the captain's adjutant came to me and told me Markham wished to speak with me. I finished the last of my flapjacks, and went to the captain's tent.

Inside it was dark and musty. The fact that the captain had not been washing was clear. I could see some book next to his cot and a scratch pad full of notes. I noticed the book was in Creole.

Markham didn't look up at me.

"I know where Bule is. Twenty miles west, in a village called Saint-Michel-de-l'Attalaye."

"Excellent," I said. "Can I ask where you got the information?"

"A young man I interviewed two days ago. He turned out to be Bule's nephew. He agreed to become a spy for me for the grand sum of one hundred American dollars. He wants to marry his sweetheart. I paid him twenty on account and

I've been expecting word from him ever since. Yesterday I received it."

I said nothing for a moment. If the boy had told him this, why wasn't I informed?

"What about Colonel Fine?" I finally asked.

"What about him?"

"He has a Colt's." The Colt's machine gun was our heaviest weapon in Haiti, besides our artillery pieces. "Should I send a messenger to tell him to meet us?" I took out my field map of Haiti and consulted it briefly. "Here," I said, pointing. "At Saint-Michel?"

"No."

"What about the men tracking us?"

Markham gave me a bored look. He couldn't even be bothered to be angry; I am not, I'm sure, enough on his level to offend him.

"Joseph has assured me he's put them off the scent, telling them that we're on our way to Cap-Haïtien to rendezvous with Fine. He's put out word that the Bule mission is over. We will proceed out of camp tomorrow, march to the outskirts of town, then turn on Joseph's directions for Saint-Michel-de-l'Attalaye, out of the sight of the villagers."

"You place a great deal of trust in this Haitian."

"We're interlopers here," he said with a sigh. "We need to learn the place to get what we want. And we need allies. I have got us two: Joseph and the nephew."

"He'll sell out his uncle, the king of their sorcerers, for one hundred dollars?"

"What of it?"

"It seems a bargain price."

"Perhaps you haven't been poor, Godwin. I have. This man would have sold him for half the money."

"Two more men are feeling the effects of malaria, and one of the mules . . ."

Markham waved me away. "Shoot the mule and have the men put into litters, or any damn thing you please. But have everything ready by eight a.m. I want to be heading west by ten at the latest. That will give us most of the day to reach Bule."

I saluted and saw to things. The two sick men were given extra water rations and said they could walk.

We left the camp the next morning by 9:15, with myself, Markham, and five specially chosen men forming our rear guard. The track was the same as everywhere. Broken ground packed hard by travelers' feet, buzzing mosquitoes, and the occasional lowing of a cow. We came on a farm that was divided into small twenty-foot plots, which we soon realized were rice paddies. After that was a string of small houses, with black faces in the windows and lank, thin figures lolling in the doorways, and then scrub jungle.

Fifty yards into the trees, Markham gave the agreed-upon signal—his left hand held out to his side—and three paces later the eleven of us simply stepped into the jungle, far enough so that even someone traveling on the same path wouldn't spot us. The mosquitoes found us, as I'd known they would—I'd given the men extra doses of quinine to ward off the malaria.

After twenty minutes, Markham emerged. A young black man stood beside him in a tattered white shirt and stained khakis—Joseph. I hadn't realized he was going to meet us, but I have stopped trying to predict Markham's maneuvers.

"He's spoken to the nephew," Markham whispered, his eyes bright with excitement. "Joseph will take us to Bule." I gave a low whistle. The other men emerged, and Joseph led the way. Not fifty paces away, Joseph made a turn and I saw his white shirt descending down a rocky path. We followed him. We were climbing down the hill and heading west. We could hear nothing of the enemy trackers; I assumed they had accepted the "cover story" and given up on following us.

We walked in silence, occasionally swatting at a bug. Joseph had chosen his route well; we rarely came upon any natives, only once surprising a naked boy leading a goat by a frayed rope, lost in his own thoughts. When he saw us, the child dropped the rope and stood as if he'd been rendered into black marble. Markham patted the boy on his head. He was in a fine mood.

By three p.m., we made the outskirts—beet fields and the occasional roadside shack, which passes for an "outskirts" in these parts—of Saint-Michel-de-l'Attalaye. I saw Joseph growing more attentive to the land, his head darting left and right as we made our way into the village. He was apprehensive, it was clear. He looked like a safari guide when you've crossed into the lion's domain.

———

October 11th, cont. Forty yards on from the last shack, we came in view of what in Haiti you could only call a fortress: ten-foot-high tan-colored walls made of concrete surrounding a compound of some sort. There were two rust-colored gates, fairly new, and they looked sturdy; they were solid iron of some sort, without openings to see inside. We regarded Bule's hideout from a small grove of pitch-apple trees that offered us reasonable cover. There was no one outside the building, and we could see nothing of the compound's interior.

"Here is Bule," Joseph whispered, pointing nervously and searching Markham's face. "It is just him and his family inside."

"Guards?"

"Two."

Markham studied the fortress.

"We agreed," Joseph said. "You pay me now and I will give the nephew his money."

Markham pulled out a small wad of notes, moist from the heat of his body. He held it up so Joseph could see it.

"Not yet," Markham said. "Not until Bule is ours."

"This is impossible. You said—"

"I don't give a damn what I said. Get us into this compound and you will get your money."

"You have no idea what you're saying. They will kill me if they suspect."

Markham unsnapped his holster and pulled out his service weapon. "And I will kill you if you delay one minute longer."

Joseph appeared to be sick; I thought he would faint. He glanced around, as if estimating his chances of escape, but they were none. If Markham didn't put him down, the rest of us would have.

"You are killing me." Keeling, he pronounced it.

Markham, tired of talking, pushed at Joseph's side with the gun. Joseph stumbled forward and walked toward the doors.

"If that gate doesn't open, I'll shoot you from here."

Joseph looked back, hate in his eyes, and walked toward the gate. His progress was slow; twice I thought he was going to turn and dash for the tree line, taking his chances on our marksmanship. But he had seen enough of it to know his odds were low. He continued, as cows lowed in the fields beyond the fortress.

Once Joseph reached the rust-colored gate, he put his hand up and banged on it, then called out something in Creole.

There were male voices from inside, barking out questions.

Joseph called back, his voice strained, and his eyes darting back to the pitch-apple grove where we waited.

"Good boy," Markham said.

There was the small report of a chain rattling, and then a bolt slid clear of its sleeve, the sound reaching us despite the considerable distance. The left gate opened, and Joseph stood back and began to argue with the man inside, whose view of us was blocked by the solid door. We ran for the nearest corner of the compound wall, keeping clear of the area that would expose us to the guard's view. Joseph watched us nervously out of the corner of his eye, his voice rising the closer we got. When we were just ten feet away, the man inside must have attempted to pull the gate shut because Joseph reached out suddenly and grabbed the door by its edge. We reached Joseph quickly, pushed him back, and went around the door at full speed. Dyer hit the first guard like a fullback, and he went sprawling into the dirt.

We were inside fast, all eleven of us, our Springfields at eye level, checking off doorways. The house was two levels, the finest structure I've seen in Haiti outside of the courthouses, and there were chickens and women and children flying in every direction. I spotted a man with a carbine cocked against his hip, and I shot him as he stood. The man collapsed. When I ran up to him, blood was pouring out of his mouth and pooling on the packed earth. He was, I determined later, the second guard.

"That's one good Haitian," Markham said as he walked by.

Prescott and I continued immediately toward the back, to prevent Bule from hopping the wall back there. We saw faces in the windows, but mostly children. At the foot of the wall, I found another carbine. I had to assume there was another guard not mentioned by Joseph, but it was clear he'd climbed over the wall and made his escape.

"Bule!" I heard Markham call from the front. "Show yourself!" And then we saw it: a man dashing from the side doorway toward an outbuilding thirty feet across the dust. All I got was a glimpse of a powerful face and a bare chest, and then the man was inside the hut like a flash.

"Don't shoot!" Markham cried, but we knew that already. The captain wanted him alive, at all costs. That he had made very clear the night before.

"Joseph!" Markham barked. Our translator was standing just inside the gate, frozen in place. "Get that nigger over here," Markham called out.

Joseph staggered over.

"What is this hut?" Markham indicated the small house Bule had run to.

"A place for his..." A Creole word, then: "For his work."

Markham's ears perked up. "For his sorcery?"

Joseph nodded.

"Weapons?"

Joseph shook his head no.

"Tell him to come out."

Joseph said nothing. Markham chambered a bullet and our translator complied.

A voice from inside, deep, in Creole.

"What's he saying?" Markham said.

Joseph cried, snot running out of his nose. "He says he will cut my testicles off."

"Tell him I'm not here to kill him."

Joseph snorted. His eyes were fixed on the hut.

"Tell him!"

Joseph shouted something in Creole. The answer came back at once, a strange name at the end.

"He says he will kill you before you leave Haiti, Captain Markham. And your blond wife will follow."

There was no need for him to translate the name.
Markham had a strange look in his eyes. A combination, I
think, of rage and . . . wonder.

"Rebecca," he said softly. "He said Rebecca." Instead of
being angered, Markham laughed out loud, almost with
delight. "I'll be damned! How does he know that?"

Joseph said nothing, just hung his head.

"Captain, let us go in there," I said.

"Check first at the window."

Prescott and I bent over and ran to the wall of the little
house. There were linen curtains covering the two windows,
moving slightly in the breeze. I put my back up against the
near wall, then swiveled and pointed my gun through the
open window, pushing the curtain aside. I saw Bule sitting
on a table, his feet up on a bench. He had in his right hand
what looked like a rosary. In the other was a statue of a small,
grotesque figure that I'd seen in the voudoun altars in the
villages we came through. The sorcerer's eyes were closed,
and his lips moved in a soundless chant. There was a candle
burning next to him, and next to his thigh was the dried head
of some small animal, well-worn through rubbing.

The room was otherwise bare. A thick wooden beam ran
the length of the room, exposed on all sides.

Bule must have run to the little house to have access to
these things. Certainly no weapons were visible.

"Don't move," I told Bule in Creole. I nodded to Markham
that it was safe, and he walked toward the front door.
Through the window, I saw him enter the place, followed by
Dyer, who soon held the witch doctor at gunpoint. I left the
window and was the third man into the hut. On the way in, I
ordered Prescott to bring Joseph.

"Look at him," Markham said to me. He was grinning.
"This is one remarkable savage. Not even hiding from us."

Bule ignored him, only raising his face to the hut's ceiling, his neck muscles straining as the intensity of his incantation seemed to increase. Joseph stumbled into the little room after being pushed by Prescott. He peered at Bule, and his face twitched fearfully. He whispered something in Creole, but Bule continued to chant silently, his body relaxed.

"Tell him I will interrogate him now," Markham said. Joseph was in a sad state, trembling and even whining at points.

"Did you resurrect the man we shot on the way to Gonaïves?" Markham demanded.

Bule had apparently finished his chant. "Go back to your barley fields, Captain," he said, as translated by Joseph. "Your power is useless here."

Markham's eyes sparked. His father grew barley on twenty acres outside Northam, that I knew.

"There are other kinds of power besides yours," Markham said. He motioned to me. "Tie him to that beam. And bring some kindling, just in case."

We did as instructed, finding some rough rope made of God knows what plant, which had been used for tethering a milk cow to its stake in the other corner of the yard. I cut it and brought it back to the hut, and we grabbed Bule roughly, then stood him on the table and secured his hands above the beam. The kindling we tossed under the bench. Bule looked at me with contempt smoldering in his eyes. He resented being handled by us, that much was clear. Joseph collapsed in the corner, and we could not stop him from crying out.

I had the feeling Bule was memorizing our faces. It was then that the coppery taste from the previous night returned to my mouth, and I spit on the packed-earth floor.

"I will talk to this man alone," Markham said to Dyer and me. "Leave Joseph."

It was my duty to speak up. I went to the captain and spoke low enough so that only us two could hear. "Captain, our orders are to bring Bule in alive."

Markham's eyes flashed at me. "Dismissed, Sergeant."

"He's not just another Haitian, Captain. Headquarters will be—"

Markham dropped his head low and fairly hissed at me, "I won't speak to you again."

I wasn't fighting for the Haitian's life. He was nothing to me. But Monk had died in pursuit of this man, and orders were orders.

I motioned for Dyer to leave. I gave Markham one last look, but his eyes were already on the prisoner.

We went out into the yard. The main house was deathly quiet. Then I could hear Markham's voice, low, and after Joseph's babble I heard the responses of Bule, even lower. But I could not make out the words.

The sun was still powerful, so we retired to the shade of a palm tree. From here, we heard the voices from inside the hut rise in volume, with Markham's insistent and Bule's haughty. Ten minutes later, Joseph came staggering out. He was babbling something.

"What is it?" I cried.

"Fou," he spat. "The captain is fou."

"What's fou?" I asked Dyer.

"I believe it means 'crazy,'" Dyer said. "Tell us something we don't know."

Before I could call back to Joseph, there was a pistol shot, and Joseph's arms splayed out in the air and he fell face-first into the dirt. He was shot in the shoulder. The report had come from inside the hut, Markham's sidearm surely.

"Goddamn it," I said, and started toward the hut, but already a wisp of smoke escaped the window. Then another.

I called out to Markham and was answered by a strangled animal cry.

"Let him burn," Dyer said behind me.

I came to the doorway, and there I saw something I will never forget. The captain had heaped the kindling—dried cane leaves and cedar branches—onto the table, under Bule, and lit it. The fire was licking at the Haitian's bare feet, and the table had already caught as well. But Bule didn't pull them away; as the smoke billowed, he was staring with a diabolical intensity at Markham.

I sensed that it was Markham, not his prisoner, who had cried out.

The smoke was thick, billowing, and I saw the flames puff out from Bule's clothes. He began to scream.

Markham stumbled past me.

Dyer ran for a bucket, and the two others propped their guns against the house and moved inside. But I could feel the heat press against me as the hut went up. I staggered back and nearly collided with Markham. He was on his knees in the yard, and on his face was a look of such horror that I called out his name and asked if he was injured.

But he was mute, even when I shook him. I found he couldn't speak. Not for another three days did the captain find his voice.

———————

November 10th: I have been down at heart and so have neglected this journal for near on a month. But an unfinished account of what transpired in Haiti will be worthless to anyone so unfortunate as to want to read this sad tale, so I must relate the final details. The public will know them soon enough, as Captain Markham is in the brig at Fort-Liberté

and will be transported back to Northam for trial and, I
have no doubt, execution. The families of Ford and McIlhane
demand this trial in Northam, and I can understand the logic
of the thing. The testimony will be given where their loved
ones can attend and stare at the murderer as he is brought in
chains. The Corps agreed to this, in part, I'm sure, to mollify
public opinion and keep the Haitian mission protected from
even further public scorn.

What I will relate is this: Markham was a changed man as
we made our way back to Colonel Fine's headquarters in Cap-
Haïtien. His unwillingness to talk troubled us all, but after the
first day we gave up trying to coax him into speech; he seemed
lost in his own thoughts and deeply disturbed by them as well.
The killing of Bule would have not affected his status with the
Corps by itself; there are tales of many such "interrogations"
that we have heard from outfits that have served us longer.
But Markham was nevertheless deeply shaken. His face was
troubled, his brow constantly beetling with perplexity, and
even his speech changed at times—he was prone to outbursts
of intense anger. At other times, he seemed lost, almost
childlike.

Four nights after the death of Bule, as we slept in
camp alongside Colonel Fine's unit, I heard the sounds of
commotion in my dreams. I woke with a start and found an
indescribable sight: Captain Markham was on the other side
of the campfire outside my tent. His form was illuminated by
the flickering flames, and they cast terrible shadows across his
face. But I will say this, and this I will testify in Northam: his
lips were curled in an expression of nothing less than joy.

His bayonet was raised above the figures of the sleeping
men. I was too late to do anything to save them. Markham
had nearly completed his crime—the murder of Privates Ford
and McIlhane.

I do not know how I sensed the situation so quickly. Perhaps I saw unconsciously the blood on the bayonet, or I intuited that the captain had lost his reason from the mad expression on his face. But I reached for my revolver and shot Markham once in the thigh, missing on the second bullet. When I came to him, dashing past the remains of Ford and McIlhane on their bedrolls and catching only a brightly lit glimpse of their savaged faces, he was raving at me, laughing and crying out in gibberish. His leg was shattered—I saw the bone at five paces—but he seemed to feel no pain. I shouted at him to be quiet, but he was beyond reason, and I had to strike him with the butt of my pistol to silence him.

I will not go into detail about the state of the bodies. There are full details in the charging documents that I provided to the Marine investigators and have no wish to revisit. As is commonly known, Ford and McIlhane were already dead or near death when I checked them. But that, of course, was only the least diabolical of Captain Markham's actions that night. When I came upon him, he had just finished removing the organs of Private Ford and had already cut up McIlhane around the midsection. Three organs—two kidneys and a heart—were carefully laid out on a clean piece of buckram that the captain formerly used for storing his sidearm. I will remember that sight for the rest of my life and for as long as my poor spirit lingers in the afterworld, of that I am sure.

I can write no more of this night. And I cannot account for Markham's actions, except to say that I believe that he was unbalanced to his core.

———

November 13th: I have only one more thing to add to this sad narrative, and it concerns our translator, Joseph. I had long been curious about what passed between Markham and Bule on that fateful day when the captain ordered me from the hut and spoke to the prisoner only in the presence of Joseph. I searched for our translator after the events; he had survived Markham's bullet, that I knew, but after being treated at one of our field hospitals, he quickly disappeared into the countryside. We hired a new translator in Plaisance, but all efforts to find Joseph were unsuccessful. The Haitians did not even wish to speak his name.

It was soon after the murders of my comrades that I came upon him. We were driving in our auto-truck toward Gonaïves to bring supplies to a unit there—tents, medical bandages, and boots, as I recall, to replace the ones that tended to rot away in the tropical heat. We were passing through a small town whose name I do not know, and Haitians were lined up on either side of the road.

I was in the passenger seat, with Private Shaughnessy from Colonel Fine's unit doing the driving, when I happened to glance out of the window and caught sight of Joseph in the mass of black faces watching the truck push its way through the streets. I cried, "Stop!" and dismounted immediately. Joseph didn't run away but only observed my approach with red-veined eyes and a slack expression.

He was much altered; the neat and even dapper man was gone, and he stood now in poor clothing: a much-used gray shirt, filthy at the cuffs and stained, with a pair of ragged black half-pants. He might have not changed the outfit he was wearing for the previous weeks, I would guess. This educated man was now indistinguishable from the mass of peasantry. I hustled him into the back of the auto-truck, made room among the provisions, and spoke to him there for the rest of the journey.

It was an odd conversation. The raw smell of clairin—

Haitian moonshine—came across the short space between us, and his speech, at least early on, was slurred. He slipped into Creole on several occasions, and I had to call him back to English, that we might continue the conversation.

"What happened in that hut?" I asked him finally.

He guffawed. "You blans! More curious than children. You must know everything. You must have everything and you must know it, too."

"Tell me what happened," I said, impatient with his new freedom with me.

"What would you like to know?"

"What did Markham ask Bule? Was it about the leadership of the cacos?"

Joseph leaned over as if he were to impart a great revelation, breathed a mouthful of clairin fumes into my face, and solemnly intoned: "No."

He sat up, laughing.

"Do not become too familiar, Joseph."

He gave me an insolent stare. "What then?" The gaiety passed out of his expression—perhaps it was the last fumes of intoxication—and the lines of his face hardened. "Why don't you ask Markham?"

"Because he's insane. He won't talk to anyone."

Joseph laughed softly to himself. "What does he eat?"

"What do you mean?"

"What does he eat, the captain? Your blan food or griot?" Griot was the local pork dish, the food of the common people here when they could afford it. I didn't respond. "He loves his griot now, yes? Yes, I'm sure."

Again he leaned over, but this time his face was serious, as if he really wished to impart a secret with no one hearing, although we could barely make ourselves heard above the shifting of the auto-truck on the road.

"Markham is dead," he whispered. "He just doesn't know it."

"What do you mean?"

Joseph stared at me contemptuously. "Just what I said. Markham believes he lives. Maybe he believes that he's been unjustly accused. Maybe he believes he's back in America, romancing some woman. Or perhaps he is suffering unimaginable torture. He experiences what Bule allows him to experience."

This was madness, and I looked at Joseph as I would a man ranting about the end of the world. With pity and solicitude. But his face was so calm, his voice as reasonable-seeming as a pastor back home discussing some minor event. It made me uneasy, and I found myself at a loss for words. What could he mean that Markham was living some kind of shadow, hermetic life?

"You are not like your captain," Joseph said finally after a minute or two of silence. "You are satisfied with the world you see, eh? Markham, oh, much different. Much. When I first met him, I expected him to carve me with his knife and ask about the cacos. That's what the Marines do, that's all they're interested in. We have a saying, you know, us Haitians: the Americans came to Haiti to see the color of our blood."

He glanced back at the receding landscape. "But Markham invited me to sit down as if we were courtiers at the presidential palace, and he offered me brandy from his private flask. He didn't ask a single question about the rebels." His eyes back on me, intent. "All he wanted to know about was Bule. You thought he was in those 'interviews' grilling the Haitians about the cacos, but he wanted to know the sorcerer's secrets. How he did his . . . magic. Yes? How he enchanted Francelow—that is the man he shot in the village—during the ceremony of voudoun. And then other questions: What had Bule done with Monk? And more so, how had he done it. Very strange questions for a blan."

I gaped at him as we bounced on the benches, the landscape of rural Haiti dancing beyond the canvas flaps.

"Ahhh, yes. Captain Markham was curious. He told me he had always been curious about the spirit world, that he had attended séances back in his home, and was a member of the Rosicrucians. He called himself a seeker."

There was a certain correspondence between what I was hearing and Markham's odd behavior.

"And that was his downfall," Joseph said.

"Why? Bule died in the fire at his compound."

Again, disdain in the Haitian's eyes. If he'd looked at me that way in the street, I might have struck him down. But I wanted to hear what he said.

"Bule," Joseph said, his eyes unfixed and his voice hoarse, "is the greatest sorcerer in Haiti for three or four generations. Since the time of Charlemagne Herivaux, or that is what they say. But even he had limits." Joseph sat back against canvas. "You see, everyone in Haiti goes to Bule, but everyone fears him, too. They will not open up themselves—" Here he put the palms of his hands together, then slowly peeled them back, as if to reveal something inside. "No, they have defenses against the likes of Bule." He slapped his hands together quickly and held them grasped together. "They know what he will do. They will not allow him in."

"I don't understand."

"Exactly. Be happy you don't understand. I told Markham this. I said, your seeking will get you more than you bargain for. But he was determined."

"So in the hut, on that final day, he didn't ask about the cacos either? He didn't ask about the rebel networks, about who was supplying them? What did he burn him for, then, if not to find out these things?"

Joseph shook his head no.

"He said, 'Bule, I admire you. I want to learn your secrets. Tell me and you will live.' "

"Impossible!" I nearly shouted.

Joseph laughed. "Believe what you want. But those were his words. I, too, was shocked. Shocked because I saw Bule thinking, thinking.

"He laughed. Bule knew that Markham couldn't grant him life. If you Americans didn't kill him, the Haitians would make them, Dartiguenave"—the president of the Senate— "and some others in the government. He'd grown much, much too powerful and now they had the chance to do away with him without being . . ." Joseph had a smile on his lips. "Contaminated. So he spit on the ground. Markham sprang at him, shouting bloody mur-deerrr. But Bule only went quiet. And soon, I knew it was done."

"What was done, Joseph?"

Instead of answering me, Joseph glanced up at the bright day. "I've been waiting for him."

"For Markham?"

Joseph laughed. "Markham is dead, I tell you. As am I. But let me ask you this—" His face was grave as I ever saw it. "The things Markham removed from the two soldiers. What was done with them?"

I gaped at him. "The organs, you mean?"

"Yes."

"I couldn't possibly—"

Joseph's voice rose. "They are part of Bule's power now. He was feeding his spirit, do you see? You must not let them be offered to the fire. If those organs are brought to the flame, Bule will grow even stronger. And that will not be so good for you."

"For me?" I said.

"How many children do you have, Sergeant?" he asked, with concern in his eyes.

"That is none of your affair."

"Let me give you this one piece of advice. When you return to America, move as far away from Captain Markham's home-place as you can." He coughed. "And should you find your family plagued by strange illnesses and terrible ends, do not think that you are the victim of bad luck. Seek the evildoer among the descendants of your squadron. The squadron, Sergeant. That's where you will find the traveler. Do you understand me?"

Joseph had clearly passed into the realm of delirium tremens, or outright madness. I could get no more sense out of him after that. He simply stared at the ribbon of road spilling out behind us, as if lost in reverie. After a few more questions, I gave up.

I felt Joseph had been wrongly done by Markham, and I was struck to see him so fallen. I reached into my pocket and pulled out a few dollars and handed them to him. He took them without thanks. "Tell your driver to let me out here."

I did, and Joseph marched off, swaying as he went, the clairin still not out of his system.

I resumed my seat next to the driver, but I saw only that yard in Saint-Michel-de-l'Attalaye and Markham stumbling from the hut. I went over and over it again, but I couldn't make any sense of Joseph's ramblings. Did he mean that Bule had cursed Markham somehow? Or were the two in league together, consorts in some evil I still didn't comprehend?

It was a long trip to Gonaïves, and I wished to God I had never come to Haiti.

CHAPTER FORTY-EIGHT

John Bailey stood in front of Stephanie Godwin's door and rang the bell. A light rain drizzled on the flagstones behind him. It sounded far off, a feeble rattle, as if the electric current in the house were running low. Nothing moved behind the three diamond-shaped windows in the wooden door; no breath of wind stirred the little lace curtains that covered them on the inside.

He took a deep breath. If he was going to tell his boss that zombies—no, *nzombes*, as Nat had told him—were running wild all over Northam, he needed to get his ducks in a row. He had to be able to say Chuck Godwin was wandering the woods and have his wife, Stephanie, to back him up on that little fact. That's why he was here. To get her on board in case he needed to go to the chief.

He didn't know what else to do. Nothing else made sense right now.

John clomped his size-13 boots impatiently on the red-colored porch. He couldn't believe he was standing here, but that was his life now. The shock of Charlie holding John's gun in his mouth hadn't left him; it had simply joined the other stream of images that had turned everything into a continuous walking nightmare.

Finally, the thin lace curtain that hung over the bottom window trembled and John saw an eye with pale flesh around it regard him from the corner.

"Mrs. Godwin?" he called. "It's Detective Bailey. Can we talk for a minute?"

The curtain dropped, and it was as if the eye had never been there. The door didn't open. No sound came out of the house. John grimaced and leaned on the doorbell. What was the city coming to, when people stopped talking to cops? John walked along the porch, whose red paint was chipping and showing the cement beneath, and ducked his head to look in the picture window.

The living room was sunk in a green aquarium light, dark at the edges. There was a red knit throw on the couch, trailing down to the carpeted floor, as if someone had been taking a nap and just gotten up.

He returned to the railing, turning his back to the house. He looked up and down the street. What the fuck was going on here?

Something caught his eye to the east. It was in the Raitliff Woods, high up on a slope. Must be half a mile away. Something glowing red. *Did some idiot start a fire up there?* John thought. He watched it for a moment, trying to remember the last time he'd seen flames in that forest. Never, that's when . . .

He shivered, gritting his teeth. He watched to see if the flames, which were sending up a pall of dirty gray smoke, were spreading. But the fire wasn't moving. Maybe it was kids, he thought; kids playing Lewis and Clark, roasting some marshmallows or passing around a bottle of cheap schnapps, had let their campfire get out of control and touched off a grove of pines. But he was uneasy, and he couldn't take his eyes from the flames that were sending a dark plume of smoke into the drifting mists that covered large swathes of the forest.

Finally, he pulled his gaze from the woods and went back to the door, pulled open the screen door, and gave the wood three hearty raps.

Silence. Then a shuffling. Like feet being dragged on a carpet.

Suddenly John heard a rasping noise as the handle of the door was being slowly turned. It caught, and then the door swung open. John Bailey lowered his head and peered into the greenish gloom as the door was pulled back.

"Mrs. Godwin, is that you?"

She was standing by the open door, her hands down by her side. She was wearing a white cardigan, a rust-colored turtleneck, and rumpled khakis. She glanced past him out into the street, her eyes startled and fearful.

"Hi, it's Detective Bailey. Can I come in?"

She said nothing, but turned and walked into the room.

"Now *she's* gone off the fucking deep end?" Bailey muttered as he followed her inside.

The house smelled of . . . tomato soup. And stale, unwashed flesh.

John walked through the living room, with a stunted Christmas tree in the corner, pine needles dropped to the pomegranate-colored Oriental carpet. He found her in the kitchen. She was sitting at the table, staring at the plastic roses in a delicate green vase that served as a centerpiece, as if she'd never seen the things before. A clock on the wall was clicking loudly into the musty air. The kitchen walls seemed to reflect the sound back so that either the ticking or its echo was always hanging in the room.

He sat down in a padded black-and-white chair, the corner of the table between them. There was a white plastic tablecloth with yellow flowers on it, and Mrs. Godwin rested her arms heavily on it.

"Mrs. Godwin, are you okay?" he said.

The woman looked in his direction as if there were no one sitting in his chair.

"Everything good?" he prompted her again.

She nodded once.

"Has anyone come to visit you?"

Her eyes shot up to look at John. "Visit?" she said worriedly.

"Yeah, your kids?" Shit, he didn't know if they had kids in the area. "Or neighbors? This can be a tough time."

"No one's come. No one needs to come." There was a light in her eyes now.

"I came to talk about your husband."

"Everything's fine," she said, and a smile spread across her dry lips.

"Fine? I believe you talked to Dr. Thayer . . ."

"Everything," she said, turning to him with her dry, sagging face, "is fine."

The clock was ticking, but he thought he heard another sound, a shuffling again. When he waited for the clock strike to fade, it was gone.

Mrs. Godwin watched him.

"No more sightings of your husband?"

Her eyes. They were that of a . . . a hardened person. One of the wiseasses he picked up for phoning in death threats to school or a homeless guy who'd been on the streets for years. A bully's eyes, maybe.

Again, the sound. It seemed to be coming from the hallway that probably led to the bedrooms in the back of the house. He looked more closely. The hallway was in shadow, with waist-high wood paneling and mint-green paint above it. The only light was coming through the window in the kitchen, dank gray January sunlight. He could swear someone was shuffling, pacing, back there. But it was the barest whisper.

Her eyes followed his.

"Is there anyone else here, Mrs. Godwin?"

The eyelids drooped. "Here?" The smile again.

"In the house."

Tock. Tick-tock. Tick.

"No, I don't believe so."

John studied her. She seemed to be waiting for a blow. She reached up and, with a finger, pulled the rust-colored turtleneck away from her throat.

"Do you want me to check?" he said.

The house was still now, silent. John's hand dropped to his lap and inched back toward his gun.

His mouth was dry. There was nowhere safe from the strangeness now. Not even this widow's house.

The whispering sound again.

"No. Everything is fine."

John felt his heart thump.

"Just give me the word and I'll do a check."

He needed her permission to search the house. But what would he do if he found Chuck Godwin hiding back there in a closet, his face all bashed up from the car accident? What would he do then?

Her eyes swung up to his. *Is this woman a prisoner?* he thought. *What's keeping her here?*

For a wild moment, he wanted out of the house. The image of Charlie flashed into his head. He had to get home, check on the boy. A crazy vision filled his mind: Charlie, his throat cut, trying to say something with the flap of severed pulpy flesh gushing little streams of blood, just like Margaret Post.

Her eyes were filled with an appeal.

"Mrs. Godwin?"

Her lips moved, but nothing came out.

"What is it?"

She swallowed. "No need."

John sat there. The shuffling had not resumed.

Games. Someone is playing games.

"Is your husband in the house?"

Her look was dead, the eyes of a drowned woman, the eyes filming over from too long in the water.

"You need to leave now," she said. "Please don't come here again."

CHAPTER FORTY-NINE

Nat was walking toward the town square. The journal of Sergeant Godwin was back home, on the arm of the leather couch. He had to get away from it, to clear his head.

The cold assaulted him, sending drafts of frigid air up his pant legs and down the back of his neck. He shivered and increased his pace.

There could be no more doubt after reading the journal. The traveler was here, among them, *in* one of them, if the translator Joseph was right. The feeling of doom that had been lurking in the back of his mind—*Nothing will ever turn out good again*—was now front and center. The only redeeming thing was that his and Becca's fates were now one. Their ancestors had bound them together, joined their hands in the darkness of the Haitian jungle.

It was as if she were with him now, as if the warmth he felt were coming partly from her touch. The almost physical discomfort he'd always felt when anyone tried to get close to him was gone—he wanted to be near Becca, and he felt that, out there in the ether, was a response from her. *Yes. Now.* He didn't feel wild or reckless; he felt that he had something he wanted, at all costs, to protect.

He turned on State, choked with shoppers. Must be the post–New Year's sales, thought Nat, merchants trying to stretch the holidays a couple of weeks. He passed a gaggle of Wartham students and an elderly couple who walked ahead of him with stooped, uncertain steps. Nat thought of Buenos Aires, of getting away from this black hole of a city in winter. But now he wanted to escape with Becca. And forever.

Nat crossed over State toward the town square, the white steam of his breath blurring his vision. There were more shoppers, a scrum of teenagers weaving through the crowd. As Nat stepped up on the sidewalk, the crowd parted for a moment, and there, sitting on one of the green wrought iron benches at the edge of the park, was Becca Prescott, wrapped in a thick coat, the lower part of her face hidden by a big black-and-red scarf. Nat stopped. He wasn't surprised or alarmed to see her, or even that he'd picked her out from the hundreds of people walking or resting on this busy square. His mood ticked upward, and he strode toward her, smiling.

She was crying, or had been.

"Becca?" he said, sitting next to her on the bench.

"Yes?"

"Everything okay?"

She nodded her head, then again more vigorously.

"Yes. Yes, Nat?"

It was the first time she'd said his name without prompting. It sounded strange and wonderful to his ears.

"What happened?" he said, moving closer to her on the thin struts of the bench.

"I remembered," she said, tears glittering in her eyes.

"You . . . What did you remember?"

Her gaze sharpened. Nat followed her eyes and saw only Hartigan's liquor store across the street and the long wool coats of Northam citizens striding past it, mixed in with the bright down jackets of the Wartham girls.

"I saw my brother. Chase."

Nat frowned. "You saw him *here*?"

"No," she said, laughing. God, he'd never heard her really laugh before, he thought; never heard this light rill escaping so naturally from her mouth. "Chase is dead. I know that. What I remembered was him giving me a ride on his shoulders when I was just eight or nine. I *saw* it, Nat."

"Okay."

"We were walking down State Street. That's why I had to come out and look at it again. We were right there"—she pointed with her finger just to the left of Hartigan Liquors's front window, stocked with bottles of every color—"and it was Easter time and I was wearing a new kelly green dress, and Chase wanted to carry me on his shoulders. To show me off, he said. My father . . ."

She turned to face him. Nat studied her brown eyes, as clear and as happy as he'd ever seen them. *Could she have been released?* he thought. *Could she be free from the thing that haunted her?*

"Walter Prescott, my *father*." And another tear escaped her eye, but Nat saw that she was crying for happiness.

"Exactly," Nat said. "Your father."

"My father said to Chase: 'If you think you're strong enough.' And Chase let out this little laugh, like, *Are you kidding me?* And he lifted me up." Becca slowly raised her hand and touched it to the side of her arm. "I could feel it, Nat. I could feel the pressure of his hand. Just a minute ago. I remembered it like it had just happened."

Nat shook his head. "That's . . . terrific."

"And he picked me up and we walked down there." She pointed to Mrs. Cathay's Ice Cream Shoppe, which had been on the corner of State and Prince forever. It had four-foot cardboard candy canes pasted to the doorway, along with lots of silver tinsel and a smattering of blue Christmas decorations left over from the holidays. Nat smiled.

Her mouth fell open slightly. "My father called it promenading. We were *promenading down State Street*. And I had a mint chocolate chip, a child's size. It cost a dollar twenty-five, and my father paid."

"Sugar cone or regular?"

She laughed again. "Sugar. Who would eat a regular?"

Nat laughed, and she joined in. Her hand reached for his. "I know they're dead, but now they're mine again. I miss them, but missing them is so much better than . . ." A dark cloud seemed to pass across her face. "Nat, maybe I didn't die. I'm here with you, right?"

"Yes."

She laughed. "Pinch me."

He did, on her thigh. The touch sent a shock of pleasure up his arm.

"Ow!" she yelped, and the bright laughter made her cheeks bunch and spilled the tears in her eyes out sideways.

Maybe I was all wrong, Nat thought. *Maybe everything will be okay.*

But then he remembered Captain Markham and the names of the squadron and he looked away.

"I have to bring you home," he said.

"No!" she said, her voice burbling with suppressed laughter. "Let's get ice cream. Cherry vanilla for me."

Her cheeks were reddened by the cold and the tips of her ears. She seemed, finally, to feel as young as she was. Nineteen. She looked nineteen for the first time.

"Okay. Ice cream. Then home."

CHAPTER FIFTY

After he dropped Becca at her house and checked the perimeter, Nat headed back to town, to the grocery store near his condo—who knew you still had to shop for orange juice and coffee when the world was falling apart? he thought. After he'd finished his shopping, he drove to the Northam Museum to have a talk with Atkins. It took longer than he expected, and he didn't emerge from the museum entrance until after one p.m. As he emerged, his eyes fell on a stack of the *Northam News* piled in a plastic display case. He picked a copy off the stack. *Disappearance of Lawyer Mystifies Officials*, read the headline.

There were now two people and one corpse missing. The body of Chuck Godwin, the lawyer whose widow had come to visit Nat, had disappeared. Elizabeth Dyer, that unpleasant woman he'd met at the morgue, hadn't been to work in two days. And another morgue employee, Jimmy Stearns, was AWOL, though there seemed to be less concern about him. Judging by his address in a bleak part of the Shan, Nat guessed that Jimmy's friends didn't have the attention span or the clout to get the city to notice the man's disappearance. But Elizabeth Dyer had been someone of substance and, more than that, a woman who hadn't missed a day of work in three solid years.

Blood had been found at the morgue where the two worked, and there were fears that Stearns had kidnapped—or killed—his fellow employee, then disappeared. The chances that they'd "run off together," as one police spokesman put it, seemed low. "We don't know what happened, we just want to talk with them," the cop had told the newspaper. Their credit cards and ATM cards hadn't been used; Elizabeth's car was still parked in the morgue parking lot. Odd. There was no connection made to the Margaret Post case, though it had to be on people's minds. There was far too much violence happening in Northam, relative to its size. It was starting to sound like Hartford or Boston.

There was a separate story on the Post murder. Her parents were offering a $50,000 reward for information leading to the arrest of the killer, with the city chipping in an additional $25,000. A Northam PD spokesman was quoted as saying the investigation was ongoing and that no persons of interest had yet been identified. The city was clearly desperate to be seen as taking the case seriously. Nat guessed the $25,000 was just the beginning.

Nat looked up and down the snowy street, almost empty of pedestrians. Three Wartham students were hurrying home to their dorms, bags tucked under their arms, their chins tucked deep in blue-and-white scarves, the school colors.

Nat pulled out his phone, thumbed to the recent calls, and hit a name.

"John."

"Yeah," John Bailey's sleep-bleary voice rasped on the other end.

Nat was watching the man at the end of the street. He turned, blowing a wreath of steam into the air, then began to retrace his steps. He reached his hand up, and it disappeared beneath the hood. *Trying to keep warm*, Nat thought.

"I found something," he said.

"What?" John said. "Nat, you there? What the hell did you find?"

"I know why people are dying," he said.

The sound of John's breathing. "Why?" he said.

"I'll be there in ten," Nat said.

CHAPTER FIFTY-ONE

Ramona steered the Altima up Hanover Road. The weather was crisp, the dome of sky above the wall eggshell blue. Ramona's heart was palpitating as she came to the tree where they'd found Margaret. She slowed down and stared at the ash's black branches spread out against the red wall. *I wonder if the killer grabbed her here,* she thought, *because he wanted every Wartham girl to have to pass the spot of her murder again and again, so that we would remember that none of us is safe.* That was one of the latest theories she'd come across online. Jezebel had done a whole roundup of theories on the Wartham murder. Ramona usually tried to steer clear of the rampant gossip surrounding Margaret's death; it was grotesque to see her life dissected by people who'd never known her. But that one little nugget had stayed with her.

She hit the gas and made the right into Wartham, passing under the arch that read *Terras Irradient,* the Altima's front end groaning as she made the wide turn. The car always made her self-conscious when she was on campus. It had made her even more conspicuous among the brightly colored Fiat 500s and the Beemer 3-series that dotted the campus like pieces of candy. The car was twelve years old and loud; the noises from its engine seemed to bounce off the Johnson Chapel with enough force to break its windows. Ramona had to get the damn thing looked at, even if she couldn't afford the repairs.

She didn't want to be any more exposed than she already felt. Ramona pressed the accelerator and made her way down

Johnson Drive, past the chapel. She could feel the girls on the paths, walking home from the dining hall, their books held high up, turning to look. *The hell with them,* she thought. *At least I have wheels.* Most of them had to wait for Mommy and Daddy to come pick them up in the Jag, but Ramona Best was *mobile.* The thought failed to lighten the darkness of her mood, which had been steadily deflating all the way up 95 North.

The Altima edged over a little hump in the road. She turned down Raitliff Road and touched the brake as the car's nose tipped downward, accelerating slightly down the little hill. When she reached the bottom, Ramona swung the car into the lot behind her dorm. She parked near the door in the back. Exit strategy.

She took out her little two-day bag and headed in the back entrance. When she opened the door, the dorm smell came rushing out to greet her—it always smelled like floor wax, baby powder, and one other ingredient she never was able to nail down. White girls, maybe.

Ramona started up the stairs. Martina Webb came down toward her, munching on a celery stick.

"Oh, hey, Ramona."

Martina was a thin, acne-pocked sophomore, plain as anything, and a generally pleasant person. Ramona never felt she needed to be on her guard with her.

"Hi."

Martina leaned back on the steel railing and pointed with the celery. "Been away?"

Ramona nodded.

"Went home?"

"Yes, Martina. I went home."

Martina made a face. "Wish I could. But I've got papers up to my tits."

"Already? Classes have barely started."

"Some leftover stuff." Martina looked more closely at Ramona. "Are you okay, hon?"

"I don't have cancer, Martina. I'm not recovering from anything. And good for what? Forgetting about Margaret?"

Martina made a face. "We all miss her."

"No, 'we' don't," Ramona said quickly. Then her face softened. "But I do believe you do."

Martina sniffled and came in for a hug. Ramona gave her a brief one, no patting on the back, then picked up her bag and started up the stairs.

The unadorned door of her room, with its plain black plate reading 2C screwed into the wood, made her tear up a little. Feeling in her bag for the keys, she glanced down and saw the white stuff along the floor at the door's bottom edge. She didn't need to touch it to know what it was.

Salt. A line of salt.

————

Nat drove to John Bailey's house. The porch light was off.

It was odd. *You want to show criminals you're home,* John had always told him. *Forget that movie shit about turning off all the lights when you think they're ready to break into your house. Most thieves and burglars are cowards. Show them you're home and they'll go away.*

But the lights were off now.

Nat pulled into the driveway and parked behind John's Malibu.

The pathway was shining palest blue in the evening light. He went up and knocked softly on the door. It immediately cracked open an inch, and Nat saw John's pale, haggard face. Nat could see the glint of gunmetal pointed straight at his belly button.

"It's not me you have to worry about," Nat said. Where had he heard that before?

But the door didn't open.

"John."

"What'd you find out, Nat?"

"It was Maggie Voorhees. She's come back to kill us all."

The eyes were remote, unamused. "What . . . did . . . you . . . find?"

Nat frowned. "A list."

Five seconds ticked by. Then the door opened.

"Sorry," John said, waving him in with the gun barrel.

Nat entered quickly and shut the door behind him.

"Answering the door with your gun?" he asked John. "Are you all right, buddy?"

John sat heavily on the couch, crunching the front section of the *Boston Globe* under him. He was dressed in a white T-shirt and his blue Pats shorts. His skin looked unhealthy, and his right hand was shaking. He laid the gun on a side table.

"I don't know what got into me. Maybe I'm losing my fucking mind."

"I'd keep it in the safe, if I were you."

John closed his eyes and rubbed his eyelids vigorously with his index fingers. After a minute, he gave a quick nod. "You're probably right."

Nat went to the window and peered out between the curtains.

"What list?" John said.

Outside the edges of things were glowing with frost—trees, mailboxes, the crust of snow over the trimmed grass.

Nat brought the book out of a zippered carrying case he usually carried his laptop in. He flipped through the pages as he walked toward John. At the back of the book was a list of the squadron members. He stopped there and handed the journal to John. "Here," he said.

John looked at him dubiously. "What is it?"

"It's a diary by a member of a squadron from the Marines

2nd Regiment. The regiment was sent to Haiti in the summer of 1919. I won't get into the reasons, but it was basically a re-store-order kind of mission. We occupied the country for the next seventeen years; the 2nd Regiment was the second wave of troops going in. They sailed from Baltimore harbor in June 1919. Part of the regiment was a squadron under a Captain Thomas Markham. The squadron was all from around here. Northam men."

John stared dully at the pages. "John Prescott," he said. "Ezra Dyer."

"Yep."

John's eye slid down the list. He stopped. "I'll be a son of a bitch. Otis Bailey."

"Your great-great-grandfather?" Nat said.

"Yeah. I knew he was in the Marines, but I never knew he'd gone to Haiti."

"He did. They all did. And when they were down there, something ugly happened. Bad enough that the squadron leader, Captain Markham, was brought back here and hanged in the town square."

"I'll be a son of a bitch," John said again.

Nat stared at his friend. "Look at the next name."

"Vincent DeMott. So what?"

"What was the name of the first guy that Chase Prescott killed when he went on his little rampage?"

John's forehead wrinkled. "Matt DeMott."

"It wasn't an accident," Nat said.

John was staring at the rug. "Margaret Post, too?"

Nat moved closer to John and pointed at the list of squadron members. The third name was Steven Post. "I checked Genealogy.com. He was Margaret's great-great-uncle."

"So Margaret is the last of his relatives?"

"No. The last one in Northam. The literature says that the

traveler can only work within a certain range, so any cousins in California or wherever are probably safe. For the moment."

"That's why Margaret's parents, the missionaries, aren't dead? Because they lived in Brazil."

"That's my guess. But I'd get them the hell out of town if I were you."

John stared at the page. His lips moved.

"Okay. So everyone who's died or gone missing recently has a relative on this list. Post. Dyer. Godwin." His brow wrinkled. "John Thayer," he read.

"My mother's grandfather."

John rubbed his eyes with the palms of his hands and then stared at the carpet. "Do we know they're related, or are we guessing?"

"We know. I just spent some time with Mr. Atkins at the Northam museum. Not the most pleasant two hours of my life, I can tell you. We went over genealogies of some of the twelve families: Markham, Kelly, Monk, Ford, Prescott, Dyer, Godwin, Bailey, Thayer, Post, DeMott, and McIlhane. I thought we might find some mysterious deaths there, some evidence that our killer had been working at, let's say, pruning the family trees before he got down to our generation. Atkins and I had the town death records for the past hundred years."

"And?"

"I underestimated him. It. In fact, his work is almost done."

"What?"

Nat pulled a sheet of paper from his right front pocket. "You want the box score?" he said bitterly. "McIlhane and Ford were murdered by Captain Markham. Unmarried and childless, both of them. Markham was executed here. No children. Kelly died in Haiti two weeks after Bule's death. He blew his head off with his Marine-issued Springfield rifle. He was just eighteen years old and had no wife or kids that we know of. Ford went insane soon after, ran amuck in the camp outside Port-au-Prince, hacking at soldiers with his bayonet. He was shot in the chest by a Marine guard, died three days later. No descendants either."

"So who's next?"

Nat shrugged. "Let's go with Private Post. He made it back to Northam, married a local girl, Sarah Bishop, and had three children."

The word *children* slowed Nat down. He cleared his throat and his voice quieted just a bit. He read from the sheet of paper in his hand. "Nicholas Post died, age twelve, as a result of a boating accident on Brooks Pond. No newspaper reports to be found, possibility of foul play unknown. Balthazar Post was employed as a forger in the ironworks over on the east side and died at age seventeen, poisoned himself with an industrial dye. Delphine Post survived, married, and had two children. Mary—"

"Enough!" John cried.

Nat stopped reading.

"They all died?" John said.

"Not all, obviously. We're here. Some members of the squadron survived long enough to have children, some escaped with a natural death. But yeah, the rate of suicides, murders, and accidental deaths was much higher for the descendants than for the general population in Northam."

John rubbed a hand through his greasy hair. "Who's left?"

Nat felt he'd burdened John enough already. "You sure you want to know?"

"Yeah."

"Of the original families? In Northam? Margaret's dad, me, you . . ." He stopped.

"Charlie," John said.

Nat was about to say, *Nothing's gonna happen to Charlie*, but he and John had never been bullshitters, so he just said, "Yeah.

And Becca Prescott," and his mind filled with an image of her face. He set his jaw. "He's in some kind of a hurry."

"You can say that again. Speaking of which, I visited the widow Godwin. She's half off her rocker."

"I had her at the clinic. She's convinced her dead husband is walking the hills."

"Crazy is what it is," John said. "But hold on. What about Jimmy Stearns?"

"No relation to the squadron. Did you find out anything about him?"

"Not a lot there. Local, kept to himself. Seemed to have a crush on the Dyer woman, from what some of his friends said."

"Maybe he got in the way."

"But why all this killing now? What happened?"

"Who knows? Maybe the traveler's found a powerful host, someone whose gifts are stronger than anyone before. The binding is the combination of two souls. Maybe the traveler has met . . . another powerful spirit."

Nat let the journal fall onto the coffee table.

"You know, my mother always said the family was cursed. Mental illness, alcoholism, strange accidents that were probably suicide."

The two men stared at each other.

"But now we know, old man," Nat said. "Now we can stop it."

"Stop it how?"

The question Nat had been turning over and over in his mind all night. "By finding the traveler."

John's eyes asked, *Then what?* As if he knew the answer but didn't want to say it out loud.

"And then we kill him or her before the spirit has a chance to jump to another host."

"But Charlie . . . ," John said.

"What about Charlie?"

John pursed his lips. "What if I took him out of town?"

Nat stared at his friend, then dropped his gaze. "Would Leah let you do that?"

John closed his eyes. "No. She wants him near her mother, to keep an eye on us."

"What would happen if you did it anyway?"

"I'd lose him for good, probably."

Nat thought that over. "I'm not sure it matters, John. When the traveler's done here, it'll move on to its next set of victims. Might as well keep him close."

CHAPTER FIFTY-TWO

The next morning, John drove down Hanover Road and parked thirty yards down from the tree where Margaret Post had been hung. He waited for two cars to pass him, then made a U-turn and parallel-parked between a Land Cruiser and a Jeep Cherokee. John killed the engine, hit the button to pop the trunk, and got out. Inside the trunk was the rake he'd placed there after breakfast. He hoisted it out and carried it across the street.

He was tired of thinking about *nzombes* and spirits and travelers and the rest of it. That was Nat's specialty; Nat was smarter than him and would figure it out. He'd decided to go back to what he knew. He was going back to inspect the crime scene again. Forensics had inspected the site, but it never hurt to look again.

Should have done it a few days ago, John thought. *This voodoo shit has me all discombobulated.* Back to basics now: hard work and a fucking Glock 19 on his hip.

But he didn't want the *Northam News* spotting him out here and coming around to ask questions. He hadn't brought any crime scene tape or any of that. He was wearing his old green Dockers work pants that he used to work around the house, and a Red Sox ball cap. If people mistook him for a Wartham maintenance man prettying up the shrubbery, it was all good. No one needed to know.

John stood in front of the tree and studied the thick branch where he'd found Margaret's wrists tied. It looked normal. Only a thin strip of bark missing where the rope had scraped against the tree as Margaret struggled for her life. The breeze kicked up, and the bare branches above his head began to knock into one another in a whispery rhythm. In between the hard *clacks*, he could hear the indrawn breath of the wind.

He inspected the foot of the tree. The day of the murder, it had been drizzling. The branches above, even without their leaves, had protected the ground from any rain falling directly on it, but eventually the water had seeped through and dripped onto the ground. There'd been a struggle when the killer grabbed Margaret, a hell of a struggle, he'd guessed. He'd remembered the ground being all mashed up, no footprints as such—he'd checked, and forensics had confirmed—just churned-up mud. Now John dropped the teeth of the rake onto the far edge of the patch and said a little prayer. *Let me just find something, God. Lead me to the killer.*

He pulled on the rake handle. The metal prongs kicked up dirt as they went, and objects shot out ahead of the moving pile of dirt. John leaned over, picked up the biggest one—a rock— and tossed it aside. When he'd reached the end of the dirt patch, he went back and sifted the freed-up dirt, sweeping through the grit slowly with his big hand. Nothing.

He took up the handle and went back to the far edge, resting the last tooth in the final row he'd made on the first run. Then he jerked back and pulled it through again.

Two Heineken bottle caps and three more rocks on the second pull. John bent down and picked up one of the bottle caps, brought it out onto the sidewalk to get a little sunlight on it. It showed faint ridges of light red rust running along the creases where the opener had bent the metal. That had to take a little time, he thought. The caps had been down in the mud a couple of weeks at least, which told him he was going deep enough with the rake.

He tossed the cap and went back to the patch, lifted the rake to the edge, and pulled. Nothing this time, just clumps of mud and a few broken twigs that had been trampled down into the earth. An SUV came riding up Hanover, a silver Honda Pilot, slowing as it approached John. He pivoted away, toward the brick wall, and leaned on the rake, pretending to rest. The car slowed even further; John stood there, willing the SUV to keep moving. Finally, the engine revved and he saw the Pilot continue down the street.

John walked slowly back, moved the rake farther to the left, and went again. He was halfway through the patch when something silver and dirt-encrusted spit out from the right side of the rake. It disappeared into the churned-up mud, and John leaned on the rake, looking for it. *Where the hell'd it go?* He walked around the edge of the patch, propped the rake on the brick wall, and returned, squatting down over the last place he saw the flash of silver. John slowly ran his fingers over the center of the mud patch, sifting, feeling for something odd. He brushed away the top layer of dirt—as light as chocolate shavings—and peered at the stuff beneath it. Nothing. He grunted, moved left a few inches, and repeated the procedure.

I'm sure I saw something, he thought. *Too heavy to be an old pull tab from a soda can, and too evenly shaped to be a piece of slate or a shiny rock. Where the hell—*

He brushed a little mound of dirt with his fingers and there it was. A little glint of silver. John picked it up and began to rub the dirt away with his thumb. It was a medal, round and heavy in his hand. It showed a bearded man striding across what looked like a river with a little boy on his back, the man's calves half submerged in the water.

John Bailey knew his saints. There it was, written at the bottom in raised letters: *St. Christopher protect us.*

I'll be damned, he thought.

He turned it over. On the back, in flowing script, was written: *To Becca, from her father, 4-9-2008.*

CHAPTER FIFTY-THREE

Charlie entered his Gmail password—*Patriots88*—and his in-box came up. There were two new e-mails, the first from someone called FoxyRedhead, but he quickly deleted it and moved down to the next one. It read *LeahSD72*. That was Mommy.

He opened the e-mail:

My big boy—

Don't worry about Daddy, he's probably just working too much. As usual. Has he yelled at you a lot? Charlie, has he hit you ever, even once? I won't get Daddy in trouble but that's something you can always tell Mommy.

I don't want you to tell Daddy this, but I'm planning a surprise visit—well, it's not much of a surprise anymore, is it?!!—in a few weeks when I can get away from work. I will come to see you as soon as I fly into the airport. There might even be an early birthday present in my luggage, but only if you can be a good boy and keep our secret. I don't know about an Xbox, baby, Mommy's job isn't giving her the hours she needs, but I will bring you something special.

Charlie, if Daddy does anything that really scares you, just let me know and I'll send Grandma over to get you right away. That might get me in trouble, but don't worry about that. We're a team, right? You and me. So if you feel afraid, EVER, just write me.

I'll see you soon, baby, and we'll go for ice cream at Mrs. Cathay's, I don't care how cold it is. The ice cream out here is so terrible you wouldn't believe it.

Don't worry, my love. I'll see you soon.

Love,
Mommy

Charlie frowned and clicked the *Sign Out* button and turned off the power. He stared at the dark screen.

He wanted to see his mother, but he was afraid of a fight between her and daddy. And why didn't she tell him what to do? Maybe there was a medicine his Daddy needed. Or a book he could get to tell him what was wrong.

Charlie didn't even want the Xbox anymore. He just wanted his daddy to go back to being normal.

———

John sighed deeply. He was sitting in the front seat of his car. Between the pad of his thumb and his right index finger was the St. Christopher's medal, turned upside down. He was rubbing it as his thoughts wandered, always returning to the same uncomfortable place. He could feel the scratchy outline of the inscription underneath his thumb.

He was thinking of Nat. *This will kill the poor bastard*, he thought. John often worried about Nat being alone, *wanting* to be alone. As much as John kidded the guy about his primo bachelor existence, Nat took it to extremes. He'd never let himself care about anyone, except Charlie and himself. It was like they were the only real human connections the man had. He was the most popular loner John had ever met, always keeping people just far enough away so that they wouldn't have any claims on him.

But Becca? Nat's eyes went wide when he talked about her. The girl had gotten to him.

And now this.

"Goddamn it," John said quietly, rubbing his right temple with his fingers. A headache was taking root right under the skull. What if Becca *had* killed Margaret Post? It was, at best, a murder by—what do you call it? Murder by proxy—he remembered it from one of his academy classes. That's when you convince someone to kill on your behalf.

But what do you do when the real killer might be some dark presence, a long-dead Haitian sorcerer? And could Becca Prescott really have slit Margaret's throat, gutted the poor girl, while that thing was inside her? Goading Becca on?

John closed his eyes tight and rubbed his temple harder. The headache seemed to shoot its tentacles to every part of his brain. *Go back to what you know, John. Police work. Bring the woman in and charge her if she's the one. At least you'll get one of the creatures off the street.*

"Ah, hell," he said, picking his phone up off the center console and dialing Nat's number.

———

In his condo, Nat sat back slowly on his couch, his cell phone to his ear.

"What's going on?" he said.

John's voice was scratchy, and sounded far away. "There's been a development in the Margaret Post case. I found something. I'm coming over—"

"Just tell me."

He heard John sigh. "I found a piece of jewelry belonging to Becca."

Nat closed his eyes, a feeling of dread rising in his gut. "Where?"

"Right under the tree. Where the struggle was."

Nat, his eyes still closed. He saw in his mind not Becca's face but the gouges in her wooden door, down the gloom of that airless hallway. He could not keep the thought away: What if it wasn't a possessed Walter Prescott who was chopping at that door, screaming to kill his innocent daughter? What if Walter seized a rare moment of sanity, when the traveler's "thought stream" was weak, and tried to kill the source of his misery and his family's destruction? What if that was the true message of those horrible murderous gashes on her door?

"Fuck," he said finally. "John—"

"Take it easy, bro."

"Listen to me. Even if it's her . . ."

"Nat, I know—"

"No, you don't. Even if it's her, it's not *really* her. Okay? Do you hear what I'm saying?"

"I hear you. But Nat, listen to me . . . what if she's the one?"

A feeling of horror spread through Nat's mind like black ink. "The one what?"

"Nat. The traveler."

"Don't you think I'd *know*?" Nat practically shouted.

There was a pause. Nat knew what John was thinking. Chase Prescott—the murderer. The random murderer who'd gone off to Williamstown and shot innocent people in cold blood, people he didn't even know. But at least one of his victims turned out to be the great-great-nephew of Private DeMott of the Marine squadron in Haiti.

Maybe the traveler had passed through the Prescott family like a snake dropping down branches of a tree. Using one member of the family, then killing him off and finding another host. Nestled in that gloom-ridden house. Orchestrating the deaths of the twelve families, including the Prescotts. History repeating itself every generation, over and over.

Now Becca was the last one.

"Nat?" John's voice was quiet again. The gentle giant. Worried about his little boy. Worried about Becca causing Charlie to hang him—

Nat shut the thought out.

"Meet me at her house," Nat said tersely. "It'll be quicker."

"All right," John said. Nat heard the ignition kick in in the background.

Nat put down the phone and closed his eyes. He began to shake. *What if it's true? How am I to know?*

He could not shake the depression sweeping through his mind. It was as if a black hood had been thrown over his head. *It's not just that the worst will come true,* he thought. *But I am part of the darkness that is coming.*

I invited evil into my life, he thought, *and now I have to pay the price.* Nat opened his mouth but nothing came out. He felt his skin go cold. He suddenly cupped his hand over his mouth.

The worst part isn't here yet, but it's coming, he thought. *It's coming it's coming it's coming.*

CHAPTER FIFTY-FOUR

Nat was waiting in his car, the driver-side window down to get some air, when John pulled up. Snow drifted down lazily like confetti. His friend's Malibu pulled in front of the Prescott driveway. Old cop trick, he knew. Block the exit, but make it seem casual.

John approached the car, slapping a long black flashlight against his thigh. Nat watched him come.

"You okay?" John said, leaning on the Saab's door.

"Yeah."

Nat took a deep breath, turned the key in the ignition to give the Saab some power, and slid the driver's window up against the snow. He got out of the car, taking a deep breath, the air so cold it had a taste, like raw peppermint.

"You look like shit, buddy," John said, a sorrowful smile on his face.

"I know."

"I can do this if you want to stay out here."

"No," Nat said grimly. "I'm okay."

They walked up the path toward the house.

Nat glanced up. 96 Endicott looked shabby in the light. It needed a fresh coat of paint. Was the thing already decaying now that Walter was gone? How odd to think that this malicious place needed primer and varnish just like any ordinary house.

"You think she's in here?" John said as they stepped onto the porch.

"Probably. She only goes out . . ."

He didn't finish the sentence. They approached the door.

"Can I see it?" Nat asked as they paused in front of the entrance.

John searched in the pocket of his thin L.L.Bean jacket. He pulled out something silver on a thin chain and handed it to Nat.

It was cold in his hand. He flipped it over to the little scene stamped on the front and studied it closely. St. Christopher was wading across a river, a shaggy-looking tree just behind him. There was a mountain in the background, topped with snow. It didn't look like a mass-produced item; he'd never seen one like this before. The craftsmanship evident in the details spoke of something that was handmade. The silversmith had been a good one—you could feel the exhaustion in St. Christopher's thin body, the concern in his eyes. *Will we make it? Can I save this child?* An acknowledgment that the world's dangers were real.

Is this some kind of macabre joke? Nat thought. *St. Christopher, the patron saint of travelers, get it? Of travelers. Is it a family heirloom, given to each host in turn?* Nat frowned fiercely. He had the urge to turn and fling the piece of silver off into the snowbanks, get it away from him.

"Ring the bell," Nat said, handing the medal back. "Let her know we're coming."

John pushed the button, but there was no answer. He tried the door; it was unlocked, and he swung it back noiselessly. They went inside. The air in the lobby was filled with dust motes, and John coughed. *It's like a mausoleum,* Nat thought, *a place of the dead.* The sounds of their footsteps traveled back to them from the interior of the house.

"Becca?" Nat called.

"She can hear us from down here?" John said.

"Should be," Nat answered, staring up at the second-floor landing, which seemed to waver behind a curtain of dust motes.

John shone his flashlight up there, but the dust only reflected the beam back.

"Why isn't she answering?" Nat said. He went up the stairs, moving quickly for the second floor. He could hear John close behind.

Nat got down the hallway in five long strides, the wood sagging behind him and the sounds of his pounding footsteps filling the passageway. He reached the door, the gouges there still visible. He pounded on the fractured wood.

"Becca, open up."

Nothing, just an eerie stillness. A watchful stillness.

"Becca, it's me."

"I gotta do this," he heard John say, and before he could turn, he saw John's thick leg snap toward the door and kick it. The door let out a metallic shriek and shuddered inward.

Nat walked inside. The bed was made up, the curtains pulled, and the room dark and empty. John got on his knees and shone his flashlight under the bed. Nothing. They searched the rest of the room in thirty seconds.

The house was echoing. Neutral.

Ten minutes later, when they came out, John took a deep breath, let it out, and looked up and down the street. The house was completely empty.

"Where could she have gone?"

Nat stamped some heat back into his feet. The porch echoed hollowly.

"I don't know. She doesn't have any friends that I know of."

"Let's check the grounds."

They tramped down the porch and turned down the driveway toward the back.

The search of the grounds took them another twenty minutes. Nothing.

They walked slowly up the drive and back to their cars.

"I'm going home," John said. "Fuck, I wanted to find her."

Nat knew he was thinking of Charlie. Becca was out there now, and in his bones, John now considered Becca the traveler. Nat worried about what John—the new incarnation of John, whose hands shook and who answered the door with gun drawn—would do if he encountered the girl.

"It's not her, John," Nat said. "He might have guided her, but I feel—"

"She's a murder suspect, Nat," John said, his voice flat. "Call me if you hear anything." He got into his car.

Nat walked to the Saab, the shadows gathering on the street and lights going on in the houses down the block. John roared away without waving. As he swept past, Nat saw John's face frozen into a mask of determination.

Nat opened the car door and climbed in. The slick leather of the driver's seat was cold. He started the engine and waited a moment or two, letting the air out of the vents get hot. Then he drove away, looking at the windows of the nearby houses to see if there were faces in them.

He got to the corner of Endicott Street. The air was pumping warm, and he felt himself relax for the first time in a couple of hours. He made the turn onto State and hit the accelerator and listened to the turbo kick in.

Suddenly, he spoke.

"It's okay now," he said.

There was no response. Nat's eyes went wide, and he jerked around, turning to look at the space behind the front seats. The coat he'd thrown in the back was still there. He reached over and touched it as his eyes went back to the road.

It stirred under his hand. He let out a shaky breath.

The pale face of Becca Prescott rose in his rearview mirror.

"Nat," she said.

The look in her eyes in the rearview mirror. Was it love? Gratitude? Or something darker—like triumph?

CHAPTER FIFTY-FIVE

Ramona Best walked away from her dorm, crossing the quad quickly toward its little-used northeast corner, which led toward the college power plant. She could see a dirty column of smoke rising from behind the Rossmore science building. Behind it lay the plant, which marked the far edge of the college grounds, and beyond that was the Raitliff Woods, ascending slowly away from the college, its trees just visible through the mist rising from the twin stacks that funneled smoke into the frigid air.

Ramona hurried down the path and reached the gap between the dining hall and the science building. The plant was straight ahead, a squat old brick building with an arched entrance that said *Wartham Power* above it, and in front was a new forest green Ford pickup with the Wartham seal on its side. There was a gate somewhere back here, Ramona knew, an opening in the red brick wall where workers brought in supplies, lumber, carpeting, and paint to keep the dorms looking respectable. She prayed it was open.

Ramona approached the plant and turned left along the path that paralleled the building's facade. There was no one back here; the path was empty, lit by a single black street lamp that glowed hazily in the gloom. Ramona angled off the path and plunged into the pine trees that lined the side of the plant. From the building to her left came a deep humming noise that seemed to vibrate the molecules of the air around her. Her teeth caught the vibration and began to ache. She clamped them tight, ducking beneath the pine branches and heading toward the Raitliff Woods.

I have to go there, she said to herself. *I have to see once and for all. To see if the little boy is real or a dream, and why Margaret is calling me.*

Ten steps later, Ramona emerged from the tree line. She was at the brick wall, which rose up only five feet away. Ramona followed the wall and soon came to the plant's gravel-covered backyard. Twenty-five feet away was a large gap in the brick, with a chain-link gate large enough to let a large truck through. A chain and heavy padlock hung loose where the two arms of the gate met. Ramona hurried toward it.

She pulled one arm of the gate, and it swung back with a metal rasp. Ramona ducked through the gap, and she was through the fence, beyond the wall. There was a snowy margin of a dozen yards or so between the brick perimeter and the ragged tree line of the Raitliff Woods. She headed straight in, her feet finding a path between two giant Douglas firs.

Once Ramona passed ten feet into the forest, the trees seemed to close behind her, like a curtain being pulled, shutting out the gray sunlight. The sounds of cars driving along the nearby Route 9 had disappeared, as if muffled by thick cloth. The feeling of open space was cut off. She could see someone had come this way recently—the trail in the dim light was touched here and there by a muddy brown where a boot had gone through the snow. The wind moved down the incline she was climbing, buffeting her face and causing her lips to go cold after a few minutes.

She felt she was in two places, her body down here walking through the knee-deep snow, with bristles raking her jeans and spiky brown burrs sticking to them, gusts of white breath appearing before her. But she was up there, too, above the trees, flying as in her dream. Because she knew the way. She recognized this part of the forest. *How can that be? I've never been here, and yet I know where I'm going.*

She'd expected to hear Margaret as she got closer, for she knew now that this was where Margaret and the others gathered. *This is where the undead stay when they aren't roaming the city*, she said to herself.

Why can't I hear her?

Suddenly a spasm of terror cut off the thought. What if Margaret was too frightened to speak? *What if she could bring me here but couldn't communicate, only let me see?*

A bird cry cut through the muffled air. Ramona stopped, her heart beating fast. She cupped her hands to her mouth to blow hot air onto them, but instead they closed over her lips, stifling a shriek.

She looked back the way she'd come. The little path seemed to have been swallowed up in darkness. She couldn't see the trail cut through the white snow. Only trees. Straight and stark, the blacks of their trunks rich and lustrous. Suddenly she ducked behind one and sat down abruptly, her back to the rough bark.

Nat waited at a stop sign. A pale blue Suburban rusting at the wheel wells made a left ahead of him, and Nat eased down on the gas pedal. He swung into a right turn and kept the Saab under 30 mph.

He circled back toward the Prescott house. Becca was quiet in the backseat, resting her head just below the window. There was an off chance they'd cross paths with John, and Nat didn't want him seeing the girl. He thought of what he was doing as protective custody. Get John away from the house. Get Becca back to her room. Make sure the place was locked up.

He made another right onto Endicott Street and rolled up to the Prescott house. John's car was nowhere to be seen.

He turned. Becca was there, whole, alive, sane—and disturbingly beautiful. Why didn't he ask her if she wanted to leave Northam with him, fly to Argentina? What was here for them except misery?

But something told him they couldn't run from what was pursuing them. It had to be faced here, and soon.

Becca was reaching for the door handle, her eyes on the house.

"I'll walk you in," he said.

"Raised to be a gentleman," she said, a hint of mockery in her voice.

He laughed. He got out, came around the car, and together they walked up the path. Becca slipped her arm through the crook of his elbow, and gently leaned on him. They walked slowly in silence. Becca opened the front door, and Nat followed her into the house.

Five minutes later, he emerged again and, after a quick glance at the sky, hurried down to the Saab.

———

Ramona sat, listening. How long had she been sitting here? The sun through the trees seemed higher in the sky, but she felt like time had stopped as soon as she entered the forest.

She had to go on. She could hear a roaring sound ahead of her, upslope. It was like there was some kind of dynamo ahead, a secret and powerful thing hidden in the forest, and it was sucking her toward it.

She didn't know if she could do it. She thought of Zuela and Ray-ray, her brother. She couldn't die up here in these stupid woods and leave them alone.

"God, please help me," she said. The cold was rising up her back, and her teeth chattered slightly as she whispered.

Finally, she gritted her teeth, cursed Margaret, and rose unsteadily. *Girls from Roosevelt don't scare*, she thought. *What's a little old forest to a girl who's traveled down Nassau Road at midnight?*

She began walking.

The angle of the ground rose ahead of Ramona. She bent forward at the waist, and her breaths began to shorten. Shards of dull light began appearing through the tree cover. She walked for twenty minutes, looking only at the trail ahead of her.

Finally, she felt the ground begin to level off a bit. The clearing was not too far away now, she knew, perhaps thirty yards. She imagined the grass swaying. Ten steps later, she caught a glimpse of brightness ahead. Just like in the dream. But this was different. Something was burning ahead. Was a part of the forest in flames? Or was it a bonfire?

Ramona stepped quickly off the pathway into the stand of maples to her left. She touched one to steady herself, and her hand came away oily with sap and water. Ramona flinched. She began to creep ahead, trying to dampen the crump of her boots as they moved through the snow. She peered ahead at the blazing field, ducking her head. A pall of cold seemed to enter her chest as the clearing came closer.

What are you bringing me here to see, Margaret?

She spotted a gap in the maples three or four yards ahead. A bright rectangle of light seemed to be floating beyond the trees, suspended, alight.

Everything was so quiet here in the clearing. No voices, just the buffeting sound of the wind.

What have you brought me here to see?! she felt like screaming.

She saw three figures ahead. The three from the dream, but completely real and present now: the old man, the bald man, and Margaret Post.

They were standing at the edges of the clearing, one on each side, the far side hidden from her sight. Margaret in her black poncho in front of Ramona.

Ramona walked to the last tree before the clearing and hugged it, peeking around its jagged bark trunk and regarding each of the three in turn.

Her heart was beating so loud that her vision shook. *They* are *real*, Ramona thought. *Not figments of my imagination. Able to turn and chase any dull-witted old girl they care to.*

But the light in the center of the clearing. She knew what it was now. Not grass lit by some mysterious light. She could hear the crackling of timber in the flames. They were standing around a giant bonfire, logs piled higher than the top of Margaret's head. The flames sent out a cracking roar—the sound she'd heard on her approach—as they burned.

Margaret's black poncho shone just in front of Ramona, not twenty feet away, throbbing darkly against the flames. To her left, the bald man slumped, his eyes closed. She could see an angry red line across his pale throat. To her right was the old man, who seemed not to be standing but hanging in the air, like a suit of clothes on a hanger.

They were staring, transfixed, at the flames. Their lips were moving.

What were they saying?

Ramona's ears buzzed horribly.

No, I don't want to know. She sank to her knees. It looked as if some sacrifice was being prepared, some rite that no living thing should see. Ramona gasped for air. But she knew if she raised her voice that something would come hunting her in the forest. The three would turn and then she would be prey. And their knives would be real and their hands would be terribly strong.

The droning, the voiceless thing, only howled louder.

The flames licked upward toward the darkened sky. Margaret stepped forward, as did the others. Ramona could see they were approaching something at the fire's edge, a figure in the snow. They were chanting something, in a language Ramona had never heard. But her eyes were on Margaret's shoulder, which was blocking the thing at the center. As she got closer, the figure was slowly being revealed. At first Ramona saw brown hair whipping wildly in the wind. The figure was kneeling, head bowed.

Ramona, dread coursing through her veins, lifted up on her tiptoes and squinted.

"Please don't let it be . . ."

Suddenly the figure lifted his head. His mouth was open as he repeated the chanted words, his cheeks pale as chalk and his red-rimmed eyes staring ahead in a trance.

"Oh God," Ramona whispered. "No no no *no no no*."

She began to run blindly through the woods, her lips white with a suppressed cry.

As she churned through the knee-deep snow, she heard a bloodcurdling scream. A high voice, screaming again and again, the notes rising as if they would never stop.

Instead of dropping away, the roar grew in her ears as she crashed down the trail. Underneath it was the sound of footsteps and twigs breaking.

CHAPTER FIFTY-SIX

Nat stared at the TV screen. A college basketball game was on. Notre Dame–Stanford, tied at 88. A tepid, mistake-filled game.

Nat watched the Stanford quarterback throw a long bomb. The ball arced in the air, and the camera caught the fans—thousands of them in the background of the long pass—rising as one. Thousands of people who knew nothing of Northam, Mass., or Charlie or Becca . . .

He felt odd, restless. Waiting for something to happen.

Suddenly, a wave of claustrophobia seemed to wash over him. Staying in the condo seemed intolerable; there was no air in the place, and he felt himself starting to hyperventilate. Nat got up quickly, grabbed the Saab keys, and ran for the front door.

As soon as he emerged from the building and felt the breeze on his face, the feeling of being boxed in the airless apartment dissipated. Now he felt only dread, rising in him until he thought he would shout.

Oh God, oh God, there's one after me, Ramona thought. Echoing crashing noises from far behind her. Heavy footsteps.

She saw a tall thick-trunked oak up a ways on her right, and when she got to it, she stepped off the trail and put her back to the tree. Her coat rubbed on the rough bark, and she felt the protection of the huge thing. The forest seemed to echo with the sound of her breathing, and her vision wavered with her rising chest. She listened now.

Maybe it would shoot right past her. Because she couldn't outrun it, that was for sure. Ramona closed her eyes and brought her fist up to her lips and pressed it there, her front teeth painfully biting into the flesh so she wouldn't scream.

The footsteps slowly grew more distant. It was as if the pursuer were breaking trail to another part of the forest.

It's not me they're after, thought Ramona. *It's someone else. They're chasing someone else.* And guiltily, she said a brief prayer of thanks.

She brought her bag around and unzipped it, then reached in for her phone. She grabbed it and hit the *Talk* button. *Searching* the little message said in the upper right hand corner. No bars.

"Damn it all," Ramona said. She listened carefully—hearing only a faraway noise of disturbance in the forest—and pushed away from the tree. She found the path again in the dim forest light and ran on, holding the phone in her right hand.

Ten minutes later, she saw the red brick of the Walter Power Plant looming through the dark branches. She stopped and brought the phone up. Two bars. She hit *Missed Calls*, brought up the call from Detective Bailey she'd ignored, and hit *Talk*.

"Come on, come on, *come on.*"

The number lingered on the screen.

"Come on, damn it," she said, giving the phone a shake. Finally the number disappeared and the calling screen came on. A faint ringing could be heard.

"Pick up, pick up, pick— Detective?"

A male voice.

"It's Ramona Best," she said.

"Ramona? What's going—"

"I'm in the Raitliff Woods, near where the bonfire's burning."

"Okay. What are you doing up there?"

"I know who they're going to kill next. Can you go now, please? Right now."

She just blurted it out. No time for messing around. No time left at all.

She thought, *He's going to ask me who is going to kill someone next*, and then she'd have to explain the gathering of the dead people in the Raitliff Woods, and the dreams, and Margaret's wanting to be allowed to die, even though she was already dead. *How can I explain all that? How the fuck—*

Ramona took a deep breath.

"Who is it?" the voice on the other end said.

And then Ramona understood. Detective Bailey hadn't asked who *they* were, or why someone had to be next, or how she was sure they were going to kill anyone. *The police know*, she thought. *But if they know and it's still happening, they can't stop them.* Her legs began to shake and she suddenly crouched down.

"It's a little boy," she said.

————

John dropped the phone and ran toward Charlie's room.

He bellowed the boy's name as he barged into the hallway.

When he pushed Charlie's door in, the first thing he saw was the open window and the curtains fluttering in and beyond it the snow, glowing violet.

————

Nat was sitting on the park bench on State Street where he'd found Becca that day, the day she remembered her family. It was the best memory of her that he possessed. His hand was placed flat on the slats where Becca had been sitting. The steel was cold against his palm.

He was trying to keep thoughts of what he had to ask her at bay. For one moment longer.

His cell phone buzzed. He reached into his pocket and pulled it out. John.

He hit the *Talk* button.

John's voice, hurried, commotion behind it. "They took the boy," he said.

Nat found he could not say it: *You mean Charlie?* "Jesus," he whispered. "Are you sure?"

"Yeah," John said finally. "Bring those two over here!" he shouted to someone on the other end.

There was commotion in the background, the sound of people hurrying. "Nat?"

"Yeah. I'm here."

"We're going to get them now, Nat. And anything I see moving, I am going to kill on sight."

Nat felt his body going cold. "Where are you going?"

"The Raitliff Woods. Ramona Best said she saw him up there with . . . those things."

He glanced up. There was a fire burning in the Raitliff Woods, the same spot he'd seen days ago from his car parked in front of Becca's house.

His mind flashed to Captain Markham taking the organs of his young soldiers, and the Haitian translator's warning that the sacrifices shouldn't be placed in fire. Or the sorcerer would become stronger.

It's coming, he thought. *My God, the end is coming.*

Ramona took a deep, shaking breath. She'd done her duty.

The forest was quiet. She could actually hear birds flitting through the branches above, and the deep hum of the power plant was shaking the air again. Like the hum could shift the oxygen molecules, get them to shiver. It was, strangely, like the droning that had filled her ears up in the woods.

She stepped onto the path and began to walk toward the gate behind the power plant. She would go back to her room. She would lock the door. She would read *The Magic Mountain* for Professor DeMint's class on the Continental novel and lose herself in the odd world of Hans Castorp.

As she drew closer, the powerful hum emitted by the power plant seemed to vibrate in her bones. Something moved off to her left. What she'd thought was a tree trunk wasn't there anymore, just white space. She was starting to imagine things.

Ramona chose her steps carefully. She didn't want to fall and break her leg here on the edge of civilization, stranded out here, yelling at the plant workers to save her. *Just make it through the gate and forget about Margaret and everything. Tonight is turkey dinner at the dining hall with all the fixin's. You deserve . . .*

A figure in front of her. Tall, tall, up close the old man was taller than she remembered. Her vision wobbled with sheer terror, and she saw the bayonet rise in the cold air. Her screaming merging with the deafening hum . . .

Ramona turned to run, but she was only three steps up the slope when she felt the blade go in and pain sprint through her disguised as blazing heat.

John Bailey twisted his body through the thick underbrush, fifty yards from the tree line. The air was damp in here, clogging his lungs with mist, and the light was bluish gray, eerie. The trees were dripping with water, and the brush underneath his feet sent brittle sounds echoing off the poplars when he broke through an icy patch. He was panting already, kicking his feet through the knee-high snow cover.

It had taken thirty minutes to get a search party organized. Dusk was falling. One hurried call to dispatch, asking for all first responders available to head to the fire burning in the Raitliff

Woods. He'd met them at the tree line, said he had information that his son had been taken and was being kept near the bonfire. That was all he'd said; he'd figure out how to explain the rest once he had Charlie in his arms.

On his left and right, he could see a broken line of men and a few women—cops, EMTs, and a few firefighters—marching through the oak scrub and pine. The ground was slanting upward. Ramona had said just go toward the fire. The boy would be there.

Just be strong for a little while longer, Charlie.

His radio crackled.

"Let's tighten it up on the right. Don't want anyone slipping through." He looked down the line, but the trees blocked his way.

"How much further?" a voice said.

He thumbed the button down. "Should be half a mile."

Kick, step, scan. Kick, step, scan.

Daddy's coming.

CHAPTER FIFTY-SEVEN

Nat stood on the street in front of the Prescott house. The sky around the rim of trees behind the house was turning a bruised black. He tilted his head up to look at the Raitliff Woods. The fire was still burning up there. Nat watched it. He thought he could hear chanting, blood oaths, but of course that was all in his mind. The fire was a mile away at least. *Something or someone is being readied*, he thought.

He walked slowly up the front path, his heels striking loudly on the flagstones. He thought again of finding her and then driving to the airport, buying tickets for the first plane to Buenos Aires. No luggage, nothing but themselves. They would escape, tonight. But he knew in his heart that it was a fantasy. *Nothing will ever turn out right again.*

It would end here, in Northam. This is where the bodies were. It couldn't be any other way.

There was no sign of Becca here, no light in her window, no note by the door. But he had to find out for sure, because if she wasn't in the house, she was on the mountain.

Does she know? he thought. *Does she even know what she's done, or does the traveler keep the blood and the gore and the image of Charlie's face away from her conscious mind so that she can survive?*

The outline of the lower story of the house was bleeding into the darkness, the edges of the wood siding slowly merging into black. High storm clouds were turning day into night. He reached into his jacket and felt the long knife he'd taken from his kitchen.

He'd removed it from the butcher's block of German chef tools in his apartment. It was barely used, its blade as clean as a mirror. He'd wrapped it in an old T-shirt and stashed it inside his coat in the inside pocket that he once used for a brandy flask at college football games.

The house felt alive tonight. Its clear cut glass reflected the last rays of the sun as it set behind him. The glass sparkled amid the hideous black shapes of columns and jutting corners. It was as if the house were some malevolent old toad, eyes glimmering, poison in its mouth, silent.

Nat shivered in his coat. He pulled the coat tighter, then began to walk. The shape of the knife pressed into his ribs.

He placed his foot on the lowest step, then put his weight on it, then the next. When the third step gave a long drawn-out creak, he saw movement behind the narrow window to the left of the front door.

Nat Thayer to the rescue, he said to himself. A grim laugh escaped his lips, and he strode to the door and gripped the doorknob. The hairs on his hand stood up.

He pushed on the door and it drifted back. There were no dust motes in the fading light this time. Just clear hard angles in the blackness.

Something whispered on the landing above, past the railing, from a place he couldn't see. A whisper and then a scuttling noise.

Nat closed the door, his left hand on the knob. As he shut it, the foyer grew dimmer. Only a few faint glimmerings of sunlight reached into the interior of the house. His right hand reached into the inner pocket and gripped the knife's handle. His fingers slowly closed on the polished wood again and again, and he found himself staring at the warping facets of the window. *Now I'm inside the eyes*, he thought. *I am in the house and the house is in me.*

Something moved behind him. A jolt of fear ran up his back, but he turned slowly.

You . . .

It was the voice of his mother. The light contralto of his mother, but hoarse.

. . . are called.

Ah, so I was right about Mother, he thought. *We're all links in a chain. How many are here tonight? Is Chase risen up? Is William Prescott?*

A figure stood on the top balcony, a face only, the body lost in interior darkness. The face was thin and bone white, with long black scabs across the cheeks and lips, like it'd been raked by a bird's talons. Nat recognized the disembodied face from the newspaper photos: Jimmy Stearns. A tremor of horror swept through him, and he found himself unable to speak.

Jimmy Stearns's eyes were black, insect eyes set into lifeless gray putty. They stared at Nat, and his flesh crawled as he stared back. *Is that what my mother's eyes looked like when she jerked the steering wheel toward the abyss?* he thought.

The face withdrew, back into the blackness as if submerging in a dark pond.

You are called.

A male voice now, deep and guttural. Was it Bule's?

He wondered if he'd really heard the voice or if the traveler was in his mind, whispering there.

"I am called," he said aloud and he moved forward.

———

Charlie gripped his Captain America figurine and tried to burrow back into the brush. But the bald man twisted around and grabbed his neck. He shoved Charlie's head forward until it was between his knees.

Twenty feet away the bonfire roared. The people around it . . .

he didn't want to look at them. Their faces were dead faces. They smelled. They were standing, looking at the fire but not looking at the fire. As if they were waiting for a signal.

The Magician was near, he could tell.

I don't want to be here, he said in his mind. *I want to go home.*

The flames sucked in air and branches snapped in the pile.

Magician, let me go home.

He was afraid the people would go rushing into the fire. And the bald man would take him and carry him in, too. The fire was big as a house. He squirmed back, but the bald man gripped his neck so tight. His fingers came around and pressed on his throat. Choking.

The Magician's voice came to him.

Do you deserve to be saved, Charlie?

The voice wasn't friendly. It wasn't angry; it was just cold.

Are you angry with me? Charlie said. *Did I do something wrong? The goblin . . .*

I asked if you deserved to live, Charlie. Do you think you do?

Yes, I think so.

Would you like to live forever?

Charlie looked at the figures around him. Is that what he meant by *live forever*? Like them?

No, thank you. I want to see my daddy.

The Magician's laugh—it was scary. Cruel. A bully's laugh.

Charlie, you are going to burn.

Charlie shook his head no, fighting the bald man's grip.

No! he cried. *No, keep me away from it.*

Charlie dropped Captain America and reached for the bald man's hands. But the fingers gripping his neck were strong as steel. They didn't budge.

He was choking. The fingers pressed into the soft flesh of his throat. Blackness closed in on the edge of his vision.

Like a little pig roasting. Will you squeal, Charlie? Will you?

His legs shaking, Nat walked quickly to the stairs and ascended the three steps to the landing. He headed up the rest of the way. The polished edges of the stairs gleamed far below his eyes, like lines of surf on a darkened beach as seen from a high cliff. That was all he could see. He reached for the railing.

He touched it and began to climb. He felt like he was pushing his face into black cloth. *Will it be a knife? Or will I step into a noose, the loose strands rough against my skin?* His neck tingled all over.

He reached the top of the stairs, the knife heavy in his coat.

Run, he thought. *It's not too late. Save yourself from this death. Don't look don't look do not look.*

But it was as if Nat were being forced around by an irresistible gravity and against his will, his head swiveling left slowly as he came to the top of the stairs and stepped onto the upstairs hallway. Half blind in the deep gloom. He felt a column of fetid breath—human breath—brushing against his face and gagged.

Submit.

A black face loomed up in his mind. Black eyes circling toward a tiny orange flame.

"I . . ."

He struggled to speak.

"I am called," he said finally.

He felt his body unclench, and he was able to turn away. The stairs beckoned, but he couldn't force his body to move. Bodies slithered away into the darkness behind him.

Where is Becca? he thought.

Nat's shoes whispered dully on the polished wood. He moved down the hallway and the feeling of black space extended in front of him like a deep pool. The light by Becca's door was off. The smell of putrefaction was getting stronger, clogging his throat. He felt as if he were lowering himself into a crypt filled with rotting bodies.

He took a breath, and the fumes nearly overwhelmed him. Nat gagged and reached out for the wall. At the last second he thought he would touch a face, and he let out a hoarse yell, but it was the wallpaper, and he leaned against it.

Becca, I'm coming, he thought.

A laugh seemed to rumble up and travel the hallways from deep in the house, displacing the air around him. It moved with a rush past him. A door had been opened and then closed.

"Who is it?" he said, a waver of fear in his voice. His words seemed to echo and return to him.

Who is it Whoisit Who is . . .

Nat stumbled forward, at the same time reaching inside his jacket and turning the knife so that the long blade faced down toward his stomach, ready to be pulled out. He could feel the edge press through his thin wool shirt.

The air seemed to tremble in front of him, and Nat sank to his knees. A huge rumbling noise filled his world, and he opened his mouth to stop his eardrums from splitting. The air seemed to be sucked out of the hallway, and Nat gasped for breath while pressing his hands to his ears.

"Stop!" he cried. "*Stop!*"

The noise was cut off suddenly.

Are you ready to die and live again?

The air brought with it a sharp, metallic smell. He heard someone moaning softly in front of him. One voice, then two, and another. Everyone that Bule commanded was in the house now, he guessed. The dead—Elizabeth Dyer, Chuck Godwin, God knew who else. And the living. Becca. A final gathering of his *nzombes.*

Nat gritted his teeth. The smell seemed to be seeping into him, penetrating his pores.

"Let Becca go," he said aloud.

He felt something move behind him, and the smell of rotting flesh swam over him. They were closing in. He coughed.

"Take me instead."

He felt along the wall. His hand touched the mounted head of the boar, and he barely paused, staggering on, his eyes open wide and his mouth gasping for air.

He came to the door, felt the gashes in the wood. A faint smell of pine. He could feel the things gather behind him, the moaning twisting and braiding together until he felt he would go deaf. Nat twisted the knob and pushed in. The door opened, and he rushed into Becca's room, rattling the door shut behind him.

He locked the two locks.

When he was done, he glanced at the bed. Becca was laid out on the duvet cover. She appeared to be asleep. There were candles burning, one on her desk, the other on the windowsill. Aromatic. He smelled pomegranate. And was that cinnamon?

He walked over to her. The handle of the knife was cool in his hand. He reached out with the left to touch her bare leg.

"Becca," he called out softly.

She slept on. Moonlight shone in through the window, throwing long shadows toward him. Her head was in darkness, but he recognized the bones of her face.

"Becca, wake up."

Leave her be.

Nat felt the strength begin to leave him, sliding out of his body like water from a cracked glass.

"Becca!" he cried.

His left hand curled over the knife handle.

Leave . . .

She came awake, the eyes fluttering and her lips repeating a word that Nat didn't catch.

Watch the eyes, he told himself.

"Nat?" she said, and it was her voice. Becca's true clear voice.

"Look into my eyes, Becca. Can you do that?"

"My arms," she said. "You're hurting me."

"Look into my eyes," he said, as gently as he could.

. . . her BE!

He looked into her eyes, and into the blackness at the center.

Something moved back there, like an eel in a dark pool. Just a glimpse of black against black.

He gripped the knife under the coat.

They were at the door, which creaked inward.

"Take . . . me!"

Becca's eyes went wide with shock. Her mouth was open and she breathed shallowly. Then suddenly, the corners of her lips curled into a malevolent grin.

The flesh of her face sagged; the cheek muscles sharpened. Even her breathing had changed. *Bule*, Nat thought. *At last.*

Becca's lips stayed frozen in the leer. *Do you know . . . what happened to the last man who taunted me?*

He must mean Markham, all those decades ago. "I know."

And you invite me to . . . ? There was a garbled word, a foreign word.

Nat felt Becca's arms push him off. Incredible power. He staggered back against the tall bookcase, which rattled back and forth on its wooden feet.

Jesus, the power in her body. Bule had killed Margaret Post, he was sure of it. And the St. Christopher's medal at the death scene was proof that he'd used Becca's body to do it. Clearly she had the strength. The thought of his Becca slitting the girl's throat . . .

But it wasn't her. Mustn't think that way.

Becca sat on the bed, her head down, her shoulders crooked, impaled somehow, though there was nothing behind her.

I like my beautiful vessel.

Nat shivered and put his hands in his coat pockets. All he could do was threaten death. Then Bule would be forced away from Becca into one of the other *nzombes.*

"You can't have her."

A smile on the mouth beneath the glossy locks of hair.

I will have her, always.

A dark look entered Nat's eyes. He brought the knife out of his coat and tipped the point toward Becca.

Her eyes went wide and she began to fall back. Nat came up on the bed on his knees and put his left hand over Becca's face, covering it. He pushed her head down into the soft mattress. He placed the point of the knife to the beating flesh of her throat.

"You've had your revenge. It's over now."

You'd never.

Nat grimaced, jabbing the knife lightly into her skin. A spot of blood appeared crimson at the base of Becca's throat. He turned away from the sight of the blood.

"*LEAVE!*" he shouted.

I know your mind.

"I will kill her, Bule."

Suddenly Becca went limp. He felt her eyelids flutter. He eased the hand back over her mouth.

Have I killed her?

"Nat?" her voice was soft, confused.

"Don't do this," he said to the voice in his head, his voice weakening. He pulled the knife from her throat and laid it on the bed under his outspread hand.

"Nat, what's happening?"

He shook his head, unable to speak.

"Na—"

Did she even remember the murder of Margaret Post? The struggle of her body, the gouts of blood?

But what did it matter? Who cared if she did it herself or used one of the *nzombes* in the hallway? It didn't really matter.

She raised up on one elbow, touching her hand to her throat. It came away with a blotch of blood on the pad of her index finger. She looked at it, and then at him.

The noise at the door spiked, moaning and shouting. The stench was growing unbearable again, the air swimming with currents of putrid fumes.

"Who are they?" she said.

"It's the others."

She saw the knife on the bed, under his hand. Her gaze came back to him. She closed her eyes, and a tremor—disgust? fear?—rippled along the muscles of her neck. She understood now. When she opened her eyes, there was terror in them.

"He's inside me, Nat?"

It was the trust in her voice that appalled him the most. She hadn't even tried to escape when she'd seen the weapon. He felt himself grow light-headed.

"Is he?"

I don't know. The only way to be sure is to kill you. And that I can't do.

The reeking fumes were choking him. His vision began to spin.

He tried to call her name, but his voice was a groan in his ears. He saw her get up and move toward the candle on the desk. It was guttering in its holder.

CHAPTER FIFTY-EIGHT

The sounds picked up, more voices and more urgent. The snapping of branches quickened, and John sensed the blurred, ragged line of men to his right surging ahead. *What do they see?* John ducked his head and peered ahead, upslope. All he could see was the bluish glow of snow and trees, ranks of bare trees.

He started to run. His heart felt like it was being stretched out, and a stabbing pain was making itself felt underneath his collarbone. *God, please don't let me have a heart attack now*, he thought.

Baying. Movement. Flashlights bobbing. They had to be getting close.

If Charlie was dead . . .

He felt the wind drop away and shift direction. It was coming downslope now, and he immediately picked up a scent. It smelled like meat charring on a grill.

The pitch of the bloodhounds' baying went one note higher.

He saw the flames through the trees, a lick of orange and then another. He turned toward them, fifteen degrees right, and began to run, spraying snow up to his face as his boots clomped through the icy crystals.

"Charlie!" he shouted. "*Charliieeeeeeee!*"

The flashlights darting in the black. The fire was growing. And the smell—oh, no, it couldn't be. He'd never smelled anything like that before.

The trees were parting, giving way. He was coming up on a clearing. Shouts from behind him.

The bonfire was roaring, the flames thirty feet high. John's eyes strained to make out the black things in it. There were logs and then on top of them . . .

Oh God. Oh, please no.

He saw a dark figure outlined against the hot orange flames, staggering toward the bonfire. John froze and reached for his gun, crying for the man to stop. But as he jerked the Glock up, the man went toward the blaze without stopping and leapt into it, his hoarse cry being sucked into the roar of the flames.

Another black figure emerged and followed him. A shower of red sparks blossomed up toward the dark sky as the body dropped into the bonfire. There was a loud popping sound and John thought, *Was that a skull or a branch?*

He ran forward the last few yards to the clearing.

Nat woke up, feeling heat on his face. Pain shot along the length of his neck at the spine. He breathed out once, then again. The air was clean and cold, but it choked him. His throat felt as though it had been crushed.

Nat lifted his head up. *Oh, you've gone and broken your neck,* he thought. He reached up, his eyes closing in pain. On his face, heat, flames. He sank back down, but in the little glimpse around him he'd recognized where he was.

The Prescott backyard. He was splayed out in the snow just under Becca's window.

He felt the heat again and forced his eyes open. He saw Becca's window open and black smoke pouring out. The smoke would billow and then part, and he saw flames then, white-orange, and he heard them beginning to roar like a wave far off but coming toward you.

He tried to raise his head, and pain screamed up from the base of his skull. *Did I fall?*

"Becca," he called weakly. He tried to turn his head, but bright stars appeared behind his eyes. He knew she wasn't with him. He could feel her absence, and a dawning horror overcame him.

He saw a hand on the window frame, the fingers pale against the dark green paint, the Dartmouth trim. Becca was standing just to the side, as if the fire and smoke weren't there. Her eyes were on him.

Behind the roar of the flames, he heard screams. Jimmy Stearns and the other *nzombes*—whoever was in there—burning, surely.

Becca caught his gaze. *Oh, no, don't look at me like that*, he thought. No accusation in her eyes, only love.

In the place where her right hand would be, he saw a glint of silver. His knife, rising through the billows of smoke toward her neck. Nat's eyes went wide, and five words echoed in his head from far away.

And . . . off . . . came . . . her . . . head.

The knife was turning in the smoke as she brought it up fast.

He cried out her name, but the blackness washed over her.

CHAPTER FIFTY-NINE

Six-month case review.

Patient: Nathaniel Thayer, 34, Caucasian male. Admission
  number 01876.

Supervising psychiatrist: Dr. Jennifer Greene.

Dr. Thayer is a former clinical psychiatrist at this facility who
was brought in on 1/31 exhibiting symptoms of catatonia. During
his initial admission, the patient was fully awake but unrespon-
sive to external stimuli, including pain stimuli. He exhibited
signs of waxy flexibility, and appeared to be mumbling a phrase
repetitively, though he would not answer the team's questions.
There were no signs of echolalia or echopraxia. His admission
followed a traumatic incident with Thayer's patient, Ms. Rebecca
Prescott, since deceased in Massachusetts Memorial Hospital. This
six-month report summarizes the patient's course of treatment,
response to care, and the extenuating circumstances that have
attended this unusual case.

As the colleague of the patient who perhaps knew him best, I was
asked to supervise his treatment strategy. I was at the facility the
night Dr. Thayer was brought in, and have been leading the team
for the past six months. Despite our friendship in the past, the
patient exhibited no recognition of me or his former colleagues on
that night or in the subsequent period.

The relevant backstory to the patient's admission begins with his
treatment of Ms. Prescott in an unofficial capacity on or near 1/5.
After he arrived in-unit, the facility conducted an extensive round

of interviews with Dr. Thayer's friends and colleagues to determine the details leading up to his intake. Det. John Bailey was the most informative of the witnesses, though he has lately become nonresponsive to further inquiries regarding the relationship between Dr. Thayer and Ms. Prescott.

Ms. Prescott was apparently suffering from a case of Cotard delusion, first reported by her father, which worsened into apparent full-blown psychosis in which she imagined she was possessed by an evil spirit. Diaries found in the partially destroyed Prescott house have been conclusively shown to be those of Mr. Prescott, and they record his daughter's progressive descent into the belief that she was, in fact, already deceased. The diary states his intention of seeking help at the Northam Psychiatric Outreach Office on or about 1/4.

Mr. Prescott apparently first encountered Dr. Thayer in that time period, and the patient continued to see Becca Prescott in a professional capacity, as well as a personal one, up until the incidents of 1/17. Dr. Thayer's failure to report Ms. Prescott's case to this or any other Massachusetts facility of mental health, and his failure to admit her to any psychiatric facility, are now a matter of record, but the reason for these lapses in judgment has not been revealed in our investigation. We will not be addressing any professional misconduct on the part of Dr. Thayer in this report.

(Soon after Mr. Prescott came to him for the first time, Dr. Thayer consulted me on the parameters of Cotard, and I volunteered to assist him with the treatment of his then-unnamed patient. Dr. Thayer declined and discussed the matter only one more time with me. I sensed then that he wished to divulge the details of the case, but apparently the strangeness of the circumstances prevented him. Our two brief conversations represent the only interactions between Dr. Thayer and other Mass Memorial staff regarding Ms. Prescott's case.)

Several days after his admittance to this facility, Dr. Thayer still presented many symptoms of a classic catatonic state. His eyes were open and fixed; his face showed a marked lack of affect, although not the usual flat or blunted appearance but one of fixed attention, what would be classed an "agitated" state but without the usual resistance and violence. The repetition of the meaningless phrases had ceased. Initially, the cause of the catatonia was believed to be the shock of seeing Ms. Prescott perish in the house fire at 96 Endicott Street, especially as Dr. Thayer has no history of schizophrenia or epilepsy and subsequently tested negative for encephalitis. The initial evaluation of post-traumatic stress reaction has subsequently proven problematic, however.

The standard recovery time for such a PTSD-related episode is several days. But after six days at the facility, Dr. Thayer showed no improvement. The only change in his condition came when he was given reading material by one of the orderlies during the normal course of his fourth day at the facility. Dr. Thayer immediately grabbed a pen from the attendant and began to draw obsessively a series of pictures (see Appendix B-1). The first set of pictures can generally be described as showing the events of the house fire, and Ms. Prescott pictured in the window of the upper story of the Endicott Street house. Other images he produced included the face of a thin woman, an older Caucasian male with a lacerating wound to his neck area, and a small hut or wooden house on fire in a heavily forested area; these Dr. Thayer drew obsessively when he was provided with more paper.

After the two-week quarantine period, it was thought that perhaps Dr. Thayer would benefit from seeing his friends and coworkers in a casual setting. But the results were disappointing. Dr. Thayer maintained his "thousand-yard stare," only breaking from this posture to work on his drawings. The pictures themselves didn't seem to the treatment team to be efforts to communicate with the outside world, but simply a phase in an internal narrative that Dr. Thayer was working through.

After the initial shock of his experience was thought to have worn off and Dr. Thayer still showed no signs of improvement, a course of medications was decided upon by this doctor, in consultation with the director. We began on 2/5 with 40 cc's of carbamazepine and continued it for a week, then increased the dose to 60 cc's, given by injection every morning. The carbamazepine had no discernible effects, positive or negative, on the patient's affect or behavior. The treatment was discontinued on 2/15, and after a period of three days, clonazepam was administered in a dose of 40 cc's every morning, also by injection. The clonazepam had the effect of making Dr. Thayer drowsy for large parts of the day and prone to bouts of shallow breathing and dizziness, but no improvement in his catatonic symptoms was observed. The drug was given a two-week course of treatment, and was discontinued on 3/1. The treatment team then tried dantrolene, with similar (negative) results, and finally olanzapine, both in similar courses as with the other two drugs. The dantrolene increased the agitation of Dr. Thayer without decreasing the catatonic symptoms, and was discontinued after only five days, as Dr. Thayer had twice injured himself, the second time seriously, by banging his head against the door frame of his room. He was treated for those injuries and returned to the facility on 3/23.

The most remarkable incidents in the last six months were the two visits by Det. John Bailey, on 4/14 and 4/22. Det. Bailey had been urgently requesting to see Dr. Thayer, but it was thought best to deny those visits, as he was intimately involved in the patient's relationship with Ms. Prescott and any reliving of those experiences could have had a negative impact on Dr. Thayer's condition. After being interviewed several times, Det. Bailey confirmed what had been rumored in the Northam community for many weeks, especially after the interview with the local historian, Wilbur Atkins, published in the *Northam News* on 2/21. Mr. Atkins detailed Dr. Thayer's obsession with some local families and their connections to a long-dead soldier, Capt. Thomas Markham, who was hanged in the town square in the early part of 1920. Det. Bailey explained that Dr. Thayer—and he, for a time—had come to believe that local individuals had become possessed or controlled by the spirit of a man Capt. Markham had killed in Haiti during the American occupation of that country.

Det. Bailey explained that he and the patient had initially connected a series of disturbing events with this Capt. Markham: the
deaths of Walter Prescott, Margaret Post, Elizabeth Dyer, Jimmy
Stearns, and Charles Godwin—in addition to the disappearance of
their bodies. But the detective stated to the treatment team that
those deaths had been solved in the aftermath of the events of
1/17. For example, it was determined by the Northam police that
Margaret Post had been killed by Walter Prescott. In the diary
found in the Prescott home after the fire, Prescott confessed to the
murder, saying that Margaret Post had come to visit his daughter
and that he feared Margaret meant Becca harm, so he followed
her back to her college and attacked her just outside its walls.
Walter Prescott had apparently killed himself subsequently, out
of guilt. The deaths of Elizabeth Dyer and Jimmy Stearns remain
unsolved, but Det. Bailey reported confidentially that police were
questioning an employee of the morgue, Claude Roke, who had a
difficult work relationship with both victims.

As for the disappearance of the corpses, subsequent to the death
of Ms. Prescott in the house fire, all the missing bodies were
found—as has been reported widely in the *Boston Globe* and elsewhere—in two locations: deep in the Raitliff Woods and at the
Prescott house (including that of Mrs. Stephanie Godwin). The
clearing in the Raitliff Woods, where some of the bodies were re-
covered, was later determined to be the original burial site for the
executed Capt. Markham. He was interred in this spot after his
1920 execution, as no church graveyard in Northam would accept
his body and the authorities at that time wanted him buried as far
away from the city as possible. The missing bodies were found the
morning after the Prescott house fire, some of them burned in a
bonfire that had been built over the grave of Capt. Markham. The
newspapers have connected this gruesome fact to some kind of
ritualistic or possibly even satanic activity in the area, which Det.
Bailey gave some credence to. Officials at the morgue are investigating the original disappearance of the bodies.

Det. Bailey explained to the treatment team that Dr. Thayer was in
the grips of a psychosis focused on a supposed "*nzombe* outbreak"

involving these dead individuals. By speaking with Dr. Thayer, he hoped to explain to the patient the actual circumstances of the recent odd occurrences.

The offer was initially refused, for the reasons stated above. However, when the drug courses failed and Det. Bailey insisted that he could help "reach" Dr. Thayer, he was allowed a visit, with the understanding that members of the treatment team would be on hand and would be able to monitor and observe the interaction.

Myself and Drs. Bradley and Chalmers were on hand when Det. Bailey visited the facility and met with Dr. Thayer in the small conference room on the second floor. Dr. Thayer was seated in one of the chairs, free of any restraints, his affect still exhibiting signs of catatonia. Det. Bailey sat opposite him and began talking to him in a quiet voice. We immediately asked the detective to speak up, as we reserved the right to stop the conversation at any point if Dr. Thayer became agitated or violent. Det. Bailey was not at first willing to do so, but we soon convinced him that the interview would be terminated if he did not. He then agreed and began speaking to the patient about his son, Charlie—someone, as he'd earlier explained to us, that Dr. Thayer had been deeply concerned about in the days leading up to the patient's hospitalization. Dr. Thayer rocked continuously back and forth during this part of the conversation, and bent his head in a listening posture. Det. Bailey told him that Charlie was safe, that he'd resumed a normal life with no adverse affects of "the thing we were worried about." Dr. Thayer nodded, and we motioned for Det. Bailey to continue, as this was the first response of any kind we'd witnessed in Dr. Thayer in several months.

"He's not dreaming anymore, Nat," Det. Bailey said, according to our transcription of the interview. "He's not talking about this Magician guy. We're good, buddy, you did it. Becca was the one."

Det. Bailey became emotional at this point, wiping away several tears and reaching out and grabbing Dr. Thayer's hand. We considered ending the interview, but Dr. Chalmers argued it should continue, as Dr. Thayer was showing some slight response, even if he still seemed incapable of speaking. But soon Dr. Thayer broke his gaze with Det. Bailey and moved his eyes up to the ceiling. It was unclear if any of Det. Bailey's remarks were registering with the patient. We motioned to Det. Bailey that Dr. Thayer was apparently getting tired and the interview was being terminated. Det. Bailey then disobeyed our earlier instructions and quickly whispered something to Dr. Thayer that we were unable to hear.

Det. Bailey left the facility, and for days afterward, we observed an improvement in Dr. Thayer's affect. He was less agitated, his rocking and jerking had lessened considerably, and there were no further instances of self-harm. His appetite increased, and we observed a general improvement in his physical health: his extremely pallid skin showed more color, and he put on a total of four pounds from 4/14 to 4/21. We then allowed Det. Bailey's request for a second interview to go ahead. The detective indicated that he wanted to bring along his son, Charlie, to show Dr. Thayer that he was in good health. After discussing this, we agreed. The improvement in Dr. Thayer's general outlook was considerable, and we thought that some of the agitation that he still exhibited could be connected to unresolved anxiety about Charlie's well-being.

The interview took place on 4/22. Charlie, six years old and suffering from Heller's syndrome, arrived at the facility with his father. We explained the conditions, and both he and Det. Bailey expressed their agreement with the terms for the interview, Charlie by nodding.

On being admitted to the room, Dr. Thayer's affect was as positive as we had seen it in months. He greeted Det. Bailey with a handshake and embraced Charlie. Both the visitors seemed very happy to see the patient, and Dr. Thayer was equally pleased and positive in his affect. When Det. Bailey noted that Charlie had joined the baseball team at his grammar school, we noted that Dr. Thayer nodded emphatically. The treatment team was very pleased with

Dr. Thayer's affect in the interview, and noted the relaxed body posture and the normative behavior that characterized the first part of the interview.

It was only when Det. Bailey excused himself to visit the restroom that we noticed a change—indeed a severe change—in the patient's demeanor. Left alone with Charlie, Dr. Thayer at first maintained a steady eye contact with the boy. The two were both silent. But about sixty seconds later, Dr. Thayer's posture and affect changed drastically. This couldn't have been caused by anything the boy did, as he sat there, still, merely watching Dr. Thayer, who began to exhibit severe paranoid tendencies. He stared, transfixed, at the boy, and then he began to mumble a series of unintelligible words. When he stood and began to move aggressively toward the child, the orderlies intervened and pinned Dr. Thayer to the floor, overturning his chair in the ensuing—and quite violent—struggle. Three orderlies had an extremely difficult job in restraining Dr. Thayer, and at one point we feared he would successfully attack the boy. Charlie, however, simply watched the patient calmly and didn't move during the entire incident.

The interview was taped, as is standard procedure at the facility, and it was only in reviewing the tape after the incident that we first noticed something odd. Before Dr. Thayer's outburst, Charlie Bailey was leaning forward in his chair, with the patient in a similar posture, their faces only a few feet apart. We observed Charlie's mouth move, forming words. Then, strangely, Dr. Thayer would apparently repeat the same words a second later. This rather eerie playacting went on for ninety seconds, in which neither subject moved. The treatment team wanted to know the content of the communication between the two, and we replayed the tape later, increasing the volume to the maximum level. But there was no sound. The tape was completely silent.

The odd colloquy between the two was broken off when Dr. Thayer became agitated. When Det. Bailey, alerted to the problem, rushed back to the interview room, we observed Dr. Thayer trying to speak to Det. Bailey. The patient became increasingly distressed when he couldn't get the words out or make himself understood. He stared with what can only be described as a beseeching, distressed gaze—a look of horror, if you will—at Det. Bailey, and his hand came up in a gesture of reaching for his friend. But the hand froze midway and stayed there, and Dr. Thayer's body maintained this posture, almost constantly, for many days to come. It was the most unusual display of catatonic onset that we have ever witnessed or come across in the clinical literature.

The boy, Charlie, could tell us nothing about the incident. When interviewed afterward, he shook his head when asked if he knew what had caused Dr. Thayer's outburst. Thankfully, he did not seem upset by Dr. Thayer, and only smiled when asked if he'd felt threatened or afraid.

On his return to the room, Det. Bailey was equally distressed by the change in Dr. Thayer and especially with the odd interaction between the patient and the boy. We felt it was time to end the interview. We have not granted Det. Bailey's many requests for further interviews and have no plans to do so at this time, for obvious reasons.

Dr. Thayer's postinterview decline was precipitous. That night, he emerged from the catatonic symptoms long enough to tear apart the furnishings in his room, screaming continuously in an inarticulate fashion that frightened the other patients on the floor tremendously and even unnerved the veteran attendants who were working that night. They said that Dr. Thayer seemed inconsolable and that he was attempting to communicate something, but his powers to convey it were frozen or inaccessible. When the attendants attempted to put him in restraints, he broke the arm of Mr. Bishop and bit the hand of Mr. Marcus. He was given 150 mgs of propofol and was put back into his room in heavy restraints. A suicide watch was posted, with a visual assessment of his condition every fifteen minutes. He slept fitfully that night and in the morning the catatonia had returned, full force. He has remained in that state ever since, and the treatment team is now reevaluating the program to see where we will go next.

One postscript to the night of 4/22 remains to be addressed. In his room, among the papers that he'd torn apart and strewn across the floor, the attendants found the drawings that I've referenced before. Dr. Thayer had completed them weeks prior to the second interview with Det. Bailey and Charlie, and he'd been allowed to keep the materials, as they represented his only outward form of expression since his admission. Many of those drawings were found torn into pieces. But on the back of one, we found a few words scribbled in an agitated hand, apparently written by Dr. Thayer on the night of 4/22. We pieced together a few fragments:

> Traveler possessed Prescotts in turn, probably from 1919 on. Slowly killed off [unreadable.] Suicides in Prescotts could be attr. to genetic mental illness. Family madness his disguise. Maybe he purposefully led me to think Becca was the one. Then hid in Charlie. Lonely and vul [nerable? Unreadable.] Maybe saw that we wouldn't want it to be Char.

And this:

> . . . he let bodies be found . . . proof traveler died . . . will find new nzombes.

Obviously, the paranoid delusions about the spirit of Capt. Markham had returned full force. When Dr. Thayer suffered his final seizure on 4/22, which has rendered him unable to talk or move, another piece of his writings was found in his mouth. He'd written it at some point during the night.

The note read simply:

WARN JOHN.

John is the first name of Det. Bailey. We have, of course, decided not to mention any of this to him.

CHAPTER SIXTY

Ramona Best sat in the Altima at the last red light before the left turn onto 95 South. The highway, now baking in the early June heat, would take her out of the valley that held Northam and then parallel to the eastern seaboard all the way to Long Island.

She glanced out the passenger window. There was a little meadow there, with a stand of pine trees, their branches so green it almost hurt the eyes. The noon sun sent the branches' shadows straight down to the ground. A heat shimmer passed over the pines, making them appear to wave like plants in an aquarium. Ramona looked away.

The engine fairly purred. After the stabbing, Zuela had come up for a week to nurse her back to health in the hospital and, when she left, gave her $400 as a graduation present. She'd spent part of the money on renting her purple graduation rope and cap, which she thought were resplendent. After paying her remaining bills, she still had $200 left over that she planned on spending at Houston's, on a dinner with Zuela. Zuela hadn't been able to make the graduation ceremony, but they would celebrate in Long Island.

Ramona understood why Zuela hadn't come. In the hospital, Ramona had refused to talk about what had happened, or who had stabbed her, and from her silence, Zuela had inferred the worst. She'd cried on Ramona's cheek as she'd leaned over to kiss her forehead. "I'm not coming back, child. But I love you."

Ramona reached over and laid her hand on the diploma that she'd received just three hours ago. Someone had told her that Wartham was the last college in New England to still use real goatskin for their degrees, which had grossed out a few of her classmates. Ramona thought it was a nice touch. Goatskin was permanent; it wouldn't shrivel up like parchment. As she stroked the document, it felt glossy and almost alive, like a beautiful leather coat. The president of Wartham, Dr. Ronald Wingate, had handed it to her up on the tall wooden stage in the quad, the same smiling, gaunt man who'd come to see her in the hospital weeks ago, right after Detective Bailey's visit.

She'd been still groggy from the pain meds when Detective Bailey came in with his sad walrus eyes. She'd shifted in her bed, the wound still like a piece of sharp steel under her skin. She hadn't been questioned about the stabbing and was expecting a barrage of questions about whom the attacker was and Margaret and the boy in the clearing and so many things. But the detective had sat down by her bed, asked her how she felt, smiled (but not in the sad walrus eyes), then told her that he was disappointed to learn that she'd contracted amnesia. That it was too bad she couldn't remember the face of her attacker, but it didn't matter so much because he'd probably died in the bonfire in the Raitliff Woods anyway. When Ramona went to object—she felt the anger rising up her chest like a streak of Icy Hot—he held out his hand and told her that they didn't have time to discuss the details because President Wingate was there to award her the newly established Marcus R. Bateman Scholarship, funded by the Bateman family of some mining corporation or other, which went to the most improved Wartham student over four years of study and provided full tuition to any postgraduate institution of her choice, which Ramona had been awarded during her convalescence, and they didn't want to keep a man like Wingate waiting.

"A full ride," Bailey said quietly. "Books and incidentals, too."

She could take the scholarship to Harvard Med, if she could get in. Or Columbia Law. And Bailey implied that once she made her decision, phone calls would be made to ensure her application to whatever program got "very special" attention.

"I know you don't need any advice from anyone, Ramona, especially not me," Bailey had said. "But listen to me. You. Take. That. Scholarship."

So maybe he did know a little about life, Ramona thought then. And maybe she could learn something about it herself by reading between the lines of the detective's offer. For instance, if Ramona didn't take the scholarship and told everyone how she'd been stabbed by the lumbering old man with the black eyes who was supposed to be dead, then she would be tangled up in these folks' business for a long, long time. That was in his eyes, too.

He didn't need to press her. She'd decided that it was time to leave this place, for good. She'd said nothing to Bailey, but nodded once and closed her eyes, and Ramona Best got amnesia right there in the hospital bed in Northam, Mass., before President Wingate came into the room, trying not to make any noise with his loafered feet.

But not before Detective Bailey took her hand and said, "You saved Charlie," and cried a little, and the Icy Hot feeling went away from her chest and she nodded once more.

Suddenly, a blast of noise filled the car and Ramona started. She glanced at her rearview mirror, her eyes wide with fear and her heart going a million miles an hour.

A fat white guy in a Chevy TrailBlazer was leaning out his driver-side window, pointing up at the streetlight.

"Hey! You wanna fucking go," he shouted. "Or what?"

Ramona looked up at the light. It was glowing green in the bright sunlight. She let her hand drift out of the open window. She gave the man the finger, vigorously, then hit the gas, turned the wheel left, and gunned up the ramp of 95 South, the Altima's engine sounding loud and smooth.

Good-bye, Wartham, she thought to herself. *See you when I see you.*

As she got to the top of the ramp, her eyes flicked to the rear-view mirror for one last look at the place where she'd spent the last four years of her life. Behind the asshole in the TrailBlazer, which was lumbering up the ramp after her, the little stand of pines stood. She couldn't tell if the thickening of the shadows behind them was because of the shift in her view or if there was something else there, among the bright green branches.

Ramona watched the pines until the Altima crested the top of the ramp and the sight of trees was replaced by a long ribbon of cars heading south.